LETTER TO THE FUTURE

MICHAEL DAVID O'BRIEN

Letter to the Future

A Novel

IGNATIUS PRESS SAN FRANCISCO

In Scripture quotations, the wording of Mark 4:22 and Hebrews 11:13 has been adapted from the New American Bible and the Revised Standard Version, Catholic edition. The wording of Psalm 12:7–8 is from the New American Bible. The wording of the Acts of the Apostles 2:17 and Joel 2:28–32 is from the Revised Standard Version.

Cover art: *Birth/Death* by Michael D. O'Brien
Cover design by Roxanne Mei Lum

ISBN 978-1-62164-787-4 (HB)
ISBN 978-1-64229-353-1 (eBook)
Library of Congress Control Number 2024950206
Printed in the United States of America ∞

CONTENTS

PART I

Sursum Corda

"For there is nothing hidden that will not be revealed; nor is anything secret except to be brought into the light."

Mark 4:22

I

THE WIND BLEW in the children's faces as they climbed the hill above the village. On this warm day, the sun danced overhead while puffs of cloud seemed held in suspension above the undulating land. The tall grass moved in waves. Wildflowers exploded their unrestrained perfumes, enticing the hummingbirds and bees.

The four children passed the beehives standing like giant's teeth at the edge of the upper fields. They waved to the keeper, and waved also to the tiny form of their mother who stood in the yard of their home below, hanging out laundry, watching them climb. She lifted one arm in acknowledgment, and they could almost see her broad smile beaming at them. From the collation of two hundred houses that formed the village there arose the sounds of children at their games, laughter, the cries of a baby, the clanging of a hammer on a forge, and the slow tongs of the bell in St. John's steeple, marking the Angelus hour, reverberating, diminishing into silence, much as liturgical voices will, at times, fall into contemplation, generating peace that flows from it like invisible water.

So, too, the falls at the river mill could barely be heard, no more than a sighing that disappeared whenever the wind shifted, the water sounds borne away by the tide of air that came down from the mountain peaks in the west and winnowed outward through the foothills and onto the quilted farm fields beyond the river, and then onward to the distant prairie.

The surrounding hills were not very high, and upon them were numerous close-cropped pastures where the village's flocks grazed. Woodlets of poplar and pine crowned the heights, and lower creeks were flanked by stands of gnarled cottonwood. In some nearby shallow valleys, patches of flax, barley, and red corn were grown, for the soil was better there and the rain sufficient. Others were little more than narrow gorges through which sheep paths wandered and sometimes circled around the bases of hills.

The children's dog, Chester, accompanied them, a black and white breed who had descended in part from border collies in times past and the more recent bloodline of wolves with which they had commingled. Chester had inherited mainly the domesticated portion of his ancestry; he was a good herder, protective of the children, sensitive to human moods, and keenly intelligent, though it must be said that from time to time he killed a household hen.

This afternoon he ranged ahead of the four children, scouting, or perhaps merely anticipating a hare or quail that he might chase and eat in the wild. From time to time he stopped to sniff the air, his eyes narrowing, his nose pointing in the direction of other dogs in the distance, relatives of his who sat alert beside their shepherds or ambled around the landed clouds of their flocks. Chester took note of it all, then resumed his customary gait.

Behind him in a line came the children, all of them following a disused sheep path that was being absorbed by knee-high grass. Their destination this day was a seldom frequented valley an hour's walk to the northeast, a place where clover and calendula grew around a series of springs. The children carried empty loose-weave sacks tucked into their belts, for gathering the flowers that their mother would compress into oils she would mix with beeswax to make healing salves and scented soaps.

Behind Chester came the eldest child, a boy of sixteen years named Bede-Thaddeus, who liked to stride over configurations of the earth and also would race ahead of the restraints of time, if it were possible, as rashness and responsibility strained for mastery within his eager nature. He carried over one shoulder a bow that he had made and a quiver of arrows. Like the other children, he wore a linen summer tunic bound at the waist by a braided leather cord, and his feet were shod in deer-hide moccasins.

After Bede came the next oldest, a girl of fourteen years named Mari-Kanti, motherly by nature but strong-willed, a singer of songs and maker of beautiful things with her weaving and sewing. The next to follow was her little sister Catherine-Josephine, who was usually called Sweetpea by her siblings and parents. She was six years old, fanciful and affectionate, a maker of straw dolls, and beloved by all. She was seated on a brown-and-cream pony named Pie (for piebald). Her sister Mari kept a firm hold on Pie's halter, as the pony had a habit of sloughing off riders and bolting for greener pastures.

Bringing up the rear was Ahanu-Paul, age twelve, growing visibly taller day by day, word-witty and overfull of information that he crammed into his mind at every opportunity, garnered through observation of the world around him, of human nature, and from the small number of books in the village. He liked to pretend solemnity but was quick to laugh and quick to tease, full of jokes and harmless mischief. He carried a cherry-wood spear, its point whittled sharply, and, strapped to his waist, a sheathed knife that his father, the village blacksmith, had made for him from a substance called kar-metal, a rare material from the olden times, retrieved on long journeys into dead cities.

The boys cherished their weapons, not so much for the possibility of spotting game, but for the manly feeling of defense against unforeseen marauders. In the mountains to the west, bears and lions roamed, it was said, though none of the children had ever seen one. Whenever the People of the High Forest came down to the village for trade in the spring and autumn of each year, they would tell stories about those ferocious animals, the cats most dangerous, for they were sly and skillful at stalking. Like the Hill people, the Foresters also raised sheep, but lost many to the predators. The bears, though enormously powerful, were brutish plodders, fish-eaters, berry-eaters, perilous only if you came upon them unawares. Between wolves and bears, there had been no killings of humans in living memory, said the mountain people.

From the east, the People of the Flatlands also came to the village for trade, always in the spring and autumn, bringing thick hides and cartloads of wheat to exchange for woolen weavings, tools, and crafts. They told of gray wolves prowling the prairies, chary of man, hunting small creatures mainly, and sometimes culling the buffalo herds that were returning in great numbers. No one had ever heard of a human attacked by a wolf in that land, though legends offered frightening accounts. Once in a very long while, a wolf pack would pass through the hills not far from the village, usually in a deep-snow winter, but the frantically barking dogs warned them off. Coyotes were ever-present, yipping at night, seldom seen, and a threat to the sheep only during lambing season. Nevertheless, impelled by tradition and symbol and enthusiasm, the boys were armed and ready.

The children knew their route well, and Chester, whose memory was long, knew it, too, for he did not cede his advance position. Each year the family visited the valley of springs during the month of August when the flower harvest was in its prime. White and purple clover were common throughout the region, but nowhere other than by the springs were the purple blossoms as large and fragrant. The calendula patches were the great prize, yellow and orange varieties, and the less common striped combinations that came about by cross-pollination. Now and then a rare pink blossom was found, much treasured by the children's mother, more for its beauty than for its medicinal qualities. The scent of calendula was an unusual blend of sweet and stringent. The leaves of geranium and tomato were like it in a way, also pleasing but lacking its unique character.

"Joy to the eyes, joy to the soul," their mother liked to say as she thrust her nose deep into the sacks the children brought home. "Healing to the flesh, healing to the bruised heart," she would add with her gentle smile.

Now they entered the valley of springs. Before commencing the afternoon's task, they took a short rest, sitting down on a hummock beside the flower patches. Catherine slid from the pony's back, and Mari set the animal free to wander. Immediately it began to graze on the rich grass as it went, swatting away flies with its swishing tail. Chester sat on his haunches, surveying the scene before him. As the children ate bread and cheese, he got up to lap water from a spring and then returned to them, settling down with his head on his forepaws, his eyes ever alert.

After the children drank from the spring, the boys set aside their weapons, and then all four began plucking calendula blooms and dropping them into their bags. Because the calendula was of higher value, they ignored the clover, leaving it for the end of the afternoon, as it was easier to pick and it filled a bag more swiftly. Before long, all fingers and thumbs were dyed a deep yellow and everyone unconsciously smiled because of the scent. The youngest worked as diligently as the oldest, for they wished to please their mother and father, and glowed with anticipated praise. From their earliest years, they had been imbued with the sense that the family was made strong and well by each member working to the best of his ability.

Mari began singing as she worked.

"We are the People of the Hills," she chanted in a high voice, "We are the Longworth family of *Sursum Corda* on the Little Jordan River."

"This we all know, my sister dear," sang Ahanu in a matching tone. "Please tell us something new."

"We are gathering flowers against the winter to come," she sang in return. "We will smell summer in the midst of blizzards' snow and ice."

"Mmm, that's not much better," said Ahanu. "Keep going."

"Soon we will make saskatoon-berry pastries for Christmas."

"Christmas is too far away," piped Catherine.

"We will pick the berries next month, Sweetpea," said Bede. "You can eat all you want then. But we have to save some for drying, too. In December, the week before Christmas, Mama will make wheat dough, and she will bake pastry."

"I will help her," said the little girl.

"My mouth waters already!" cried Ahanu, and they all laughed.

The summer day was long, with sunset still far off. By the time the sun had slipped a little on its downward arc, all the sacks were full save Catherine's. The three older ones helped her pick until her sack was full too. Opening fresh sacks, they harvested clover for another hour.

"No pinks this year," sang Mari.

"But more stripes," warbled Ahanu.

"And all the orange we need!" declared Bede with a grin, straightening his back and lifting both hands to show them his stained fingers.

Without warning, he leaned over and drew his forefinger down the bridge of his brother's nose, leaving a bright orange streak. Ahanu yelped and retaliated. The boys tussled, trying to apply more streaks to each other's faces, while the girls convulsed with laughter. Finally, Bede and Ahanu exchanged a conspiratorial look and sprang into action, going after the girls with hands outstretched like claws. Mari and Catherine screeched and ran away hand in hand. The boys soon caught them and struggled to make their marks as Chester barked and danced in circles. Mari and Catherine fought back, and the boys feigned defeat, tripping and falling to the ground. Instantly the girls leapt upon their brothers, smearing sticky orange flower oils over their faces.

"Don't!" cried Ahanu in a high wail. "Stop!"

"Don't stop? All right if you say so," said Mari, as she and Catherine continued to overwhelm the boys, anointing their foreheads and cheeks with the color. Flat on their backs, the brothers pretended desperate resistance, rendered powerless by their helpless laughter.

It was Chester's whining that first alerted the children to something amiss. They stopped their play and got to their feet, gazing in the direction where the dog's quivering nose and worried eyes were pointing. There in the west, a mass of purple and black cloud was engorging above the mountain crests and moving swiftly toward them. Within minutes it had darkened a quarter of the sky and was steadily growing. Flashes of lightning appeared, followed by the rumble of thunder.

"It'll be a bad one," said Bede. "Let's go home."

"We'll never outrun it," observed Ahanu with a wrinkled brow.

"The trees," said Mari. "The trees," Catherine copied her in a whisper.

"Right, the trees. If there's hail, we can shelter there," said Ahanu.

"We'll get a little wet but not knocked on the head," Bede contributed.

Quickly they gathered up the full sacks while Mari chased after Pie and caught her halter. Then they all hastened up the slope to a stand of older pines. They arrived there safely and huddled together under the thickest branches, awaiting the advance of the storm. Its first wave was a blast of wind that flattened the foliage in the valley below and swayed the branches on the heights. The pine trunks began to creak as they bent under the oncoming force. The children turned their backs to the storm, as did Pie and Chester.

Lightning cracked close on the surrounding hilltops, followed almost instantly by shocking thunder booms. Then the rain came, hard and hissing, the roaring wind blowing it sideways. This was followed by light hail and then a pelting of larger white stones, carpeting the forest floor inches deep. Smaller tree branches fell all around them, and the large pine under which they sheltered was now not only bending and creaking, but screeching with the sound of tearing wood.

During a pause in the hail, Bede shouted, "I hope it bypasses the crops."

Mari clutched his arm, her face white with fear. "This tree's going to fall," she cried.

Ahanu stood and pointed deeper into the trees, higher up the slope.

"There's a big rock up there. See the shadow beneath it, maybe an overhang. We can hide under it."

Abandoning the flower sacks, the children linked hands and ran with wind and rain at their backs, trying not to slip on the ankle-deep accumulation of ice. Catherine lost her footing once or twice but did not cry out, though her eyes were wide and her lips compressed into a line. Ahanu helped her up, and together they stumbled on. Arriving at the rock, which was now completely coated with white, they found that it was as large as a house. At first the shadow Ahanu had seen appeared to be no more than a shallow incline. Even so, the formation continued around to the leeward side, where it sloped deeper beneath the massive stone, offering a few feet of shelter. The children crawled in, along with whimpering Chester, while Pie stood at the entrance, blocking some of the wind, looking patient.

"Poor Pie!" sobbed Catherine.

"Don't worry, Sweetpea," Mari comforted her. "She's got a warm fur coat, and she's seen worse than this."

A tree fell nearby and shattered on the rock. Two or three more trees fell, and then the hail ceased, the wind abated, the rain dwindled to a light drizzle, and the worst was over.

When the sun broke into the forest, the children scrambled outside to survey the scene around them. From all directions came the sound of dripping water. The white carpet began to melt into patches, exposing the layer of leaves and moss on the forest floor. The ice on the rock slid to the ground. Three of the children beat the ice from Pie's back. The pony whinnied and trotted away a few feet, shaking herself and standing still in a wide bar of sunlight to soak up the warmth.

"Where's Bede?" Ahanu asked with a frown.

"Still here!" came the answer from the shadow.

"You can come out now, dear brother. Don't be afraid."

This was greeted by a chuckle. "I'm not afraid. I've found something interesting."

The three younger children knelt by the shelter's entrance and peered within.

"It's bigger than we thought," said Ahanu.

"A little cave," said Mari.

"Yes, the ceiling is higher back here at the end," Bede called.

Dimly visible was his form bending over what appeared to be a curved piece of wood, which he gripped with both hands.

"Look at this."

The three others crowded inside.

"It's metal, rusty, probably iron," he said.

"Maybe an ancient tool," Ahanu suggested.

"Let's take it home to Papa," said Mari.

"It won't move," said Bede after tugging mightily for a few minutes.

Clearing away several inches of dirt surrounding the object, they saw that it was a half-circle of metal as thick as a man's thumb. Both ends of it were locked into the stone beneath. Clearing away more dirt, they found that the stone was perfectly flat.

"That's very strange," Ahanu mused. "How would anyone do that?"

"You mean embed this metal in stone?" Bede replied. "I don't know."

"Papa will know," Mari said.

"I'm hungry," said Catherine.

All four scrambled out through the low entrance and into the warm air. It was now late afternoon or early evening by their reckoning. The position of the sun told them that there remained only a couple of hours before sunset. The last of the storm clouds were shrinking in the east, and the sky was mainly clear.

Leading Pie back down the hill, they came to their abandoned flower sacks, finding them soaked and a little flattened. After shaking as much water out of them as they could, they tied the bundles to Pie's back and set off for home.

They had not gone far along the path when they saw the figure of their father loping down the hillside toward them.

"Thank God!" breathed Isaac Longworth when they came together. "Thank God!"

"We're fine, Papa," said Bede.

"We're very fine," chimed Catherine.

Their father smiled, and then his eyes examined them with a look of calmness that they knew masked his underlying worry. "You're soaking wet, the lot of you. Let's get you home and into dry clothes."

"You're very wet, too, Papa," said Mari. "It looks like you came for us through a downpour."

"I did," he nodded. "I came as fast as I could."

On their way back to the village, Ahanu asked, "Are the crops all right, Papa?"

"Yes, the worst of the storm narrowly missed us. The hilltops are white, but only rain fell on the fields. Heavy showers, but that will do no harm, as the corn sorely needed it."

When they reached the village, they led Pie into the barn and undid her halter. After depositing their flower sacks in a bin, they made straightway to the house, a small stone and log dwelling with a thatched roof.

"What have you done to your faces?" asked their mother as she met them at the door, her tone half scold, half amused.

"Go wash up now, and then get into some dry clothes. Bede and Ahanu, I'll need more firewood brought in before dark."

"Yes, Mama," the boys answered, and with their sisters went off to the water pump in the yard.

Over supper they related their adventure to their parents, who were keenly interested in every detail and expressed pride in how the children had protected themselves from the storm. Bede described the unusual piece of metal he had found in the cave, which intrigued their father greatly.

"Metal embedded in stone," he mused. "That's not really possible, unless Nature has developed a new trick."

"You mean like a rock growing a metal tree?" Ahanu asked.

Isaac Longworth smiled. "It sounds very much like cement."

"What is cement?" Mari asked.

"You know how we chink the chimney stones and the walls with a mortar of clay and lime," their father answered. "It grows hard when it dries."

"But it makes chips if you hit it," said Catherine.

"In the old days, they made a kind of mortar that didn't crumble. It became as hard as rock when it dried. That is what they called cement."

His wife, Theresa, said with a note of whimsy, "How curious that someone left the metal bar stuck in wet cement, and when it dried it looked like a rock sprouting a sapling."

"Why would anyone do that?" Bede asked, as his brother Ahanu furrowed his brow and mentally chewed on the question.

"And why in a cave?" said Ahanu.

"I don't know," said their father. "Tomorrow, let's go take a closer look."

And the children beamed with anticipation.

After breakfast the next morning, the children helped their mother empty the flowers they had harvested into metal tubs of water, to simmer throughout the day over an outdoor fire. When this and other chores were done, they gathered at the door of their father's smithy and pleaded with him to leave aside the horseshoe he was hammering at his forge. He smiled and dunked the shoe into a bucket of water, then wiped his hands on his apron. He hung the apron on a peg and gathered a few tools to bring with them on the expedition. To add to the day's mood of adventure, Bede brought his bow and Ahanu his spear.

The weather was again fair, warm, and cloudless, with a light breeze to keep the insects at bay. A spirit of eager anticipation gripped the young Longworths, with Chester dashing ahead and the older children trying to keep up with him. Pie took up the rear with Catherine on the pony's back. Isaac walked beside them, hand on the halter rope, his paces intentional and leisurely, which was his way. They were last to reach the valley of the springs. The older children waited for them at the base of the hill, and then they all commenced to climb.

Arriving at the great rock, Isaac went down on his haunches and peered into the shadowed recession.

"It's hardly a cave," he said.

"You have to go deeper inside, Papa," said Bede, scrambling under the overhang, the heels of his moccasins disappearing into the dark. Isaac followed on hands and knees, the tools on his work belt clanking. Ahanu came after him.

The girls remained outside, knowing how crowded it would be within the small dark chamber.

With his flint kit, Isaac lit a waxed splint, kneeling upright, for the ceiling of the cave was a little higher than the tunnel. Bede showed him the metal bar growing out of the stone. After handing the flaming splint to Ahanu, Isaac used his flat trowel to clear away more of the humus, which was inches deep, formed by countless years of decomposed leaves that the wind had blown inside, mixed with the droppings of wild animals.

"This has been here for a very long time," Isaac said. "And it is definitely cement."

"*Cement*," the boys echoed, fascinated.

"It's very smooth," Ahanu noted, stroking the surface with his fingertips.

Their father scraped away more of the humus until a pattern became visible—a crack in the shape of a square surrounded the metal bar, each of its sides about a foot in length. Now he gripped the bar and tried to pull it upward. It remained immovable. Next, he took a hammer from his belt and with a sharp-edged chisel proceeded to strike along the lines of the crack.

"Whoever made this had a certain skill," he observed, wiping sweat from his brow. "It was designed, I think, to keep water out. There's old resin in this crack."

"You mean hard pinesap?" Ahanu asked.

"Yes, or something like it."

Ahanu drew his forefinger along the trail of amber dust that the chisel had cast up. Putting it to his nose, he sniffed and then sneezed.

"It doesn't smell like pine," he said. "It smells like nothing."

Isaac returned to his chiseling. When all four sides had been gouged as deeply as possible, he once again tried to lift the bar. With a scraping sound, it moved a fraction. Again and again Isaac pulled upward, straining every muscle of his mighty arms, but with little progress. Then a thought came to him, and he asked Ahanu if he might borrow his cherry-wood spear. The boy ran outside and was back in a minute. Isaac inserted the stout spear through the loop of metal bar and, using a loose rock as a fulcrum, he slowly levered it up. With aching slowness the cement square lifted and finally broke free. Bede and Ahanu, grabbing its edges lest it fall back down, shifted it aside.

Around two inches in thickness, it was now revealed as a lid, for beneath it was a pit or chamber. Isaac lowered the burning splint into the hole, the light filling the recess below. The boys crowded around their father.

"A cave within a cave," whispered Ahanu.

"A cave made by human hands," said Isaac. "Its floor and walls are cement. There are a few things stored here. I wonder what they are."

Clean and dry, perhaps two feet deep, the chamber was only a little larger than the lid. It contained a number of items that were not immediately comprehensible, as they were each wrapped in what looked like a dark cloth. Reaching down, Isaac removed them one by one, six in all. As he picked up each package, pieces of the wrapping began to slough off in large flakes.

"Let's take all this out into the sunshine," he said, "and we can have a better look."

When everything had been removed from the cave and set on the moss outside, the children dropped to their knees in a circle around the trove, while their father examined each item one by one. Beginning with the largest package, he carefully removed its fragile wrapping, which fragmented and blew away in the light breeze.

"It's not animal hide," said Mari. "Can it be an olden times cloth?" She rubbed a piece of the black flake and puzzled over its thinness and the way it disintegrated between her fingers. "It has no weave. What is this material?"

"The people of old had many inventions that have not come down to us over time," said Isaac. "But certainly it is a covering to protect what is within from being corroded by moisture."

Even as he spoke, he brushed off the last layer of black leaf, revealing a stack of yellow papers, bound by a fine cord.

"It's paper," gasped Ahanu. "A lot of it."

His father nodded. They were not unfamiliar with ancient paper, since Fr. Maurus possessed a few bound books that he had retrieved over a lifetime on expeditions into dead cities, and sometimes under his watchful eye he permitted the older children to attempt deciphering the print, with little or no success. Such paper was an extremely rare thing, very thin, and though much worn and stained by time, hints of its original fineness were evident. Northward at the Abbey of the Savior, the monks possessed a larger collection, carefully preserved. They also had their own paperworks, producing a thick parchment made from their linen crops. With it they quilled copies of missals and the Sacred Scriptures, which they gave to newly ordained priests to ensure the true teaching of the flocks entrusted to them and, moreover, to pass down the Word of God to coming generations. The abbey library owned three copies of Scripture from the time before the darkness fell—*Biblios* or *Bibles*, which meant *book*—one in Old English, another in Old French, and the third, which was oldest of all, in a language called Cree, though it was a mixture of the Blackfoot, Cree, and Saulteaux languages. *Dialectis*, Fr. Maurus called them.

Now, the Longworth family gazed in amazement at the largest collation of antique paper that any of them had ever seen.

"There is much writing on it," observed Isaac, tracing with his forefinger a few letters on the top page.

"What does it say, Papa?" asked Mari.

"It is Old English, I think, though I cannot understand many of the words. This, you see, is the word *beloved*, and there is *children*, and here is *time*."

"The same words as ours!"

"The same words as ours, but it may not be the same meaning we hold for those words. We must show this to Fr. Maurus."

"What is in the other packages?" Ahanu asked, agitated with curiosity.

Isaac unwrapped a second item, which fit into the palm of his hand. It was a thin slab, a rectangle of black substance with a glass front, beneath which were numerous small buttons.

"What is this thing?" Bede asked with a furrowed brow.

"Perhaps a tool," said his father. "Or a *machina* of ancient kind."

"A *machina* without wheels and pulleys?"

"The people of old were marvelously clever in their inventions, with powers that have long fallen beyond the reach of memory."

The third package contained something more recognizable, for it was a crucifix made entirely of silver, the craftsmanship of exceedingly high quality, the lifelike precision of Christ's corpus unlike anything they had seen before.

"I. N. R. I.," Mari whispered.

"The person who buried this was a Christian, wasn't he, Papa?" asked Catherine.

"It would seem so," Isaac replied in a musing tone.

"Then he was just like us!"

"He may have been like us in some ways, in the important ways, we hope."

"But why would he bury these *here*?" Ahanu asked.

"And why was he *hiding* them?" Bede said with a frown.

"Maybe it was a surprise, Papa," said Catherine. "He was having fun, like we do in hide-and-seek and find-the-treasure?"

Isaac did not respond. Instead, he unwrapped a fourth package, which contained a small book bound in frayed red leather, with the word *Psalms* inscribed on the cover. Inside the cover page was a loose card, illustrated with a picture of a winged angel carrying a sword in one hand and what looked like a hammer in the other; inked on the card's reverse side were the handwritten words:

> *To Cleve, best house slave in the world.*
> *Try these on for size, buddy.*
> *Your benevolent overseer and master,*
> *Rafe*

"Do you know what the words mean, Papa?" asked Mari.

"No, they are difficult to read," her father answered regretfully.

The fifth package contained a wooden box with rusted hinges. Inside it was a small piece of tarnished metal sculpted in the shape of a heart. Rubbing it with his thumb, Isaac felt sure it was made of bronze. Engraved in its surface were two words, *Cleve* and *Anne*, joined by a simple cross. There was a gold ring as well, fit for a woman's finger.

The sixth package contained a curious collection of odd little objects the size of a baby finger, each with a metal lip at one end. They were of various colors, faded now, though the letters USB and numbers were still legible.

Isaac stood. "Several mysteries," he said, dusting his palms and slapping the dirt from his knees. "We will have much to ponder this coming winter."

He went back into the cave and dragged out the cement lid by its handle. The children gathered up the discoveries. Their father asked Bede to carry the paper manuscript with greatest care, exacting a promise that not a sheet of it would be lost to the wind.

Isaac and Ahanu, using the boy's spear, thrust through the loop of metal bar, lifted the cement lid and together they carried it homeward to the village.

When they showed the find to Theresa, she expressed her surprise and her wonder, then grew thoughtful as she touched the crucifix, the heart, and the ring.

"Swift as the weaver's shuttle flow the years," she said, lost in her thoughts.

On the following morning, after Mass, the family waited at the door of St. John's carrying a large wicker basket containing the items from the cave.

"Oho, a flock of Longworths," said the priest when he came outside after his thanksgiving prayers. "An invitation to lunch, I hope."

The children grinned. Isaac smiled and said, "You're welcome to come to lunch, Father, but this is about something else." He gestured to the basket. "A rather big surprise. I would be grateful for any insights you could give us about it."

"Well, well, let's go into the rectory then, and we'll talk it over."

Unlike the stone church, Fr. Maurus' residence was a square hut made of logs and roofed with thatch, only a few steps away. When they had all gathered inside, the priest put his kettle on the fireplace hob and gazed at his visitors curiously.

Isaac explained the discovery the children had made in the Valley of Springs. He took the thick manuscript from the basket and placed it on the table before the priest. Fr. Maurus leaned over it with keen interest, his eyes flickering left and right, reading a few lines.

Isaac said, "I spent a few hours last night trying to decipher it. I can make out some of the words, Father, but I can't seem to string them together to make sense of the whole thing." He scratched his nose. "Not that I've read far into it, just a dozen pages before my mind couldn't take it anymore."

"So you think it's a kind of English?"

"I think so. In any sentence I understood a third to a half of the words. The rest were a complete mystery. I tried guessing, to fill in the gaps, but . . ." Isaac spread his arms wide in a gesture of helplessness.

Fr. Maurus glanced down at the stack of fragile papers before him and resumed reading.

"It is certainly English," he said, looking up. "And very old. The paper alone indicates that several centuries have passed since it was written. As you know, over the course of long years, many words in our Common Tongue have come down to us from Old English, but language changes, little by little, a continuous process. Words that were once recognized by everyone fade out of memory, almost unnoticed, usually replaced by new ones. Then there are expressions and idioms, which are even more fleeting."

"But you were a scholar at Jarrow when you were younger.

And you told me once that you had made a study of trying to decipher old books rescued from the dead cities."

"There aren't many of them in the abbey library. So few had been found in the ruins. And not a dictionary among them, sad to say. If there had been, my work would have been far easier."

"Would you try to translate this, Father?"

"I would be most happy to. Of course, you understand that it will take some time."

"I understand," Isaac nodded. "And there is this," he said, handing the priest the book of Psalms.

"Oh my," said Fr. Maurus with widening eyes, turning a page and reading a few lines. "This is a great treasure."

One by one, Isaac removed the other items from the basket, the children crowding in close, eagerly anticipating their pastor's reaction.

"This crucifix and heart are strong indications that the manuscript was written by a Christian," said the priest.

"Yes, that seems certain enough. But what are these?" asked Isaac, pointing to the other items he had spread on the table, the black object with its buttons and glass top, and the small, colorful oblongs the size of his baby finger.

"I do not know," said Fr. Maurus.

"So, what should we do with these things?"

"They are your discovery, so the decision is yours regarding what is to be done with them."

"Father, I would like to leave the manuscript and the book of Psalms with you. I'll take the other items home with us. I know that Theresa will be overjoyed to have such a fine crucifix. She'll want to place it above our family altar."

"This is good."

"Papa, could we put the gold ring on a peg at the foot of the crucifix?" asked Mari-Kanti. "And the heart too?"

"A beautiful idea, Mari, we will do it."

"The glassed object and the little fingers will provide an intriguing puzzle for you all to solve," said Fr. Maurus with a fond look at the young Longworths.

"My very intelligent children, no doubt, will come up with good guesses about what they are," said Isaac.

The children grinned and wriggled.

"They are certainly most excellent investigators and explorers, Isaac, considering that it is they who made this amazing find. In addition to your good guesses, as I go through the manuscript I will be alert for any hints in the text that could shed light on these mysterious objects."

Throughout all the known lands, there existed no habitation similar to the cities of old. There were hundreds of villages and small towns, and these were mainly farming communities, connected by a network of trails and dirt roads.

Twice a year, the closest villages sent trade parties to *Sursum Corda*, one in the spring and one in the autumn. That week eight People of the High Forest arrived. Very weary, they had come a five-day journey by down-trails winding out of the mountains, bearing metal ingots in shoulder packs and on travois pulled by dogs. Their home village was known as *Habemus Domini*, a shortened version of "We have an Abundance from the Hand of the Lord", and their lives were worthy of the name, for they possessed a good smelter fed by the community's small mining operations, producing copper, tin, bronze, and iron. Isaac had visited that place in years past and knew the men well.

The party of eight was composed of two fathers and their adolescent sons. They camped in the Longworths' hayloft, which was warmer and drier than their deerskin tents, and Theresa fed them from her own abundance. Isaac as blacksmith was the main customer for metals, but whatever he did not take was deposited in the trade master's shed, awaiting the coming of the People of the Flatlands, who were also scheduled to arrive that week.

Two days later, the party from the plains duly arrived from the east, twelve people, mainly men and boys and also a few older women. Their journey was considerably easier than that of the mountain folk. The route from their home village of *Pacem in Terris* was through rolling grasslands with well-defined trails, and they were also aided by horse-drawn carts. There was a shallow ford across the Little Jordan not far below the mill dam at *Sursum Corda*, but it offered no significant obstacle.

A particular joy for Theresa was to be reunited with her youngest sister, Miriam, who was married to a man named Micah Jacobson, a hunter and farmer with a small holding near Pacem. She was now three months pregnant with their first child and wanted to tell Theresa the good news in person.

Though the villages of Sursum, Habemus, and Pacem engaged in trade with communities farther afield, they were especially bound to each other by intermarriages, by strong affections, and by a tradition that had its origins in time out of mind. The semiannual meeting of the three peoples was for everyone a long-anticipated event. It was a time for the barter of necessities, the trade of rolled buffalo hides for new woolen blankets, of sacks of fat-wheat for rods of metal, and many other diverse items. It was an event also cherished for the recounting of noteworthy changes in their communities, of shared rejoicing, feasting, song, and prayer.

The mountain people had no priest, and thus, day after day, the church was happily overfull for Mass and evening psalms. Fr. Maurus was engaged morning to night with confessions and catechesis, as well as long conversations, during which his counsel, much respected, was sought by those who did not live in Sursum. The prairie people were as devout as the mountain people, but they lived closer to the seat of the diocese at Jarrow and had more frequent access to the sacraments. Some of them knew Fr. Maurus personally from his days as a young monk of the Abbey of the Savior, and most others knew of his high reputation now that he was old.

Bede and Ahanu were much engaged in reuniting with boys their own age, and many an evening was spent with the young visitors making arrows and spears, telling stories, or playing endless games of peg board by lamplight, and, each evening after chores, the much beloved target competitions. Mari, never one to linger on the sidelines, was nearly as involved in this as her brothers, sharp of aim and fleet of foot. Several of the outland boys regarded her thoughtfully, but whenever she met their eyes, they glanced shyly away. Catherine stood far back, as no children her age had come with the visitors, but she was content to jump up and down as she watched the games, cheering her siblings on.

The week went by too swiftly. On the eighth day, as the visitors prepared to depart for their home villages, east and west, Isaac gave each of the visiting youths a newly made knife. Theresa gave the men pots of her salves to take back to their wives, and, to her sister Miriam a finely woven baby blanket of lambs' wool. And then they were gone, leaving among the people of Sursum a sense of fullness that was not without a brief sadness over the parting and yearning for the next reunion, six months hence.

One of the benefits of their time together had been the examination of the metal bar found in the cave near the valley of springs. The mountain men had worked with Isaac in his shop, firing the bar and testing it with hammer and tong, heat and cold. In the end, they all agreed that it was a form of iron, but unusual in that it contained a residue of carbon. This, they concluded, had been an ingenious invention by the men of old, a device that had the surprising effect of not only strengthening the iron but greatly reducing its corrosion by rust. Both Isaac and the mountain men determined to experiment with the new method and to compare their findings when next they met.

But of course, the great discovery was the manuscript. For a time, little progress was made in the translation. Summer and autumn were the seasons most full with the needs of the community, and the parish priest was as involved as others in cutting firewood for the coming winter, harvesting crops, processing and storing food, and a thousand other tasks that had to be accomplished before the first snows fell. Moreover, Fr. Maurus lacked the paper necessary for making a full copy of the manuscript. The use of vellum parchment made from deerskin or lambskin was not impossible, but making it in quantity would demand long labors and the investment of valuable hides, and the end product would be very bulky.

"We are not a scriptorium in a medieval monastery," he would sometimes say to Isaac. "Yet the good Lord provides, and I think we may achieve better results with other methods."

Over the years Fr. Maurus had attempted making fiber-based sheets of "papel", with no great success. Now he applied intense thought and observation to a variety of experiments. He used linen mainly, gleaned from his plot of flax in a field across the river. He had learned that wool was useless for his purposes, but that tufts of bog cotton performed well enough. Wood pulp, too, was surprisingly versatile, as long as it was shredded very finely. It had mysterious chemical properties that helped with the binding of particles. Though it was acidic and produced sheets darker than desired, the recipe could be altered by the addition of a little calcium derived from powdered eggshells, and even a few droplets of rabbit skin glue. He was endlessly experimenting.

During the months after the discovery in the cave, Fr. Maurus used all his free time to simmer vats of his diverse mulches and to pour the resulting "soup" onto the metal trays Isaac made for him. An alternative method they tried was to spread a thicker soup or gruel onto a flat wooden plank and cap it with another plank, then add stones on top to increase the compression. The results were uneven, yet little by little the process was perfected, and by the end of the year the priest had accumulated about a dozen satisfactory pieces. It was a small fraction of the sheets that would be needed for the project, yet it was an accomplishment full of promise.

Throughout those months Fr. Maurus had written letters to his fellow priests in the region, penning his messages with quill and ink on bulky, malformed, and torn sheets—his "failures" he called them. He advised the pastors that the newly discovered manuscript bore every mark of being a unique testimony to the mind and soul of people who had lived in that tragic period long past, almost certainly the ancestors of present inhabitants of these territories. There was much to be learned from this phenomenal artifact, he felt sure, and begged the pastors to contribute any spare *papel* that might be in their possession. If his hopes were well-founded, he said in conclusion, he would in the coming years be able to produce his own supply in abundance and would not only be pleased to share it with them, but desired to make copies of the new manuscript to be added to their own collections.

These letters he sent off in several directions, borne in the hands of horse riders and sometimes in the carry pouches of walkers. He did not write to the elders of the people at Habemus in the high mountains, as he knew they had no paper whatsoever, but placed his hopes in the priest at Pacem in the east and the priest at Kalvaria in the south, the town at the mouth of the pass into the Great Southlands of Dakota, Mount Anna, and Idaho. Most importantly, he wrote to his friend the abbot of the monastery at Jarrow. This town of 2800 people, a five-day journey to the north of Sursum, was thought to be the largest community in the Westerlands and was situated on the Lake of Galilee (its name in the Dark Ages was now lost), which most people referred to informally as The Sea. Fr. Maurus prayed that either in the abbey or in the town itself, sufficient paper might be begged or purchased.

He included in his letter to the abbot a duplicate letter addressed to the bishop of the Northlands, who had his episcopal seat close to a dead city, which had been renamed St. Edmundston in time out of mind. Though his request that the letter be forwarded to this bishop was in earnest, he felt that due to the distances and natural obstacles that must be crossed in order to reach him, it was an exercise in hope rather than practicality.

In any event, he waited and he prayed. In the interim, he began to translate the opening few pages of the manuscript and was rewarded not only by the thoughts and sentiments it contained, but by a surprising fact—the identity of its author. This he kept to himself for the time being.

In the first week of October of the following year, on the feast of St. Thérèse of Lisieux to be exact, a walker arrived from Pacem, bearing the gift of forty sheets of very fine paper. The pastor of that village had himself been much occupied with developing methods of papermaking, as he had always felt that heavy vellum copies of the Scriptures, liturgical missals, and lives of the saints might be reproduced in less bulky ways, which, if Providence and inspiration permitted, would render the Sacred Scriptures more available to layfolk. The forty sheets of paper were a most welcome boon, though they were far from sufficient for translation of the manuscript.

Earlier that autumn, the eldest child of the Longworth family had broached the subject of the priesthood with his pastor and his parents. Bede-Thaddeus told them that, after much prayer about the question, he was feeling the yearning to try his vocation and asked their permission to apply to the Schola at the Abbey of the Savior. They readily and joyfully granted their permission. Fr. Maurus wrote letters of recommendation to be delivered to the abbot and the Schola master. In late September, Bede set out, riding on Pie the pony, accompanied by a boy from Habemus named Jerome Lyon, one of the miners' sons, who was determined to pursue the same path. Jerome rode a pony loaned to him by a farmer whose barley fields lay on the far side of the river. Abraham Morrow by name, he and his wife, Rose, had no children of their own and took great pleasure in helping other families.

Escorting the aspiring young scholars was Isaac Longworth. The route was winding and physically hazardous in parts, and neither of the boys had ever ventured that way before. Isaac had visited Jarrow more than once since his childhood and was familiar with the paths to the north. Mighty in build and long in stride, he chose to travel with them on foot. Due to his great size, there was no horse in the region of Sursum large enough to bear him for so lengthy a journey. While the route to Jarrow presented no dangers that the boys could not surmount, he wanted to "write into their bones"—as he later confided to Theresa—the unspoken message that the hearts of their families and communities were with them.

Three weeks later, Isaac returned, leading Pie and the second pony by their halter ropes. All had gone well.

In the evening of the day of his return, after a fine feast and recounting of tales, after prayers and thanksgiving, Isaac threw a log onto the throbbing coals of the fireplace and beamed at Fr. Maurus, who had been a supper guest. For a time they all sipped at apple cider.

"Out with it, Isaac," said the priest. "You're bursting with a secret you want to tell me."

Isaac laughed and said, "Abbot Placidus sends you a gift, Father."

With that, he retrieved the backpack he had taken on the journey, opened it, and removed a thick package wrapped in soft hide. He handed it to the priest.

It contained four hundred sheets of fine papel.

As the winter months progressed, villagers observed that their pastor seemed unusually preoccupied. His ministries and his love for his people were no less diligent, no less warm than they had been before, but it became obvious to all that his mind was now gripped by an entirely new interest, which he did not discuss with others. During the following spring, he joined in the planting of crops and sheepshearing with his usual concentration, yet an elusive pensiveness prevailed in the man.

In April, a lone rider arrived in the village, bearing a package for Fr. Maurus that had passed through many hands on its journey from the far northlands. It was a gift sent by the bishop of St. Edmundston, a very ancient, very tattered English dictionary.

Now and then, Isaac or Theresa would ask their pastor, "How is the translation going, Father?"

"Oh, very well, very well indeed. There are layers of difficulty with handwriting, of course, in contrast to printed text. However, I believe I am deciphering it accurately. Then there are the colloquialisms of those times . . . and the idioms . . . hmm, a challenge, to be sure."

"What is an idiom?" Ahanu-Paul once asked him as the family relaxed by the Longworth fireplace after supper.

"An idiom is an expression peculiar to a specific time and culture, unique to its own sensibilities, one might say. For example, in these very lands where we now live, the people of ages long past once said things like 'It is raining cats and dogs.' What they meant by this was that the rain was falling heavily."

"But cats and dogs don't fall out of the sky!" protested Sweetpea in her high voice, her forehead crinkled in confusion.

"Maybe they did in the old days," remarked Ahanu with a mischievous smile.

"It would be terrible, terrible!" the little girl cried. "Think of poor Chester!"

Which made everyone laugh and Sweetpea blush.

In June, Bede-Thaddeus and Jerome returned, arriving on foot after an uneventful four-day journey, the travel time reduced by their eagerness to be reunited with their families. Both boys were glowing with health and a quiet happiness, and they seemed to have grown inches taller during their absence. It was the Schola's policy that outland students should return to their home villages to help their families with the heavier demands of summer work. Only when a student had been accepted into the novitiate would he remain year-round at the abbey. Jerome spent the night with the Longworths, and in the morning he went on into the mountains, carrying an extra backpack filled with baked treats from Theresa, both savory and sweet, some to eat on the way and some for his parents and siblings.

On an evening shortly after the completion of corn planting in the surrounding fields, Fr. Maurus appeared at the Longworths' door carrying a leather satchel. He was invited in and given a steaming cup of *kaffeeya*, a pungent drink that Isaac enjoyed making from his own recipe of chicory, roasted barley, and dandelion root, usually taken with goat's milk and a spoonful of honey. When everyone had settled around the hearth, nursing their drinks, Fr. Maurus opened his satchel and took from it a bundle of papers wrapped with twine.

"I have completed the translation," he said diffidently.

Everyone leaned forward expectantly.

"I have translated it as best I can into the Common Tongue. The dictionary was immeasurably helpful in this regard, yet not everything in the author's text was completely intelligible to me. Certain references to the *machinas*, or 'technology' as they called it, remain beyond my understanding. Clearly these referred to various forms of transportation and communication."

"Nevertheless, what you have accomplished is a great blessing, Father," said Isaac. "You have worked long and hard on this, and we are grateful."

"My friends, it is I who am grateful for the opportunity

to read it. It gives us a glimpse into the hearts and minds of a people surrounded by many woes, as they struggled to keep themselves faithful within the choking cloud of darkness that lay over those times. The influence of the evil one's malice and his multitudinous deceits is evident throughout. Wherever the spirit of murder and falsehood dominates, that is an indelible sign that he is active. For those whose story is recounted here, the adversary's activities must have seemed all-powerful, and they would have been tempted to feel abandoned by God. Yet it was not so. The devil raged because his time was short."

Silence filled the room as the listeners absorbed what the priest had told them. A brief chill of an ancient fear washed through them.

Fr. Maurus glanced pensively at the crucifix, the bronze heart, and the gold wedding ring enshrined on the wall above the family altar.

Theresa cleared her throat. "Father, do you think it best that Isaac and I read it first?"

"That would be prudent. There is much in the account that would be profoundly disturbing. We must take care lest the devil's malice reach across these past centuries of peace to bring new infections."

Bede-Thaddeus spoke up. "Father, the Bible is full of wicked characters and dire events. Even so, we hear the readings at Masses, and we are free to read from our own copy."

"This is true, Bede. Yet not everything is read at once. You learn from the Scriptures in stages befitting your age and understanding. I think you would come to no harm reading this manuscript. There are several young people in the story who were much like you."

"May I read the manuscript?" asked Mari-Kanti who was next oldest to Bede.

"And me too?" asked Ahanu-Paul. "I will be fourteen next month."

The priest smiled. "Mari and Ahanu, I suggest that you let your parents read it first and then you can ask them."

"And me, too?" chimed in Sweetpea.

"Ah, Catherine-Josephine, perhaps you should wait a few more years."

"I know my sums and letters! I can read!"

"This is a different kind of reading," Isaac answered and pulled her onto his lap.

Looking down at the manuscript in his hands, Fr. Maurus said, "It is very long, and therefore I suggest that you read it over time, with silent pondering and with prayer that the Spirit of the Lord will reveal to you what He desires you to learn from it."

After removing the top two pages, he handed the manuscript to Isaac. Turning to Bede-Thaddeus, he said:

"It was your discovery, Bede. I would ask you to read to us the author's opening words. It is a short letter that introduces the major body of this writing. Indeed, we might call the entire manuscript *Letter to the Future*."

Bede reached over and took the two sheets of paper the priest offered.

Standing before the gathering with a quiet dignity, he prepared to read aloud, swallowing, taking a deep breath, and finding his voice.

Bede-Thaddeus read:

Beloved ones, you whom I cannot see, for you do not exist at the time of this writing. Children of the ages to come, hear what I would say to you, I who lived in the past. This past is my present; this past, which for me and for all those left alive as I write, is our knowable existence. For you it is, perhaps, deep antiquity or legend, lost in the mists of time.

Each person sees his own life as a lengthy story: ten years is a long time for him, fifty seems immense, and as it nears its end, the frontier of eternity races to meet him. My long life, so brief in the history of mankind, now seems to be little more than a breath. The frontier is close at hand.

Do you believe that I yearn forward to you, you who have not yet come into being? Do you believe that I love you? I call you *beloved* because I do love you. I love you as if you were my own, knowing that beyond all time we will meet face to face, there where no more tears will fall and rejoicing will flow without ceasing.

What gulf do you gaze across as you ponder my times? How many years, decades, centuries? What remains in your world of what we once were? Do you speak my language still? Can you read it? Is the full spectrum of thought, ideas, vocabularies available to you? How much has been lost and how much retained?

The human mind—I expect that yours is not so different from mine—perceives the reality around us as a semblance of eternity, and all the changes that happen in life, such as personal growth, environments, economies, governments, war and peace, and even radical shifts in the configuration of the world, in fact everything, usually come about as a gradual progression. For us, they were barely perceptible as they happened. By contrast, the historian who assesses long ages and the passing of civilizations is able to see the emerging shape or form. For us, the aspects of these multiple dimensions of human life are not so much solid breaks as they are currents that run simultaneously, parallel, or intertwined, or, at times, clashing. When there comes a convergence of crises, confusion reigns in the mind as it seeks to make sense of it all. Then fear distorts our perception and interpretation. We grasp hastily at templates that offer an explanation, a semblance of knowledge, thinking that knowledge will save us.

Indeed, knowledge destroyed us—knowledge poisoned by pride.

This is not to suggest that knowledge is necessarily bad. Good, decent knowledge is a form of charity. It can aid life but never replace it. It is my hope, dear children of the future, that you are able to make the distinction. I hope that our follies will never again be repeated.

Will this letter reach someone? If you are reading it a hundred years from now, or a thousand years from now, please pray for my soul and for the souls of my wife and children and our grandchildren. I have not asked our Father in heaven for the survival of our flesh, but I beg Him to bring our souls through these dark times unto Paradise.

Love, always,
Cleveland Longworth

PART II

Letter to the Future

You, O Lord, will keep us
and preserve us always from this generation,
While about us the wicked strut
and in high place are the basest of men.

Psalm 12:7–8

2

WELL, HERE I AM, pen in hand, embarking on the writing of the *belles-lettres* I've always wanted to compose—the failed aesthetician, or diatribician, even the would-be novelist, one of the several variations on my life that I had envisioned for myself in my younger years—all of them brought to naught for reasons that will become obvious in these my partial memoirs.

It is surprising how vividly the events resurface, how clear are those scenes and dialogues, which I would guess is what happens when one lives through a trauma. Deeply imprinted, or in my case *burned*, into the consciousness, it plays again and again in the mind's eye, and one relives the emotions until arriving, hopefully, at a point of detached resolution. The process of healing has been a long one, and perhaps it is not yet complete. The trauma, after all, was catastrophic, global, even cosmic, entailing so many grievous losses that I scarcely know how to describe it. So I will begin at the beginning.

The yearning for shelter has been with me since I was very young. It was not fear that impelled me then but rather the glee of a child playing at hide-and-seek. At age eight, I dug a hole in the sand on the edge of the suburb where my family then lived, not far from a city in the dry Okanagan region of British Columbia. I covered the hole with pieces of cardboard and crawled under it. I liked hiding there, feeling the thrill of secretiveness and invisibility. I helped my friends in the neighborhood to make them, too, so that we could have a little town of our own. But mothers put a stop to this pretty fast, fearing snakes and black-widow spiders. After that, I made a bower of dead branches farther out in the semi-arid expanses that stretched away toward the mountains. This, too, I shared with friends my own age. We spent all our free time in the bushes, perfecting our hideouts, running and shooting toy guns at each other, making explosion noises with our mouths, dying gloriously when shot, laughing and yelling and developing skills of elusion and aggression. We killed gangsters, foreign invaders, pirates, and extraterrestrial aliens bent on exterminating the human race. We paused only to eat what we called our cowboy picnics and to read comic books within warrens of thorn brush.

In retrospect, I see that my gang was something of an anomaly, a throwback to the 1950s. In my childhood, the great majority of my peers had become glued to electronic screens, in mansions and trailer parks alike, playing games while disengaged from their bodies, save for their thumbs manipulating the virtual reality through remote control. I suppose I was the catalyst of an alternative culture because my family had never had television or internet—just books and more books, as well as library cards. Add to this my amazement when I learned that the toy sections of certain dollar stores still carried gunslinger pistols and rolls of caps. Totally bad, totally violent male. But the satisfying sound of a real *bang* captured me immediately, and I soon spread my thrilling discovery to a small number of willing desperados.

The grandfather of one of the guys had boxes of antiquated comic books stored in his attic, and he was glad to get rid of them. We couldn't believe our luck. While it is true that the oldest of the comics displayed blazing battles in which "Indians" (the Wild West) and "Orientals" (World

War II) were dispatched with shocking callousness, we did not question the rightness or wrongness of it. We merely needed something to resist, an "enemy" in any kind of costume. We did not share this information with our parents.

Years later when I was at university, I had a Japanese girlfriend, whom I loved to the point of constant distraction, and regretted my earlier exploits, though she dropped me for another guy. As I was majoring in Canadian literature with a minor in anthropology, I visited native reserves north and south of the border, wrote papers on their cultures and pasts, growing ever more critical of stereotypical narratives, and, shamefacedly, of myself. It was a period of my life when I did a lot of rethinking about my assumptions, even as I had to bat away a whole new set of assumptions, ranging from ideological to primitive instincts. My moods at the time were generally low, and my consumption of alcohol high.

Somewhere along the way, it dawned on me that the mass obsession with extraterrestrial invaders in film (I was addicted, at the time, to movies and internet) was really a transference of our feelings of terror in the face of our own inner demons—exteriorizing the enemy, so to speak. The Enemy 'R' Us, not to put too fine a point on the matter. I also came to see a pattern in the tsunami of apocalyptic and neo-apocalyptic and post-apocalyptic media adventures: they not only exteriorized our fears of the future but offered solutions: technology, muscle, swift reflexes, creepy supernatural powers, and constant foul-mouthed bravado would save us. With the added spice of semi-nudity and later total nudity. The consistent underlying message: Using evil means to defeat evil is the assured path to victory. Killing is the most effective solution to all our social and personal problems.

I should pause here to mention that despite my early

infatuation with shooting bad guys with cap pistols, I never for a moment felt a desire to dispatch real people with a real gun. That was a role for others, such as detectives. The death of gangsters I never regretted.

The political gangsters who ruled the nations were another category altogether. A criminal might shoot a dozen individuals in his lifetime. A duly elected head of state might kill millions. I learned over time to mistrust every word that came from the mouths of such people. I tried not to hate them and sometimes succeeded in this. By slow growth, I came to understand that, with a few notable exceptions, politicians were never pure evil. Not infrequently they were idealists. They tried to achieve good for the sake of those who lived in their territories, combined with their own sense of personal glory. On the whole, they were moderately intelligent, but they did not make decisions based on absolute principles. They were driven by impulsive expedience in the pursuit of their long- or short-range goals, which they invariably perceived as the highest good. Left, right, or moderate center, not a one of them would risk his career for the sake of defending a truth. Hence, the state of my world.

For two or three years after graduation, I suffered from the self-delusion that I should become a writer. With the dregs of my student loan money, I moved from my room near the UBC campus in Vancouver to an apartment in a low-rent district on the edge of Calgary. I had hooked a job as a roving reporter with a small-town newspaper that served the region south of the city. This sixteen-page weekly was crowded with advertisements, obituaries, reports of elderly lady craft sales and high school sports events. I found the job unspeakably boring, but it allowed me plenty of off-duty time and the means to develop my own webpage, where I could air my opinions on anything and everything.

To my great surprise, within a year my initial online readership of about ten extended family members, and my somewhat disapproving but indulgent editor at the paper, grew to number close to eighty. I was elated by my success and began work on the draft of a novel that I felt would be an astoundingly brilliant literary masterpiece. The central character was a heroic libertarian who just happened to be a courageous roving reporter. He would die gloriously at the end, shot by state agents, so much more satisfying than death by cap pistol.

My parents then lived in Edmonton, just far enough away that I had an excuse to visit them rarely, reducing the guilt I always felt in their presence. I was the black sheep of the family, you see, and my brothers and sisters were faith-filled folks living orderly lives, with plenty of nieces and nephews to sweeten the pot. They were scattered across the country and into the States, due to employment, leaving me, the misfit, closest to home.

My mother and father had loved their children with total dedication, and to their credit, with fairly good parenting skills. Despite our differences, I loved them too. They were honest, kindhearted people, very religious, worried over my apostasy, and no doubt praying for me incessantly, trying not to let their anguish over me show. I had chucked all that, you see, in favor of becoming the brave new man, free of myths and other restraints—and of course unconsciously spinning a new myth that permitted me plenty of ego-enhancement with minimal discomfort.

While the newsy pieces I wrote for the local paper were articulate, they were uniformly banal. By contrast, the opinion pieces I wrote for my online journal were stunningly insightful and beautifully expressed, I thought. By the second year, my blog readership was creeping upward with glacial slowness and crested at around one hundred and twenty regular visitors. Now and then I was afflicted by the suspicion that my followers were people who had been recruited by my parents, trying to show their support for a ne'er-do-well son.

Nevertheless, a couple of times I was quoted by the big provincial newspapers (not flatteringly, but hey, there's no such thing as bad publicity). That I was noticed at all, I took to be a sign of immense hope for the country—Yes! They were listening to me out there! I was confident that if I just continued to explain things well enough, people would wake up, shake themselves, and get down to the business of building (rebuilding, actually) a sane civilization and genuine democracy.

Overlooking the fact that literally millions of articles were published each year, and millions of blurtings posted each day, I forged onward, composing essays critiquing the mass mesmerization of the West, indeed the propagandizing of the entire globe. Though none of my essays was published in the mainstream media (it was wholly enslaved by that point), a few appeared in the beleaguered, shrinking number of free online journals. Not the hysterical fringe, you understand, but rather those platforms where serious thinking was displayed.

Even so, it took me a while to see that my arduous efforts at writing rational, articulate, convincing pieces had no positive effect. Everyone was writing or talking, no one was really listening. Perhaps a few readers agreed with my points, nodding sagely before going on to read something else or to write something of their own. Of course, there was also a backlash of vitriol in the comments section, written by the truly demented or the terminally enraged, or simply by those who had no other forum in which to express their grievances against life. In summation, we were all of us walled into a ghetto dialogue.

And thus, I decided to become a carpenter.

3

DECIDED IS PROBABLY THE WRONG WORD. Let me explain. During my third year as a writer, my editor at the local paper had come to the conclusion that my sociopolitical nonconformity was becoming a threat to his financial health. There had been complaints from his subscribers, people who had stumbled across my more daring writings posted on the internet. There had been cancellations. Furthermore, he was alarmed by a feeler-warning from a federal agency about a possible "hate crime", meaning that I persisted in using traditional gender pronouns in my articles. I argued vehemently that my opinions were aired only on my private little corner of cyberspace, but, vehemence being almost always counterproductive, he was not convinced. Fearing guilt by association with my online blog, he terminated my employment.

I had been calling phone numbers in employment ads for weeks, trying to get work at construction sites. I was sick to death of intellectual verbiage, and, with a kind of reverse Thoreauian desperation, I wanted manual labor. But whenever I showed up for an interview, prospective employers took in my underdeveloped physique at a glance, listened to me verbally download my overdeveloped curriculum vitae, and realized I was a no-hoper. Invariably courteous, they told me they would let me know, and, of course, they never did.

Indeed, I was very much becoming a man without hope. Week after week, then month after month, I paced around my bachelor apartment each night, my credit cards maxed out, rent overdue, car repossessed, music console, cell phone, and computer pawned, and now skipping meals to save money, and trying to resist the lure of alcohol. I resisted, as well, the gentle inner promptings to get down on my knees and plead for divine help. But, like a five-year-old suffering from high octane willfulness, I kept declaring, "I can do it myself!"

Yup, that was me in those years. Mr. Independent. Autonomous man. I could have called or written my father asking for help, but he was a retired high school teacher surviving on a limited pension and was trying to pay the astronomical bills amassing from my mother's medical treatments and special care during her final years of life. She was still alive, clinging to life in a nursing home, the costs of which were not covered by their health insurance. In his exhausted and stressed state my father was now considering selling our family home to pay the bills, making plans to move into a cheap apartment in some run-down neighborhood in a galaxy far away, and was probably skimping on meals just like me. I could not bear to add to his burdens and, probably more to the point, admit to him that all my grand dreams for my life had come to nothing. It was pride, of course. It'll get you in the end, one way or another.

One night during the final stage of that period, I had a dream in which I was running away from something dark and awful, maybe a specter of civilization in its end-phase, my feet going slower and slower as the *thing*, or whatever it was, chased me faster and faster, until it caught up with me and surrounded me and would have swallowed me whole. Paralyzed, choking with terror, I shouted, "O God, help me!", and found myself suddenly wide awake, sprawled on the floor beside the bed, sweating and trembling, my heart pounding, and my mouth yelling in real-time, "O God, help me!"

It was close to dawn. I could hear the go-to-work traffic beginning to rumble on the street outside. So rather than return to the perils of dreamland, I got up and went downstairs in my pajamas to check my lobby mailbox. As expected, nothing. At that moment a guy came in the front entrance and dropped a bundle of newspapers on the table by the mailboxes.

"Free," he grunted, eyeing me up and down with something like disdain.

"Thanks," I said, and took a copy.

A few minutes later, I was seated at my chrome table, eating the last slice of bread I had in the house and sipping a weak cup of coffee, made from the pitiful grounds I found at the bottom of an empty can. Scanning the want ads in a mood bordering on genuine panic, I stumbled upon one that offered a flicker of promise.

RAPHAEL'S CONSTRUCTION AND RENOVATIONS
SKILLED LABORERS NEEDED

Well, I was skilled. I could drive a car, tell time, ride a bike, add and subtract. I went down to the pay phone in the lobby, and with my last coins I called the number and got an answering machine. It gave an address where applicants should appear in person for an interview. The office opened at eight A.M.

Hurriedly I got dressed, scrambling into jeans and hiking boots and an old checkered lumberjack shirt. Forgetting to shave, I set off on foot to my appointment with destiny (I hoped). I had no car and no money for the bus, and my mountain bike had been stolen weeks before, lock, chain, and all, so I walked briskly for forty-five minutes until I came to an industrial enclave in a suburb. Within its labyrinth I found the yard and office of the construction company. The office was a trailer raised on concrete blocks, alongside a huge shed filled with lumber racks and stacks of plywood sheeting and drywall. Three pickups were parked by the trailer, all of them dusty, one of them with a dented cargo box. The Raphael's Construction logos on their doors presented a flying angel with a sword in one hand and a hammer in the other. I went up the steps and knocked on the trailer door. It was opened by a young guy about my own age, dressed in work clothes, wearing a tool belt, and carrying a steaming cup of coffee.

"Morning," he said.

"Morning," I replied. "I saw your ad in the paper."

"Great, come on inside. We're short-handed this week so your prospects are good." He grinned. "Hope you don't mind working for free."

I chuckled nervously. "I don't mind at all; I need the exercise."

"I'm Brent," he said, offering a hand for a shake. "Pour yourself some coffee. I'll go get the boss."

He went off to a back room and left me surveying the interior, trying to get a fix on just how successful this business was. The room was crowded with desks and computers, filing cabinets, a couple of old landline phones, and a counter with a burbling coffee maker. By way of decoration, there was a wildlife calendar with a picture of an antlered stag, alongside a huge whiteboard covered with black marker notations, probably indicating projects. I poured coffee into one of the stained, chipped mugs and added some cream from a carton—real cream, I noted with surprise. I added more, craving the nourishment. I had just taken my first euphoric sip when Brent returned, followed by a tall, muscular man in his early forties, presumably the "boss." Predictably, he was dressed in faded blue jeans and a red checkered shirt with colored pens clipped to the chest pocket.

"Hi, I'm Raphael," he said in the deepest bass voice I'd ever heard. "Human, not angel."

"I'm Cleve," I answered, deepening my own voice for effect.

His handshake was a crusher.

"Well, let's go talk," he said, and led me back into his office. The room was even more cluttered than the other. He sat down behind his desk, and I took the hard wooden chair facing it.

"So, you're looking for a job," he began. "Tell me about your work experience."

I drew a breath. This was the hiatus point of hope and despair. I was painfully aware that I had nothing to recommend myself in the way of physical labor and was top-heavy with activities in the realm of words alone, my contribution of useless verbiage to the vast sea of Babel.

As I described my education and my experiences as a writer, his face became still, his eyes soberly surveying mine. I knew that I was probably shooting myself in the foot, because my skill-set was definitely not what this company needed. Nevertheless, I forged ahead, despite my sinking heart, fully expecting to drown in a septic pool of fatalism, knowing that the word *fatalism* was all too close to *fatality*. But he listened without interruption.

Having been inoculated against the lure of stereotypes, but by no means immune, I slipped, without realizing it, into inter-racial autopilot. Not prejudiced, please understand, but wanting to reassure him that I wasn't a bigot and not knowing how to do it. Wanting to treat him as an equal (oblivious to the condescension inherent in this). Almost on its own volition, my accent wandered into his ethnic zone, and I also wove a little street jargon derived from movies into my presentation, just to let him know I was cool, which I wasn't, and he knew it. Raphael, you see, was a black man.

When I was finished, I sighed in resignation. He smiled. It even looked like a sympathetic smile. He leaned way back in his swivel chair and gazed out a window, saying nothing.

"Uh," I added as a postscript, "I can tie my shoelaces and ride a bike."

This made him chuckle and he returned his gaze to me.

"You look sturdy enough, and I need good men. Ever worked on construction?"

"Yeah, I used to build houses."

"Ah," he said, leaning forward. "Why didn't you say so?"

"Well, they were made of cardboard and tumbleweeds."

He laughed.

"Me and my friends built 'em for years, ages eight to twelve approximately."

"How did they stand the ravages of time?"

"Not very well."

"Okay. Look, at the moment I need a yardman, stacking lumber, offloading supply shipments into the shed, that sort of thing. Think you could take it on?"

"Absolutely."

"We'll ease you into more skilled labor bit by bit."

"Truth is, sir, I've never done anything like this. I don't have any skills."

"Oh, don't worry your head about that. I can teach you. Question is, are you teachable?"

"I'm willing to learn."

"Good enough," he said with laughing eyes and a blaze of white teeth, as if he half believed me. "You're hired."

"Whew," I exhaled loudly, hardly believing my good luck.

"Payday every Friday afternoon," he concluded, rising to his feet. "Couple of bucks above minimum wage to start, but if everything works out it'll climb rapidly. You all right with that?"

I nodded. Oh, yes, more than all right. It was so much better than starvation and sleeping on the streets.

We shook hands.

"Brent'll show you the yard and get you launched. Take care now, Cleve."

"Take care, uh, Mr. . . ."

"Morrow. But you can call me Rafe."

"Thanks, Rafe."

My first morning's work was an exercise in extreme arduousity (is that a word?). Put another way, it was hard. Brent got me teamed with a yardman named Carlito, and together we unloaded a truck that had brought in a load of drywall sheets. My coworker lent me his extra pair of gloves—more grip, fewer blisters, he explained—and we moved the sheets one by one to a stack in the largest shed, out of the elements. By break time, every muscle in my body was aching, my stomach was growling, and I was feeling lightheaded. Carlito drank something steaming from a thermos, and seeing my somewhat haunted eyes observing him, he offered me a cup—it was tea and most welcome it was. Watching the way I gulped it, he broke an energy bar and gave me half. I wolfed it down.

"Hey, man, you look seriously challenged in the diet department," he said.

"I forgot to pack a lunch," I lied.

"Okay, don't worry. Come lunch time I'll give you some of my sandwiches. My wife she's always tryin' t' stuff me like a roast turkey. I hate to hurt her feelings, so I have to throw a lot of it away. Don't tell her, okay?"

"Please don't throw *any* of it away," I pleaded, going all squeaky voiced, to my shame.

He looked at me with some concern.

"I won't tell," I added.

Wordlessly he handed me his half of the energy bar.

Somehow I got through the rest of the morning. And at lunchtime, Carlito divided his food, making sure my portion was larger than his. From the corner of his eye he watched me eat in record time three burritos, an orange, and a bag of salted corn chips. I also availed myself of the coffee machine in the trailer, three cups, each of them half full of cream.

At the end of the day I knocked on the boss's door.

"I've got be honest, Mr. Morrow," I said to him.

"Rafe."

"I've got to be honest, Rafe. I don't have a dollar in my pocket and no food at home. Do you think you could bend the rules a little and pay me for today's work?"

"Sure," he said. "I make the rules, so let's bend 'em a little." He reached into his pocket and brought out a roll of money. He counted out $160 in twenties.

"You coming back tomorrow?"

"I sure am," I said, "and any day of the week you want me back."

"We never work on Sundays, and we knock off on Saturdays because the guys want to be with their families, or they have their own projects on the go. We'll need you Mondays to Fridays, that's if you feel strong enough for it. You look kind of run-down, my man, if I may be so bold."

"I'm getting stronger by the hour. I'm dependable. I won't let you down."

"Great, great," he said and handed me my pay.

Looking up, he added, "Need a ride home?"

I nodded gratefully.

Well, that should give you an idea of what kind of people

I was working with. The first week went by with plenty of muscle aches and pains but a full stomach. By the end of the month, I'd paid off my overdue rent and I was buying solid, nourishing food—a whole lot more protein and a whole lot less quick-fix carbs. I started to sleep better. My energy levels were rising.

The following month, I bought a replacement bicycle, but took care to park it inside my apartment whenever I wasn't using it. I rode to work and back each day, which further helped build up my stamina.

The month after that, I was able to pay my rent on time and also purchase good work boots. I toyed with the idea of redeeming my cell phone, computer, and music system from the pawnshop, but in the end I decided I could live without them. It felt good to be free of my old life-support possessions. The sense of liberation, even elation, surprised me.

Occasionally I mailed a check to my father, with post-it notes affixed. *Pay-back time*, I scribbled, and beneath it a smiley face. The checks were never cashed.

I had been hired in the middle of a mini-boom of sorts. Raphael's Construction and Renovations was becoming a steadily busier enterprise, with Rafe overseeing the building of three houses, as well as a larger number of reno projects. During my first months with the company, he had to hire a couple more men, and as a result I graduated to our smaller flatbed trucks that delivered materials to the job sites. I loaded and offloaded and, from time to time, was told to stay and work on the projects, hammering together wall frames, helping lift them into place and securing them, installing insulation and drywall, and so forth. Sub-contractors for plumbing and wiring were not as reliable as we were, but they did eventually show up. We didn't overcharge our customers, and we didn't waste time. As our reputation grew, the waiting list kept filling.

Once a month, Rafe would host a Friday afternoon levy at a nearby Irish pub. All employees welcome, the boss pays the tab. There was always plenty of good cheer, shop talk, jokes, friendly jibes. Rafe loved it whenever one of us underlings teased him for being so devoted to Celtic culture. "I'm black Irish," he'd shoot back, "I got rights." No one stayed more than an hour or two, as most of the guys had wives and children to get home to, and they wanted to do it walking straight. I still thought of myself as a free radical, an unstable molecule in this organism, and would have kept chugging the tap until midnight, but there was a kind of unwritten, unspoken code among the crew. Despite their various personalities and backgrounds, they all had a kind of mutual respect, dignity maybe, certainly integrity. I never saw evidence of insobriety, not even the less offensive margins of it. Odder still, there was a complete absence of foul language and off-color jokes. Little by little I realized I wanted to become more like them and a lot less like me.

Eight months went by with me hardly noticing the passage of time. The sweetness of making tangible things became my life, of gathering raw materials and shaping them into dwellings in which people could live. There were changes in my nervous system, brought about by the thoughtful intentionality that is needed when fitting pieces together and by the smell of fresh sawn wood, the satisfying sound and feel when a nail is driven home with a solid hammer (I hated nail-guns, considered myself a traditionalist craftsman). There were changes in my thoughts as well, the decline of rage and dread as the positive action of physical labor replaced endless obsessive hours staring into a computer screen and trying to fight monsters with text, a Quixotic, one might say Sisyphean, exercise that had nearly consumed my former life.

4

FIVE YEARS PASSED IN THIS WAY. They were good years full of learning real things, doing real things. Gone was the subconscious desperation that had been my previous mode of existence, replaced gradually by a peace that suffused my labors and my days of rest. How this happened deserves some explanation:

Near the end of my first year working for Rafe, he took me aside late one Friday afternoon (not a pub night) and invited me to have supper with him. His wife and their three girls were away visiting family in Toronto, he explained, and he wasn't much of a cook. Would I be his guest at a restaurant? Surprised as I was, I heartily accepted. We hopped into his truck, and he drove us to a diner that was a favorite of his, named *Mom 'n' Pop's* on the south side of Calgary. The invitation puzzled me, though. While Rafe was a man of warm temperament, he never tried to be intimately buddy-buddy with employees. He was an outstanding employer, to say the least, always fair, great at decision-making and communication, firm and commanding without any hint of authoritarianism, tolerant of mistakes as long as you diligently applied yourself to improvement. A certified Master Carpenter, he was extremely knowledgeable about the trade.

Above all, there was his inherent dignity. Without doubt, he was our employer, and consequently, to some degree, our fates were in his hands, but he never threw his weight around. Though he liked to laugh, and could be subtly, intelligently witty, it was never at the expense of others. He enjoyed bantering, but would not tolerate blatant disrespect. Interestingly, if someone tried to cross the line, Rafe would not grow angry or engage in intimidation of any sort. Instead, he merely grew very still, very quiet as he looked the offender steadily in the eye. I believe that the recipients of this look turned away in shame rather than fear. I'm not sure how to define it, but suffice it to say, there was never a false note in the man. It was hard to get a fix on him, but that didn't really matter, because, to tell the truth, I was just glad he had dropped into my life. Or I into his.

He ordered fish and chips, I ordered a hamburger and fries. Both of us added salads and a glass of red beer. Our beers arrived first and over these we settled into casual chat. To my astonishment, he brought up the subject of my online blog posts.

"I enjoyed that article you wrote last year about the violation of ontology in imposed social revolutions," he began, tossing off the comment as if what he said had no great significance.

Ontology? Where on earth had Rafe picked up a word like that? He read my mind, smiled.

"Um . . . uh . . ." I mumbled, probably openmouthed.

"You made excellent points," he continued. "I was sorry to see that you shut down the site."

"You've read my stuff?" I asked, shaking my head, still trying to get my mind around it.

"Yes, fairly regularly," he nodded. "Couldn't agree with everything you wrote, but I liked the way you put up some resistance to the socio-gestapo. Did you study Polysci at university?"

"No, it was Literature. Did you go to university, Rafe?"

He broke into a grin. "Uh-huh, managed to get a Masters in Philosophy."

"Hence your use of the word *ontology*."

"Hence indeed."

My internal lenses were revolving a notch or two, bringing the picture of my boss into clearer focus: the powerful body of a basketball player/superhero, African muscles nourished on American vitamins, with the face of a whimsical philosopher.

Our food arrived, and we began to eat. I noticed that Rafe first bowed his head and closed his eyes, his lips moving silently.

When he launched into his meal, I asked him if he had known who I was when he hired me. Still chewing, he nodded in the affirmative.

"Your name isn't all that common," he said. "Plus, in your résumé you mentioned being a journalist and creative writer. I put two and two together pretty fast."

"So is that why you hired me?"

He smiled in reply, but didn't answer.

"Was it curiosity?" I pressed. "You wanted to see how a brainy nerd would handle real work, right? Or was it pity?"

"Well," he said with a reflective tilt of his head, "We were desperate for laborers at the time."

"I see."

After a few more bites, he looked thoughtful and said, "The loss of genuine metaphysics has pretty much messed up the whole world."

"You may be overlooking Islam," I said. "They're messed up, but they do have metaphysics."

"Is it *genuine* metaphysics? I wonder. Maybe I should say the *corruption* of metaphysics has messed up the world."

Hoo-boy, this was a whole new side to my boss. I was still trying to absorb it when he added:

"In reality, it's *both* loss and corruption, depending on the person, depending on the specific society and culture."

Maybe because my stereotypes were falling all to pieces, I

inanely asked, "When did your people first come to America?"

He had a way of smiling with his eyes, keeping his mouth neutral even when tossing off humorous remarks. "Oh, my ancestors arrived here with Brendan the Navigator," he said with barely a quiver of the lips.

"Huh?"

"Maybe the Vikings."

"I could be jumping to conclusions, but I presumed a slave ship."

"Mmm, a natural enough supposition. However, since it seems you've noticed my pigmentation, I might hazard to say that my ancestors did not arrive but actually never left."

"Pardon me?"

"The indigenous people of this continent are also part of my ancestry."

"Really?" I said like a little kid, wide-eyed.

Which made him laugh outright and then wipe his mouth with a napkin.

"You're playing with my mind, Boss."

"Just playing. But with an underlying point. I guess I'm trying to say that we're all immigrants, survivors of a big shipwreck, take it back far enough. Take it back even farther, and you get our shared Mom 'n' Pop."

"You've lost me."

"Adam and Eve," he said, growing suddenly serious.

I nodded that I understood, but quickly applied myself to finishing my hamburger.

He pushed back his plate and watched me, frowning a little, as if he were trying to come to a decision.

"What do you do with yourself on Sundays?" he asked.

I didn't tell him that I spent an unhealthy amount of time staring at the walls of my apartment. Instead, I explained that when I wasn't catching up on sleep, I took leisurely bike rides, visited my fitness club, and tinkered away on a novel I was writing.

"A novel!" he said, leaning forward, interested. "Can you tell me what it's about?"

I enthused over the adventures of my superhero libertarian Autonomous Man with a cap pistol, dying a glorious death for the cause of Freedom.

He listened attentively, making no comments, though I detected a certain sadness in his eyes.

I can't recall the exact chronology, but I think it was about six months later that he again invited me to a restaurant meal, this time on a weekday. Whatever Rafe's motives for fraternizing with me might be, I was glad to accept the invitation. Unlike the rest of our crew, outside of working hours I was generally at loose ends, uncommitted to any relationships, and thus I was probably the most likely candidate to fill in a blank spot, as his wife and children were once again away in the east, this time for the funeral of an aunt. I had yet to meet his family, though I sensed that my boss enjoyed a happy marriage and adored his children, glowing with pride whenever he talked about them. Moreover, I had no social life, the novel was going poorly—well, to be frank, it had stalled entirely—and my mother had recently died. I was grieving, increasingly dispirited, listless even, though I made sure I worked up to par on the job. Going out for a free meal offered a much-needed diversion.

We drove to Rafe's favorite café and settled into a booth.

"This time I'm paying," I said.

"No way. I invited *you*."

"In that case, I'll pay for my own meal."

"That's a gross failure in logic."

"I insist."

"Then you're fired."

"Oh. Okay, then. Do you mind if I order anything on the menu?"

He waved a hand in courtly beneficence.

"Feel free. You know, Cleve, you look like the kind of guy who always—I mean *always*—orders the cheapest thing on a menu, even if you don't like it."

"Out of necessity. Ever been hungry, Rafe?"

He fixed me with a grave, analytical look.

"Oh, yeah, I've been so hungry I was ready to boil my belt and boots to make soup."

I laughed. But he didn't join in, which told me that he wasn't joking.

"Seems to me, Cleve, that having experienced that sort of desperation a person can let himself be driven in different directions."

"Such as?"

"You either get reckless and greedy, on one hand, or you get miserly, on the other."

"No third options?"

"We are engaging in one, even as we speak."

I had no chance to reply, because the waitress arrived just then and asked for our orders. I still couldn't bring myself to select anything expensive, even though the thought of a juicy steak made my mouth water. Instead, I chose a low-budget burger and fries. Rafe observed this with a wry look, then asked the lady to bring, in addition, two servings of an item called The Bronco-Buster Sirloin.

"One for me, one for my friend here," he said.

"Is it horse meat?" I asked after she headed off to the kitchen.

"Nope, it's the kind of beef that bronco-busters eat out on the range."

When the food arrived, I hardly dared eat it, it looked so

good—too good for the likes of me. Then Rafe did what he'd done the last time we ate together, bowing his head and closing his eyes before taking the first bite. Clearly, he was praying a private grace. Conversation dwindled as we heartily tucked into our steaks, me smiling stupidly throughout, whenever I wasn't chewing.

Over vanilla ice cream and apple pie, we sat back, sipping our coffees.

"Thanks, Rafe. That was really wonderful," I said.

"Glad you liked it. It's good to do this now and then. Not as a habit, mind you."

I nodded as if I understood, though this kind of eating was a habit I would very much like to get into, if I could ever afford it.

"I was sorry to hear your Mom passed away," he said in a quiet voice.

"Thanks."

"You hanging in there?"

The way he said it, combined with what I knew about the man, reassured me that he wasn't just checking to see if I would become a less productive employee. No, there was basic human concern in his voice, his eyes.

"Need some time off?"

"That's generous of you, Boss, but I think I'm all right. Besides, the work keeps me focused and moving forward."

"Okay, if you're sure. If you need a break, just ask."

I lowered my eyes, sensing myself beginning to choke up. When I could manage it, I changed the subject. I told him that my father was trying to sell the family home to pay bills, as his pensions were inadequate to cover the debts accumulated during my mother's final years of life, round-the-clock nursing, hospice care, special medications not covered by insurance, and so forth.

"I could help with that," Rafe said in his quietest voice, so quiet I almost didn't hear it. And that did make me choke up.

Maybe it was his unusual combination of strength and kindness that overwhelmed me. I had met so few people like him in my life.

Finally, I managed to say, "My father would never accept it, Rafe. He won't even let *me* contribute financially and, hey, I'm his son."

I went on to explain that I was bussing back and forth to Edmonton most weekends, helping Dad repair things around the house and sprucing it up in preparation for a better sale. It would all work out, I said in conclusion.

5

FAST FORWARD A FEW MORE MONTHS. By then I had bought myself a new cell phone and was loving that good ol' electro-dopamine rush, feeling reconnected to the world, feeling cool, no longer a dysfunctional misfit.

About the same time, I bought a used Toyota pickup truck, small cab, two-door, sort of white with a liberal splattering of rust, but more or less reliable in terms of mobility. Brent and Carlito helped me install a Raphael's Construction logo on both doors, angel and all, a magnetized shield with a few added screws for durability. I didn't mind putting new holes in the vehicle, it had so many already. I felt proud to be part of an elite team. I also enjoyed the sensation of being all grown up, with a ride of my own: I can do it myself! Yup, that was me, late-twenties but still an adolescent. This I acknowledged, though in more objective moments of self-assessment, I noted that I had become, under Rafe's tutelage, unfailingly responsible, capable of putting my impulses aside, obeying orders without resentment, building my physical strength and prowess, and growing more attentive to the feelings of others.

However, I still lacked my own "metaphysics", so to speak. Which brings me to the day that Rafe and his wife hosted a barbecue at their place in a suburb of Calgary. The event was to mark the completion of a house in record time, with no loss of excellence. We would also salute the recent signing of contracts for five more houses. It was a major leap forward for the company, and Rafe wanted to celebrate.

Forgetting to bring my GPS-loaded phone, which I'd thoughtlessly left in the pocket of my work jacket at home, I was forced to revert to a booklet map of the city. After some trial and error, I located the Morrows' street in a maze of middle-class houses in an older neighborhood, not an insta-mansion among them, with thick poplars, birches, and an occasional western maple soaring high above every property. The trees were turning colors, the days were still unseasonably warm, though the nights were beginning to hint at coming winter.

There was no need to check house numbers, as dozens of parked cars and trucks lined the curb, centering on a two story residence that looked like it had been built in the 1940s or thereabouts. As I cruised past, I could see that it needed some minor repairs and cosmetic care, which made me smile. I parked a block down and walked back, merging into clusters of people standing on the front lawn, talking and laughing, kids of all ages running around everywhere, guests going in and out the front door, or heading through an open side gate leading to what I supposed was a backyard. Billows of delicious smoke were coming from that direction, so I followed my nose.

There must have been sixty people milling about in the yard, a lot of noisy conversation, smoke signals rising from two barbecues, and Rafe with spatula in hand officiating over the making of burgers and hotdogs. The smell of spicy sausages and frying onions was also in the air. My mouth began to water. A long trestle table made of four sawhorses and plywood sheets held platters of charbroiled meats, mountains of buns and numerous condiments. Another table offered punch bowls and bottles of wine. Beside the tables, thermos coolers were full of beer on ice. Nearest to me was a table with a coffee urn and the fixings, cartons of cream, bowls of sugar, jars of honey, and ranks of new white mugs, each with our logo on them.

Raphael's Construction and Renovations employed twenty-six men, last I had counted, maybe more now. It looked like everyone had chosen to come to the party, many with their families. I knew most of the guys by name, but not all. Standing by the coffee urn were two whom I had never worked with side-by-side, as they were roof shinglers, very above my head, literally, though we had chatted a few times at the Irish pub soirées. Farley Crowshoe and Albert Goodrider by name, they were brothers-in-law and members of the Blackfoot people. In their early forties, both men were noticeably overweight, but they had a sinewy strength that took them up and down ladders with amazing dexterity. They were slow speaking and slow moving, deliberate and painstaking in their work. They were nondrinkers, restricting themselves to diet colas at the pub. Farley was head of the A.A. group on his reserve, which he referred to as the Siksiká Nation.

His sense of humor was of the droll kind. One night at the pub he showed me a number of photos on his cell phone, his wife and children, and a single newborn grandchild. There was also a shot of a very lifelike stuffed buffalo that stood guard on the front lawn of his house, tilted slightly at an angle.

"The taxidermy bill for this babe cost Farley an arm and a leg," said Albert.

It crossed my mind that the days when a Blackfoot on horseback chased a buffalo herd with bow and arrow were long gone.

"I call her Eileen," said Farley with a near microscopic flicker of a smile.

Albert grinned broadly. "Get it, Cleve? I *lean*."

So here we were at the party, and though I really wanted

a beer from one of the coolers, I accepted a cup of coffee from Farley. We talked shop for a while, agreeing on what a great breakthrough the contracts for the new houses were and worrying a little about the risk of pouring concrete foundations this close to freeze-up. They talked about their plans to go deer hunting in November, or whenever the snow came and stayed. Rafe always gave them a couple of weeks off for it.

"He's crazy about venison sausage," Albert explained. But I knew that the boss was equally or more "crazy" about keeping these men linked to the company. He liked them a lot, and so did I.

I was intrigued to see that Farley wore a crucifix on his chest, superimposed on a red and white beaded disc of native design, this hybrid arrangement hanging from a leather cord about his neck. I'd never seen him wearing it at work, so maybe he kept it hidden inside his shirt whenever he was up on roofs. Maybe not. It could be he showed his mixed colors, and mixed symbols, only on special occasions.

Their wives sauntered over, and we were introduced. Farley's wife, Albert's sister, was a classic mother-type named Kateri, all heart, all soul, asking me questions about my family, looking sad when I told her I wasn't married, but she did not indulge, as so many women of all races do, in kindly advice that at my age I really needed to settle down. Albert's wife was Sharon Kanti, a psychologist by profession, with four grown sons and daughters, and a keen analytical eye. I expect she sized me up pretty quickly as a man adrift in the cosmos, but refrained from prodding. Albert the explainer jumped in to say that his wife was not Blackfoot; she was Cree, born and raised in the Ermineskin reserve near Pigeon Lake, south of Edmonton. Their eldest child was a Catholic priest working in a parish in the inner core of that city.

"His name's *Ahanu*," said his father proudly. "In Cree it means 'He who laughs'."

"And he surely does," contributed Farley the uncle dryly. "Maybe a bit too much."

Kateri the aunt reproved her husband with a look and said, "Underneath the laughter there's deep waters in that boy. He takes his calling seriously."

"And maybe you should be called 'He who needs to laugh more'," contributed Albert with a waggish look at his brother-in-law.

"Ha-ha," grunted Farley humorlessly, which made everyone grin.

This was all culturally interesting, and I was enjoying the conversation very much. However, my eye was caught by Brent waving to me from across the lawn. He lifted a bottle of beer in one hand and pointed to a cooler with the other. I said so long to the Goodriders and Crowshoes and moved through the crowd to join him. On the way, I bumped into Carlito Reyes and was introduced to his sweet wife Guadalupe and their five shiny-faced children. We made small talk for a while and then they had to get food for their kids. I forged onward toward Brent, who was the only nearby team member I knew well.

I had almost reached the cooler, when suddenly I was stopped dead in my tracks. Standing about ten feet away was the most beautiful, awesome, heart-gripping young woman I had ever seen in my life. She was deep in conversation with another woman, with whom she was holding hands in a sisterly fashion. She wore a blue dress, almost turquoise, with a shimmer of aquamarine scarf around her neck, sandals on her feet. Her open face was full of affection. She was tallish and graceful, her gestures a little reserved but unselfconscious. A quiet person, a listening person, fully attentive to the other woman.

While I am very often captivated by the sight of attractive women, a few years ago I had stopped acting upon the impulse. Penury, near starvation actually, had put a damper on what amounted to my social life at the time. Dates were expensive. Relationships were emotionally expensive. And, besides, I had been totally wed to my life as a heroic journalist. This didn't mean that I had stopped noticing the other half of the species. Nor did it keep me from desiring them. Indeed, I had noted a number of good-looking ladies scattered throughout the crowd around me, some of them unmarried I guessed, a couple of them a tad prettier than the lady in the blue dress but lacking her whole gestalt. Now, as I observed this extraordinary woman, I was not so much driven by the usual habitual buzz. It was more like shock and awe, to borrow a phrase. Time went into slow motion and stopped. My heartbeat also.

"You okay?" asked the voice of Brent. I tore my eyes away from the vision of loveliness to find him standing by my side.

In a casual tone of voice, I asked, "Who are those two women over there talking by the picnic table?"

"Oh, the black lady is Rafe's wife, Cora. I'm not sure who the other one is. Want me to do some sleuthing?"

"No, no, not necessary. Just wondering who they are."

"*They*? I think you mean *she*—the other one."

I ignored this.

"Ah, come on, Lone Ranger," he said with a knowing grin, "you're all agog. You really could use an intermediary."

That was Brent for you, a regular working-class guy who frequently used words like *intermediary* and *agog*.

"Nah, forget it," I said.

"I'll charge you the discount rate. Of course my full-suite matchmaker service will cost you more."

I shook my head, mouth firm, a bit of a scowl on the brow.

With a sympathetic look, he said, "Okay. But you looked pretty interested a moment ago. Why don't you just introduce yourself to her?"

No more was said, or done, because he suddenly rushed off to rescue one of his children, a toddler teetering too close to the barbecue.

I took a last wistful look at the wonderful woman, turned in the opposite direction, and strolled to the far side of the lawn as if nothing monumental had happened. I knew that someone like her wouldn't be interested in a guy like me. If I were to "just introduce" myself, I would be setting myself up for swift and permanent disappointment. It would be too painful. Life is not fair.

For the rest of the afternoon, I lingered around the edges of the party, straining to keep my eyes directed away from the radioactive core of the woman's presence. I busied myself greeting and receiving friendly greetings from coworkers, meeting their families, chatting. Two or three beers and a spicy hotdog later, I noticed Rafe approaching with his wife beside him.

"This is my wife, Cora, Cleve," he began. "Cora, this is Cleve."

She extended a forthright hand to me, with an equally forthright look. As we shook hands, I noted her warm personality, her graciousness and lack of guile. Clearly, this was a *real* person, an excellent match for my boss.

"So glad to meet you, Cleve. Rafe's told me a lot about you."

What? I thought.

"You're a writer, I hear."

"I used to be a writer, now I'm a carpenter," I said, checking quickly to see if the boss would squash this bit of presumption. "Not a very good one though," I added as a preemptive correction.

"He's learning, Cora," said Rafe with a fist-bump on my bicep. "This lad's a quick study."

"Well, don't give up on your novel," Cora said, making me wonder if she had intuited I wouldn't last long in the construction business or had heard something to that effect from her husband. On the other hand, maybe she liked to encourage creativity in people. How on earth had she heard about my novel?

"I used to be a philosopher," quipped Rafe. "Not a very good one though."

Cora leaned close to her husband, looping an arm through his. With the other she reached out and put a hand on my forearm. It was so intimate a gesture, as if I were part of their family circle, it disarmed me completely.

"He's Mr. Self-deprecation," she said with a sideways smile at her man. "Taught Medieval Philosophy, published papers in obscure journals, won a medal for his research."

"Yeah, yeah, then I got turfed out as the social revolution gathered momentum and the Humanities departments shrank."

"Their loss," said Cora.

"The students' loss, honey. That's the real tragedy. Now they have to live with blanked out zones on the existential spectrum. More and more of those vacant spaces every day, and the young people don't even know there's anything missing."

I stirred uncomfortably, feeling my own private blanked-out zones. Then, in a moment of weakness, I let my eyes flash left and right over their shoulders in search of the wonderful, beautiful woman whom I would never get to know. Where had she gone?

Cora glanced at her wristwatch. "Oh, dear, I'm going to have to run. I'm driving Annie to the airport. Great to meet you, Cleve." And off she dashed toward the house.

"Who's Annie?" I asked Rafe.

"My wife's best friend from college. She's been staying with us this past week while looking for medical work here in Calgary. She's a surgical nurse in Vancouver, or was, until she refused to assist in euthanasia at her hospital."

"Brave lady," I said.

"She is."

"I don't think I met her."

"You'd remember her if you had. Didn't you notice the very lovely woman in a blue dress?"

"I might have."

Annie, I thought. *Your name is Annie.*

Rafe explained that he had to go say good-bye to the said Annie and encouraged me to hang around as long as I liked, get to know people, mingle, have a go at faking extroversion. I promised to make an effort, then watched him head toward the house, his three children bounding after him like puppies. I strained for a last sight of their departing friend, but no such luck.

I will love you forever, Annie. Forever.

The crowd thinned eventually. I didn't want to go back to my empty apartment, so I sat down on the picnic bench where Annie had been, closing my eyes, feeling the background radiation of her presence. People came up and talked with me. I smiled and responded appropriately. But I didn't want to leave. Rafe wandered by and handed me another hamburger, fried onions, sesame bun, blue cheese dressing.

"How did you know?" I asked.

"Creature of habit, you are," he said and went off again.

I wondered anew over this unusual fellow, my employer, and also maybe a kind of friend.

An hour later everyone else had gone, but I lingered by the picnic table, cleaning up the scattered plates and cups, scrubbing the cooling BBQ with a wire brush, all in all just basically loitering without intent. I heard car doors slam from the front driveway, some shouted camaraderie, and then Rafe returned to the backyard.

"Yo, Cleve."

"Yo, Boss."

"Looks like we're the last men standing," he said with two beers in hand, giving me one. "Wanna sit down?"

We found lawn chairs under a flaming red maple tree.

"My baby," said Rafe patting the trunk. "Rare in our neck of the woods."

I nodded. Most maples in the west turned golden in autumn.

"Symbolic," I said.

"Nope, just beautiful."

The sun was touching the peaks of the blue mountain range on the horizon, with theatrical streaks of rose and tangerine, above which lime green bled seamlessly into indigo. Crimson leaves fluttered down about our ears. Solar yard lights were beginning to glow.

"Wonderful party, Rafe. Thanks for asking me."

"Good to have you with us. You're part of the crew, Cleve."

"An amazing crew, Boss, your band of merry men. It's not what I expected."

"What did you expect?"

I shrugged, made a ponderous facial expression. I didn't

answer him directly, just veered tangentially around the question.

"I notice most of the guys are married with kids," I said.

"Uh-huh. And . . . ?"

"They all look pretty happy. Even the unmarried ones. A lot of believers here today."

"Believers?"

"You know, churchgoers." I gave it a pause, took a sip of beer. "So, do you hire people based on their religious beliefs?"

"I hire people based on their character, which is a good indication of how honest and diligent they'll be as craftsmen."

"I'm glad you made an exception in my case."

"Knock it off, Cleve."

"It?"

"The chip."

"Okay," I said, and blew a loud breath across my shoulder. "Just curious, but how do you know what a guy's character is when you first hire him?"

"I don't, really. It's more a sense I've come to rely on. Now and then I'm wrong, of course, but even when I'm off-radar, the poorer hires usually shape up. Over the past ten years, a few of them have quit, but I've never had to fire anybody."

"That's an amazing track record."

"It is, thanks be to God."

God? I repeated lamely in my mind.

I wasn't a mind reader, but his reference to a deity must have triggered something in his thoughts. He leaned forward, elbows on knees, fingers of his hands twined together around the neck of his beer bottle.

"Cleve, I've been wondering if you'd ever like to come with us to a Sunday service at our church."

I stared at him, surprised. He was risking something here. This was definitely a violation of employer-employee relations, possibly illegal. Moreover, it was my first glimpse ever of his vulnerability. He had made the offer in a somewhat subdued voice, with a tentative look in his eyes that told me he was preparing himself to be disappointed.

"What kind of church?" I asked him, matching the subduedness, giving away nothing.

"We go to Sacred Heart parish," he said with a grave look, as if he felt that Catholicism compounded upon Christianity might be pushing the boundaries of tolerance to the outermost limits.

"Um, well, I used to be Catholic," I tossed off.

"No longer?"

"Nah, no longer," I murmured with a shrug, arguing to myself that if God had answered my prayer with a newspaper ad, it didn't mean I had to take on the whole package of belief.

"Why not?" he asked in a kindly voice, not wanting to sound like the Grand Inquisitor, I suppose.

I snorted. "Oh, lots of reasons. Scandals in the Church, a busy life, you know the scene."

"Yeah, I know the scene. Went through it myself, one time, long ago when I was a teen. But for me it was more a case of wanting sin without guilt feelings. The psychic drift just reinforced the subconscious, or maybe conscious, choice. I don't know which, but on some level, I did decide to turn my back on Christ."

I said nothing. *Sin?* Yup, mine had been a case of sin too—let's be specific here: it was a case of sex drive, cotton-candy wrapped in serial romances. But I didn't want to admit this to the man I had come to admire most in this world. How could I confess to him that I'd become a follower of another kind of religion, my own congregation of one—sinning and gulping down anti-Catholic propaganda. Glutting myself on electronic entertainment culture, from which the very thought of God had been banished, religion permitted in the storylines only for mockery and representation of ministers of faith as sociopaths, tyrants, abusers, or gullible fools. I had discarded the outmoded myth in the name of progress, had embraced social revolution as liberation. A very specific kind of revolution, however, for mine wasn't about loud aggression but rather the protection of civil liberties in the face of the insidious neo-totalitarianism that had infiltrated into positions of power everywhere. Neither was it about the lower forms of that same beast, the street anarchists shrieking their shopworn jargon into your face. I had enough honesty left in me to realize that both echelons of the new cultural uniformity were symbiotic fronts of a psyche war. And I knew that a good deal of this revolution business was based on distorted history, ongoing lies, hype and hysteria, Nietzschean smash-and-bash as the necessary prelude to a brave new utopia, weirdly mixed with Marxist templates, all draped in a thin veneer of democracy. I hated every bit of it. I believed myself superior to both sides, left and right—to all sides, actually. I was a man alone.

"*Psychic drift*, interesting phrase," I said to Rafe.

"Portions of the moral conscience shut down in me, you see, and that blunted the unwelcome feelings of guilt, which in turn dialed down real thinking, springboarding this huge case I made against the Faith."

"Uh-huh," I nodded.

"Or maybe the stages weren't so clear cut. I call it *drift* because a lot of it was overlap, some of it simultaneous, though it all started with me telling myself it was no big deal to fornicate and watch pornography and all the trappings that come with those activities. Told myself I wasn't harming anybody. Convinced myself it was all about love." He paused, looked down at the grass by his feet, shook his head, and then looked back at me. "Easy to lie to yourself when it feels so good. Funny thing, though, after a while it didn't feel so good. Fact is, it just got darker and more miserable."

"What about freedom? What about our right to choose?"

"Oh yeah," he replied with a grimace. "Some freedom that is, choosing to make yourself weaker and sicker. Then comes the day you realize you're an addict, hooked on the very thing that's killing you. And if you're honest enough with yourself, you admit that you've turned yourself into a slave . . . in the name of your precious illusion of freedom."

Now I was getting a fix on him. He was like a certain genre of reformed alcoholic who becomes the most preachy teetotaler prohibitionist in the world. It made me sad. Made me cringe a little, too, because I understood from experience everything he was saying.

"So, how did you get from there to asking your loyal employee to come to church with you?"

He took a sip from his beer bottle.

"I met the devil."

"You met the devil?" I tried to suppress a smile.

We were both rescued at that moment by his wife Cora calling across the lawn from the open patio door. She was back from the airport. It was bedtime for the kids, she said, they needed his blessing.

"Duty calls," said Rafe, as we both stood up. I waved to Cora, shouted my thanks for a great party, and said goodnight to the boss.

6

THREE WEEKS LATER, the monthly soirée at the Irish pub lasted the customary length of time, but for some reason I wanted to linger longer than was usual for me. Rafe, too, seemed reluctant to go. When we found ourselves alone, sipping the dregs, I ventured a delicate question:

"Boss, can I ask you something?"

"Fire away."

"You're my employer, and yet you've also become a kind of friend to me. You've shared some sensitive stuff from your past, the sort of things only true friends entrust to each other. It's hard to get my head around it sometimes . . . like where the lines are."

He pursed his lips, looking thoughtful, considering the question.

"I mean, I hope you'll feel free to fire me at any time, any place, at your convenience."

He chuckled. "That comes with the territory," he said.

"But friendship doesn't come with the territory."

He leaned way back in his chair, tilting it so it balanced on the two hind legs. Still pondering, he was not quite looking at me.

"You know," he said at last, "maybe it has something to do with those articles you wrote when you were a journalist. Somehow I came to feel that I knew you. We had a lot of the same ideas, and those ideas are fading out of the colloquium of public discourse. In fact, they're becoming rare. And soon, maybe sooner than we think, they're going to be outlawed."

Colloquium of public discourse? I wondered. Rafe was going all intellectual on me.

"I thought that most of the time your analyses were right on the mark, Cleve. But I kept asking myself, okay, this is a sharp guy, he wants truth, and I see what he's *against*, but what is he *for*?"

I took a moment to absorb this. "You're saying I was good at diagnosing cancer but a failure at offering treatment."

"Uh-huh. No offense."

"No offense taken."

"True friends can think together without frontiers, without blanked-out zones. Maybe that's all I mean."

I nodded. "So we have both employment and friendship. It's kind of unique."

"Not really. I think it happens all the time in all kinds of environments. Employment doesn't mean subservience. Call it a mutual exchange of goods and services, but if it's done right, it's way more than that. It's media, it's communication."

"Huh. *Media*. I'll have to think about that."

"When I hire someone, I'm always thinking this unique *person* is joining our community labor—a community of persons that's bigger than the sum of its parts, because human beings aren't reducible to functions, we're not mechanisms."

"Okay, I see it. That's a noble vision you've come up with."

He smiled. "Oh, I didn't come up with it. There have been papal encyclicals on the dignity of the worker and his labor."

"It's Catholic, then."

"Very much Catholic—quintessentially so; uniquely so."

"Is this why you became a Catholic?"

"Good heavens, no."

"Uh, you met the devil, right?"

"Right, I met the devil. Or one of his more vicious lieutenants. In any event, an evil spirit. Want to hear about it?"

"Okay."

I didn't really want to hear about it, because I was sure that whatever he was about to tell me was a figment of his imagination. The mind was all about chemistry and imprinting tracks in the brain. Angels and demons were arbitrary symbols, had been manufactured over millennia to express psychological conditions, our human dreads and hopes, just as other man-made symbols embodied the poles of pleasure or threat and everything in between. The mind was endlessly creating its subjective myths about reality.

He drew a breath, looking serious but apparently not burdened by the memory—rather, what he perceived to be a memory—of an objective experience.

"Maybe you recall me telling you about a dark time in my past, late teens, early twenties it was," he began. "My general condition was not good. I was deep into sin and addicted to it. As a result, not only my conscience but my mental state kept getting darker and darker. Depression set in. Not clinical depression, just a gloomy cloud that seemed to cover everything with meaninglessness. A void inside of me kept getting bigger all the time, and nothing would fill it. Nothing. Oh, there were constant thrills and pleasures, but I always felt emptier in the aftermath. Like a drug user, I had to keep increasing the dose to get the same high. I fought the darkness in every way I could, filling every waking hour with frantic activities, achievements, scrabbling for financial security, faking happiness, faking joy so I could tell myself I was just fine.

"I was working on my master's thesis, aiming for a

doctorate. My thesis was titled *The Death of God: The New Metaphysics*. Or to put it in plain English, it was about the necessity of killing any remnant of the culture of the divine as a prelude to finding the god within oneself. Intellectualizing everything to death but really just trying to build a rationale for my rejection of God's authority over me. I was reading plenty of existential philosophy and fiction that confirmed I was in the vanguard of civilization. That I was a visionary, like them."

Rafe paused here to chuckle. "Yup, I was right up there among the elite, at the cutting edge of evolution. But at night, I still had to look at the dark wall of the future. The black pit of meaninglessness, the void. Things just seemed to get darker and darker no matter how brilliantly I articulated it with my oh-so-superior intellect. And then in the wee small hours one night, a presence showed up at the foot of my bed. Well, this was quite a shock, because it was my first encounter with a real metaphysics."

"What do you mean, *real*?" I interrupted Rafe.

"It was a demon, Cleve. It was a conscious entity, it was present, and it was intent on devouring me . . . I should say, more like *possessing* me. Total control. And I felt waves of its hatred coming at me."

Rafe patted the top of his head. "My hair stood on end, which as you might guess is nearly impossible for a guy like me. I've been badly scared a few times in my life, but nothing like this. This was absolute, radical terror. At the same time it paralyzed me."

"Sleep deprivation, anxiety, it can do funny things to the mind, Rafe. Maybe you were projecting inner conflicts."

"I saw it with my own eyes. It was darkness made visible. It had a shape, and it sent its thoughts to me, its hatred of me, and it was moving toward my mouth, which was open in a silent scream."

"Okay, but it could have been a temporary hallucination caused by extreme emotional stress."

"Could have been, but wasn't. What happened next confirmed this."

"Uh, what happened next?"

"I cried out to God—the God I didn't believe in. Something basic in my soul, covered over with layers and layers of garbage, but still there. It was like a huge yell from my soul, not a sound from my lips, you see, just this pleading for help with my whole being. Instantly, this devil stopped advancing toward me. In fact it recoiled. I was still semi-paralyzed, but no longer totally. I rolled off the bed and onto the floor, still pleading with God. Then forgotten prayers rose up in me, words I'd been taught to pray in my childhood, lines from the twenty-third Psalm, parts of the Our Father, all swirling and mixed up but still pouring out of me soundlessly. The more I prayed, the more the thing backed off. And then an incredible peace fell over me, poured through me. I wasn't terrified any longer, wasn't paralyzed at all. I knelt up and kept praying, saying the name of Jesus over and over, now with my mouth. Then the black hole just sucked itself out of the room."

"Ever have any repeats of the episode?" I asked.

"During the following months, it returned three more times. Each time, the moment it appeared, I just got down on my knees and prayed. By then I'd returned to the sacraments, and was a lot more savvy about this kind of encounter. I was learning to pray better, with more clarity and consistency. Finally, I got smart and told the devil that if he ever bothered me again this way, I would increase my prayers even more and start praying for the most hardened sinners I knew—a category in which I included myself. After that, it never came back."

"So when was all this?"

"About fifteen years ago, before I met Cora, before I launched the company. I had to scrap my thesis, of course, because I now realized that it was a pile of clever drivel. I'd learned that there was an authentic metaphysical realm, mostly hidden from our eyes, and that it was a war zone. I'd nearly become a casualty. Around that time, I started reading the medieval philosophers, then the Fathers of the Church, the teachings of the saints and the holier sort of popes. I began to see that we'd been robbed by modernity and post-modernity or post-post-modernity or whatever the popular religion is now. A whole new world opened up for me. A kingdom, actually."

"And the rest, as they say, is history."

"And the present and the future. It's not a black wall, Cleve, it's the greatest adventure of all. It's the ultimate real."

The ultimate real, I thought to myself, still unconvinced. But I could see that *he* was convinced and that this conviction had somehow forged a stellar kind of man. Well, if it helped him get through life . . .

We both took sips of our beers. His must be growing warm.

Almost as an afterthought, he said, "But that's not why I became a Catholic."

"No? Seems to me you're implying just that."

"It had its role to play, shattering my illusions. At first, it was a case of me running from the portal of hell that had opened in front of me, that wanted to devour my life. But as I began to get fed real food, I got steadily stronger and more hopeful, genuinely happy at times. Fears declined, love started trickling in, the lights went on. Soon it was no longer a running *from* but a running *to*."

I said nothing, taking it all in, uncertain about how much objective truth there was in what he had told me.

"And that launched me on a whole new life, Cleve. Little by little, step by step, I began to discover what I was intended to be from the beginning."

To his credit, he let the matter rest that night. He might have pressed onward trying to bring down my mental and spiritual resistance, to overwhelm me with his preaching, but he didn't. His was a faith that never forced itself on others, never tried to sweep aside human freedom.

During my years of unbelief, as I wobbled back and forth between atheism and agnosticism, I had not for a moment considered that I had been inducted into a cult—the cult of the self as god. After my religious discussions with Rafe, however, I began to entertain the notion that there just might be something much bigger going on in existence and that it could very well be a cosmic war, mostly invisible to the eyes and senses. If this were the case, then I was dangerously close to becoming a casualty myself.

There came a time when I accepted his invitation to attend a church service with him. I argued to myself that I would do no more than go and see what it was all about. I would maintain my skepticism. After that, I would be able to decline any further involvement by pointing out that I had tried it and found that it wasn't my cup of tea, or rather my favorite brand of booze. So I went. And it wasn't anything like what I had imagined. It was quiet. It was kind of beautiful in an unostentatious way. It was peaceful. The peace especially moved me, because I hadn't felt anything like that since my childhood when my mother and father had brought me to Mass faithfully, where I sometimes felt an indescribable joy and consumed the Host unthinkingly, presuming that its sweet warmth radiating through me was no more than my due.

As a boy, my nature had been endlessly distractible, short on memory and understanding, dominated by my ever-changing secular enthusiasms. When adolescence got underway, my passions and my impulse to rebellion ramped up simultaneously. My parents continued to insist that I attend Sunday Mass with them, and I went along, enduring it, secretly fuming. And as soon as I could make my escape, I was off into the wild blue yonder of academia and pride and ten thousand wolf-traps of mind and soul.

My return to the faith of my childhood came about in fits and starts. It was a process, to be sure, but one not initially comprehensible to me. I began to read books that Rafe lent me, inhaling for the first time the bracing atmosphere of a magnificent universe—dangerous and beautiful and true. As Rafe's experience had been, my darkness lifted little by little, love trickled in, slowly but surely changing from seepage into a brook. As I began to understand the toxic consequences of modernist myths, the brook became a river. To continue the metaphor, there came a moment when I made the decision to plunge into the deep water. I made the longest confession of my life to a wise old priest who knew the ways of God and man and how we creatures tell lies to ourselves. Like a doctor of the soul, he patiently guided me through, and, above all, he gave me absolution, which to my amazement was a liberation that felt like no other I had ever experienced. When I received Communion for the first time in years, I wept silently, joyfully, all the way back from the altar rail to the pew where I knelt down beside Rafe and Cora and their girls.

This is not a book of apologetics. It's a narrative of momentous events, but I cannot leave out the part about my conversion, because what later happened to me and my family and circle of friends depended a great deal upon it. Suffice it to say for now that my transformation has never ceased during all the years since then. It was, and is, a journey of restoration to what I was intended to be from the beginning.

I should mention one encounter that occurred shortly after my return to the Church. By then my father had done what he had planned during my mother's final months of life: he had sold the house, paid most of his bills, and was now scrimping out an existence in a two-room apartment in a run-down inner city district. He persistently refused any financial help from his children, insisting that he didn't need much to live on, he had his books and his faith—"I feel the Lord closer than ever before," he would say in response to our various sorts of pressure. "You and my precious grandchildren are my joy, my inheritance. What more could a man want?"

One weekend I drove north to Edmonton to speak with my father face-to-face about what had happened to me. I knew he deserved that much after all the grief I had put him and my mother through. When we sat down at his kitchen table over cups of coffee and I told him, his reaction wasn't what I expected.

First he said nothing, then he covered his face with his hands and began to cry. This was a dignified, educated, highly respected teacher, a responsible and even-tempered man beloved by all who knew him. I had seen him cry only once before in my life, at my mother's funeral.

When he looked up at last, I took his hand across the table and said, "I'm sorry for all the worry I gave you, Dad. Please forgive me."

"I forgive you, Cleve," he said in a choked voice. "You know I forgive you."

"I only wish Mum had lived long enough to see me come back to the faith."

He smiled and wiped his face. "Oh, she knew," he said.

He was speaking in the past tense, which made no sense to me.

"We prayed so much for you over the years, son. Your Mum told me that three times she heard a voice speaking to her when she was praying for you—praying desperately, I hope you don't mind me mentioning."

"Voices spoke to her?"

"Yes, twice in the voice of Our Lady, she said, and once in the voice of Our Lord. Each time they said, 'He will return.'"

Then it was my turn to cry.

7

MY CONVERSION OCCURRED during the third year I worked for Raphael's Construction. From then on, I continued to attend Sunday Mass without fail and as many daily Masses as I could get to, usually in the evenings. Most parishioners of Sacred Heart parish attended a morning liturgy during the weekdays, but our pastor, Fr. John, also offered one every evening so that working people could attend. Confession times were frequent, and he could be counted on, as well, to hear your confession any time you knocked on his rectory door.

He was a wonderfully kind man, endlessly patient and serene, despite the ever-increasing turns of the screw from government agencies. The perpetual twinkle in his eyes was the visible form of the love that emanated from him like a pilot light that never ran out of fuel, that nothing could blow out.

After Sunday Masses, there was always a coffee and doughnut social in the parish hall, down in the basement under the church. It provided a means for me to meet a wider circle of people with strong faith. They began to feel like family—soul family. All the human damage was present, just as it was out there in the wider world. There was, however, no evidence of despair. Somehow these folks bore their physical and/or occasional mental infirmities with grace. The majority in the parish were older people, and as I got to talking with them, I heard stories about the apostasies in their extended families, broken marriages, a suicide, cancer, a sword in the heart from offspring who had broken off contact because of their parents' or grandparents' supposed "religious fanaticism." These people suffered, but they all found strength and consolation in prayer and sacraments—and, I came to realize, in each other.

My own age group was limited to a few solitaries who socially didn't quite fit in and who were consequently very focused on Christ himself. They were charitable and eager to help anyone in need, but they were, as I had been, a displaced generation. There was also a growing minority of young marrieds, with a surprising number of children. It seemed to me that by an immense miracle of grace they had stumbled out of the darkness of our times and were finding in the Faith the strength to raise their families in peace and hope. In low moments, I wondered how long it would last. The churches still functioned in plain sight, but they were being increasingly surrounded by government strictures that sought to neutralize any positive effect religion might have on society. As the noose slowly tightened, a great sifting was underway, with some churches compromising and some standing firm, willing to live with the consequences.

The federal government had just revoked our diocese's charitable institution status, after the bishop—a man with spine—refused to silence his priests on matters of the sacredness of life and gender. Charged with alleged "hate crimes", i.e., preaching the Gospel, he was currently waiting for his day in court, a pending hearing at our "Human Rights Tribunal." He might soon be off to prison for a very long time.

I was angry about the insanity that was gathering momentum on every front, and in recent weeks found myself returning to my old street-fighter mode, composing blistering articles in my mind, knowing full well that there was no longer any venue for their publication. The internet had by then come under total governmental control. Moreover, the state could block access to any dissident voices trying to enter the country from outside sources. Not that there *were* many remaining sources. And, I wondered, was there much of a remaining audience? The entire continent was now populated by three generations who had been force-fed Huxleyan *soma* swill.

I often discussed the infuriating state of affairs with Rafe and Cora, whenever they invited me over for supper. However, I was careful not to vent my spleen in front of their children. By then I had been pulled into a kind of uncle role with the three girls, who made me read them stories after supper, demanded endless games of checkers, and at times exhibited a disconcerting lack of guile, saying things like "Why aren't you married, Cleve?" or making me laugh with their charmingly naïve comments, such as "Cleve, did you know Mummy and Daddy were children once?"

"No!" I would reply, shocked. "It can't be true!" Which made them break into a fit of giggling.

Their names were Josie ("I was named for St. Josephine Bakhita," the girl explained). She was eleven years old. Next came a sweetheart named Rose, age nine, and finally bright and shiny Penny, age seven.

I really came to love those kids, and at one point it struck me like a revelation that, despite all evidence to the contrary, I might, somehow, miraculously, make a good father one day.

Occasionally, after night prayers and last kisses and the girls were tucked into bed, Rafe and Cora and I would discuss the state of the country. As was my wont, I fumed. I gave free rein to my darker thoughts. I tried not to hate, but my feelings were strong. Over time, I believe my friends helped me a lot in this regard. The way they maintained their inner peace was infectious, and Rafe kept feeding me sane, rational analyses devoid of anything like my old habitual rancor.

"Those baby-boomers!" I once seethed with disgust. "They destroyed our civilization!"

"No, Cleve, they didn't destroy civilization. They were floating on a wave of victory over evil, trusting that right had prevailed against tyranny and that progress would sweep us into a prosperous future. They didn't foresee that the imposed transvaluation of all values was coming. They didn't recognize it when it began to seize hold of everything in the sixties. And when they finally realized what was happening, they didn't know how to resist."

"Yeah, and they gave birth to the Gen Xers, who in turn begat the Millennials, and now we're living in a Post-Millennial society that kills a helluva lot of innocent people."

"Each successive generation became more confused, rootless, unmoored from fundamental principles, and ever more vulnerable to indoctrination. Our parents had to deal with a rapidly dechristianizing society. We've had to cope with the results—a dehumanized society."

"And what will that lead to, Rafe? What will our children inherit?"

"If worse comes to worst, a diabolical society," he answered grimly.

"Unless something big happens to shake the world to the foundations."

"We mustn't discount the revival of the Faith that's spreading everywhere among the young—an incredible new generation."

"But if their efforts don't turn things around, Rafe, then

what? God'll *have* to send a huge shakeup—maybe some kind of global shock."

"Have to? Mmmm. Be careful what you hope for, Cleve. Who can measure the consequences of a global shock? Some people might wake up and change their lives, but others might go deeper into evil."

Rafe loved to quote from his favorite authors, invariably writers from the past.

"You know, Cleve, Chesterton once wrote, sometime in the 1930s, that in the future it would become necessary to argue that the grass is green and the sky is blue."

"Who is Chesterton?" I asked.

"A unique kind of genius, a journalist among other things. More importantly, he was a convert who somehow worked his way out of every mass delusion of the late nineteenth and early twentieth centuries. He was a singularly honest man, which helped him in his journey to the Catholic Faith."

"That's a century ago, when the Western world was still basically Christian," I said with a sigh. "Nowadays you could make a Supreme Court case in favor of green grass and blue skies, and you'd probably lose. Even if you won it technically, no one would care."

"Ooh, sweetie," said Cora. "Don't lose your faith in humanity. People can change."

"If they want to," I replied glumly, and then had a backflash of my own mental attitudes during my years of unbelief.

Something melted in me whenever she called me *sweetie* in that tone of voice. Like an auntie soothing an errant nephew. Like I somehow belonged.

Regrettably, there was one incident when I failed to control myself, having foolishly listened to the national news on the truck radio while driving over to their place—the "news" courtesy of our own posturing, sycophantic, mass-produced influencers, reporters, and editors—our Fourth Estate, supposedly objective, supposedly champions of freedom, who would have been the envy of Dr. Goebbels' Reich Ministry of Public Enlightenment and Propaganda. *Pravda*, too, for that matter. But I digress.

After supper I vented aloud to Rafe and Cora, forgetting for the moment that there were children in the room. They stopped their play and listened with worried faces. Catching myself, I brought my torrent to a halt.

"Let's pray," said Rafe. He and his wife and the girls slid down onto their knees right there in their living room. I followed their example. Rafe asked God for strength and grace and peace in the midst of the rising storms. Cora asked for wisdom and prudence, for protection of their children's minds and souls. The children unabashedly asked Jesus for various intentions, the eldest daughter for success in her coming school exams, the middle daughter for a "fun trip" to the Rockies next summer, the youngest for a new baby for the family. The eldest kicked in once more at the end and said, aloud, "Please bring someone for Cleve to love so he'll be happy again."

Cora intervened quickly, and led the sign of the cross, then hustled the young ones off to the kitchen to prepare treats.

"Sorry about that," said Rafe with a look of chagrin. "I hope you know we don't talk about you in front of them."

I nodded. "My sorry, Rafe. I really have to watch this bitterness thing in me. It sure rears its nasty head without warning."

"The ferocious articulator that you once were, my man, was not without his redeeming qualities. However, I think the Lord would like to show you that we now have to fight in a better way."

"I know, I know," I whispered with a shake of the head. "I've still got a long way to go."

He smacked the arms of his chair and said, "Would you like a beer? I just capped an experimental home-brew a couple of days ago."

"Would I be risking my life drinking it?"

"Definitely. But think of the alternatives."

"I am."

We laughed and moved on.

During the several months since encountering the magnificent, radiant, wondrous, beautiful, impossibly inaccessible Annie at the barbecue party the previous summer, I had not given in to the urge to ask the Morrows about her. Nonetheless, I thought about her all the time and even dreamed about her in my sleep, which says a lot. I was totally, hopelessly in love—emphasis on hopelessly.

Once a month a pancake brunch was offered by the Knights of Columbus, an organization that had been recently outlawed in our country, but whose members cheerfully soldiered on without regalia and swords. Yup, there's nothing like trials and tribulations to reveal who the true knights are. One spring day after Sunday Mass, I went downstairs to the basement hall, looking forward to the brunch.

And there she was, standing in the lineup moving slowly toward the serving table manned by knights.

At that very moment, I was struck by an illumination that seemed to come out of nowhere, like a flash of lightning. It informed me that I would get to know her and that we would be married. I wasn't sure how true this was. Everything argued against it. Was it wishful thinking on my part, even wistful obsession, generating a longed-for chimera of the mind? As I found a place at the end of the line, my heart beat faster and I kept swallowing, overcome by awe and fear.

Fear of loss, perhaps. Even so, by the time the knights were filling my plate with pancakes and sausages and scrambled eggs, the dream of our shared future, Annie's and mine, had grown to the level of a mysterious kind of knowledge. I was either totally unbalanced or was suffused with a grace sent by the Holy Spirit. I did not bother to consider the former possibility because my life now depended entirely on the latter being true.

She had already taken a seat on the far side of the hall, at a table with Rafe and Cora's girls, who were busily eating their brunch and chatting merrily with her. She did not see me approach. My hands were trembling so much I dropped the silverware onto the floor, making the children look up. They beamed, and the youngest girl cried, "Oh, yay, it's Cleve!" and the eldest said, "Sit with us, Cleve, c'mon sit with us!"

I seated myself on a vacant stacking chair across the table from Annie. For the first time in my life I looked her in the eyes and almost fell into the pool of those eyes, unable to say anything, unable to look away. Realizing that my mouth was hanging open, and remembering also the knife and fork and spoon scattered on the floor, I jumped up to get them, knocking over the chair. After righting it with a red face, I retrieved the cutlery, returned to the table, and sat down.

"I'll get you clean utensils," said Annie in the sweetest, most beautiful voice I had ever heard.

"Oh, no, no, please, I'm . . ." But she was up and gone before I could stop her. I bowed my head and prayed silently. "Thank you Lord for this food, please bless it in your holy name, and thank you for bringing her here . . . please don't let me make a mess of things." I made the sign of the cross and looked up.

She was back. Regarding me with a small smile, she handed me clean utensils.

My mouth was still half open, my eyes unblinking. The girls giggled.

"My name's Annie," she said, extending her hand for a shake.

"I know," I said, and reached across the table and shook it. Her grip was warm, firm but gentle. Mine was vibrating. I didn't let go of her hand. She began to look a little uncomfortable, but disentangled herself graciously.

"And you are?" she asked.

One of the girls broke in. "He's Cleve, Daddy's friend."

I cleared my throat. "And employee," I added.

"I'm staying with the Morrows right now," she went on. "Cora's an old friend from university years."

"I know," I said again, idiotically.

She gave me a quizzical look and turned her attention to her pancakes.

When the girls had finished their meals, they ran off, carrying their dishes to the kitchen, leaving me alone with Annie.

I took a deep breath. "I realize this will sound strange," I began. "You don't know me, but I would be so pleased and grateful if you were to agree to take a walk with me."

She half smiled. "That's a rather formal sounding invitation. But, sure, we could take a walk together sometime. When were you thinking?"

"Would now be appropriate?"

"Appropriate?"

"I mean, would it fit in with your schedule?"

"Um, well, I don't know. I'll have to ask Cora and Rafe when they're planning to head home. I'm dependent on them for a ride."

"I could drive you home."

She didn't reply immediately. She gazed at me with a quiet,

noncommittal expression. I think she was assessing me and the implications.

"I'm quite harmless," I said, which made her smile. "And my intentions are honorable, in fact the highest." Which broadened her smile.

Finally she blinked and said, "Well, we *have* just consumed too much sugar and starch, and it would be good to walk some of it off."

"There's a nice park with walkways around the city reservoir, not far from here. Would you like to see it?"

"Yes, all right," she answered tentatively.

She went away to the kitchen to consult with her hosts. Within a minute, Rafe in an apron was shooting me a big wave from the kitchen's service window. I waved back.

Out in the church parking lot, I led Annie to my battered pickup truck.

"Nothing fancy," I said apologetically.

"This is fine. I prefer plain and simple."

"Just give me a moment," I said and hopped inside to clear off the passenger seat, stuffing all kinds of litter out of sight, brushing away dust and wood chips, and shifting my tool kit to the rear carry box.

All kinds of scenarios were bouncing around in my head—I mean dialogue scenarios, such as the options of me being witty and charming, or serious thinker loaded with insights, or the clownish joker, or even the strong silent type. None of it seemed right. I think I was a bit disoriented actually. I opened the passenger door for her, and she climbed in.

We drove across a bridge on the Bow River to the west side of the city and then down the Sarcee Trail, and after skirting the Tsuu T'ina native reserve, headed east again toward the park I wanted to show her. Since we left the church, there had been no further conversation. Annie seemed relaxed, her long brown hair billowing in the breeze that came through our windows, open a few inches for ventilation. I felt from time to time her face briefly turn toward me, probably trying to figure me out. I kept my eyes on the road. For most of the drive, she drank in the view, the pale green trees budding in early spring sunshine, the blue sky feathered with high cloud. Yup, green and blue, just the way colors are supposed to be. Finally we arrived at the Glenmore Reservoir. This was a large artificial lake on the southwest borders of the city, fed by the Elbow River, with the downtown skyline in the distance and bordered by pathways and trees flanking the water. I parked the truck in a public access lot, and we got out.

The pathway sloped down close to the water's edge, then meandered along the embankment among copses of trees and swaths of grass turning from winter-brown to green. A lot of birds were singing. The air was pure, no hint of urban exhaust. We walked for a few minutes until we paused by a slip of water reeds to watch frogs leaping away from us in panic.

I wondered if Rafe or Cora had informed Annie that I was a frog that was hopefully morphing into a prince. In the age of fairy tales long past, the metaphor would have been apt, but now it was far more common to see princes changing into frogs. Maybe most boys still started off as a potential prince and even matured partway into one. But how many of them got sidetracked along the way, as I had.

"I suppose Rafe or Cora told you about me," I said.

"Nothing much, since it's hard to condense a life into a minute's summary," she replied with a smile. "Rafe just said that you're a 'good guy'. Cora told me that a walk would do us both good."

I was inordinately pleased by the reference they'd given

me. Relieved, actually. It meant there might be a glimmer of hope. Lightning flashes were fleeting, after all, and subjective human judgments were always front and center in relationships.

We walked on.

"Are you looking for work in Calgary?" I asked.

"I'm giving it one more try. Last year I lost my job in Vancouver because I refused to assist in abortions and euthanasia. Alberta's a little more lenient in respecting the conscience rights of medical practitioners."

"For how long?" I said. "The government's just extended the assisted death laws to include people with mental illness, depression, anyone who asks for it, really."

She nodded somberly. "And sometimes people who don't ask for it."

"So what are you going to do?"

"I'm not sure. This past winter I worked among the Dené people in the Northwest Territories. A remote outpost nursing station. Delivered babies, sewed up cuts, tried to keep teenagers from killing themselves . . ."

"Killing themselves?"

"It's almost an epidemic in our native communities. It breaks my heart. Drugs and alcohol are part of the problem, but I think it's something deeper. The fracturing of family life, of course, but that's universal now. I believe the real problem is that many young people feel so worthless, adrift, not knowing who they are or what they came from."

"That's also pretty universal," I said.

She nodded, her face solemn. We walked on in silence.

"I don't mean cultural or historical identity, as important as that is," she said at last. "It's more like they've inhaled a poisonous toxin in the atmosphere. Whenever I talk to the young, I find there's so much depression. At root they have no sense whatsoever of their eternal value."

"Why did you leave?"

"I didn't want to. But, like every place on earth, there was a division in the community between people with deep insight and others who think that politics and money are salvation. The band council voted by a slim majority to terminate my employment. The rage-and-politics people wanted me out, you see. The minority urged me to stay, said they'd try to raise funds to keep me there, maybe doing some counseling or catechetics. It was a hard choice for me, because I really loved them, and some of them really loved me."

Who could not love you? I thought.

"How did you arrive at a decision?"

"I prayed a lot for guidance. In the end, this light just came, a gentle certainty that I should go see the Morrows and take it from there. There was peace in it, which surprised me. I really grieved over leaving my friends up north, but I wanted God's will above all. So here I am."

"Here you are," I echoed somewhat breathlessly.

Not much more was said that day. As we walked along, I felt no compulsion to blab my intellectual ruminations. I was merely grateful to be in her company. As we circled the lake I hoped that she couldn't hear my loudly drumming heart, hoped as well that she would be open to more encounters with me. But I knew that my general physical appearance was nothing a woman like her would find attractive, and my personality or character, such as it was, wasn't helping any, being somewhat obscure, due to my silence.

When we returned to my truck, I opened the passenger door for her, then went to the driver's side and got in.

As we drove away, she said with a pleasant smile and look, "Thank you. That was really refreshing."

"If you like, we could come back here another time," I said.

She didn't respond immediately, during which hiatus I understood that she had completed her assessment of me and found me wanting. My heart sank.

Then she said quietly, "I would enjoy that very much," making me almost run through a stop sign. I braked hard.

"Sorry," I said.

"Not to worry," she replied with eyes full of mirth.

When we arrived at the Morrows, she turned to me and said, "Why don't you come in for a few minutes, Cleve."

Cleve. The first time she had used my name.

And that led to Rafe and Cora inviting me to join them for supper. Throughout the late afternoon, I didn't say much, mainly just watched Annie interacting with the children. I pulled some carrots for Cora from the backyard garden and helped Rafe move some summer lawn furniture out of storage in the garage. Nobody probed. No hinting, no curiosity about how my time with Annie had gone. Business as usual. Everything normal, though in my heart I knew that the balance of the universe had radically shifted.

After supper, I stayed and stayed. Annie and I joined in family prayers, and later we listened to Rafe reading to the three girls from a children's book—a nightly ritual. When their father told them it was time for them to get into pajamas, I stood to make my goodbyes.

Annie gave me a farewell smile. Cora gave me a hug. Rafe walked me to the front door. As I was about to step out onto the porch, I overheard Josie the eldest say to her mother, "Annie is so pretty and Cleve is *sooo* handsome."

Rafe gave me an arch look, and I beat a hasty retreat.

Sooo handsome. Hoo-boy, the endearing delusions of childhood. I had trouble getting to sleep that night, playing and replaying the walk with Annie, every word, every facial expression crystal clear in memory. Somehow I managed to slide into sleep.

The next morning, after brushing my teeth, I looked more closely into the bathroom mirror, trying to detect signs that I might be going downhill. Nothing had changed since yesterday. The fine crow's feet were suitable for my age, the shadows under my eyes were no darker; my face needed a shave, and my sandy hair was overdue for a trim. Though it was not my habit to spend more than a few seconds a day looking at my reflected appearance, it struck me that my face and arms were now a healthy looking tan-bronze, the result of frequently working outdoors the past few years.

Off went the sweaty tee-shirt. I straightened my spine, flexed my biceps, and squared my shoulders. Well, this was something of a surprise. It seemed that without me noting the changes, I had been metamorphosed from a skinny computer geek into a robust man. Uh-huh, I had unknowingly graduated from Not-a-Great-Catch category to an Okay-Catch, maybe even to Pretty-Good-Catch in environments with subdued lighting. There was hope after all!

There is too much to tell about how we arrived at our wedding day. Needless to say, there were hundreds of hours of conversation, many walks, much kindly repartee and wholesome laughter. I loved her laugh, as warm as honey. I was always moved by her deeper insights, her wise thoughts about faith, people, human relationships. In time, all of this led to hand-holding. And then came the autumn day when we walked around the reservoir, stopping now and then to look up at the arrowheads of geese flying south for the winter, honking in bird conversation.

"Geese mate for life," I said.

She turned to me and smiled.

I went down on one knee and took her right hand in both of mine.

"Annie, will you marry me?" I asked.

"Yes, Cleve, I will," she answered. Without hesitation. Without qualm or reservation.

Stunned, I got up and wrapped my arms around her. She held on tightly.

"For life," I whispered. "Forever."

"Forever and a day," she whispered back.

We kissed. Our first. Short and intoxicating.

"To be continued," she said with a laugh, pulling back.

I was momentarily distracted when I spotted over her shoulder an elderly lady sitting on a park bench ten feet away. She was propped upright with both hands on a cane, her back was bowed, her face lifted, beaming at us, nodding and nodding and nodding her approval.

We were married by a priest friend of Annie's family in a parish in Vancouver. The parish had been closed down by the provincial government, chains and padlocks on all the front doors, yellow crime-scene tape across the steps, and warning signs posted. It wasn't stated, but I thought to myself, *Scene of Thoughtcrime*. The former pastor, a man now living unobtrusively somewhere in the city, still had the key to the back door of the sacristy. Hundreds of people attended the Mass, which was illuminated by candlelight only. It was so cold in there you could see everyone's breath, but this didn't put a damper on the festive atmosphere. Cora was bridesmaid, Rafe my best man. The Anti-happiness Police must have had their eyes turned elsewhere that day, because there was no state interference. Amazingly, no informers, no brainwashed neighbors had blown the whistle. Doubtless an entire brigade of angels was hard at work.

After the evening pot luck banquet held in a rented meeting hall, Annie and I drove away in my pickup truck, launched on our honeymoon, a short drive up the Fraser River valley to the town of Hope. There I had reserved a room for the night in a hotel overlooking the river, surrounded by close mountains and canopied with a dazzling display of stars.

I do believe we conceived our baby there that night.

The next day we headed northeast on the Coquihalla highway, which took us deeper into the Rockies. After a few hours climbing higher and higher, we turned east onto 97, which brought us to the city of Kelowna in the Okanagan Valley, a region that sported countless fruit orchards surrounded by barren hills. I took Annie on a side tour of the little town where I had lived as a boy, told her about my summers picking peaches the size of softballs dripping syrup and building secret shelters in the arid soil beyond the reach of irrigation systems. How I and my pals had died a thousand deaths as we practiced bravado and, at times, real bravery. I told her about the venomous rattlesnakes and showed her the cacti growing anomalously in the midst of our chilly nation.

Beyond Kelowna, we spent our second night in a motel room near the town of Oyama. Arising early, we swam in the jade-green, freezing cold Kalamalka Lake, had breakfast of bacon and eggs and dark roast coffee, and pressed on. We drove northward through Vernon and Enderby, and when we reached Salmon Arm, we turned right onto number 1 highway, the Trans-Canada, which would take us through some of the most staggeringly beautiful mountains in the

Rockies. It was a long day's drive, but we didn't feel the passage of time.

We passed through a snowstorm around Revelstoke, then I drove more carefully through Kicking Horse Pass, onward to Lake Louise, and finally we stopped for supper in the resort city of Banff, where the snow had eased off. We might have stayed overnight there, but the plows had been busy on the highway, and by mutual agreement Annie and I continued on through the dark, observing the night-glow of Calgary rising on the eastern horizon. Two hours later, I was unlocking the door of our own little palace on the south side of the city, about halfway to the satellite town of Okotoks. I had recently purchased this bungalow in a street of similar dwellings, all of them older and poorer than the houses typical of the economically prospering city. It was the only house on the market that I could even remotely afford. Annie loved it when I first showed it to her. "It has character," she said.

We had spent weeks cleaning and decorating, hardly believing that it would one day be ours. Each night we had kissed each other goodbye and returned to our separate places of residence, me to my hollow apartment, she to the happy hubbub of the Morrows.

Now we stood hand-in-hand in the entrance hall and looked all about us.

"We're home," I said.

"We're home," breathed Annie, joyful light shining through her.

8

THE DAY THAT CHANGED EVERYTHING began as usual. I awoke from a muddled dream that was mildly dramatic, in technicolor, and fairly ridiculous in the way of such dreams. Something about a bird and a giant. Within seconds it began to fade.

Another day, was my first semi-conscious thought. *Another day at the end of the world.* Then added the necessary corollary: *as we know it.*

As quietly as I could, I got myself out of bed, noting the rise and fall of Annie's breathing in the bed beside me. Yawning, barefoot, and in pajamas, I shuffled along the hallway and into the kitchen.

Coffee, coffee, coffee, coffee.

A look through the window over the sink told me that it would be a fair summer day, nearly cloudless, the eastern horizon glowing with a pale rose tint.

I turned on the coffee maker and got it rumbling, hoping that the sound and smell would not awaken my wife. *Mr. Zombie on autopilot*, I thought. Then, after filling up the mug with the Raphael's logo on it, I opened the back door carefully and went out into the yard, carrying my steaming wake-up drink with me. The grass was overdue for a mowing, ankle high, damp on my feet, a not unpleasant, natural sensation. The air was still cool, and as I dragged large bellows of it into my lungs, I couldn't help smiling, thinking that no matter how crazy the world was, I was relatively young and strong, and a whole lot of good things hadn't yet been made illegal or socially anathematized.

After seating myself on top of the picnic table, my feet on the bench, I took a few sips, thinking that it was a good thing I'd remembered to get coffee at the black market yesterday, good thing I'd oiled the door hinges not too long ago. It was a Saturday morning, allowing me the luxury of basking in a leisurely planning of my day, itemizing the things that needed fixing around the house: replacing some roof shingles on our beloved little wreck of a bungalow, mowing the lawn, phoning my Dad, then shopping and other chores I would run for Annie. I would make a nice supper for her. Afterward, we'd sit arm in arm, dreaming of the future, soaking ourselves in the long, slow thrill of anticipating the baby's gender (we wanted to be surprised) and his or her name.

My given name is Cleveland, though I was born in Cincinnati. My father, a Canadian, had been studying at Mount St. Joseph University in that city, where he met my mother, an American, at a meeting of the Catholic Youth Organization in a parish close to the campus. They fell in love, married, and lived in cramped student quarters until his graduation. Then they moved north of the border, teaching in several places, including the Okanagan, until finally settling in Edmonton.

My mother's family was rooted in Cleveland, and she missed them a lot. Thankfully, she named me after *her* birthplace. Consider the diminutive if she'd named me after *my* birthplace. *Cleve* was okay, but it convinced Annie and me not to name any of our children after cities.

The sun rose gently over the horizon of high-rise office towers to the north. Now I could hear the nearby hum of the highway slowly coming awake. It all looked so normal—so like a beautiful morning in Pompeii, with only a wisp of vapor rising from Vesuvius.

Bits and pieces of the dream returned to me, the bird, the giant, the hilly forest. And with them came a certain uneasiness that had no obvious explanation. I attributed it to my ongoing worries about the degenerating condition of our society, nation, world.

Wars and rumors of wars, I thought. *Pandemics and rumors of pandemics. Fear and franticness in the populace at large, decline of civil liberties in the name of health and security, mesmerization by constant propaganda, the cold calculators, on one hand, the ragers and haters, on the other, the ecclesial confusions, the betrayers, the strutting of the wicked, the machinations of the basest of men and women who rule in high places—*

Catching myself, I cut off the mushrooming editorial in mid-rant. I bowed my head, remembering how blind I, too, had been before encountering the light of Christ. The social revolutionaries, left-right-center, high and low, were no worse than I once was. Oh yes, I had avoided being infected by their politics, had critiqued their endless scheming, but I, no less than they, had succumbed to the lightless core hidden beneath it all—the elevation of the self as supreme god, a sad little love affair with myself.

I got down from the picnic table and knelt in the damp grass, trying to shake the dark mood that had appeared without warning on this bright shining morn. I prayed:

"Forgive me, Lord, please forgive me for whatever of that old blindness remains in me. Please bless Annie and our baby. You know what they mean to me. They're the best gift I've ever received, after knowing *you*, and I love them so much. Please show us the way through these times."

For the thousandth time, I reminded myself of the liberation I had found, the wonder of deep friendship combined with blessed passion. *Love stronger than death*, said the Song of Songs. I now had hope in the possibility of making an island of good living in the midst of the surrounding madness. I had so recently come to believe in God's love. Now, through Annie, I had come to believe in indestructible human love.

I lifted my head when I heard her voice through the open bedroom window.

"Cleve to me," she called.

"Cleve coming to a bedside near you," I answered, reciting our well-worn banter.

Back in the kitchen, I made her a cup of peppermint tea the way she liked it, with a dab of honey, and carried it into our bedroom. She sat up and took the cup gratefully.

"Thanks," she whispered, blowing steam off the top. "You look suitably rumpled this morning. Why are there wet grass stains on your knees?"

"I was greeting the dawn enthusiastically. Did you sleep all right?"

"Off and on. Three or four times a foot or elbow jolted me awake."

"The baby's exercising." I gently patted her rotund belly. She was seven and a half months pregnant with our first child.

"It was *your* foot and elbow, buddy," she said.

"Ooh, sorry, honey."

"You were mumbling, too, having a bad dream by the sounds of it."

"Mmm, not really a bad dream, just kind of mysterious."

"You were so restless when we went to bed last night, Cleve. I know something's worrying you."

"Nothing's worrying me."

"C'mon, you can tell me. What's bothering you? Things not going well with Rafe and the company?"

"Rafe and company are doing fine."

I took a sip of coffee, she took a sip of her tea.

"The dream's mostly faded now," I said, avoiding her next question. "I can remember a few details. It was something about a giant striding along a road, with a little bird flying ahead of him, singing. See what I mean; it's nothing to get worried about."

She took another sip, examining my eyes. "The bird was singing or the giant was singing?"

"Both of us. The bird was way up high and ahead of me—"

"So *you* were the giant!"

"Er, no. I wasn't the giant, I was *with* the giant—it's hard to explain. Anyway, this bird was about a hundred feet ahead of us, and it was tied to my finger by a golden thread." I chuckled. "I thought I was controlling the bird, you see, but in reality it controlled me. Well, not exactly control, more like it was leading me somewhere. The thread was so fine, I could have snapped it at any moment."

"Led by a wily canary," she said with a laugh.

"It wasn't a canary. It was blue, the most astonishing blue I ever saw in my life, turquoise at the head with the tiny feathers changing color along the body, gradually becoming a kind of royal blue and finally indigo at the tail. It was just amazing the way the color changed without any breaks."

"Deeply significant, psychologically," she grinned. "Did you find out where it was taking you?"

I strained to recall more of the evaporating bits.

"It was taking me into hilly country with mountains in the distance. We were on a dirt road winding through a forest, and we arrived finally at a log cabin. I think it was my uncle's."

"Your uncle?"

"My Uncle Dave, my Dad's older brother. He had this cabin in the foothills down by Waterton Park, not far from the U.S. border. He spent every summer there, and after he retired, he went to live there full-time. Dad and I visited him once, when I was about ten or so. Uncle Dave died a few years ago and left the cabin to Dad."

My heart sank at the thought that my father was now fighting stage 4 cancer, living his final days in an Edmonton hospice, which was itself in major crisis because the government was demanding that "medical assistance in dying" be provided by all health-care facilities, even in private Catholic institutions. The hospice board had been fighting battle after battle in the courts, losing and appealing and losing again. No way would Dad accept euthanasia, nor would I as next of kin permit it, but if the higher courts continued trampling religious freedom and conscience rights, the hospice would eventually either cave in or be forced to close.

"I'm not going to be shuttled to a state holding tank," he had told me during our most recent visit. "I'm not going to spend my final days on this earth with people being murdered in the surrounding beds."

I had reassured him that, if worse came to worse, he could come and live with Annie and me.

"Just as the baby's being born, an old fellow dies in the next room? No way would I do that to you, Cleve."

"People have always lived that way, Dad," I countered. "It's natural, the generations living together. Birth and death, it's all part of life."

"I don't want to taint your joy with grief."

"You'd grieve us a hundred times more if you crawled away into a motel room and died alone."

"I'll think of something," he said, and gave a little extra squeeze on the morphine pump. Indicating, I thought, that the tension of our discussion was adding to his pain. I hoped he wasn't signaling that he intended to self-overdose.

I pointed to the control mechanism. "Don't even think of it. You do that and you'd be killing more than yourself. You'd be killing *us*."

He shot me a puzzled look, followed by a feeble grin.

"You misread me," he said with his scratchy voice.

"As always," I shrugged, producing a fake smile.

"And . . . I love you."

"I love you too."

"You should go see your dad," said Annie, interrupting the memory. "It's been, what, three weeks?"

"I don't want to leave you, honey. It's getting too close to B-Day."

"Nonsense. I'll be fine. No contractions yet. There'll be plenty of warning."

The drive from our house to the hospice in Edmonton was four hours each way. At least eight hours round trip, traffic and weather permitting. Add on visiting time, and it would make for a long, long day.

"I'll call him," I said to Annie, and took another sip of coffee.

"Uh-huh," she answered sleepily with heavy eyelids. She was drifting off again, maybe into one of those maternal naps she was having more frequently. I got up and went into the small den off the living room, checked the clock to see if it was too early, and then decided the nurses would probably already be bustling patients into their day's routine. I tapped the number into the landline wall phone beside the desk.

Dad answered his bedside phone after three rings.

"Hello."

His voice sounded groggy.

He wanted to hear first about how Annie and the baby were doing. I told him the latest, and then apologized for not seeing him as much as I wanted. He verbally batted this away. This was a fundamental principle of my father's existence. He never—*never*—wanted to be a burden on anyone. He had always been a giver, a sacrificer, a man of faith. But I knew that his self-effacement could easily make a mess of things here at the end of his life.

"We've got to get you moved down here," I said. "If you refuse to move in with us, we can still try to find a facility someplace close."

"Nah, buddy, they're all the killing fields now. Where I'm at is the last holdout."

"Yeah, but for how long?"

"Hard to say. Miracles happen."

Miracles happen. Yes, they do, but we'd need a global-size miracle to change the hearts of millions—no, billions—of brainwashed citizens and their democratically elected lethal governments.

I kept the bitterness out of my voice. "We'd just like to see you more."

"Cleve-boy, don't you worry about me. Apropos of that, Fr. Chen from St. Clement's came by last night and gave me the Last Rites."

"The Sacrament of the Sick, you mean."

"However you want to think of it. I feel better this morning, my soul for certain, my body kind of iffy, but it's plain as day that my days are numbered."

"I hate it when you talk in clichés."

This made him laugh.

"After the priest left, I fell right asleep, without any pain. I had a dream about you. You and Annie and the baby."

"A dream?"

"Uh-huh. It was a good dream, though kind of oddball. You know how dreams are. But this one was a little different. In it, you and a couple of other families were driving teams of oxen pulling covered wagons. You were looking desperate, trying to go faster and faster, but the whole bunch of you kept going slower and slower, meeting all kinds of obstacles. It really frustrated you. And every time you got blocked, you picked up a hitchhiker, then another and another, so the wagons soon got crowded with everyone you were helping." I heard my father's rasping chuckle.

"Good to hear you can still laugh," I said.

"Oh yeah, my philosophy of life is, you stop laughing, and it won't be long before you're wailing."

Now he laughed outright.

"Something funny?" I asked.

"That dream. You were wearing a big sombrero, two six-shooters on your hips, chaps on your legs, but underneath you had on those bunny pajamas your Mum and I got for you for Christmas when you were five or six. Remember?"

How could I forget. I had hated those pajamas, had pined for cowboy pajamas with images of pistols and lassos all over them. In any event, I didn't bring it up at the moment.

"No accounting for the imagination, Dad. Better than going to the movies, eh?"

"Sometimes. That dream now, I think it was trying to tell me something."

"Really? Even with bunny pajamas on a full-grown man?"

"Oh, that was just window dressing. The real thing, the deep thing, was I was supposed to pray for you, because there was a purpose in it all."

"What purpose?"

"That was never explained. Anyway, the point of the

whole thing seemed to be that you had to learn this big lesson."

"And the lesson?"

"You had to learn to trust. I mean, you had to go deeper and deeper into trust. And hope. Higher and higher into hope might be a better way to put it."

"Quite a dream, Dad," I said, shaking my head.

Trying to change the subject, I asked him about the cabin his brother had left him. He said, yes, the cabin was still there, last time he visited it, before the cancer hit.

"I've left it to you in my will, Cleve. It'll be yours soon."

The reality of his impending death struck me anew; I could say nothing by way of gratitude.

"Monday morning, I'll pop a map and directions in the mail, in case you want to go look at it sometime."

I knew he meant regular snail post, as he had always refused to "get wired"—one of his terms for involvement in the electronic universe—"strapping your brain to a microwave oven" was another.

"Has the doctor been in to see you?" I asked.

"He came by yesterday. Had to dig it out of him, but he told me I've probably got three or four more weeks."

"I'm coming up to see you today."

"Nah, you stay where you are and look after that princess you married. Tell her I love her, and tell her I think she's the best thing that ever happened to my son."

"She knows, but I'll tell her anyway. Look, I'll be there by noon, one o'clock at the latest."

"Ah, please don't, Cleve. This is Bingo day. I hate to miss my Bingo."

"Your Bingo? You gotta be kidding. You've always despised Bingo."

"I'm hoping to win the pink flamingo floor lamp. I'll put

that in the will for you, too. Besides, I have an appointment to play chess in the lounge with another old derelict at three P.M. He depends on it, you see, no family, never any visitors. So, look, lad, I don't want to be rude, but I'd prefer you not to mess up my schedule."

"Okay, I won't mess up your schedule," I replied glumly.

After an exchange of *love you*'s, we ended the call.

Returning to the bedroom, I found Annie awake but still drowsy. I told her what my father had said about her being the best thing that ever happened to me.

"No argument there," she said.

I related the doctor's prognosis, which saddened her. I also mentioned the current status of the cabin in the Rockies, that it would one day be ours. Annie received this news noncommittally, but she smiled when I recounted Dad's Bingo gambit.

"We do need a floor lamp," she said.

I sat down on the end of the bed and arranged my facial expression to convey calm dependability, allowing her to see that I was not Irrational Man. This was a necessary preparation for what I had to say.

"Maybe we should go there."

"Where?"

"The cabin. My uncle's cabin."

"Following a dream, Cleve?" she said with her compassionate look that had always melted us into one consciousness. The look that also said we should never let anything disturb our unity.

"I know, crazy isn't it."

"Well, I like you, crazy as you are."

"I like you, too, sensible as you are."

"So, you're suggesting . . . what?"

"Let's go on a holiday."

"When?"

"Soon."

"You've had your annual vacation, pal. No way Rafe is going to let you go on a holiday."

"A weekend, then."

"I'm willing, but we'd just get there and have time to cook a hot dog, and then turn right around and come back so you could show up at work on Monday."

"I might wrangle an extra day or two out of him."

"At the height of the building season? He'd want to know why. And if you tell him you need to follow a bird into the mountains, he'll never agree. He knows you might never come back." She punctuated this with a sweet grin, as if to tell me that she was pretty sure I was kidding or just following a thread of imagination, which was a longstanding habit of mine. Savvy lady that she was, she knew that Rafe would keep me from going off the deep end.

"He knows you might never come back," she said again, underlining her point.

I gave Annie a scolding look and said, "*We* might never come back. We're a couple, remember. A family."

Now she was beginning to frown a little, eyes all serious.

"You're presuming we should just pack up and leave? Without thinking this through?"

"Why not?"

"But when?" she asked for the second time.

"How about today, after I clear it with Rafe?"

"Today? That's a bit sudden."

"Tomorrow, then. We could leave right after Mass."

"Cleve, is this the right time for a jaunt? It sounds kind of impulsive to me."

"Okay, how about sometime after the baby's born?"

She looked dubious.

"Yeah," I mused, "something temporary but open-ended."

"Temporary open-ended. Now there's a cute expression. What do you mean by temporary? And if the open-ended business means we don't come back, how would we live?"

"I'd figure something out."

"But for what reason? And for what kind of life?" Shaking her head. "It's not realistic, Cleve."

"I know," I said, looking away from her. What was wrong with me, I asked myself. What glitch in my higher brain functions was causing this, manifesting as a blue bird, pulling me—and my wife and child—into a radically insecure future?

Bluebird of happiness? Clichés rising from the subconscious directing the future of our family?

"Wake up, Sleeping Beauty," she said, giving me a love tap on the cheek.

"I'm Wide Awake Ugly."

She smiled but pressed on.

"Cleve, flight of fancy or daydream or nightmare, whatever you want to call it, it's not reality. We can't just walk away from everything we've built together."

"They're taking it away anyway, bit by bit."

"But this is our *home*."

"Uh-huh. For how long? A few months, a year. Maybe a couple of years if we're lucky."

She fell silent, swung her legs over the side of the bed and sat upright. Another sip of tea, the frown deepening.

"To keep all this going," I said with a sweep of the arm, "to protect our home and our life, they're demanding more and more compromise, more and more complicity with their laws and evil agendas."

"Yes, but we don't have to cooperate with it."

"They'll make it impossible for us not to cooperate. We'll have more kids, God-willing. They'll hold our children hostage, without even taking them away. Propagandize our own children with the new social norms, or we're unfit parents—dangerous ones. They've been putting the pressure on families for years, and it's getting worse all the time."

"I know, I know. But it hasn't happened to us, and there's no guarantee it ever will."

"There's no guarantee it ever won't."

"So you're saying run for the hills, just in case?"

"No. Look, honey, we've been watching the snake mesmerize the world, watching so many people we know—even sensible people—succumbing to the mind-bending through media and school and endless new laws. And sometimes—not often, but *sometimes*—children are taken away from perfectly healthy families because the parents' politics aren't correct, or their religion, or their psychology."

"I understand. It's bad. But how can we know if they'll go farther?"

"The beast has an appetite, Annie. We keep hoping it's satisfied, but it never works out that way, does it. No, honey, they're going for total control—"

"Total devouring," she said with a quiver in her voice.

I put my arm around her shoulders. "We'll get through it."

"We'll get through it, Cleve. I believe that. Or I hope it's true. But . . ."

"But will our children get through it? That's the crucial question. Ordinary Catholics like us, we're characterized everywhere as cult members. Children of cults need to be rescued, right?"

She sighed.

"I'm sorry, Annie, I didn't mean to depress you."

"You didn't depress me." She sighed again and wiped her eyes. "It's just a bit early in the morning for end-of-the-world discussions."

"End of the world as we know it," I corrected her.

She gave a thin laugh. "Oh dear, *Gotterdammerung* on top of maternal hormones."

"Bad combination."

"Would you make me another cup of tea?"

"Glad to." I jumped up and headed off to the kitchen, carrying our empty cups, man of action, squaring my shoulders so she could see me in protector-of-the-family posture. But as I fixed our drinks, I wondered where the little blue bird was at the moment.

9

THROUGHOUT THE MORNING I accomplished a few chores around the house, did the laundry, fixed a leaking tap in the bathroom, and then I went shopping for groceries. There were big posters on the supermarket windows flanking the doors, dramatic eye-catchers I hadn't seen before. One of them portrayed an ecstatically happy young couple, both of them beautiful women cradling a baby in their lissome arms. The other was a mirror image of two handsome young men, equally happy, with *their* baby held in muscular bare arms. Off to the side was a similar poster, but in this one the parents were male and female, looking pleasant enough but not quite ecstatic. The three images were the typical virtue-signaling that always made me groan. I'd seen plenty of this kind of advertisement during the past several years, in banks, post offices, schools, businesses, and wondered why it had taken so long for the food chain companies to fall into line.

However, the captions on the three posters before me were not what I expected. Uniformly they proclaimed:

> WE SIGNED UP OUR FAMILY FOR DIGITAL CURRENCY!
> BEST DECISION WE EVER MADE!

And below this:

> 30 MORE DAYS TO REGISTER FOR YOUR 10% FEDERAL BONUS.

Followed in smaller font by:

> *PENALTIES WILL APPLY FOR LATE REGISTRATION.

Penalties? I had read a lot about the government's relentless plodding toward imposition of universal digital commerce, the gradual shift to a cashless society. Supposedly it would eliminate theft and fraud, and put a stop to much of the black market as well, enabling taxation agencies to oversee all currency flow and suck off taxes that until now had eluded their grasp—goods and services exchanged for cash, under the radar.

I was stunned. I had expected that this would come one day but felt we had plenty of time left before it became universal and mandatory. I had been sure the population as a whole would resist. Polls said that eighty-five percent of the people didn't want it. We were already one of the most heavily taxed countries in the world—studies said that the average person paid forty-eight percent of his annual income to the myriad gaping maws that demanded taxes. I suspected that the majority of people conducted a little alternative economy on the side, just to get by.

I went into the store and loaded up my shopping cart, then went to the check-out and paid with cash.

"Have a good day," said the pretty young girl at the till with a show of brilliantly white, orthodontized teeth. Along with my receipt, she handed me a shiny brochure, color illustrated with the ecstatic couples, headlined *SECURITY and EFFICIENCY*. With a quick perusal of the text, I realized that it explained the coming shift to digital economy.

"You have a good day too, miss," I replied with a somewhat strained smile.

For some reason she found that funny. Then I got it—*miss*—good old antediluvian me.

After loading the groceries into the back of my truck, I drove a few blocks in the direction of home. But when I came to a traffic light, I stopped and turned the other way, heading to the city, specifically to Rafe and Cora's.

I spent much of Saturday afternoon with the Morrows, the three of us seated on lawn chairs at our usual spot under the maple tree in the backyard. As we talked, Rafe and I sipped slowly from bottles of his home-brew. Cora joined us for parts of the discussion, listening attentively, saying little. I could sense her concern, though she didn't seem distressed. Mainly she was busy playing badminton with the girls, and after an hour of that they all went off to the local library.

"It's begun," I said to Rafe, handing him the brochure from the supermarket.

He quietly read it to himself, showing no surprise.

Looking up with a sigh, he said, "It began some time ago. The erosion of civil and religious liberties, step by step. Now they're moving to the next stage. For the past six months, I've been receiving advance federal and provincial documents about this. And of course the largest news channels have been pushing it hard."

"Sorry, I haven't been paying much attention to their nauseating hype. We already have enough nausea at our house."

"You've been distracted with the baby coming, Cleve. A healthy approach, in my opinion."

"Thanks. The news channels are pushing it hard, you say. A few months ago, I read a poll that says the overwhelming majority of people are against it."

"Uh-huh, people do get agitated if their wallets are affected. But the government just keeps rolling on, ignoring all the flak."

"I gotta believe there's *some* media resistance."

"Oh yeah, there's some. A minority of the big papers and

networks are pushing back with a few opinion pieces, blah-blah-blah, never front page, never prime time. It's a token, Cleve. It's cosmetics."

"Don't worry, folks, all's right with democracy?"

"Yup, that's the message. So, any idea how you and Annie are going to handle this?"

Feeling at a loss for an answer, I shook my head despondently. Then, after some hesitation, I said:

"Um, I had this dream last night."

"Tell me about your dream."

I got back home just after five o'clock, worrying about the perishable groceries going bad and sorry that I would be late making supper for Annie.

I found her in the kitchen, standing watch over a pot of rice and little pork chops sizzling in the frying pan.

"Howdy, stranger," she said with a welcoming smile.

"How do, ma'am," I drawled as I crouched down to put the groceries into the fridge.

"Supper in twenty minutes. Hope you've got an appetite." She proceeded to toss a spinach and avocado salad.

"Sorry I'm late, honey. I really wanted to cook you something special. I got sidetracked at Rafe's. There've been some developments."

"Oh? Good or bad?"

"Challenging. I'll tell you more after we eat."

After I finished the dishes, we sat down on the couch in the living room, her head on my shoulder, our arms pressed warmly together.

"Developments?" she prompted.

First I told her about the supermarket posters and then showed her the brochure on the upcoming digital economy. She read through it slowly, carefully, her brow furrowed.

"This is totalitarian," she said quietly when she was finished.

"Uh-huh, it seems we're in final countdown to a state of total control, total surveillance."

"Culminating in total manipulation."

"Looks like that's where it's going. Did you notice how many times they use the word *freedom* in this little marvel of newspeak?"

"Mmm, freedom from crime, freedom from hunger, freedom from lost purses and wallets, freedom from feeling abandoned in the universe with no big brother to watch over you. They don't say freedom from responsibility, but that's what it's about, ultimately."

"Isn't it interesting the way the people who want to control everything always present themselves as anti-totalitarian?"

"If it walks like a duck, talks like a duck, maybe it *is* a duck."

"Exactly."

"*Security and efficiency*, it says. Cleve, that's what every dictator in history has offered the trembling masses."

"Right. Except that people aren't *masses*. We're not a feedlot full of cattle." I snorted. "And we don't have to tremble."

"So . . . you're saying . . . ?"

"I told Rafe and Cora about my uncle's cabin. He was interested."

"In what way?"

"He believes that malevolent governments always prepare the ground with a massive psychological assault against people's natural instinct for independence. Begin by making us think we have no choices, get us convinced we're powerless and resistance is futile."

"Well, that's certainly happening. But I don't see any Gestapo or KGB knocking on doors."

"Not yet. And when they do come—"

"*If* they come."

"If they come, they won't be wearing sinister uniforms. They'll have good manners. They'll talk to us in reasonable tones and make us feel awful about our sociopathic tendencies. They'll appear to have our best interests at heart and present the new laws as protective measures for the greater good—for *our* own good."

"But they'll be immovable and relentless, you're saying."

"Yes, and Rafe agrees that it's coming down the tube very soon. When I told him about my dream—you remember the giant and the blue bird—he thought it might not be a bad idea to check out the cabin. He said I could take a week off."

"Rats," she said. "I was hoping he'd squash it like a bug."

"Did you now. Well, strange thing, he said he's been having unusual dreams too, and plenty of worrying during daylight hours."

"That's not like him, the most laid-back guy on the planet."

"Not like him at all. He was also unusually literary today, which tells me he's really chewing on the state of the world, lots of clips about politics and laws and such. He even quoted Chesterton."

"Chesterton? Oh, yes, the writer you've been reading lately. Rafe lent you the books, didn't he?"

"That's right. He's Rafe's favorite author, who famously said, 'If men will not be governed by the Ten Commandments, they will be governed by the ten thousand commandments.'"

"Mmm, that's astute. Well, we're living in a world that can't even remember the Ten Commandments, let alone obey them. And here we are choking to death on ten thousand laws and regulations from every level of government and social agency."

"And there's more to come."

"Does Rafe think it's going to get worse?"

"Not in the immediate. There's no doubt the country's in an enforced transition period, gradually accelerating, but how fast it'll go is hard to tell at this point. He believes he can keep the business in operation for a while, keep paying wages and buying wholesalers' supplies, as long as he's able to pay the penalties for non-compliance with the new economy. He'll be doing some fancy juggling, and he's willing to do it for the sake of his employees putting bread and butter on the table. It'll probably wipe out any profit he makes."

"Oh, poor Rafe, poor Cora. You said he's having unusual dreams too."

"Uh-huh. Actually, the word he used was *weird*. I guess the deteriorating situation, combined with his dreams, made for interesting chemistry."

"Were his dreams about running away?"

"Not exactly *running*, but his latest was about him and Cora and their kids buying a little boat and sailing off into the Pacific, finding a tropical island where no one ever goes."

"He's aware, I hope, that we live a thousand miles from any sizeable body of water."

"Fully aware."

"Well," she sighed, "we all have our metaphors of escape."

"What's yours?"

"I don't think I have any. Or maybe I do, if you count big strong arms around my shoulders, and plenty of refills from the tea pot."

"I like it. Let's keep that one."

"Wait! That's not escape. It's foundational."

"We could always stay put, I guess, like running on the spot. Or maybe we could find some place small and semi-invisible here on the prairies. Alberta has a quarter million square miles, most of it empty. Then there're the other provinces, all of them half empty. Big sky gives you vistas."

There was a long pause, which informed me that she was silently absorbing what I had told her—perhaps trying to refute it mentally or maybe just letting it sink in.

"The illusion of vistas," she said with a huge sigh.

"What do you mean, Annie?"

"The feeling that we're surrounded by infinite space, with plenty of room for freedom. Big horizons. Except there aren't any true horizons left."

"Mental horizons, you mean?"

"It's not just perceptions and illusions, Cleve. I mean, there really is no place to run and hide. The time of the end is the time of no room."

"That's kinda dire coming from you, honey. It isn't the end by any means."

"So, then, what do we *do*?" There was a plaintive emphasis on *do*, a catch in her throat, the sound of fear.

"Well, what we can do is have a trial run. Rafe suggests we make the trip to the Rockies, to my uncle's cabin, both our families driving in convoy."

"Really? They'd come with us?"

"Yes. It'll be like a game, pretending we're running from the threat of a nuclear attack."

"Or from a government that wants to arrest all Christians who won't cave in?"

"That too. Anyway, we'll think of it as an adventure and learn what we can as we go along. The real thing might never happen, but at least we'd have some kind of contingency plan if it ever does. It'd be a very valuable experience, don't you think?"

"Well, okay, I can see it that way. But what about your business? You guys now have eight houses in progress."

"Brent would be the overseer while the boss is away."

"Uh-huh, so when would we go?"

"Rafe suggested some day this week. Dad's sending me a map in the mail, and as soon as it arrives we'll go. Probably Wednesday, or Thursday at the latest."

"Cleve, this is really through the looking glass. You're sure we should do this?"

"It's worth a try. It might be fun."

"Fun. Oh, great, I'll go pack a little kit with scissors and thread for tying the umbilical cord when you deliver the baby on the side of the highway."

I laughed. She didn't.

True to his word, Dad posted the map on Monday, and on Wednesday after work I found it delivered in our curbside mailbox. I opened the large manila envelope on the spot. Attached to a folded hand-drawn map was a penciled note in his now-shaky handwriting:

Dear son,

First get yourself to Pincher Creek on #3, the Crowsnest Hwy. No need for me to draw it here. What I've drawn is the route you need to take south of Pincher on #6. Just follow my squiggles and jottings, and it will bring you to the cabin without a hitch. I've written some prompts and landmarks to watch for, which you'll need because roads aren't always well marked down there.

Don't forget to wear your bunny pajamas and sombrero (just kidding).

Love, always,
Dad

The map was a rough sketch of highways and country roads, with the prompts written on the back.

Over supper, Annie and I examined it closely. Using my cell phone, I checked out Google Maps for the region south of Pincher Creek, zeroing in close to ground level. The satellite view gave me a lot of bush, farmland, and mountain topographics, but nothing quite matched Dad's map. I booted up my laptop for a bigger screen, and the results were the same.

"Mmm," said Annie, "it looks a bit like a scavenger hunt."

"What do you think?" I asked her. "Should we go?"

"All right, let's do it," she said with a definitive nod.

That evening I telephoned Rafe, and we agreed to make an early start the following day. He and Cora and their children would drive to our place, arriving around eight A.M., and from there on we would travel in convoy.

I found Annie in the kitchen, mixing a bowl of oats, raisins, and cinnamon, preparing to bake oatmeal cookies, her classic *pièce de résistance.*

"All systems Go!" I said. "We launch at eight tomorrow morning."

Her eyes brightened, her cheeks coloring at the prospect of adventure.

"That's great!" she said with real enthusiasm, for which I was grateful, considering her doubts in recent days. I now recalled that this was the woman who had ventured north to work as a frontier outpost nurse, had resisted the mandates of a lethal government, and was consistently able to think outside the box. Yup, that was my Annie. Even in her slow-moving maternal condition, she was essentially a spirited, intrepid person.

I hugged her close and wouldn't let go of her. Or perhaps it was she who wouldn't let go of me.

10

WE WERE UP AT DAYBREAK, bleary-eyed but looking forward to the journey. I wouldn't call it eagerness, yet we both were feeling the stimulation that often comes with a change of scene.

While Annie was having a shower, I busied myself in the kitchen brewing the coffee. As the machine began bubbling and hissing, I stood there watching it and doing some mental percolation of my own, a final private quibble. I wondered if this whole trip was a big overreaction. Maybe the looming economic system was nothing more than a new way of exchanging debits and credits. After all, it was only about numbers. It needn't be about politics at all. Had we been reading too much into it, presuming that participation in the system would be enslavement—a slavery of biblical proportions, maybe even taking the Mark of the Beast upon ourselves? No buying or selling unless you had the mark inscribed on the palm of your hand or your forehead, and then you were on the highway to hell?

The psychology of perception had always fascinated me, the way our minds could select myriad facts and assemble them in such a way that they seemed to confirm an *a priori* theory or fear. Was this our family's first skirmish with paranoia?

Anyway, the outing would do us good. As Annie made a breakfast of toast and scrambled eggs, I carried our gear out to the pickup and began loading the cargo bed. Not knowing what possessions Uncle Dave had left at the cabin, I made sure to bring sleeping bags, a few extra blankets, an axe and hatchet, a pack of butane lighters, and a roll of newspapers for firestarter. Then came the big thermos cooler filled with sandwiches, bananas, a bag of apples, mini-bottles of orange juice, a carton of milk, baggies of nuts and dried fruit, and a scattering of freezy packs. The sack of oatmeal cookies wouldn't fit, so I ate a couple on the run, then a third, and finally put the sack on the front seat, where I knew that Annie would guard me from further excess. To these I added a prayer book she especially loved and the book of Psalms that Rafe had given me shortly after my conversion. It was my habit to read one of the psalms each night before lights-out, and I didn't want to miss one during the trip.

Noting that the sky was hidden by thick overcast, I covered the cargo hold with a blue plastic tarp, tying it down with bungee cords. It was a mild June morning, but I thought it better to play it safe in case of rain.

Annie and I ate breakfast without saying much. She sipped at her herbal tea, I gulped a cup of coffee and was pouring myself a second when we heard the sound of a vehicle pulling into the driveway.

We went outside to greet the Morrows, and I was surprised to see a vehicle I didn't recognize, a long, sleek, passenger van, forest green in color. The boss's usual transportation was his company pickup, and for the family they had an older Dodge Caravan, somewhat the worse for wear. As Rafe and Cora stepped out of the new van, the girls spilled from the other doors and raced to be first to hug Annie.

"Wow, Rafe, I've never seen you in a luxury ride before," I said.

"A shade this side of luxury, Cleve. I couldn't afford a European import, but this Ford Explorer is nine passenger. With the five of us, that leaves plenty of room for baggage and human company. Also, a few seats can be removed to make a sleeping space."

"Good for long trips. Uh, did our conversation on Saturday have anything to do with it?"

He smiled knowingly. "As a decorative touch. No, in fact I bought it a week ago, before you told me about your dream."

"What prompted you? With the financial troubles brewing, I would have thought you'd be counting your pennies."

"Penny-wise but pound-foolish? Or is it the other way around? To tell the truth, one night last week I had this peculiar dream about buying a big green van and driving it up a mountainside—defying the laws of gravity. The dream woke me around 3 A.M., and I couldn't get back to sleep, so I went to the online auto-trader—something I never do—and there it was, staring me in the face, the first thing my eyes lit on. Private sale, only 57,000 miles on the odometer, nearly new tires. A great price too. A few dents and scratches, as you see, but they saved me thousands."

"Congratulations."

"Thanks. So, should we take a look at the directions your father sent you?"

I fetched Dad's hand-drawn map from the cab of the Toyota and spread it open on the hood. Rafe joined me there, bringing his provincial road atlas with him.

"I checked the online satellite map last night," I informed him, "but it wasn't much help."

"Uh-huh," he nodded. "Well let's see what the old-fashioned method has to tell us."

We studied every detail, not that Dad's penciled lines and squiggles made much immediate sense to us. I suggested that they would sharpen into focus the closer we got to our destination. Getting to Pincher Creek by way of Fort Macleod and the Crowsnest highway was no problem for either of us—we both had good atlases. However, the area south of Pincher was a semi-blank zone on the official maps, just a few major lines with the highway number and a black dot or two. Clearly, the region was so relatively unpopulated that the cartographers didn't have much to define.

Opening his atlas, Rafe used his index finger as a pointer. "I did some computing last night. In ordinary conditions, the entire journey from Calgary to the U.S. border station at Chief Mountain is theoretically five hours, based upon driving straight through from start to finish."

"Theorists usually don't factor in the bladders and tummies of children and pregnant women."

"True. So, here's how I see it: Heading more or less south on number 2 highway, it's around a hundred and ten miles from Calgary to Fort Macleod. Factoring in a bathroom break for the little ones, that leg of the journey should take us two hours, conservative estimate."

"We might think about taking a break at Macleod, top up the gas tanks, get a bite to eat."

"Good idea. After that, we turn onto number 3 Crowsnest Highway and head west to Pincher Creek, a thirty-five-mile drive, which should take about thirty to forty minutes, depending on the speed limit. At Pincher Creek we turn south onto number 6 highway, which is the last leg of the route to the border. Supposedly it's about a forty-mile drive, but it winds through mountains, so we can't presume we'll be able to maintain the speed of the major highways. My guess is the drive south after Pincher will take between one and a half to two hours."

"You're probably right," I said. "Plus, it's not quite clear where we leave 6, but the way Dad's drawn it, the turnoff looks much closer to the border than to Pincher. Then when we get off 6, we'll be heading west on a back country road, and there's no way of telling at this point how good or bad the route is."

Rafe nodded. "Will it be paved or gravel, you mean? Also, we'll be getting into steadily rising terrain, so we may be going even slower than we now estimate."

"Hopefully we won't have to defy your laws of gravity."

"Hopefully not."

"Okay, to recap: south on number 2, west on number 3, south again on number 6. Then we turn west again onto the backwoods road to the cabin—if we can find it."

As we tossed these details back and forth, I could hear with one ear Annie and Cora talking in tones that were cheery but low volume.

"The boys are looking awfully serious, don't you think?" Cora said to my wife, unintentionally loud enough for us to overhear.

"Looks like a grave consultation, to be sure," Annie replied. "They're really enjoying their Great Adventure. For these lads, the *gravitas* is part of the fun."

Cora said in a high-pitched voice, "Whee, *fun!*"

Simultaneously Rafe and I peered over at the ladies, both of us with cocked eyebrows and mock censorious expressions, communicating that we were onto them. Linking arms, they burst into giggles, and I caught a glimpse of what they must have been like as young college girls.

Back we went to our consultation. I flipped the map over.

"These prompts of Dad's don't mean anything specific to us at the moment. What on earth does 'Calvary' represent? And this note about a 'rickety ravine' could mean anything. Then there's 'Joe's Freehold' about halfway along this side road."

"I expect they'll make sense when we spot them."

"I guess we'll find out."

"Cleve, another factor is, see where he's noted 'about 20 m. from 6 to cabin'? It indicates that the distances he's drawn are out of scale. Your Dad made the wilderness parts of the route with disproportionately longer lines, compared to highway distances."

"Yes, you're right," I said after a closer look.

I folded up the map.

"All set to go?" Rafe asked.

"Ready to launch, Boss."

"Lead the way, subservient underling."

However, departure was delayed an additional twenty minutes, due to the three little girls needing final trips to the bathroom. Annie went back inside the house and returned with plump pillows she had forgotten to pack, explaining that these would help make the journey in our truck more comfortable. "Shock absorbers," she explained.

I shook my head ruefully. "Sorry, honey, I've been meaning to replace the shocks."

"What, and ruin the ambience of our luxury vehicle!"

Cora invited her to ride in their more modern van. Annie thanked her, but said she'd like to have "quality time" with me. "Our big date," she added with a laugh.

While the others were climbing into the vehicles, Rafe gave me a small gadget with a stubby antenna, a duplicate of the one he held in his hand.

"I bought a six-pack of these transceivers—two-way radios. I thought they might be useful on the trip; you never know."

"Thanks, Rafe. These'll be a big help if we get separated."

"Batteries are fully charged, frequency's set."

We did a test call on the spot, and the radios worked just fine.

"We good to go?" I asked.

"Ten . . . nine . . . eight . . . seven . . ."

"Lift-off!"

"See you on the moon!" Rafe said with a final salute.

With everyone loaded up, I backed out of the driveway and onto the street, then drove the ten-minute route to Highway 2. At the junction, after checking to see that Rafe was close behind, I turned right and accelerated.

The journey south was pleasant and uneventful. The overcast seemed thinner. A band of aqua sky appeared ahead, with washes of golden light crossing the rolling landscape. I loved the broad sweep of seemingly limitless farmland and rangeland, the yellows and greens, and the glad feeling of driving away from pending entrapment. Or more like an exuberant bird escaping through a cage door someone had inadvertently left open.

Annie's expression was peaceful, relaxed, gazing west to the variegated wall of mountains in the distance, mauve and gray and blue under their shrinking winter snowcaps.

She asked me what the cabin was like. There was very little I could tell her, just that I remembered a simple log dwelling, a few rooms, a wood stove, shelves of books, and windows with dazzling views of mountains very close. There was an outhouse, I recalled, and a hand-pump for water. Oil lamps at night. It was somewhat primitive but comfortable.

"My memory of it is blurry," I explained. "I was ten years old the only time I saw it. More than twenty years ago."

"Your uncle may have made improvements over the years since then," she suggested.

"Could be. He lived there full-time in the last years of his life."

A flock of black birds rose en masse from a field beside the road, catching our attention. Shortly after that, we spotted a brown jackrabbit sitting on the center line just ahead. I swerved slightly to get around it. A transport truck I hadn't seen blared its horn at me as it roared past in the left lane. My little pickup shook with terror. The rabbit bounded away just in time.

"Some people," I grumbled, shaking my head.

"Look, Cleve—deer!" exclaimed Annie pointing off to the right.

I smiled, because seeing deer was almost a daily experience for anyone living in our part of the world. I had more than once had to chase whitetails out of our backyard vegetable patch.

There were three standing in the grass by the side of the road, a buck, a doe, and a fawn. I slowed to catch a better glimpse of them. They lifted their heads to watch us pass by.

"They're not deer, honey," I said, "they're pronghorn antelope."

"So beautiful, so beautiful," Annie breathed.

Yes, beautiful, I thought, but a real hazard while driving at night.

Annie fell into a doze for a while, her face tranquil, her hand warm on the knee of my jeans. When I placed my right hand over hers, she gently smiled in her sleep. I loved her so much, so much. I could hardly believe how my life had changed in one short year.

Just north of Fort Macleod, I spotted a truck stop in the distance, with what looked like half a dozen eighteen-wheelers parked in a lot behind the gas station and restaurant. I clicked the transceiver mic and called the Morrows' vehicle, which was following about a hundred yards behind me.

"Rafe, why don't we pull in here and top up our gas tanks. Maybe get a bite to eat."

"Good idea," came the reply.

Our voices had awoken Annie, who sat up and asked, "Where are we?"

"Halfway to heaven," I said.

Rafe and I parked side by side in a row of gas pumps, and the women and children went into the restaurant to find us booths for a late breakfast or early lunch.

"Huh," I said when I tried to prepay at the pump with my charge card. "It's not working."

"Mine neither," said Rafe.

A voice came over an intercom: "Please pay inside."

The cashier in the station part of the complex looked frustrated.

"Problems with your card reader at the pumps?" Rafe asked her.

"Problems with the whole shebang," she said, pointing to a reader by the cash register. "Internet's down, so you can't do digital pay here, either. I hope you fellows have cash."

We paid her in cash and then turned left to enter the restaurant. The ladies and children were seated in booths beside the plate glass windows facing the parking lot. There weren't many other people present, but I noticed that they were all checking their phones with worried faces as they picked distractedly at their meals.

A waitress took our orders, pancakes for the Morrow girls, and "Trucker's Special" for the grown-ups, which was bacon and eggs, mini-sausages, hash browns, toast with jam and unlimited coffee refills. Annie ordered milk instead of coffee.

While we waited, Rafe took a cell phone from his pocket and began checking for messages.

"Odd," he said. "It's alive, and there seems to be wi-fi, but nothing's coming in. Brent was supposed to call me about glitches in the project he's supervising over in Two Guns. Carlito was checking on a supply truck due to come in early this morning to the site at Nose Hill Park. He was going to call me or text me before nine."

I checked my watch. It was now 10:30 A.M., inching toward 11:00.

Rafe tapped a number into his phone and waited. We could hear it faintly buzz-ringing. Then it went silent.

"That's strange," he said. "If Brent wasn't picking up, it should have gone over to voice mail. But it just went dead."

He tapped in another number. This was followed by the faint ring and then silence.

"Same with Carlito's number," he said. "I'll try texting."

I checked my own cell phone, tapping the speed dial for Dad's bedside phone at the hospice. A ring, then silence. I tried a few other numbers with the same results.

"Texting's not working," said Rafe.

When our food arrived, I asked the waitress if she knew anything about the connection problem.

"I've no idea," she said, patting her apron pocket. "It wasn't working when I got up about six A.M. this morning. That's never happened before. I've got plenty of data. We do get a power outage sometimes in big storms, but we have a generator for backup. And nothing can knock out the satellites."

"So you're saying you've no idea why we've lost connection?" Cora asked.

The woman shrugged. "We've got connection, but nothing's coming through the servers."

"I just made a call, and it seemed to work, but then it suddenly went dead," said Rafe.

"Weird. Well, I'm sure some techies will figure it out. Sorry for the problem, folks."

"No problem," our group severally replied with reassuring smiles.

As we ate our meals, Rafe kept checking his phone. After forty minutes, there were still no rings or text beeps. He tried calling out again, with the same non-result. He clicked it off and put it back into his pocket.

"We might have a long day ahead," I said to him, "and we have no idea how widespread this thing is. I have about six hundred in cash with me, which should take us to the cabin and back again next week."

"I have three thousand with me," he said.

I raised my eyebrows. "You're not serious."

"Uh-huh, I never leave home without it." He indulged in one of his wry smiles, mouth engaged. "You never know what will happen in the entropic universe."

"What does *en . . . tropic* mean, Daddy?" asked Josie, his older girl.

He grinned. "It means lack of order or predictability, and a gradual disintegration into radical disorder—"

"Rafe, please," interjected Cora. She turned to her daughter and said, "It means life is full of surprises, honey."

We were on our second cups of coffee when we were distracted by a commotion at the cash register. There stood a professional looking, fortyish woman in a pantsuit, carrying a briefcase, head-to-head in heated debate with a young police officer. The woman was waving her cell phone at him and talking too loud.

"This is insane. You can't just turn around and go back."

"Listen, lady, I just got a radio call to return to the city right now."

"But we're halfway to the border."

"Sorry, but we have to abort this. It's not high priority,

so we need to take the minor back to the detention center. I'll drop you there and get on with my duties."

"But I'd have to see a judge of juvenile court to rescind the order, and then go through the process of readmitting her to the center. No way can I get all the paperwork done on time. And I can't take her home with me; I've got vulnerable people living under my roof. Children and teens!"

"She's not dangerous."

"But she is a flight risk. Why have you left her alone there in the car? She could run off again."

"The doors are locked. I suggest you try to get ahold of a judge by phone, and call your office and ask them to wait until you arrive—"

At this point the cash register clerk intervened, apparently observing the exchange with the keen interest of a soap opera devotee. "My apologies, people, but we've got no cell phone reception, no internet, either. Looks like all systems are down."

The professional woman turned red in the face and fumed, then checked her cell phone. She tapped and tapped, looking increasingly frustrated. The policeman did the same on his own phone.

"What's going on?" he mumbled. "There's nothing."

"You'll have to call my people on your radio."

"It's not permitted, lady. And it looks like we've got a major crisis in the city, so I can't waste any more time on your problems."

With deadly intensity the woman said, "Waste, is it? Well, let me inform you, I am a *social worker*, an agent of the *government*. I am responsible for this girl, who is a minor and an illegal alien, and she is mandated by juvenile court to be returned *immediately*"—the word was shouted—"to the custody of her grandparents who are waiting for her at the U.S. Customs and Border station."

"Cool down, ma'am, just cool down. Let's go talk about this outside."

They went out through the doorway, still engaged in heated debate. Both of them kept stepping aside from each other, pausing to check their cell phones.

We ordered more coffee, and a dish of ice cream for each of the children. Rafe checked his phone again, shaking his head.

"My message log says nothing came in after midnight last night, not even ads and newsfeeds."

I fished out my own cell and checked the inbox and log. An ad at 11:45 P.M., then nothing.

We were both staring at our blank screens—alive but dead—when our attention was caught by the sight of a vehicle parking close by our windows. It was an older model Aspen SUV that had seen better days. Emblazoned on the driver's door was a red Sacred Heart image with its crown of thorns and flaming cross, and beneath it a decal of two crossed feathers. To our complete surprise, out of the doors stepped Farley and Kateri Crowshoe and a young man in a Roman collar.

"Did you call them?" I asked. "Did you tell them about our trip?"

"No," said Rafe, rising to his feet.

He went out to greet the newcomers and brought them inside.

The Crowshoes and the young priest accompanying them sat down at a table facing our booths. I noticed that Farley was wearing his crucifix on his chest, the one with the disk of beaded red and white native motif. I had last seen it well over a year ago at the Morrows' barbecue.

"What on earth are you doing here?" asked Rafe, grinning but puzzled.

"What on earth are *you* doing here?" Farley threw back at him.

"You tell us first."

"Okay. But before I do, let me introduce you all to our nephew, Fr. Peter Ahanu Goodrider, Albert and Sharon's boy."

The fine-featured young priest stood up and offered his hand to the adults and said Hi to the children.

I now recalled that Albert had told me the Cree name *Ahanu* meant 'He Who Laughs'. At present the young man looked pretty serious, worried even.

Kateri prompted her husband, who began his story.

"Last night, Fr. Peter appeared on our doorstep at Siksiká. He asked if he could stay with us. His archbishop up in Edmonton sent an email message early yesterday morning to all his priests. In prayer before the exposed Blessed Sacrament, he'd heard a voice speaking to him. The Lord Jesus told him that he'd be arrested the next day and that all the priests would be put to the test. The government would try to make them swear to abide by the new laws about life issues, and sex and gender. No more preaching about it, no writing or publishing about it. No more counseling young people who have identity issues or want to have an abortion, no more trying to argue with people who want to kill their old folks. Government will say just roll over and be a good boy or else you go to jail. All priests will have to sign an affidavit swearing they'll obey the new laws. If they refuse, they'll be sentenced to long prison terms. Hate crime doubles the prison sentences, you see, at least ten years in the pen, and huge fines nobody could pay. It'd shut down all the churches for good."

"This is so crazy," Cora exclaimed in a low voice.

"It's a violation of our constitutional freedom of religion," I pointed out.

"Oh, that was whittled away long ago," said Fr. Peter. "So, in this email from my archbishop, he instructed every priest to pray fervently for the Lord's will. He was uncertain about how long it would last, or how severe it would be, but he ordered us to never sign anything that goes against the Faith, even unto death. He was told by the Lord that some of his priests would be martyred, and others would go into hiding, so that the light of the sacraments wouldn't disappear from the world. All the bishops of the western provinces and the northern territories made an agreement a couple of days ago. Your bishop in Calgary signed it too. Any priest in good standing is free to offer the sacraments anywhere now, no need to do the chancery permission thing, seeing as how we're going underground."

"Underground?" whispered Cora with a shake of her head. "Is this for real? It's so hard to imagine."

"Underground," Fr. Peter affirmed with a nod. "He said that all churches would be locked up soon, maybe within a few days. If a priest wished to stand firm in place and be a 'sign of contradiction', the archbishop called it, he had the archbishop's blessing. If a priest discerned that he should go underground, he had his blessing too. It's a time for courage, he said. It's a time of witness. Our path ahead is one of martyrdom, either the red of shed blood or the white of more suffering. For himself, he said he would choose red."

This dark and sobering account left everyone speechless for a few moments.

"How are your mother and father taking it?" Rafe asked, referring to the Goodriders.

"They're fine. Dad's buzzing with excitement, of course, since he loves the drama. They're staying on the reserve; they want to hide our pastor out at Dad's hunt camp, and then they plan to stick close to home to look after the other kids."

Farley continued, "The bishop said in his message that the priests who go into hiding shouldn't go to their parents or near kin, because that's the first place the manhunters would look."

"Albert and Sharon asked us to give Fr. Peter shelter, and we are happy to do it," said Kateri.

"God bless you," said Rafe. "But this doesn't explain why you're here."

The couple and their nephew exchanged glances.

"You ever hear about Black Elk?" asked Farley.

We shook our heads.

"He was a man of the Oglala Lakota, of the Sioux people. He was a boy at the battle of the Little Bighorn—you know, Custer's Last Stand—and he survived the massacre at Wounded Knee. He was a cousin of the warrior Crazy Horse. But the important thing about him is he was very gifted spiritually. Even as a child he had visions, and later he became a medicine man revered for his ways of healing and visions. You gotta have heard about that book *Black Elk Speaks*, huh?"

Again we all shook our heads.

"Oh, the New Agers and occulters just love that book, because it seems to prove that our early religion was as good or better than Christianity. Problem is, that book stops at the wrong spot. It doesn't tell what happened the rest of Black Elk's life. When he was still a young man he was baptized a Catholic, took the name Nicholas, and for the next forty-five years until his death he worked among his people as a catechist. His daughter said that her father was always on fire for the Faith. Over the years he brought at least four hundred people to Christ. Nicholas understood that his early visions had been partly true, as the Holy Spirit showed him how it was only a shadowy portion of the great vision brought by Christ to all the world."

"Through a glass darkly," said Fr. Peter.

"Last night Nicholas Black Elk came to Farley in a dream," said Kateri, and then prodded her husband's arm. "Go on, tell them."

"After me 'n' Kateri finished the rosary, I fell asleep. In this dream, I saw the world on fire—an evil fire, the flames invisible, licking up so many souls it was like a sea of souls; no, it was like a prairie full of wheat all in flames, and each stalk of wheat was a soul. I was mourning and grieving and crying out to the Lord over it. Then a light pushed back the flames and Nicholas steps out from it. He says, 'Farley, you love the Heart that was pierced for all peoples, He who burns with love for each and all with the fire that does not destroy; it is sweet and gives light. Rise up and take your wife, Kateri, and Peter Ahanu and go down to Fort Macleod and wait there.'

"I ask him, 'For what should I wait?' and he answers, 'For the lambs who will be pulled from the evil fire.' And I ask him, 'But how will I know the lambs?' and he says, 'It will be shown to you. You must carry them.' Then he disappears and I wake up with my heart drumming real hard."

Kateri said, "Just then we heard someone knocking at our door. It was Fr. Peter. He told us the Holy Spirit had said to him while he was in prayer that he must go to his aunt and uncle and travel with them to an unknown place, so the light won't go out. He got up and did what the Lord told him to do."

"And here we are," said Fr. Peter with a smile. "Though we don't have a glimmer about what we're supposed to do next."

"Next, you should come with us," Rafe answered. "We'll explain on the way."

Farley looked uncomfortable. "Okay, but you sure you

don't mind a crazy man who has dreams tagging along on your holiday?"

"You're not a crazy man, Farley, and it's not a holiday. And we have a few things to tell you about dreams. For now, we really must get moving."

Rafe turned to the children and said with a smile, "Finish up your ice cream, gals, we're going now."

Turning to me and Annie, he said with urgency in his voice: "When I went out to get Farley and Kateri and Fr. Peter, I overheard the cop trying to calm down the ballistic lady. He kept his voice low, didn't want anyone listening, but as I went past him I heard him tell her that all police are called in to duty, a major security crisis, they're blocking city exits."

"Blocking city exits?" I said in a quiet voice. "It sounds like the situation is more complicated than we thought."

"Yup," he nodded. "Let's hope it's not sudden entropy."

"Yeah, let's hope for gradual. But in any case I think we should get on the road as quickly as possible."

On the way out the door, I showed Farley and Kateri the map my father had sent me, pointing out the general area of our destination.

"It's somewhere in there, a valley near Waterton Park," I said in conclusion.

Outside in the parking lot we could see the social worker and policeman still at it. They were now gesturing wildly in front of the squad car, both of them yelling at each other, neither of them listening.

As Cora and Annie got the children into the Morrow van, I gave Farley and Kateri an abridged summary of the contentious scene in the restaurant, still loudly underway a few feet from us.

"Whew," said Farley scratching his head. "Things are getting messy. Why would they be locking the city down?"

"Something big's happening in the realm of providence, Farley," said his wife.

"What d'you mean, Kateri?"

"We can't read the whole weave, and we can't untangle it. But maybe our part is to take hold of a thread that's been put in front of us, and that'll be our role in keeping things from falling to pieces. Remember what Nicholas said in the dream? The lambs would be shown to us. We must carry them."

"Uh-huh," he grunted, chewing over what she had said.

"That girl is going to fall through the cracks, Farley. We could take her down to the border and get her reunited with her family."

"That's out of our way according to what Cleve's map says."

"Not out of our way, just a bit farther. After the girl's safe with her grandparents, we can double back and meet up with everyone on the highway, the place where we're supposed to turn off onto those side roads."

"Well, okay. Looks like it's a day for surprises, so let's go with it."

"Let me talk to them."

Kateri, with Farley trailing behind, walked over to the police car, where the social worker and the police officer were continually interrupting each other with their respective protocol arguments.

"Excuse me," said Kateri with a warm smile. The combatants stopped talking and turned to look at her, frowning.

"I'm Kateri Crowshoe and this is my husband Farley. We couldn't help overhearing your conversation. Sounds like you're caught in a bit of a predicament. We have a suggestion that might help all three of you."

The social worker looked dubious as she inspected the Crowshoes' faces and apparel. The police officer's expression went neutral. They both said nothing.

Farley removed his wallet from a hip pocket and opened it, showing them a card. He said, "I'm a part-time constable with the Siksiká Nation, member of the Blackfoot Confederacy." Opening his jacket he exposed a metal badge clipped to an inner pocket, and then pointed to the police crest sewn onto the jacket's shoulder.

Kateri fished about in her purse and brought out her wallet. She showed them a card. "I'm a certified youth counselor on our reserve. We're heading south, very close to the U.S. border. If you like, we could take the young lady there to meet up with her family."

The two whites looked at each other, still frowning, undecided.

"Well, Lucy *is* Blackfoot," said the woman, nodding to the girl, who was taking all this in and glowering at them from the back seat of the cruiser.

"I'm Blackfeet," she grumbled through the open window.

"South of the border they call their tribe Blackfeet," said the officer.

"We're not a *tribe*, we're a *nation*," snapped the girl, tossing her black ponytail.

Kateri took a few steps toward the car and said, "That's how we feel too, Lucy." She put a hand inside for a shake. The girl looked at it a moment, gave it a desultory shake, and then dropped it, looking away.

"It's a solution," said the social worker.

"Yeah, it could work," said the officer. "But if it goes wrong, it's not on me."

"No, it's on me," pronounced the woman in an officious tone. Turning to Kateri with a suddenly sweet, largely artificial smile, she said, "Her name is Lucy Medicine Stone. I'll need you to sign some paperwork, taking responsibility for her. And you'll have to hand over some other documents to the Americans when you deliver her."

"I'm no stranger to paperwork," said Kateri.

The woman opened her briefcase and extracted a file folder full of papers. She handed them to Kateri, saying, "For the border people."

Then came a form. Using the hood of the car for support, she wrote on it and then jotted down details from Farley's ID, including his police number, and Kateri's driver's license number and counselor card. She signed it, as did the Crowshoes, and stuffed it back into her briefcase.

The officer unlocked the back door of his car and beckoned Lucy out. "These people will drive you to meet your grandparents, okay?"

"Okay," said the girl, looking somewhat more compliant, but retaining her rights to sullenness. She wore jeans and an open jean-jacket, with a tight orange tee-shirt underneath. Fluorescent green feathers hung from her ear lobes.

Kateri helped her get into the Crowshoes' vehicle and made sure she buckled in beside Fr. Peter, who greeted her in Blackfoot, "*Oki*, hello," and received an *Oki* back from the girl.

"Let's go," growled the social worker to the officer as she got into the passenger side of the cruiser. With a long-suffering look, he eased himself in behind the wheel and waved goodbye to those of us standing about. The woman offered no farewell. They drove out of the parking lot onto the highway, turned right with a screech and sped away northward toward Calgary.

"Are you gassed up?" Rafe asked Farley.

"Yup, filled the tank before we parked by the café. Had to pay by cash."

"I know. Look, Farley, here's a two-way radio for you. Cleve and I have them too, so we can all stay in contact on the road."

"Hmmm, nice. Walkie-talkies."

"Uh-huh. The manual says talking range is around 1.5 kilometers, which should be optimum here on the flatlands, but once we get into the mountains it'll get shorter. Need me to run you through how it works?"

"Nah, me and Albert use 'em all the time when we're huntin'."

After calibrating the broadcast frequency, we all got into our cars. The three vehicles drove out of the parking lot and turned left onto highway number 2, heading south away from the city. A mile farther on, we came to the junction of number 3, the Crowsnest Highway, turned right onto it and headed due west toward the range of mountains low on the horizon.

11

THE TRAFFIC FLOW WAS MODERATE on the eastbound and westbound lanes. It looked like life was going on as usual. It did strike me, however, that a surprising number of cars and an occasional transport truck had pulled off onto the paved shoulders. I chalked it up to drivers wanting to check their phones.

We had gone only a few miles when three police cars screamed past in the eastbound lane, doing eighty or ninety miles per hour, their sirens wailing and lights flashing in panic mode.

"An accident?" Annie queried.

"Some kind of crisis," I said.

Shortly after, an army truck passed us in the left lane, an armored personnel carrier of some sort, heading west at high speed. Immediately after it, came a duplicate truck, and then a long white van of unknown type, with the letters DRDC on its side and a small satellite dish on its roof. Two more olive-green vehicles followed it close behind.

I clicked the mic on my transceiver. "Anyone have a clue what that's about?"

Rafe and Farley both replied, "No."

"Are there military bases around here?"

Farley answered. "There's one up in the drylands by Medicine Hat, outside a town called Suffield."

"Is it a big base?"

"Big enough. They have eight laboratories there, that much I know. It's a chemical and biological center."

"You mean biological warfare?"

"They call it chemical and biological *defense*. The people on the Blood Reserve and my people in the Siksiká, which is uncomfortably close to Suffield too, they make protests now and then. And every time, the government tells them there's no danger, it's safety inspected regularly, no threat to humans and wildlife."

"The white van that just passed us with the army trucks had the letters DRDC on its side."

"That's Suffield, all right," said Farley. "Defense Research and Development Canada."

"They were in quite a hurry," Rafe's voice broke in.

"Maybe a bug escaped from a test tube and got out the back door," Farley replied.

"Or maybe it's just an exercise," I suggested.

Farley, at his most droll, commented, "A lot of exercises going on today."

"Try the radio," I said to Annie. She began cycling through the frequencies. No news, no commentators, just the usual spectrum of country-and-western and pop rock. She tried AM and FM with the same results, other than the national radio network, the government's propaganda pet. They were playing something soothing by Bach, though I thought that Wagner would be more appropriate for the weird opera we were now involved in.

Finally she dialed past a talking voice, paused, and returned to it. Reception faded in and out, but we caught enough:

"This is Maverick Radio, broadcasting to you good folks out there who want all the news that's fit to print and tons of unfit too. It's happening, people! This is the showdown I've been telling you about for years, Apocalypse Now, baby. Government won't tell you anything, EMO broadcasts say the situation's under control, stay at home, stay off the roads, don't panic. Is it nuclear war, is it invasion? Nobody knows, nobody knows, and that's the way they want it . . ." The voice was ramping up from intense to frantic. "So if you have firearms for self-protection, now's the time to lock and load."

I reached over and shut it off.

"It tells us nothing," Annie said.

"Yup. But manages to inject a dose of fear in all of us good folks out here."

We could not have gone more than five miles when a cavalcade of roaring beasts began to pass us, thirty or forty bikers on Harley-Davidsons. With all baffles removed from their mufflers, the noise was deafening. I steered a few degrees to the right and eased up on the pedal, enough to let them get around us as quickly as possible. They took their time. As they passed me, I glanced at some pretty hard faces, noted their black leather clothing, the studs and chains, the logos celebrating death and destruction. Though a few were younger, most of them had long, gray or white beards divided in the slipstream, their ponytails flying behind them at horizontal. All of them, whether they met my eyes or not, emanated cynical contempt. After passing, the motorcycles cut in front of me too quickly, and I was forced to tap the brake.

Annie gave a little yelp.

"Are you okay?" I anxiously asked her.

"Just surprised. No harm done, Cleve."

Like darkness visible, the bikers disappeared over a rise in the highway, leaving a cloud of exhaust in their wake.

"Everyone all right?" came the voice of Rafe from the transceiver.

"Fine," I said.

"Just dandy," said Farley.

"A bit of local color," said Rafe.

As we went over the rise, I could see the pack of road warriors now far ahead. Hopefully, it was the last we would see of them.

Another half mile, and a new surprise greeted us. Parked on the side of the pavement was a small sedan with steam pouring out from under its hood. Two young women stood by the vehicle's trunk, jumping up and down and waving their arms frantically, trying to get our attention. I slowed and eased to the shoulder, coming to a stop behind them.

As they hurried toward me I got out of the truck and met them halfway.

"Car troubles?" I asked, rather disingenuously, eyeing their older-model Honda Civic.

"No, no, it wasn't a breakdown," said one of the women. "We were shot at."

"With guns," said the other.

Both of them had been crying. Their eyes were wet and swollen—and afflicted with terror.

"Did those bikers bother you?"

"The motorcycles? No, it was . . ." But before she could explain, she broke into sobs.

The other one put an arm around her shoulders.

I heard, rather than saw, Annie getting out of the truck and approaching. The young women instinctively turned to her.

"I'm a nurse," she said. "Are you hurt? Any bruises or scratches?"

Both women shook their heads and tried to dry their eyes on their sleeves. They were in their early twenties, slim and pretty, one dark-haired, the other blond. The wholesomeness of their faces was obvious—clear-skinned, no paint, no piercings, no telltale signs of habitual sulking. A further anomaly was their apparel: both of them wore loose-fitting summer dresses hemmed halfway down their shins, one dress robin's-egg blue, the other pale mint. Hints of white undershirt just covered their collarbones. Their sandals were plain leather.

Despite their emotional distress, the goodness of their personalities was evident too. They could have passed for my wife's younger sisters.

"I'm Annie, and this is my husband Cleve. Tell us what happened. We'll help you in any way we can."

"Thank you, thank you," they responded in unison. "I'm Theresa," said the dark-haired one. "I'm Alice," said the blond.

By now, Farley and Fr. Peter were standing beside us. Rafe and Cora arrived a moment later.

Alice said, "We were just driving along, minding our own business, and this pickup truck followed us for miles, driving too close. I'd speed up, and it would speed up. I'd slow down and it would slow down."

Theresa took over the narrative: "Then they tried to ram our bumper. They did it again and again. Two young guys. They were drunk, I think."

"Finally, they sped up and passed us slowly, shooting at us."

"Shooting at you?" I exclaimed.

"Yes, really shooting at us."

"I don't think they wanted to kill us, just to scare us."

"The bullets hit the trunk of the car," said Alice. "And when they drove ahead, the guy with the gun—not the driver—he shot at our headlights. They were laughing and yelling all the time."

"Was the shooter using a rifle or a hand gun?" asked Farley.

"A pistol, I think, or maybe a revolver, whatever you call it. And those were real bullets."

Rafe and I stepped around to the front of the car, and saw three holes in the radiator, steam jetting from them. Rounding the back end of the car, we found that the bumper was dented and out of kilter, with four puncture holes in the trunk lid.

"Does anyone have a cell phone?" asked Theresa. "Ours aren't working. We have to call the police."

"I'm afraid none of our phones are working," said Cora. "And I don't think the police are able to respond right now."

"Some raced by about ten minutes ago with their lights flashing. We waved and waved, but they wouldn't stop."

"There's some kind of crisis in the cities," I said. "We're really not sure what's happening, but there are troublesome signs that things could get worse."

"Worse? What do you mean?"

I tried to explain, but to no avail. Alice broke into fresh sobs. Theresa did not, but she clamped her arms tighter around her own body.

"We don't know how long it will last," said Annie in her calmest tone. "But it wouldn't be wise for you to stay here on the highway waiting for help, when the help might never come."

"We're heading the way you were going," said Rafe. "Do you live around here? We could give you a lift home."

Theresa said, "We're students at university in Saskatoon, doing summer jobs there. Our families are way far east in Manitoba and northern Ontario."

"To tell the truth, we don't really know why we're here or where we're going," Alice added.

While we absorbed this, they in turn were taking in Annie's large belly, Farley's crucifix, and Fr. Peter's collar. The young women looked at each other, sending unspoken messages with their eyes, then back at us.

"Um, we're following a dream, I guess you could call it," said Alice with an embarrassed look.

"A dream of seeing the Rockies?" I asked.

"No, it's not like that."

"So you decided to take a trip, just on a lark? But it's the middle of the week. Didn't you say you have jobs?"

"Yes, and we've probably lost them."

"Sorry, I guess we don't understand."

"We're roomies at college; I'm studying early childhood education; Theresa's getting her teacher's certificate in ESL. We're sharing an apartment for the summer. During the academic year we also work at . . . evangelization among the students. Do you know what *evangelization* is?"

Everyone in our party nodded in affirmation. "Yes, we do," Annie gently replied. "That's a beautiful apostolate you're involved in."

With this, the young women relaxed a little. The stress of feeling alone with their crisis was beginning to subside.

"Have you ever heard of St. Thérèse of Lisieux?" asked Theresa.

"Oh, yes," said Annie with a smile, reaching out and touching her arm. "We love her very much. I think all of us do."

"Well, I hope you won't think I'm crazy, but—"

"*We* hope you won't think *we're* crazy," Alice interrupted.

"The night before last, I had a very powerful dream," Theresa resumed. "It felt more real than real. In the dream, St. Thérèse came to me and told me to drive out west with Alice. I should say she asked me, she didn't order me or anything like that. So I asked her—I mean I was inside the dream asking her—where should we go out west? She just smiled at me and said, 'A shepherd will help you.'"

Alice now chimed in, "Then she said—I mean the saint said—there'll be trouble on the way, but we shouldn't be afraid."

"Not exactly, Alice. She said we *would* be afraid, but we should overcome our fear, turn away from it and put our trust in the Lord and the angels."

"The guardian angels."

"Yes. So I woke up then, and I woke Alice straightaway and told her the whole story about the dream. I expected her to tell me to go back to sleep, but she didn't. She took it seriously. But then I was starting to have my doubts, and I mentioned the line from Scripture about 'dreams put fools in a flutter,' you know."

Most of us looked blank, but Rafe nodded and said, "I think it's in Ecclesiastes somewhere."

"Ecclesiasticus," said Farley, to everyone's surprise. "It says you might as well clutch at shadows and chase the wind as put your faith in dreams."

Which struck me as pretty odd, since Farley and Kateri had just made a huge act of faith in their own dream.

"Well, anyway," Theresa continued, "Alice reminded me that Scripture is also full of dreams sent from heaven, and for the people who listened to the dreams, it all worked out for the best. For the people who ignored the dreams, things didn't go so well."

"So we prayed and felt much more peaceful about it. We packed a few things and hopped in the car."

"I'm sorry we're talking a mile a minute like this. We're pretty shook up. We just don't know what to do."

Rafe said, "Ladies, anyone would be shaken up by what just happened to you. Seems to me you're doing well for people who've been assaulted by first-class yahoos."

"Well, it's our mistake in the first place, listening to a dream and leaving home without rhyme or reason," said Alice.

Evidently their doubts still lingered beneath the surface, probably due to the road-trauma they had just experienced.

"There could very well be a reason," I said. "Think about it—are you the type of women who would ordinarily just get out of bed in the middle of the night, jump in the car, and drive into the west without a plan?"

Both of them shook their heads.

"Sounds to me like you were given a light or a grace," said Cora.

At the word *grace*, the young women's faces became attentive.

"Ever done anything like this before?" I asked.

Alice and Theresa again shook their heads. "Never," said one. "It's crazy," said the other.

"Or ultimate sanity," said Rafe in his sagest tone. "I'm not a shepherd, but I think we're the ones sent to help you. Your car is a goner, for sure. The police are beyond contact, and there may be more barbarians roving around taking advantage of the situation. There's some kind of widespread collapse going on. We don't have any idea how short or long it will be before order reasserts itself, but for now, I suggest you come with us."

"Where are you going?" asked Alice.

"To a safe place."

"You don't really know us," said Fr. Peter. "We wouldn't blame you if you don't feel comfortable trusting us, but I hope you'll believe that these are good people here. Would you consider coming with us?"

The young women hesitated a moment only.

"Yes," said Theresa.

"Thank you," said Alice.

"Good," said Cora. "Let's get your things, and we'll find you seats."

Alice and Theresa opened the trunk of their car, Rafe and I standing by to take their luggage. It wasn't much, just a couple of carry-on bags and a wicker picnic hamper. Suddenly, the roar of motors invaded our attention. Looking up, I spotted the cloud of darkness approaching from the west. The bikers were returning.

Or so we thought. This time there were only four motorcycles, which slowed to a crawl as they neared us. Like the rat pack that had passed us half an hour ago, the riders were all in black, with Nazi helmets, beards, and ponytails, but I could see that each bike had a passenger riding pillion. The bikes braked in a line parallel to our cars, and legs shot out to steady the vehicles in idle. The drivers gunned their engines repeatedly.

Above the deafening rumble I heard Annie's voice cry "Cleve!" I stepped in front of her to block whatever devilry the riders might do. At the same time, Farley hot footed it toward his vehicle, which was parked at the tail end of our convoy. By the time he made it there, the pillion riders were holding up soft drink cans in one hand and flicking butane lighters with the other. Realizing that they were igniting the wicks of makeshift Molotov cocktails, I shouted, "Get down!" and pulled Annie behind Alice and Theresa's vehicle. They scrambled to join us. We all crouched low.

One of the riders hurled his can at the Honda and would have done serious damage had it not bounced off the hood and landed in the field behind us. When it boomed and burst into flames, Alice and Theresa screamed. I covered Annie with my body, feeling the heat on my back.

There were three more booms, followed by the howls of blasphemies, expletives, curses, and hoots of gleeful victory.

This was followed by the gunning of motors, which rose to a crescendo and then declined in intensity as the bikers raced away down the highway.

Now we all rose from behind our vehicles.

I helped Annie to her feet. She caught my eye. "Whew!" she whispered. "More fun."

There had been four booms in all. One had hit the Honda. I walked back to see what other damage had been done. A second bomb had struck my Toyota's front left fender, spreading flaming gas across the hood and roof, but, thankfully, not cracking my windshield or igniting my tires or hitting the gas tank.

Rafe and Cora were talking to their girls through the open doors of their Explorer, checking to see if they were all right and giving them reassurances. The van looked unscathed. Beyond its tail lights I saw that the third bomb had missed them altogether, and ignited a burning epicenter in the field. Farley and Kateri's Aspen had been hit on the side, leaving black scorch marks radiating backward from the Sacred Heart logo. But its tires were intact, and the SUV seemed otherwise unhurt.

The fires in the field's damp grass burned out, with only thin tendrils of smoke remaining. Now and then, cars passed us going east or west, none of them looking in our direction, none of them slowing. A single transport truck thundered by, its horn blowing in rebuke, I suppose because we weren't as far off the pavement as we should have been.

"Time to get moving," said Rafe, coming up to me.

"The girls are settling down," said Cora. "They're kind of excited actually."

"Nothing like a bit of drama," Rafe replied.

Cora said to Alice and Theresa, "Why don't you ride with us. We have plenty of seats, and our daughters will probably have lots to ask you, if you're all right with that. I was a teacher before I married, so I'd love to ask you about the latest developments in education."

It was the perfect touch. The message communicated—life continues, back to normal, all will be well.

Alice and Theresa carried their luggage to the open door of the van.

"Cleve," said Annie, with the palm of her hand on her tummy, "would you mind if I rode with Cora?"

"Sure, honey. Softer seats and less chance of a shock a minute. Also, you'll be a reassuring presence for the college girls."

She kissed me on the cheek.

"Cora," said Rafe, "how about you drive the van and I catch a ride with Cleve?"

"Sounds good. I need the practice anyway. Driving this behemoth is no small learning curve."

"Use the power button to raise the seat."

"Will do, big man."

Farley cleared his throat. I hadn't noticed him standing behind us. Turning, I saw that he was carrying a shotgun.

"Couldn't get to it fast enough," he said, patting the weapon. "Next time, I'll be ready."

"Hopefully there'll be no next time," I said.

While the others were loading up their vehicles, Rafe and I pulled grass from the field to wipe the black grime off my windshield. With the aid of a full jug of washer fluid, this cleaned the glass and wipers. A few additional jets from the squirter completed the job.

Rafe inserted his large frame into the passenger seat, I took the wheel and *beep-beeped*. After checking for traffic, I pulled onto the highway and drove on, the other two vehicles following closely now.

The crisis had passed. Rafe looked consummately unruffled, and I felt calm enough, though there were residual tremors in my hands. We did not speak for a couple of miles.

I noticed that the sack of oatmeal cookies was missing. Annie must have taken it to share with the people in the Morrow van. However, she had left four cookies in a row on the seat between us.

"Care for a cookie?" I asked.

"Delighted," said Rafe, taking one.

"I warn you, it's not gluten-free."

"Excellent. I devour all the gluten I can get."

"Have another."

"I will."

I ate one too.

Between bites I said, "A week ago, Annie told me the idea of making this trip was through the looking glass. It's sure turning out that way."

"We even have our own Alice," Rafe said. After a long pause, he mused, "And another dream."

"A little uncanny, isn't it?"

"Definitely. You, me, Farley, and now this young lady. What are the odds?"

"Astronomical, I would think."

Farley's voice broke in over the transceiver. "We're passing through the Piikani reserve. That's the Oldman River bending in close on the right. Town of Brocket is coming up fast. After that, it's five, six miles to Pincher."

"Thanks, Farley," Rafe replied on his mic. "Pincher's where we turn off onto Highway 6 South."

"Don't make the mistake of turning right into Pincher. That's just a whistle-stop. Turn left to go to Pincher Creek, which is a bigger place, four thousand people, my atlas says. How's the Toyota doing?"

"Steady as she goes. You?"

"Having a grand ol' time."

"Once we're on 6, we'll be hitting the town in short order. No telling what we'll find there, so let's stay close together."

"Roger that. Over and out."

We were still passing through rolling croplands, horizon to horizon, save for the rising massif of the Rockies ahead of us. Then, before we knew it, the route signs appeared; right to Pincher, left to Pincher Creek and number 6 South.

I duly turned left.

The first warning that there might be trouble ahead was at a huge Walmart shopping plaza on the northern edge of town. There must have been more than a hundred cars and pickups jammed close to the main entrance, with even more people crowding around the doors, trying to get in, and very angry that they could not. I turned in to the lot and parked far enough away to avoid getting sucked into the conflict but close enough to see that employees in blue vests were vainly trying to quell what looked like the beginnings of a mini-riot. It was now early afternoon and the store should have been open, but for some reason it had been closed.

"Not propitious," Rafe said, observing the scene.

"They've probably shut down because credit and debit cards aren't working," I conjectured.

Just as I said this, things turned ugly. A few young men pushed the employees aside and began jamming tire irons into the crack between the double doors. Two others were battering the windows with crowbars. There was a lot of yelling and pushing.

"It might be wise to beat a hasty retreat," I said.

Circling the lot, I went out the exit. A glance in the mirror reassured me that Cora and Farley were close behind.

In the next few hundred yards, we drove past a Ramada

hotel, an A&W hamburger joint, a Dairy Queen, and similar fast-food enterprises, all of them with people in their lots arguing and checking cell phones with manic obsession. We had not gone far before we were brought to a halt at the tail end of a line of idling vehicles. More cars closed in behind us. At first it looked like we had been caught in a gridlock, but little by little the line inched forward, bumper to bumper. The barely suppressed road rage, fore and aft, produced a cacophony of blaring horns.

"Canadians," commented Rafe, "the nicest people in the world."

"So polite, so docile."

"From sea to shining sea."

More than twenty minutes passed as we crept forward in a series of jerks and stops. I fought back an overwhelming urge to lean on my horn. Ahead of us I could see the big yellow scallop of a Shell station beyond a traffic circle. The hands on my wristwatch slowed; the same for the digital clock on my dashboard. My blood pressure soared. Finally, finally, the cars ahead of us declined in number, some rocketing down the highway, most of them being funneled into the gas station, one at a time. The entrance was blocked with sawhorses and cardboard signs announcing, "Cash only." When the car ahead of us turned into the station, I pressed the accelerator, and we were free.

Immediately after, we passed a large medical center with a big blue H on its upper story. With a start, I realized we were now going deeper into the town proper, a maze of houses and businesses, with no highway sign in sight, only street names. Somewhere back there, probably at the traffic circle, we had left 6.

A few blocks farther on, we were slowed by more congestion, dozens of cars and a preponderance of pickups trying to get around an accident scene. A couple of men were standing in the street waving and trying to guide vehicles through. As we passed the accident, I noted a white pickup truck with its front end smashed and driver's side caved in. It bore the green logo of the Alberta Fish and Wildlife Service. A second pickup had rammed into the government vehicle and was crippled and stationary at right angles to it. Beside the wrecks, a young man in an olive-green uniform sat on the curb with his head in his hands, bleeding. Nearby, a man wearing a crumpled Stetson hat was staggering in circles, distressed, yelling incoherently. One arm dangled loosely; his other arm was held against his chest and twisted at a bad angle. Solicitous people were trying to help the injured parties by offering first aid, and others were attempting to make calls on their cell phones, doubtless hoping to connect with an ambulance service.

I braked and rolled down my window, but one of the men trying to guide traffic shouted at me, "Keep moving, keep moving!"

"My wife's a nurse," I shouted back. "She could help."

"We already got an off-duty nurse looking at these guys, and somebody's hoofing it to the health center to get an ambulance. Just get moving!"

I rolled slowly onward, maneuvering around other cars and pickups halted this way and that across the road, some with shattered headlights, leaving only a narrow opening for traffic to go through. There was a lot of glass on the road, and plenty of honking added to the mayhem. More vehicles were approaching, getting caught in the tangle.

I clicked the mic. "There has to be a way around this mess. I'm turning onto that street just ahead, and from there we'll try to zigzag out of town."

"Okay," Cora answered. "We'll follow you."

"Lead the way," said Farley's voice.

I turned right onto a wider avenue called Main and drove along it with no certainty about where I was going. I kept hoping that a way out would soon present itself. Passing a few shops and cafés, I noticed that their doorways were blocked by clusters of unhappy people, several of them trying to get a response from their phones.

Within four or five blocks I spotted a church spire on my left, and turned toward it on a cross street, thinking that it might be a good place from which to reconnoiter. Maybe there would be a minister there who would be helpful enough to give us directions. Our three vehicles parked in front of the building, which was quirky modernist in design with an asymmetrical bell tower. A sign on the front lawn informed us that it was St. Michael's Catholic Church, with Mass times posted.

On one side of the building, a gang of teenage boys and girls were throwing glass bottles at the windows. One of them was spray-painting the brick wall. I leaned hard on my horn, which caught their attention, but it wasn't until Rafe stepped out of the truck and strode toward them that they scattered in all directions.

Fr. Peter joined us, and we three went hunting for a door to a parish office or priest's residence. Circling the building, we discovered that every door was locked, with an X of yellow tape across each one. Most disconcerting of all, stapled to each were police posters announcing that the church was closed "pending investigations."

Arriving at the church's main entrance, we came upon a person whom we hadn't seen at first, an elderly lady seated on a four-wheel, heavy-duty electric wheelchair, parked in an alcove half shielded by potted plants. She was sobbing convulsively and fingering her rosary beads.

Fr. Peter went down on one knee beside her and said, "Are you all right?"

She looked up with total misery in her old pale eyes and said something in a language that sounded vaguely Slavic.

"I'm sorry, I don't understand," Fr. Peter said.

She stared at him but gave no answer.

"You seem distressed, ma'am. Is there any way I can help you?"

"No one can help me now," she cried in an ancient raspy voice. "I warn them and warn them and warn them. For years I warn them, you think this country is the free land, the democracy land? But nobody listen, nobody listen. I tell them, we were just like you before the Communists come. One day we have *Sejm*, we have Senate, just like you, then next day Nazis come and then Soviets come. Blood and fire, blood and fire . . ."

As her voice trailed off, Rafe gently said, "This lady is Polish. Ask her what happened here, Cleve."

"Madam," I said, "we are friends. We are Catholics like you. Can you tell us why the police have closed the church?"

After a flash of anger, she sniffed back her tears.

"They take Father away this morning. I come early every morning to pray before the Mass, and I see what they do. I try to stop them, I stop them with my chair, but they just smile at me. They smile like I am stupid old lady. Very nice, very polite. They tell me Father is *kryminalny*—criminal."

"Did they tell you what crime he's accused of?"

"They tell me nothing. But no sex, no money steal, because Father he is saint—real saint. It is *polityka*."

Once again she broke down crying.

"They take him away to their car, not RCMP, it was another kind of car. It was van with wire on the window. Father shout to me, he say, Call the bishop. I go home. I have my tea because I must clean my brain. I try to call bishop on my telephone, but it is not working. I come back here to pray to *Matka Boża* for protect him."

"Our Lady?" asked Fr. Peter.

"Yes, our Mother."

Cora now knelt by the woman's side.

"Where do you live?" she asked. "Can we take you to your home?"

"No!" the old woman cried sharply with a jerk of her chin, as if Cora had threatened to arrest her. Then, recollecting herself, she pointed down the street. "I live there. Close. I have motor chair."

"We need your help, madam. Can you—"

"I am Zofia."

"Zofia, I am Cora. This is Fr. Peter, and this is Cleve and my husband Rafe. We mean you no harm."

"I see it now. No badness is in your eyes. You are young. You are strong. You must call the bishop and tell him."

"I'm sorry, our phones aren't working."

And the bishop is in jail, I thought to myself.

"You may be able to help us," said Cora. "You see, we're travelers, and we've become lost in your town. Can you tell us how to find highway number 6?"

The woman seemed to rally at the request, her eyes now fully focusing on Cora. She pointed. "You go down this street, Christie Avenue." She paused, her expression straining, her mind searching.

"Oh, oh, oh," she cried plaintively, rubbing her forehead with a bone-and-parchment hand. "I forget so many things. I have lived here forty-eight years. I used to drive a car. I know every street. I see it in my mind, but the words don't come out right. Forgive me, forgive me . . ."

"That's all right," said Cora, taking Zofia's hand in her own. The old woman didn't seem to notice.

"Before he pass away, my husband, Bronis, depend on me to drive him everywhere because of the stroke." After more tears, she looked up at Cora and said, "Oh, now I remember. You go down Christie and turn left where it ends at . . . at Broadview. No, that is wrong. You turn *right* at Broadview and go to Range Road. Turn there and go past golf course. Then . . . ."

"And then?"

"Then you go on first road after golf course, and it bring you to highway."

"Number 6?"

"Yes, 6."

"Thank you, ma'am. God bless you."

"*Niech Bóg idzie z tobą*. May God walk with you."

With that, the woman grasped her vehicle's joystick and with an electric hum she set off down the street. We watched to make sure she would turn onto a front walk leading to a house, and when she safely did so, we returned to our vehicles.

Rafe and I were climbing into my truck when we were startled by the sharp crack of a gun being fired not very far away. It was followed closely by two more shots. Then a fourth that seemed to come from a different direction.

"Let's go," I said.

"Did you get all that?" he asked me as we drove away. "The directions I mean."

"I think so," I said. "First we head south on Christie to Broadview. Turn right on Broadview and take it as far as Range Road. Range Road will bring us to the highway."

"Sounds right."

Five minutes later I made the stop at Broadview and

turned right. It didn't quite make sense to me, as we were now facing the mountains and I knew that 6 was in the other direction. A few blocks later, the town petered out and the street merged into Township Road.

"This isn't working," I muttered to Rafe.

"The lady may have got a couple of things wrong, but there's a chance this road will swing around to the east and link us up with the highway."

"I don't see any golf course."

"Let's go a little farther."

After checking the rearview mirror to confirm that the other two vehicles were behind me, I drove on. But I could see that the road was still taking us steadily westward. We were now passing mixed fields and woods above a winding creek, with an occasional house or barn breaking the pattern of smaller cultivated holdings.

"We have to go back," I said with a sigh. "We'll retrace our steps. It's less than a mile to town."

"All right, Cleve. Why don't you pull into that laneway, and we can do a reverse."

I turned onto a circular driveway, at the head of which was a small house nestled among trees on the edge of the creek. Four boys, a couple of them in their teens, were busy kicking a soccer ball around on the front lawn, and a man stood at the edge of the game, watching them. He looked up as our three vehicles came to a stop in front of the house.

Bending quickly, he picked up a hockey stick and held it at the ready across his chest.

12

I GOT OUT OF THE TRUCK and approached the man. Estimating the radius of a nasty swing from the stick, I halted several paces away from him.

"Hello," I began. "I'm afraid we're lost. Can you tell us how we might get to Highway 6 south?"

He considered this a moment, a look of caution firmly fixed on his face. He was a thin, wiry fellow in his mid-forties, slightly balding, on the short side, no more than five-foot-eight. He was dressed in white tee-shirt and khaki trousers, with incongruous Oxford shoes on his feet.

"I regret I don't know," he said at last. A distinctly British accent.

"You're not familiar with the area then?"

"No."

I cleared my throat. "Well, sorry to trouble you. We'll be on our way."

As I turned to go, a voice called from the direction of the house's open front door:

"Wait!"

A woman in her late thirties came tripping down the steps, barefoot, wearing blouse and slacks, and carrying a dishcloth.

"Please wait," she said. "I'm not sure why, but I think we're supposed to talk with you." Her accent was also British.

"Colleen," said the man, switching his attention to her with a worried frown. "What's this?"

"I'm . . . I'm not sure, Richard. I just woke up from my nap, and I had the strangest dream."

"A dream?"

Without answering him, she turned to us and said, "I'm Colleen Lyon, and this is my husband Richard. These are our sons."

The four boys had stopped their play and were sidling closer to listen. I saw from the corner of my eye that Cora and Annie had joined us. Rafe and Farley, perhaps prudently, had held back.

"Colleen," said the husband, "these people just stopped to ask directions. I wasn't able to offer them any help, and I think we should let them go on their way."

"It's more complicated than that," she said. "You see, not ten minutes ago I woke up from a vivid dream, so real, so insistent, it startled me awake. I got up not knowing what sense to make of it, and thought I would clear my head by cleaning the cupboards. I happened to look out the kitchen window just as your three cars drew up to the verge in front."

"You're not making yourself very clear, darling," said Richard, lowering the hockey stick.

"In the dream, three camels came out of the desert, carrying people who were—I'm not sure how to explain how I knew it—but I knew that they were servants of God. They were crossing a dangerous desert and had lost their way. They stopped at our house as if it were a caravanserai, and we were supposed to help them."

"Help them, how?"

"I'm not sure. Food and water, I think. And shelter. Temporary shelter."

Feeling somewhat stunned, I struggled to find something to say in reply. Annie stepped into the breach.

"I'm Annie Longworth," she said with an outstretched

hand. The two women shook hands, and my wife continued. "My husband, Cleve, and I, along with our friends, are trying to reach a place that's south of here. We've wandered off our route somehow, and we need advice on how to get back on track. Highway 6 is the route we're supposed to be on."

"I simply don't know what to suggest," said Richard. "We've just arrived ourselves."

"Late last night," added his wife. "We've only started unpacking."

"So this isn't your home?" I said.

"It's the first time we've ever seen the place. It's owned by a colleague of Richard's who's renting it to us for the summer."

Rafe and Farley had now joined us.

"Where have you come from?" Rafe asked.

"Winnipeg," the woman answered.

"I teach at a university there," said her husband. "Er, I should say *taught*." The man and wife glanced at each other, frown lines appearing on their foreheads.

"Did you have any trouble along the way?"

"Trouble? No."

"How did you buy gas?"

They looked puzzled. "With our credit card."

"I should explain what's been happening since early this morning," Rafe said. "It may be hard for you to believe. I'm having trouble believing it myself."

He described the mounting number of anomalous incidents we had encountered since leaving Calgary. He began with the lockdown of the cities. When he came to the loss of phone and wi-fi connection at the truck stop, Richard removed a cell phone from his pocket and tapped on its keyboard. "I'm listening," he said. "Please go on."

Next came the attack on the college students from

Saskatoon, then the rat pack of bikers tossing Molotov cocktails at our vehicles. Hearing this, Colleen Lyon stepped closer to her husband, worried now.

Richard shook his head. "The phone's on and ostensibly alive, but it's not performing a single function. Strange." He looked up. "Did I hear you say Molotov cocktails?"

We nodded. I pointed to the blackened scorch marks on the sides of our vehicles.

"What on earth!" Richard exclaimed. "Did the police do anything? I hope they're after the culprits."

"The police themselves were busy elsewhere, and we now have no way of contacting them," said Rafe.

I stepped in to recount the disturbing things we had seen at Pincher Creek, the Walmart mini-riot, the long lineup at the gas station, the traffic snarl at the accident, and finally our arrival at the parish church.

"The church is locked," I said. "It's been closed by the police."

"What! We were planning to attend Mass there later today," Richard said.

"A person we talked to there said that the priest had been arrested. From other accounts, we think that priests are being arrested everywhere, though the bishop directed some of them to go into hiding. Almost certainly the bishop himself is in prison."

The Lyons looked shocked.

"This is awful, awful," said Colleen.

Richard clenched his jaws. "Police readily available for arresting innocent men, but can't be found when criminals are abroad."

"It seems so," said Rafe. "While we were passing through the town, we witnessed other scenes of disorder. There was some gunfire."

Colleen Lyon put a hand to her breast. "I heard shots about forty minutes ago, but I attributed it to hunters."

Richard said, "I did notice cars and trucks roaring by on the road out there, heading into the town. I made a joke of it to Colleen. So this is what rush hour in the countryside looks like, I said. Welcome to the quiet life."

Suddenly, the booms of gunfire came to us from the direction of town, making everyone flinch.

"That's louder," said Colleen nervously. "Do you think they're coming this way?"

"Maybe," said Farley. "But maybe not. That was a heavy-gauge shotgun." As more shots were fired, a few of them contrapuntally, he cocked his ear. "Two shotguns, or could be three. Some kind of shoot-out."

Richard and Colleen eyed the crucifix on his chest.

"In any event, I think we'd better get the boys inside," said the husband.

Their sons, who had returned to their soccer play on the front lawn, were so focused on their footwork they were unheeding of the noise coming from town. Their father waded into their midst and told them to go inside the house. Reluctantly they obeyed.

I turned to Rafe. "We should have arrived at the cabin hours ago. Let's get going."

Annie took my arm. "Cleve, before we leave, I need to make a quick rest stop."

Colleen Lyon stepped forward and said to Annie, "How many months along are you?"

"Seven and a half, going on eight. Would you mind if I use your bathroom?"

"Come in right now. I'll show you the way. Is there anything else you need?"

They went off in the direction of the house's front steps,

the woman with her hand on Annie's elbow for support, guiding her. My wife was moving more slowly than usual. I could see by her posture that she was suffering from a sore back, due to the long ride.

The rest of us visitors waited outside, listening to more gunfire.

"It's not getting closer," said Farley.

"But it's still going on," Richard said. "Maybe we should all step inside."

I walked back to the vehicles and put my head through the open windows. "We're taking a short rest stop. Why don't you all get out and stretch your legs?"

One by one the doors opened, and out came the passengers: The three Morrow girls, Kateri and Fr. Peter, Lucy the runaway, and the two young college students, Alice and Theresa.

"These kind people have invited us in," I told them. "We're still an hour or so from the cabin, maybe longer, so it might be a good time to take a bathroom break."

Clearly, this idea had been on more than one mind. Everyone headed toward the house, where Richard greeted them and courteously directed them inside.

I glanced at my wristwatch. It was now after 2 P.M.

Presently, everyone was seated in the living room and the connected kitchen-dining room.

"Introductions are in order," announced Richard in a buoyant tone, the first indication that he was becoming genuinely open to the invasion.

We learned that their children were Edmund, age sixteen, Gregory, age thirteen, James, age eleven, Elias, age eight, and a fifth child, who arrived from a back room, holding a book in her hand and looking agape at the extraordinary number of people who had appeared in the house. She was a lovely fifteen-year-old girl named Clare. The Morrow girls, Josie, Rose, and Penny, gravitated toward her and wanted to know about her book (*Anne of Green Gables*) and showed her their own reading material, which they never left home without. They all sat down around a stone fireplace and chattered about the stories, the Lyon girl listening with real attention and asking questions. Her brothers, disheveled in sportswear, were scattered throughout the room, not conversational, but keenly interested in what the adults were discussing.

After we visitors had introduced ourselves, Colleen jumped up and said, "I'll make tea."

"I can help," said Cora. Annie tried to rise from the couch, but Colleen waved her back down and told her to rest.

Afterward, when all the guests had tea or water or fruit juice in hand, Colleen retold her dream about three camels to those who hadn't yet heard it.

I noticed a look in Kateri Crowshoe's eyes, a simmering pleasure and motherly fondness for the narrator.

"I know it sounds irrational," Colleen said in conclusion. "Of course, it could mean nothing, but on the other hand . . . when you arrived . . . the timing, you see. God's servants riding the camels. It all seems to be coming true."

"Three wise men from the west," said Richard.

I looked at my watch. It was now after three in the afternoon. I wondered how much longer we would be on the road, and if we would be able to settle in at the cabin before nightfall—if we found the cabin.

"I'm curious," said Colleen. "Has anyone else here had dreams the past few days? I mean dreams about getting up and doing something . . . irrational."

I raised my arm, as did Farley, Rafe, and Theresa.

"Four of you, five counting me."

Six, I silently added, thinking about Dad's dream of me driving a team of ox carts,

Why these dreams all of a sudden?" Colleen asked. "And wouldn't you agree it's rather uncanny the way several of us who've had these dreams have come together like this? Some of us strangers to each other?"

"It is uncanny," said Annie. "But I don't feel you're strangers. I'm not sure I can explain it, but I feel I've known your family for years."

"I feel the same about you," said Colleen, and then swept her eyes around the circle. "About everyone, really."

"Me too," affirmed Richard. "And what are the statistical odds on that? Any probability theorists present here today?"

"One. Me," said Rafe, with the eye-twinkle I knew so well. "Strictly amateur, mind you."

This evoked a few smiles around the room.

The Lyon's oldest boy walked into the living room, waving a paper in his hand, his face animated but hesitating to interrupt.

"What is it, Edmund?" his father asked.

"I found this in the little desk in the hallway. It's a map showing where we are."

Richard took the paper and unfolded it. After a quick perusal, he said, "A map of the town, plus a few surrounding roads." Looking more closely, he tapped the paper with a forefinger. "Well, you're not terribly lost. If you follow our road a bit farther in the direction you were going, you'll come to a junction where you turn left onto Township Road 60, and that will bring you to Highway 6. You make a right onto 6, and you're on your way."

Farley stood up and said, "It's been real nice meeting

you folks, but I have to go. I'm supposed to drive Lucy to the U.S. border to meet up with her grandparents." He turned to Rafe. "It should be about an hour's drive to the border crossing. Maybe a half hour doing the paperwork there. Then I'll drive back as soon as I'm done. How about we meet up somewheres on the road, close to the place you're turning off?"

"The problem is," said Rafe, "we don't know exactly where the turnoff is. It's going to be catch-as-catch-can getting there, and maybe hide-and-seek finding it."

Richard Lyon stepped in. "Wouldn't it make more sense for you to meet here at this house? That way Mr. Crowshoe would know precisely where you are. If the situation continues to be as volatile as you've described, you could be unnecessarily exposing yourselves to danger if you were forced to wait for him by the side of the highway, miles from anywhere. He might be delayed."

"That does make sense," Rafe replied and glanced at Farley.

"Yup, it's a better plan," Farley affirmed.

Richard said, "Of course, I realize it would make a longer day for you, but you *are* welcome to wait here. Truly."

"You should consider it," said Colleen.

"Okay, we'll do it that way," said Farley. "Thank you."

"Keep your shotgun handy," Rafe suggested in a low voice.

"Oh, I will."

"I'm coming too," said Kateri in a tone that would abide no nonsense from her husband.

They locked eyes for a few moments.

"I dunno. There could be troubles," said Farley.

"We'll be covered," his wife answered.

Farley gave in with a sigh. "I been resisting this woman

all my life, and losing every time," he said to the rest of us. "No reason for me to start winning now. Looks like I'll be bringing a secret weapon along."

Turning to Lucy, he said, "Okay, girl, let's make tracks."

Fr. Peter stood and spoke to the Crowshoes in their native tongue. They bowed their heads, and he prayed a minute in Blackfoot, and finished by making the sign of the cross over them. They crossed themselves in response. When he blessed Lucy Medicine Stone, she simply averted her eyes.

As they went out the front door, Farley said, "We'll be back without a scratch. Three hours at the most."

Three hours, I thought uneasily. That would bring us to early evening. What time was sunset? Around 10 P.M. in June? Between now and then, how many more delays and sidetracks would we face? Would we be scrambling to find the cabin in the dark?

"That settles it," said Colleen, breaking into my thoughts. "You're going to be here some time yet. I'll get supper started. Is spaghetti all right for everyone?"

"That is so kind," said Cora. "You've been wonderful to us, people you hardly know."

"We know you now," said Colleen with a pleased laugh.

"We're such a lot of mouths to feed."

"Don't worry. When we passed through Lethbridge yesterday, I bought half a dozen family-sized packages of hamburger, some for the freezer in the basement. There's plenty already there, mainly older meat that Richard's friend, the owner, encouraged us to eat up, because it's been there awhile. You'd be doing us a favor, you see."

"We've brought some travel foods with us. We can bring those in too."

"If you wish, but really we're going to have more than enough, and some to spare."

Richard turned his paternal face to his sons. "Gregory, James, go down to the cellar and get two packages of hamburger from the freezer. Elias, you go too, and make sure the freezer's shut tight when you've got it all."

"Okay, Dad," the boys cheerily replied and thundered off toward a staircase.

Richard and Colleen insisted that the visitors should relax and make themselves at home. They would prepare the meal for us. Rafe and Cora talked quietly to each other as their daughters plunged into their books. Fr. Peter read silently from his breviary, which he had retrieved from the Crowshoes' car before their departure. Alice and Theresa sat in easy chairs by the picture window, looking out at the landscape. They said little, and after a while I noticed their lips moving in whispers as they prayed a rosary together. Annie and I were side by side on the couch. I held her hand as she slipped into one of her light dozes.

From time to time, through the kitchen doorway I noticed the Lyons with their heads together, deep in earnest conversation between spells of frying the meat, chopping onions, and opening cans of sauce. Delicious smells soon drifted into the living room, while their children worked as a team to bring silverware and napkins to the dining room table, along with salt and pepper, bowls of salad and grated cheese, butter, and a stack of brown bread. There weren't enough ceramic plates for everyone, but paper picnic plates and cups were carried in and added to the growing array. There was a lot of good-natured chatter among the children—a beautiful family, a happy one.

I closed my eyes and thanked God for these people. And as my mind drifted, I also thanked him for the inexplicable outpouring of dreams that had led us here.

Supper was a bit of a free-for-all, what with the five children, three adolescents, and nine adults, but it all transpired with a certain order, not to mention the taste of well-spiced pasta sauce. Afterward, Josie Morrow joined with Clare Lyon to wash the dishes while the younger boys James and Elias did the drying and putting away.

While that was in progress, the adults regathered in the living room, Richard on the floor with his legs outstretched and crossed at the ankles, Colleen sitting on the raised hearthstone beside him, and Fr. Peter cross-legged on a rug to their right.

"Father, I have a question," Colleen began. "I'm still trying to grasp what's happening. I don't mean the social unrest. I mean what could possibly be the reason for five people from different backgrounds, most of them unconnected to each other, having dreams that bring them together for an unknown purpose?"

Fr. Peter gave her question some thought before answering. "All of us are wondering about that, Colleen. Of course, it goes without saying that these may be purely coincidences."

"The most remarkable set of coincidences I've ever encountered."

"For me as well. No, I think what we're trying to absorb here is the presence of Divine Providence acting in a new way in our lives—or I should say a more *manifest* way. We don't yet understand why it's happening, and we can't foresee where it's leading, but if we give it time, I think the meaning will become clearer."

"But why dreams? If God is planning something unusual with all of us, why not send an angel to deliver a message? Why not a loud, clear voice from heaven, telling us what to do?"

"The human mind is a very busy place when it's awake. It's hard for us to hear. In sleep we're at rest, and then the Holy Spirit can gently whisper his still, small voice through images in the imagination, which can be a kind of language."

"Though not all images," Richard objected. "The imagination's a three-ring circus."

"It can be. Or a theater stage on which true stories are enacted at times, and false stories at other times. We're all subject to promptings from the spiritual realm, the good and the bad. The key is to develop a gift of discernment—to *pray* to receive the gift, I should say. God will never push our nature aside; instead, he seeks to ennoble it and perfect it in the way of love and truth. He never forces. He invites us to cooperate with grace. For example, you could so easily have ignored your dream about the three camels. You were free to do so."

I raised my hand for attention: "Uh, speaking as one of the camels, I'm glad you didn't."

Fr. Peter laughed with the others, but returned to his exploration of the question:

"Sacred Scripture reveals a lot about the communication between God and Man." He picked up his Bible, lying beside him on the floor, and opened it.

"I was reading this in the car on the way here from Calgary. It's a passage in the Acts of the Apostles, where St. Luke describes what happened immediately after the first Pentecost in Jerusalem, when the apostle Peter stands up with the eleven and declares to the crowd that the prophecy of Joel is being fulfilled in their midst. He cries out in the words of Joel, 'And in the last days it shall be, God declares, that I will pour out my Spirit upon all flesh, and your sons and your daughters shall prophesy, and your young men shall see visions, and your old men shall dream dreams.'"

"Dream dreams," whispered Colleen.

Fr. Peter flipped pages to a marker and read on:

> The prophet Joel says more: "And I will give portents in the heavens and on the earth, blood and fire and columns of smoke. The sun shall be turned to darkness, and the moon to blood, before the great and terrible day of the Lord comes. And it shall come to pass that all who call upon the name of the Lord shall be delivered; for in Mount Zion and in Jerusalem there shall be those who escape, as the Lord has said, and among the survivors shall be those whom the Lord calls."

"But didn't this already happen?" I asked. "What about the destruction of Jerusalem by the Romans in 70 A.D.?"

"The prophecy was fulfilled in part but not the whole," said Fr. Peter. "Salvation history isn't a single linear track. Throughout the millennia, there are preludes, you could call them, gathering momentum and getting worse and worse, whenever a critical mass of people refuse to obey God's laws and won't turn from their sins."

"Trial runs, you mean?"

"In a sense. More like incremental warnings."

Rafe said, "Culminating in a final crisis for mankind. Do you think we're in the midst of that, Father?"

"It's beginning to look a lot like it. All that's left is portents in the sky and universal fire and smoke."

"Not to forget the sun turning to darkness and the moon to blood," said Cora.

"That has to mean it turns blood-red," Edmund Lyon contributed.

"I think you're right about that," said Annie, turning to the boy. "But if it's going to happen to us in the near future, even then it won't be the uttermost end."

Colleen nodded. "There will be some who escape, the

prophet said. Among the survivors will be those the Lord calls."

"It sounds like God's going to reach down and supply extra help to bring the chosen ones through," said Richard.

Fr. Peter resumed: "Whether or not we're living in the times the prophets foretold, it's clear to me that we *are* being blessed with quite unusual help. Which brings us back to the question, why is this happening."

Rafe said, "Since my own conversion many years ago, Father, I've always felt that history was approaching a climax. Nevertheless, I've also felt that it's dangerous to want too much knowledge about coming events. Many people are now relying on private revelation as if it were a fifth Gospel. They prepare materially for whatever they imagine is a way of surviving. But are they preparing spiritually, I wonder?"

"The two aren't mutually exclusive," Fr. Peter countered.

"Agreed. I often think about the patriarch Joseph in Egypt, storing up grain during the seven years of bountiful harvest in preparation for the seven years of famine. He did it for the sake of the people. He didn't do it for himself. In practice, so many people who follow the seers of our times pay lip service to devotional life and spend vastly more energy on self-preservation." He paused and took a breath. "My bottom line is, God will show us what we need to know, *when* we need to know it."

"Isn't it possible that our dreams *are* him showing us?" Theresa asked.

"We surely can't rule that out," the priest replied. Turning to Rafe, he said, "You're putting your finger on a core spiritual problem in human nature, Mr. Morrow."

"Rafe."

"Rafe, I think you're saying that, without knowing it, we

can easily slide into putting our faith in our own strengths and resources. Consciously or subconsciously, we come to believe that insider knowledge, money, intelligence, and so forth, will save us."

Annie said, "In what do we ultimately place our trust? In our heart of hearts, what do we believe is our security?"

"It should be *who* not *what*!" piped Clare Lyon, evoking smiles around the room.

"Yes, exactly," said Fr. Peter to the girl. "I haven't had any special dreams, not like your mother and my Uncle Farley and some of you others. But the night before our bishop warned us to go underground, I couldn't sleep. I went into the church and knelt in front of the Blessed Sacrament, and began pleading with the Lord for guidance, kind of anguishing about how to help my parishioners get through these times. Then I got all snarled up thinking to myself maybe these aren't the end times, maybe this is just a bad patch we're going through, maybe I've been reading too much private revelation without careful discernment. There's tons of it out there—a tsunami, really.

"Tossing things around in my head, I asked myself if I'd succumbed to paranoia. I asked the Lord that, too. Then an incredible peace filled me, and with it came an inner command—gentle, but a command—to open a book of meditations I often bring with me to Adoration, the sayings of the Fathers of the Church." He held up the book for everyone to see. "It's a weighty tome, but just a sampling of what they wrote back then. In our rectory library we have eighteen volumes of the Church Fathers' writings and homilies, and this book just skims the surface of those. Anyway, I opened to a page I hadn't read before. And this is what my eyes lit on. Should I read it to you? It's not long."

"Yes," and "Please," replied a few voices.

"All right, this is what it said:

As many as shall believe the enemy and unite themselves
to him,
shall be marked by him as sheep;
but they who shall refuse his mark
will either flee to the mountains, or, being seized,
will be slain with studied tortures . . .
All things shall be confounded and mixed together against
right,
and against the laws of nature.
Thus the earth shall be laid waste,
as though by one common robbery.
When these things shall so happen,
then the righteous and the followers of truth
shall separate themselves from the wicked
and flee into solitudes."

Fr. Peter looked up and concluded. "It's by Lactantius, a Father of the Church from the early fourth century."

Richard said, "And the next morning your bishop instructed you to flee into solitudes."

Fr. Peter nodded. "I was willing to stay on deck, give my life, if that's what the Lord wanted from me, but the anointing that came with Lactantius' words basically told me there was another way of giving my life for the flock."

Richard shifted uncomfortably, cleared his throat, and said, "The situation has every earmark of going from bad to worse. For instance, the violent incidents you've encountered on your journey. The vandalizing of the church and arrest of the parish priest. There's been rioting, and it sounds like looting too. With looting happening so close by, then our family isn't safe. We don't have any weapons to defend ourselves."

I thought of Richard's hockey stick and almost made a quip about it, but stopped myself. This was no time for levity.

"Colleen and I have been talking it over. What would you think about us coming along with you?" he asked.

"That would be fine," said Rafe.

"Just for a day or two. This crisis will probably be short-lived, and then we'll feel very embarrassed for over-reacting. However, it still could be dangerous while it lasts. When it has run its course, we'll return here and get on with our summer."

"It might not turn out to be as short-lived as we hope," Rafe said.

"That's true," said Richard, his face falling.

I said, "The cabin we're going to is somewhat remote. It's not very large, but I think it can accommodate several people. If you're willing to sleep in a tent—"

"We have camping tents; one of them is an alpine dome tent, which sleeps six people. We had planned to hike in the mountains this summer, you see; we wanted to give our children the experience of a lifetime."

"A thrill for all of us, actually," said Colleen. "But we'd hate to encumber you."

"There's strength in numbers," Richard added.

"We were just about to invite you ourselves," said Rafe with a reassuring smile.

Rafe's executive decision took me by surprise, but I saw no immediate reason to argue against it. The adage, *strength in numbers*, was a good one, as long as the numbers didn't include any neurotics or control freaks trying to make things go their own way. So far, there hadn't been any sign of that.

"Please be reassured, you wouldn't be a burden," I said.

"Oh, I do hope not," said Colleen. Then, all in a rush, she went on:

"We can help, we'll pull our own weight. The boys are good hard workers, real yeomen, just like their Dad. I call my husband 'Richard the Lyon-hearted', which he is. So are the boys. And Clare is my right hand, I don't know what I would do without her. We have camping gear and some food. We haven't even unloaded the trailer yet."

The discussion went on for some time, veering to the topic of our various backgrounds. We learned that Colleen had been an archaeologist before marriage, had obtained her Ph.D. in the field and had taught the subject at a university in Yorkshire, where she met her future husband.

The Lyons were intrigued to learn that Rafe had been a doctoral candidate in philosophy. Cora mentioned her husband's scholarly articles, the medal he had won, and his expulsion from the university where he had taught. This precipitated an exchange between the Lyons and the Morrows of their respective battle stories and war wounds.

"We had to leave so much behind," said Colleen. "But we've brought things we couldn't bear to lose, photo albums, some artwork, and Richard's books, I mean the six that are published. They've had excellent peer reviews by other scholars."

"And malicious reviews as well, my dear, let us not forget those."

"They're very important historical works," countered his wife. "He's an excellent writer and teacher and most of the students loved him. He made them think, do real history, real research. But the social engineers who rule the universities these days didn't like what he wrote, because it confounded their revisionist version of history. And a tiny minority of students made complaints about him harassing them. Meaning poor marks for poor essays. Offending their sensitive hearts by questioning their ideological assumptions." Momentarily, she looked indignant. "We had to leave his personal library behind."

"Now *that* hurt," said Richard with a grimace. "Well nigh a mortal blow."

Colleen continued, "Even so, though it wasn't easy, somehow we felt so much freer after we made the decision."

"To come here, you mean?" Cora asked.

"Yes. This was supposed to be our summer away from the madness, you see."

Richard took over for her. "After I was fired and no other university would take my application, we wanted to find a quiet place and try to think, try to figure out our way ahead as a family, wrack our brains for a solution to the employment problem, how I might find work to support us. We sold everything in the city, and after a lot of prayer, we were given a real peace about it. Colleen and I just knew—we knew we had to come here and wait."

"Pray and wait," said Colleen.

I noticed that there was no bitterness in the way they told it. The Lyons and Morrows were saddened by the state of academia, but seemed to have dealt with it maturely.

Not so, yours truly. I broke into the conversation and held forth:

"The tyranny of the anti-humanists!" I declared with disgust. "So cleverly disguised as humanists, when in fact they're lying murderers."

"Ah, Cleve," said Rafe in the tone he usually employed to cool me down. "Who can say how conscious they are of what they're doing?"

"Poor, poor souls," said Cora. "They don't know history. They're unable to see that once the revolution becomes the establishment, the first wave of revolutionaries is liquidated by its successors."

"It's the dictatorship of moral relativism," said Fr. Peter. "It blinds people."

"The *addiction* of moral relativism," I growled. "It *kills* people."

Annie gently elbowed me in the ribs and pointed toward the dining room, where the children had set up a game of Monopoly and were avidly throwing themselves into the thrills and perils of capitalism. Little Penny wasn't one of the players, and she alone had heard me, lifting her eyes from her reading with a worried look.

"Cleve was a journalist and a novelist," said Annie to the others.

My heart sank at the memory.

"He's a very fine woodworker now. You should see the beautiful cabinets he made for our house."

Richard came to the rescue.

"It's rather a commonplace that ignorance of history is the necessary context for corruption of historical understanding. Rationalist or irrational templates then fill the vacuum, providing the justification for no end of horrors. Narratives as weapons, you see."

"Like Marxism or Fascism?" Rafe asked.

"Yes, they're obvious examples. I mean *any* narrative that dehumanizes others. Destroying freedom in the name of freedom. Destroying human beings in the name of humanity."

"Are you saying this country's choking to death on a *narrative*?" asked Cora.

Richard nodded. "Yes, precisely."

"And a spirit," Fr. Peter quietly added.

Annie said, "Dr. Lyon, I know we all have bits and pieces of the puzzle, our own take on what has caused the corruption, but wouldn't you agree that nothing entirely explains it?"

"I very much agree." He lowered his eyes. "Forgive me, dear people, I've been waxing didactic."

At that point we were startled by a knock at the door. Richard jumped up, grabbed his hockey stick, and went to answer it.

Farley and Kateri stood on the porch looking apologetic, with Lucy slumping behind them.

"Come in, come in," said Richard.

"What happened?" I asked.

"Border's closed," Farley grumbled. "Blocked on our side and theirs. No one gets in or out. U.S. Border Patrol cars and an army truck across the road, soldiers with automatic weapons. Same on the Canadian side. Hard to say if the Americans were protecting themselves from us or we were protecting ourselves from them."

"Is it about protection?" asked Rafe. "Or is it part of the general lockdown?"

Lucy threw herself onto the nearest empty chair, doubled over and began to sob. Kateri put an arm around her, whispering soothing words in Blackfoot.

Farley said, "I argued my way through our depot and got as far as U.S. Customs, but the damn paperwork didn't make a bit of difference."

"Did they say why?"

"Nope. Just, they had orders. Nobody's crossing. We had to turn back."

"I want my grandma!" Lucy cried, rocking back and forth.

"Did you have any trouble on the way?" I asked.

"A few rowdies and orangutangs on the way there, shouting insults when they passed us, but no gunplay. On the way back, a couple of drunken cowboys fired empty whiskey bottles at us."

"They missed," said Kateri.

I looked at the front window. Dusk had given way to night. What now?, I wondered.

"It's getting late," said Richard. "Do you really want to go searching around in the dark for your cabin? You could get lost again, and then where would you be?"

"Let's pray," said Fr. Peter.

The Lyons broke up the Monopoly game and herded their children into the living room. Fr. Peter knelt down on the rug, and we all followed suit. Lucy remained seated, still rocking and sobbing.

Fr. Peter led the prayers, and we joined in, reciting with him the Our Father, the Hail Mary, the Glory Be, and the invocation of St. Michael's protection and that of the guardian angels. He concluded by asking aloud for divine guidance. Should we drive onward tonight and try to find the cabin? At the end, he stood and made the sign of the cross over our bowed heads. In the silence that followed, people waited, listening in their hearts for an answer, a sense, an illumination.

"There's no doubt in my mind," said Colleen at last. "You're staying."

"I'll find more blankets and sleeping bags," said Richard. "Boys, let's set up the dome tent in the backyard."

The sleeping arrangements were somewhat haphazard, but places were found for everyone. Farley and Kateri were offered the pull-out couch in the living room; Lucy a foam slab on the rug. Rafe, Cora, and Penny would sleep in the back of their stretch van, after removing a seat. Josie and

Rose would share a set of bunk beds down in the basement. Alice and Theresa would take one of the three bedrooms, Colleen and Clare the other. Richard would camp with his sons in the dome tent. Fr. Peter insisted on sleeping outside in his pup tent. This left Annie and me.

"You're taking the master bedroom," said Colleen.

"But it's your room," Annie protested.

"This is an argument you can't win," Colleen said, brooking no discussion on the matter. "You're pregnant and it's the only queen-size bed in the house."

Reluctantly but gratefully, we obeyed.

After I turned off the bedside light, Annie and I talked quietly, arm in arm in the dark. It was our habitual wind-down routine before drifting off to sleep.

"Who could have foreseen what this day would bring?" she murmured drowsily.

"I know. It's hard to believe we left home only this morning."

"So much drama packed into such a short time."

"How's the baby?" I asked, putting my hand on her belly. I felt a tiny knee or elbow push back.

"The lil' Longworth is having a fine old time. He or she is enjoying our great adventure."

"I hope you are too."

I didn't hear her laugh, but I felt it. Dear Annie, she could always rise to the occasion, Molotov cocktails notwithstanding.

"Could be worse," I said.

"Could be worse, Cleve. You know, I think we've had a perfect storm of bad things happening all at once. So I'm wondering—if life can do *that* to us, couldn't a perfect storm of good things happen?"

"Mmm, you've got a point. We're very much in need of such a storm at the moment."

"*Storm*'s probably the wrong word. How about a congress of coincidences?"

"Or a convention?"

"Not bad, but both of those are organized events, which doesn't really fit our situation."

"Then a convergence of happy accidents, or a traffic jam of good fortune?"

"Accidents and traffic jams are too negative. How about a providential meeting of diverse roads?"

"Good, but a bit wordy."

"Okay, then, a party at the end of the world."

"How about a hitchhiker's guide to the apocalypse?"

"Or chuckling our way through calamity?"

"At least we're still laughing," I said, "and not wailing."

13

FR. PETER HAD BROUGHT with him a portable Mass kit and vestments. He asked Richard and Colleen if he could offer Mass in their home, and they heartily agreed. As he set up a temporary altar on the dining room table, the three youngest Lyons jockeyed for the privilege of being the altar boy. With Solomon-like wisdom, he invited all of them to serve, allotting to each a single task of the several usually performed by an acolyte.

Beforehand, Edmund asked if Father could hear his confession. They took a stroll in the backyard for the sake of privacy, and when the boy returned to the house, his face peaceful and aglow, Alice asked if she might also go to confession. After that came requests from Farley, and then Cora.

The first liturgical reading described the malice of Jezebel who was seeking to kill the prophet Elijah, and Elijah fleeing into the desert, where from fear and discouragement he pleaded with God to take his life. Instead, God sent an angel to feed the prophet and strengthen him.

The Gospel of the day was a passage from St. Matthew, where Jesus told the disciples, "You have heard it said that you shall love your neighbor and hate your enemy. But I say to you, love your enemies and pray for those who persecute you."

I had not heard Fr. Peter preach before; indeed, I had met him only yesterday. His homily was short and simple, as insightful as his thoughts had been last night, but now tailored to a congregation of young and old.

"Though the darkness deepens around us," he said, "and the malice in men's hearts is no longer restrained, we must not let hatred have a place in our hearts. Fear of evil can drive us to hatred of evildoers, and then this hatred, once it gains ground within us, breeds more evil, and thus evil wins a double victory. Instead, let us permit the Lord to fight for us in *His* way."

Fr. Peter concluded by exhorting us to trust God in all circumstances.

"*All* circumstances," he repeated with solemn emphasis.

As the Mass continued, I found it moving to watch this young native celebrating the ancient rite with such profound devotion. A son of the people to whom French missionaries had been sent centuries ago, *he* was now the missionary. I wondered how France was faring? Was it time to send our missionaries to evangelize darkest Europe? Or had the entire world become mission territory? Increasingly distracted, my mind drifted farther afield.

We should get on the road as soon as possible, I thought. How many miles until we reached the cabin? What would happen when we did? How long would we be stuck there? My eyes wandered to the window, noting the golden light of sunrise spreading across nearby fields and woods, the cloudless sky, a day that promised to become one of rare beauty. Good, no complications from the weather. Human beings might be another matter . . .

Seated beside me on a wooden chair, Annie pressed my arm with her shoulder. She knew me well. *Focus, Cleve*, her eyes were telling me. *Focus. This is the most important thing that will happen today.*

She was right of course. Turning away from my reverie,

I knelt at the Consecration and bowed to the living God, feeling the return of peace. At the Elevation, as little Elias Lyon rang a hand bell with great vigor, I worshipped the incarnate presence of the Lord in His Body and Blood. At Communion time, the gentle fire radiated through my heart. I felt the peace deepening, time dissolving. A brief taste of eternity.

Then, beyond all thought, in the realm of soul-speech, words arose from some inner reservoir in me: *Our lives are in His hands.*

After the final blessing, people got up and moved around, either heading to the kitchen to help with breakfast preparations, or thanking Fr. Peter, or seeking a bit of solitude. Annie remained with closed eyes, deeply recollected.

I noticed Penny, who had not yet made her First Communion, walk across the room to the only other non-recipient, Lucy Medicine Stone. Stationed on the stone shelf of the fireplace, Lucy had not absented herself from the Mass, but she had brooded and observed throughout. I wondered if she was an unbeliever or was just too conflicted to allow herself any participation. Dear, guileless Penny sat down beside her and, with a huge smile and a look of love, took Lucy's hand in both of her own. Surprisingly, the older girl did not fling it away.

With haunted eyes, Lucy had been sucking on something attached by a thin chain around her neck, an amulet or teenage costume jewelry I presumed. I couldn't hear what Penny said, but in response Lucy pulled the object from her mouth and dangled it before the little girl. From a distance it looked to me like a turquoise blue medallion. Lucy whispered an explanation. Penny leaned forward and kissed it.

Woah, I thought. *Not a good idea in a microbial universe.*

By that point, a buffet breakfast was being served on the

dining room table. Piles of toast, jars of jam and marmalade, coffee and orange juice. Penny hugged Lucy and ran off to get a bite to eat.

Within a minute, Kateri sat down beside Lucy and offered her a plate with a stack of toast. The girl accepted a slice, stared at it, took a nibble, and looked away.

Then Kateri spoke to the girl in Blackfoot. After a moment's pause, Lucy stood up and said in English, "Cream and sugar?"

"*Aa! Noohkani'takit! Kako, kako!*" Kateri replied. This utterance made Lucy, despite her moroseness, indulge in a soundless laugh, which she quickly masked as she headed to the dining room.

I caught Kateri's eye. "What did you say to her, Kateri? It seemed to break through her wall of gloom."

"I said yes to cream and sugar. Then I told her to please hurry. I am a grizzly bear in the morning without my coffee. Ask Farley, he'll tell you."

"Her predicament can't be easy," I said. "Far from home, unable to get back, trapped with strangers in a foreign land, and the poor girl doesn't have faith to sustain her."

"Oh, she has faith," said Kateri. "Buried under a ton of stuff, just like so many kids these days, but it's there. Deep down it's there. That medal she's wearing—her grandmother gave it to her—you can bet our Mother isn't going to abandon her."

Confused, I tried to puzzle it out in my mind—grandmother, mother?

"Our Lady of Guadalupe," Kateri explained. "We call her *She who will crush the serpent* and *She who overcomes the devourer.*"

Lucy returned bearing a cup of hot coffee in a mug, which she handed over to Kateri.

"Thank you, daughter."

"No problem, old mother."

"Be wary of using words like *old* around me," grumbled Kateri and took a long sip of coffee. The girl tossed her chin insolently, but her eyes shone with amusement.

As our expanded company reloaded the vehicles and found places, Annie asked if I would mind her riding with the Morrows again. I was fine with that, since I was concerned about the baby's well-being and Annie's back. Rafe decided to ride with me.

With that, the convoy set off on the next and final stage of the journey. My pickup went first at the head of the cavalcade, followed by the Morrows' van, then the Lyons' car and its overloaded, squeaking trailer, with the Crowshoes' SUV taking the hindmost position.

Without fail, the local map brought us to number 6 south, and I turned onto it with a sigh of relief.

At last, I said to myself.

For the first few miles, the highway was devoid of other traffic. The morning was turning out to be sunny and warm, the breeze fresh through our half-open windows. All seemed normal, as if civilization were puttering along without a hitch, the planet turning reliably on its axis, God's in his heaven, all's right with the world. This wasn't the case, I knew, but it was good to experience a respite from the disorders we had encountered yesterday. And we were close, very close to our destination.

We were about seven miles south of the Lyons' house when we rounded a bend and came upon an accident. A six-wheel cube van had rammed into the ditch at a dangerous angle, its left tires now suspended inches above the pavement. The right front had hit a rock, I guessed, as the hood was buckled on that side, with the passenger door hanging wide open.

As I slowed to see if anyone had been hurt, I noticed two people on the roadside grass at the rear. One, a man, was seated with his head in his hands and blood streaming down over his fingers. His shirt front was soaked with it. A boy of about thirteen years stood beside him, looking worried. I pulled over to the side and parked. The others drew in behind me.

The man and boy looked up apprehensively when they spotted Rafe and me getting out of my truck and approaching. The man—the driver, I presumed—was frightened, staring apprehensively at Rafe.

"Black lives matter! Black lives matter!" shouted the very white driver, throwing his hands in the air, as if in surrender. A lot of blood was washing down one side of his face from a cut on his forehead. A large bruise was swelling above it.

"This poor guy is a bit disoriented," I said under my breath. In a flash I saw how Rafe might appear to strangers. To put it simply, he was formidable. Six feet and several inches tall, packed with muscle, and when his face frowned with concern, it could easily be misinterpreted as hostility by someone who didn't know him, who couldn't see his essential kindness.

"Black lives matter!" the wounded man blurted earnestly a third time, as if to ward off retribution.

"I appreciate that," said Rafe in a pleasant tone, his eyes going subtly ironic. "Look, guy, you've had a bad blow to your head. One of the ladies here is a nurse. Let's go to the van and ask her to take a look."

The accident victim looked nervously at our vehicles. "Okay," he said. The boy said nothing.

"You can lower your arms too."

The guy lowered his arms. When he tried to stand up, he stumbled sideways. Rafe took one of his arms and I took the other, and we walked him unsteadily to the van's open side door. The boy trailed along behind.

Annie quickly assessed the situation. She told the driver to sit down on the back passenger seat. After getting out of the front with some effort, she walked around to inspect the man's wounds through the open door.

"Cleve, do we have a first aid kit?" she asked. I nodded and went to the cab of my truck and retrieved a white metal box with a red cross on it.

"Black lives matter, black lives matter," the man kept whispering as she gently dried the wound with an antiseptic swab and then applied a gauze pad over the still-bleeding cut.

"Press firmly on this, sir, as much pressure as you can stand. It'll help stop the bleeding."

He did as she asked.

She peered into his eyes to examine their condition. Then she patted her belly. "All lives matter, my friend, including yours. Looks like you've had a concussion, your pupils are dilated, and that cut will need stitches."

"Call the police," he replied. "I can't leave the scene of an accident, need to report it. I've got insurance."

I stepped in at that point.

"This is an emergency," I told the man. "You need medical help right now, and besides, the police have all vanished, we don't know why. If any show up, we'll explain everything to them. You won't get in trouble."

He seemed placated by this.

Richard Lyon, standing beside me, said, "Yesterday when we were coming in, we passed the regional health center, just a block off Highway 6, which runs through town. I'm pretty sure it has an Emergency section."

"I'll find it." Turning to the boy, I said, "We'll go in my pickup. You can ride up front with your Dad."

He looked away furtively, mumbling, "He's not my Dad."

"What's your name, son?" asked Rafe.

The boy mouthed something inaudible and looked down at his torn running shoes. He thrust his hands into his jean pockets.

"Okay," said Rafe. "Well, you still have a choice. You can go to the hospital with the man who isn't your Dad, or you can stay with us."

"Where you going?" asked the boy.

"We're heading south. Our friend here has a cabin in the mountains where we're planning to camp out."

"You have any food?"

"Some. You're welcome to a share of it."

The boy looked up at Rafe, then down again.

Rafe went off to the thermos picnic hampers and returned shortly with a package of sandwiches, a banana, and two energy bars.

The boy took them without thanks and walked to the edge of the pavement where he sat down on the roadside grass with his back to everyone. He tore into the food.

"I'd better get this guy to the hospital," I said. "I should be back in twenty minutes or so, if the situation hasn't got crazier in town."

"We'll be waiting," said Rafe.

"Be careful," said Annie.

"If you're not back in an hour, I'll drive in and find you," Farley said.

"If it comes to that, don't bring any passengers with you, Farley. We don't know how hot the situation is."

"I'll come by my lonesome. I'll be bringing my shotgun though."

With no more to be said, I led the wounded man to the cab of my truck and helped him climb inside. Doing a U-turn on the highway, I accelerated back toward town. I was frustrated by this new delay, but felt determined to do what I could to help. I wondered what new madness I would encounter.

Within fifteen minutes, I was navigating through streets on which there appeared to be ongoing confusion. I didn't see any violence, but sidewalks were clotted with knots of angry people arguing and gesturing intensely, some of them trying to make their cell phones work. In passing, I noticed random columns of black smoke rising above rooftops a few streets away. Some storefronts had suffered cracked or broken windows. Seated in front of the doorways were men on lawn chairs, rifles at the ready.

The Pincher Creek Health Centre wasn't difficult to find, and I pulled into the access lane for the Emergency wing. Here, too, there was evidence of disruption, with cars and pickups parked helter-skelter, and anxious people milling about in the parking lot.

I guided the man through the congestion to the building's entry and brought him into a crowded waiting room. Collaring a frantic triage nurse scurrying back and forth, I explained that this accident victim had a concussion, wasn't walking straight, and had a severe laceration on his forehead. She took over and led him by the arm toward an open double door, beyond which I saw ranks of curtained beds. I tried to follow.

"Wait here!" she barked at me angrily over her shoulder and pointed back to the waiting room, where there were no vacant seats and plenty of standing people.

I didn't wait. There was nothing more I could do.

Another traffic jam obstructed the access to number 6, so

on impulse I executed a dangerous U-turn, narrowly missing a collision, and headed south on the major avenue bordering the hospital. I hoped to find a connection that would bring me to the highway, but the streets I passed didn't look promising. Much to my surprise, the avenue crossed Main Street and became Christie. Dead ahead, a thick column of black smoke churned skyward.

It was St. Michael's Church. Flames shot from all its broken windows. No fire fighters were present, no neighbors trying to put it out. I made the sign of the cross, breathed a prayer, and got out of there.

Half an hour later, I was back with our convoy. Annie gave me a relieved hug. Farley said, "Good to see you. I was just putting together a posse."

"How did it go?" Rafe asked.

"No real interference. I delivered the man with the head wound to the hospital, and the staff took over without much delay."

"Did you have any trouble along the way?"

"There's plenty of entropy in town, Rafe. Traffic rules have gone out the window. People with rifles are guarding shops and homes. I heard gunshots, but whoever was shooting was nowhere near where I was. A few buildings are burning. I swung by the church we visited yesterday, and it was in flames. It's gutted. It's gone."

"Did you talk to anyone?" asked Fr. Peter. "Do you know if the Blessed Sacrament was saved?"

I shook my head. "There was no one there."

Pain crossed his face, and he dropped his eyes.

"Time we were moving," said Rafe in his usual calm voice. We all returned to our vehicles. The boy from the accident found a place in the Morrows' van. Annie chose to ride with me. She wanted to hear more about what I had seen in town. I described it and then asked her if anything untoward had happened during my absence.

She shook her head, and then she related the following.

The boy had been sitting by the side of the road, dejected, ignoring everyone else. Annie went over to talk with him, lowering herself to her knees, which at this stage of her pregnancy was no small challenge.

She began by asking his name. He wouldn't answer. Under the soft waves of her cajoling, however, he finally grunted a little.

"Garfield," he said, his lips hardly moving.

"Is that your family name, honey?" she asked.

"First." He hung his head again and heaved a great sigh. With hands over his eyes he muttered incoherently.

"What's the trouble, sweetie?" she said with a hand on his shoulder. He shook it off.

"They call me after a *cat*. And *he* changes it to *garbage*."

"The truck driver, you mean?"

"No, not him. The guy my Mom lives with. When they're shooting up, he calls me *Garbage*. Sometimes he hits me. They're always screeching at each other, when they're not in the bedroom doing—"

"So, you decided to go away for a time, is that right?"

He nodded mutely and a suppressed sob escaped from his throat.

"Did you leave a note? Did you tell them where you were going?"

He shook his head. "They don't care."

"Um, maybe they're worried, Garfield."

"Don't call me that. I'm no-name. Yeah, my name's No-name brand."

"I'm not going to call you that," Annie said in a subdued voice. "How about I call you *Son* for now."

"I ain't nobody's son."

"Well, you are now. And for as long as you want to stay with us."

He looked up at her with eyes full of mute misery, his cheeks wet.

"We'll take care of you," said Annie. "And none of us are into screeching and hitting."

"I don't need no looking after."

"I can see you're an independent boy. I understand how you'd prefer to be on your own." She paused. "How did the accident happen?"

"That guy in the truck, he picked me up at a gas station outside Fort Macleod, where I was trying to hitch a ride. He'd been drinking, I could smell it. He told me he had a load to drive down to Montana and needed someone to talk to him as far as the border, to keep him awake. I was thinking, yeah, if I can get into the States, then I can lose myself down there, no one will ever find me. I'll get a job, make a new life."

"And the accident?"

"We came through town around sunrise. It was all screwed up there, but he barreled on through, ignored the red lights and stop signs. He was going way too fast, and he kept speeding until he hit the gravel shoulder on that curve and spun out into the ditch."

"Are you feeling sore anywhere?" Annie asked.

"Just my chest. I had my seatbelt on."

"Would you let me check out your chest, see if there are any cracked ribs?"

The boy looked at her suspiciously. "I don't like nobody touching me."

"All right. I can't see any blood on your shirt. Could you at least take a few deep breaths for me?"

He took a few deep breaths, grimacing with discomfort.

"It hurts to breathe doesn't it?"

"It ain't bad."

"Good. You look pretty strong, and you should heal up fine. Probably no more than bruised muscles. If you had a fracture in there you'd be yelping with pain. But I suggest you take it easy for a few days, which will help you mend more quickly. Would you like an aspirin?"

He said, "Okay," looking at her directly, with a flicker of curiosity. She got up and walked back to the van, opened the first aid kit, and found a bottle of ASA inside. This and a thermos cup of water she brought back to the boy. He had returned to sitting with his head bowed low over his knees. She put her hand on his shoulder, and this time he didn't shake it off. He looked up at her.

"You've got a baby coming," he said after he had washed down the pill.

"Uh-huh. Five more weeks to go. Hey, can I ask you a question?"

"What question?"

"For the next while, I'll be going slower and slower, and it'll be harder for me to do things. Standing up and getting down to ground level are a major challenge already."

Abruptly, with a worried look, the boy scrambled to his feet.

"I'm sorry," he said. "I didn't know it's so hard for you."

"Well, Son, my guess is you've probably never been pregnant, so how could you know?"

For an instant a smile almost appeared on his face.

This last exchange took no more than a few seconds, but Annie at once learned several things about him. He had immediately jumped to his feet out of consideration for her, which indicated a person capable of caring about others. He had apologized. He had smiled—or almost smiled. And he hadn't reprimanded her for calling him *Son*.

"You wanted t'ask me a question?" he said.

"Oh, yes, I started to, but pregnant ladies get easily distracted. What I wanted to ask is, would you consider coming along with us for a while? The roads are becoming more and more dangerous. We've witnessed some bad things on our trip, and I don't think it's wise for you to go on alone."

He said nothing as he pondered what she had told him.

"We have a lot of children here, and just a handful of adults to look after them," she continued. "We need to protect them."

He stared at her, weighing what she had said.

"Besides," she added with a smile, "we're all runaways."

"What?"

"We'll explain it to you when we have some time to go into details. For now, let me just say that none of us will report you or try to make you go back home."

"You ain't lying to me, are you? Making me stay here until you can call the cops?"

"Leaving aside the fact that my word is my word, no one here tells lies—"

"Everybody tells lies," he said with a sour look.

"Not these people, not a one of us. Another thing, our cell phones have suddenly stopped working. Even if we wanted to call the cops on you, which we definitely don't, we wouldn't be able to. I doubt there are any cops for a hundred miles in any direction, because right now the situation's getting crazy in the cities and that's where police and rescue people will be concentrating their efforts."

He looked down at his feet.

"We need your help, Son."

He looked up and met her eyes. "Okay. I'll help."

As Annie and I drove on, I said to her, "You handled it well. He trusted you."

"He's a good kid, Cleve. He's been banged around by life, but he's basically intact."

"I wish I had a portion of your compassion, Annie. You see into people the way no one else does."

She left that unanswered.

"When we started out yesterday morning," she said, "I thought the worst thing we'd encounter would be mosquitoes keeping us awake at night."

"Me, I thought it would be too long a stretch between doughnut shops."

"Not to mention clean bathrooms. Funny how one's nagging little anxieties evaporate in the face of real trials. Life's about people, isn't it, Cleve. Ultimately, it's about how we treat each other."

"Yup, the good, the bad, and the ugly . . . and the horrendously awful. We've been very lucky so far: first the Crowshoes, then the college students, then the Lyons, and now this runaway kid."

"And don't forget the runaway girl."

"Hoo-boy, what are the odds we'd pick up an American runaway trying to go north and a Canadian runaway trying to go south? You called it through the looking glass the other day, Annie, and I think you're right in a sense."

"And it just keeps getting curiouser and curiouser."

"It sure does. But I think there's a difference. Wonderland was all about mental distortions, drug-induced illusions, weirdness, even madness. My sense is, what's happening to us, bizarre as it seems, is in the hands of a higher sanity. Do you know what I mean?"

She put a hand on my arm and left it there.

14

THE HIGHWAY CONTINUED AS BEFORE, the rolling landscape remaining more or less the same, with forested foothills on the right and the hard jawline of white peaks not far beyond. On both sides of the pavement, pastures and cultivated fields hemmed closer, east and west, with occasional farmhouses and copses of leafy woods. Now and then we passed the entrances to gravel side roads, but none of them corresponded to my father's sketchy map. We were now about sixteen miles south of Pincher Creek, and I estimated another thirty miles to the international border. Somewhere ahead, we would have to find our turnoff or admit defeat and retrace our steps.

There was a single moment of alarm, when a red muscle car sped by us going in the opposite direction, doing ninety miles an hour—a Trans Am Firebird, I thought. As it roared past with open windows, I heard the beat of frantic music and yowling males and caught a quick glimpse of a driver and three passengers, all young and seedy, baring their teeth at us like aggressive, growling dogs. A single rifle barrel pointed our way, but wasn't fired.

Not long after, we came to the first cluster of habitations we had seen along the route, a crossroads hamlet with the name of Twin Butte, boasting a few houses, a general store, and outlying farms—no more than a dozen buildings all told. The store didn't look open for business, and we didn't make a stop, as it was guarded by men with rifles who warned us off with granite faces and threatening gestures.

Three miles farther along, a clearing on the left appeared, a dirt parking lot in front of a single-story log structure with a covered porch. A sign on the cedar-shake roof advertised it as *The Burnt Café*. The place looked deserted, though a pickup truck was parked beside a propane tank on one side. I signaled left and entered the lot, hoping that someone inside would be willing to help us find our turnoff.

I thought it an odd name for a café, but then realized that it was surrounded by bushland pierced by the blackened spires of dead trees—the skeletal remains of an old forest fire.

The entrance was wide open, and its screen door had been partly wrenched off.

"Hello," I called, going up the front steps.

"Anyone home?" shouted Rafe, close behind me.

Farley, who had joined us, called out, "Police!" Which was true of the constable.

As we entered the building, the first thing I noticed was a sign on the wall above a checkout counter: WE BURN EVERYTHING EXCEPT OUR COFFEE—THE BEST IN THE WORLD. Beneath it, a big smiley face made sure customers got the joke. Beneath that, in smaller font: *Colombia, Kenya, Vietnam, Brazil—we roast our own beans daily!*

The cash register looked plundered, with the cash tray open and empty and the wires of a digital terminal ripped out. A glance to the left revealed a scene of devastation. Tables and chairs overturned, smashed dishes scattered across the floor, a pool of dark liquid . . .

Rounding a corner, we found the source. The body of a young man lay face-up with his limbs flung out, his mouth gaping, his eyes wide open, unseeing. Blood from a hole in his chest had copiously soaked his shirt and pants, and created the pool.

"Oh, no," I groaned, feeling a sudden vertigo.

"O Lord, what happened here?" breathed Rafe.

Farley squatted beside the man's body, put on his reading glasses, and inspected the glistening pool of blood. He touched its surface with the tip of his forefinger and rubbed the purple-red drop he obtained between thumb and forefinger.

"Fresh, less than an hour old," he said.

Farley had seen murder victims before, I guessed, but neither Rafe nor I had ever encountered this kind of horror. It shocked the mind. It paralyzed. It was unlike anything one might see and feel while watching violent death enacted on film. No matter how gory, fictional murder never quite overwhelmed the mind's protective filters.

"Look," said Rafe, pointing to a trail of droplets and bloody shoe prints leading toward the back of the café's guest area. As the three of us followed the tracks, we passed through an open doorway into the café's kitchen and, after that, into rooms that looked like living quarters. An open door at the end of a hallway led outside. There we came upon a second victim, a young woman sprawled face-down on the back steps, with her face turned to the side.

None of us said a word as we took in the scene. The sight of the murdered man had been shocking enough, but this was worse. The woman had been shot twice in the back. Her eyes were wide open in the stillness of death, her mouth frozen in a soundless scream. Her blood dripped down slowly from step to step.

I gasped and then gagged. Rafe put a hand over his eyes. Farley shook his head back and forth.

"Oh hell, oh hell," he groaned.

Faint mewling or whimpering sounds caught our attention, coming from somewhere in the backyard area—a line of outbuildings, a garage, a chicken coop with pecking orange hens, and an open-front shed in which a cast-iron oven was venting wisps of coffee-scented steam. Visible between the shed and coop were rows of cultivated bushes. The sound came from that direction.

Making wide steps around the body, we proceeded in haste through the yard and into what proved to be an extensive raspberry patch. Its rows were loaded with unripe green berries.

As the sound grew louder, it became clearly recognizable as the cries of a child. Or two children. We found them huddled together under the thorny branches at the end of a long row, a girl about four years old and a boy around six or seven. Their faces and bare arms were scratched, but they looked otherwise unharmed. When they saw us coming they burst into wails of terror.

I went down on my knees before them and said, "Don't be afraid. We won't hurt you."

"We want to help you," said Rafe, his voice just above a whisper.

Their wailing subsided into shuddering sobs.

"Bad mans shoot guns," whimpered the younger one.

"Mama said run to the berries," cried the older child, his eyes still wild with fear, his chest panting with rapid inhalations. "She went back to help Papa."

"Cleve, get Cora and Kateri," said Rafe.

I ran. When I reached the vehicles, I asked the two women to accompany me.

"There've been fatalities," I explained. "Two children have survived, and they're badly frightened."

Without asking questions, the women hurriedly followed me around to the rear of the building, where I pointed the way to the berry patch. That done, I carefully made my way up the back steps, avoiding the blood, and entered the living quarters. In a bedroom I tore sheets off a bed and used one to cover the dead woman's body and the other to cover the man's.

Returning to the patch, I found Cora and Kateri kneeling by the children and trying to reassure them. Rafe and Farley stood off to the side, consulting with each other in low voices.

"This is a crime scene," said Farley. "But no police'll be showing up. Leastways not for a while."

"It could be days," said Rafe. "Even weeks. We have to get these children to some kind of shelter, but we've no idea whether they have family living nearby."

"We don't know *anything*," Farley growled. "Dang, this is bad business. What're we gonna do now?"

"Obviously we can't just leave them here on their own."

"We could take them to that village we passed; maybe someone there knows who they are."

"It's a possibility. But those people looked very hostile and—"

"Yeah, the guns and all. We take these kids to that village, and we could get shot at before we even open our mouths."

"There's a chance of that, Farley, and even if it's only a small one, we can't risk taking our own children into danger. If we've learned anything the past couple of days, it's that people are behaving dangerously and irrationally."

"Uh-huh, and we can't camp out here either, waiting for who knows what to happen."

"What do you suggest?" I broke into the discussion.

"We aren't left with much of a choice," said Rafe. "As a temporary measure, I say we bring the children with us and get them out of harm's way."

"Could be interpreted as abduction, Rafe."

"Yes, if there are any 'interpreters' still functioning. The real issue here is the children's welfare. We'll live with the consequences later."

"I've covered the bodies," I said. "We could leave a note explaining what happened, with a description of how we can be located."

"It's not a great solution, but there *are* no great solutions in this situation. Okay, let's do it that way."

We returned to the vehicles, where we found Kateri and Cora standing by the Crowshoes' SUV cleaning the two children's faces with damp cloths. Fr. Peter and Annie were standing to the side, looking very worried.

"What happened, Cleve?" Annie asked me.

I nearly choked trying to formulate a reply. I took her hand. "It's so bad, honey, I can't begin to describe it. It's the worst."

She stared at me uncomprehending.

I gestured to the children. "I'd better speak in code. Parental fatalities."

"Oh, Lord, no," she said in a hushed voice, putting her hand to her heart.

"A homicide. Thankfully not witnessed by the survivors. We're going to bring them with us. There are no other options at this time. We'll try to reconnect them to family members, if we can find any. For now . . ."

"For now, protection and nurturing. But how will we explain it to them?"

"Can we leave it to you mothers? You'll know what to say."

"All right, we'll try to do our best without traumatizing them."

We were suddenly interrupted by the boy bursting into tears. "Where's Babby?" he wailed. "Where's Babby?"

"Who is Babby?" Cora gently asked.

"Our brother. I was supposed to hold his hand tight, cause he's too little. He runned away. Mama'll be mad!"

"Don't worry now," soothed Cora, pulling the boy into a hug. "Don't you worry. We'll find Babby."

"Thank God they didn't see anything," said Kateri. "They don't know."

"Let's keep it that way," said Farley. "Rafe, Cleve, why don't you look around for the missing boy. The rest of us will load up."

We were about to head to the most likely area of search, the berry patch and nearby bushland, when the boy said through his tears, "Babby runs away sometimes on the road. Papa told him no, no, no, but he doesn't listen. He's too little. He doesn't understand."

"Do you think Babby ran to the road, son?" Rafe asked.

"I don't know. I didn't see him. I was crying."

"It's all right to cry," said Rafe. "It's not your fault. We'll find your brother."

With a nod to each other, Rafe and I jumped into my truck and gunned out of the lot. I turned south, because in the other direction we hadn't passed anyone on the road since Twin Butte.

Rafe said, "Go slow, Cleve. We don't want to miss him if he's wandered off into the roadside bushes."

A hundred yards farther, and there he was, slapping his little bare feet on the pavement as he toddled along half-naked, with a loose diaper in one hand and an exposed hind end befouled with excrement.

I screeched to a halt. Rafe jumped out, scooped up the boy, and carried him back to the truck.

"Hey there, Babby," he said in his softest voice. "Good to have you with us."

The two-year-old giggled and babbled, snuggling down

onto Rafe's lap, with consequent results—the smell of the toddler's bare bottom was overpowering.

Minutes later we were back in the café's parking lot. By then, all the adults had been informed about the crime and were reacting in various stages of shock. Mainly stunned silence and looks of horror.

Colleen Lyon instantly assessed Babby's condition. "This will require some skill," she said, approaching with towel in hand. Together with Cora they cleaned up the boy, who seemed delighted by the attention. His brother and sister kept trying to hug him.

Taking a holy water bottle from his pocket, Fr. Peter said he wanted to bless the bodies. He and I went back inside the café. I followed the priest, who despite his young years, and despite his obvious shock at what he was seeing, anointed the bodies and recited certain prayers for the dead with solemnity and relative calm. He looked heavily burdened when he left.

I remained in the café, searching for anything that might give us clues to the children's identities. After stepping around the father's body and the congealing pool of blood, I entered the family's living quarters. In a filing cabinet I found, among other items, a folder with birth certificates and health cards for the children. Babby was actually Robert, the girl was Susan, the other boy was Samuel. The parents were Drew and Stephanie Hearne. A men's wallet lay on a dresser, and I added this to my collection, along with a purse from which I took the mother's wallet and a small booklet of photos. Spotting a framed photo of the entire family on a bedside table, I realized that this could be important for the children's future and took it too. In the bathroom, I found a box of paper diapers. In the children's bedroom I selected a cloth doll, a toy firetruck, and a stuffed teddy bear.

Loaded down, I maneuvered my way back to the front entrance, avoiding stepping on blood, overcome by the feeling of how surreal this all was. Rafe was standing by the cash register, penning a message on a sheet of paper. I read over his shoulder:

To whom it may concern,

Having arrived at this scene of two murders after the occurrence of the crimes, I and the undersigned wish to inform you that all three children of the deceased parents are unharmed. For the sake of their protection and health, we have taken them under our care temporarily, due to the extreme social disruption and absence of local law enforcement at this time.

Our only intention is to ensure that they will be entrusted to the appropriate authorities and/or family members without delay. Regrettably, the exact details of our destination are uncertain at this time. We will be camping near Waterton Lakes Park.

Please be assured that we will make every effort to establish contact, as soon as reasonably possible.

Sincerely,
Raphael Morrow

He signed it and jotted down his home address. I signed it as well, and added my own address. That done, we took the paper out to the waiting cars and obtained the signatures of the other adults. Hoping to underline the message that the children were not being kidnapped, Rafe asked Farley and Annie to put in brackets their occupations—police constable and nurse.

After locating a roll of adhesive, I taped the note to the cash register. Then, steeling myself, I took one last glance at the body of Drew Hearne under its sheet, walked out and closed the front door behind me.

The Hearne children were now seated in the Morrows' van, with a mother beside each one—Annie, Kateri, and Colleen. I told the ladies the children's names. As Cora got in behind the wheel, Josie, Rose, and Penny tried to engage the orphans in chatter. Shy of strangers, the older boy and his sister barely responded. They no longer looked terrified, however, though tears were not far away. Freshly diapered, Babby was having the time of his life, grinning and babbling. They all brightened a little when I gave them their toys.

"Where is my Mama?" asked the boy, putting the fire-truck aside after a token play with it.

"Your Mama wants you and Susan and Babby to come with us now, Sam," Cora answered.

"Where is Papa?"

"Your Papa wants you to come with us too."

"He says we shouldn't talk to strangers. We shouldn't get in a car with strangers."

"Your Papa is right. That's what I tell our own children. But we're not strangers now, because we're helping your mother and father."

"Bad mans shoot guns," said Susan and began to cry again. "I was scared."

"Yes, it was a very loud noise," said Annie, and stroked the girl's hair away from her wrinkled brow. "The bad men made a mess in your house, and it needs to be cleaned. We are looking after you until it's all better."

Annie cast a pained look in my direction. I knew she was thinking that nothing could ever make it better for these children, but for now what they most needed was reassurance.

Rafe and I returned to the Toyota, and I drove out of the lot, leading the way down the highway.

The miles rolled up behind us, and still no sign of a turnoff. I was looking, but it wasn't easy to focus. Both of us felt like we'd been slammed between the eyes by a two-by-four. There was nothing much to say. What *can* you say in the face of such evil? I recalled what Fr. Peter had told us the night before about not letting hatred into your heart, because that would give the devil a double victory. Well, I would try . . .

"You all right, Rafe?"

"Feel like roadkill. You?"

"The same."

"Keep a brave face. Those kids need to feel secure."

"I know."

"My course of action from now on is to give them the impression that they're in safe hands."

"They probably suspect that something very bad has happened."

"The older boy especially. But they need to believe that the bottom hasn't fallen out of their universe."

"Which it has."

"Which it has," he said with a grim nod. "Our task is to write into their hearts the message that they're not in freefall and good people are there to catch them."

The aroma in the truck's cabin was becoming heady. Rafe's soiled jeans.

I rolled down my window and turned the dashboard fan on high.

"Sorry about that," said Rafe.

"Don't worry. We'll find a mountain creek and make you stand under a waterfall for a couple of hours."

"I won't resist."

"Can you pull over, Cleve?" came a scratchy voice on the walkie-talkie.

I slowed and eased to the edge of the highway, letting the motor rumble in idle. A minute later, the Crowshoes' vehicle parked close to my tailgate, with the Morrows' and Lyons' pulling in close behind. Farley got out and ambled up to my open window.

"I came this way yesterday," he said, pushing back his cap and pointing to the south. "We go much farther and we'll be getting into the Blood Reserve, and right after that comes the U.S. border." He pointed to a valley opening up to the southwest. "And that way you're into the national park. Did your father say the cabin was in the park?"

"No. He mentioned that my uncle's property bordered on crown land, which could mean anything."

"Let me see the map, wouldya, Cleve?"

I unfolded the map and handed it out the window. Farley perused it with a frown, absentmindedly scratching his temple.

"Make any sense to you?" I asked.

"Nope. Just that we should be turning right, not left off the highway. And then we go on this snaky little road. He didn't write any name for it."

"Some of the side roads we passed didn't have name posts. All he jotted down here is we have to go nineteen miles to a river where the road ends—*if* we can find the road."

"Dang," said Farley, taking his cell phone out of his jacket pocket and staring at the live but very blank screen. "If Google Maps was up and running, we could check it that way." He pecked at the screen, shook his head, and with a sigh he stuffed the cell back into his pocket.

I showed Farley the few notes Dad had penned on the backside of the map, visual prompts to watch for, one of which was *After Twin Butte a ways Three Trees on Calvary—turn west.*

"Calvary. Maybe a town?" I suggested.

"Mmgh," said Farley. "Maybe."

He opened his road atlas, put on his reading glasses, and peered closely at a page.

"This map doesn't show any place named Calvary. Twin Butte is listed, see here this dot on the highway, and it's no more than a handful of houses. Calvary means something else, seems t'me. Maybe a cemetery?"

"Well, let's push on and see if the meaning gets clearer."

Rafe said, "I'm going back to my van, Cleve. Cora's been doing well with the driving, but she's overdue for a break."

"Good. Tell Annie hi."

At that moment we heard the rumble of engines from farther south on the highway, still out of view but approaching fast.

Farley walked quickly back to his car, reached in the open doorway, and took out his shotgun. He braced his legs and made his face go Scary Indian, holding the gun vertically across his chest in present arms position. Within moments, eight motorcycles rose over a hump in the tarmac and bore down in our direction.

Darkness visible again! Since we were running out of highway, I wondered where they had come from. From the U.S.? Or were they our northern variety of the species? If so, they had probably been turned back at the border. Or, more worrisome, they had an encampment somewhere nearby.

They slowed when they saw our four vehicles, and then when they spotted the armed man staring at them coolly, they sped up again with an ear-shattering din. The riders were all gray-bearded, wearing helmets with skulls and crossbones painted on them, their black leather coats emblazoned with images of fanged devils. As they passed us going north, they uniformly turned their heads toward us and gave us the notorious finger. A couple of them pointed their fingers at us, as if firing pistols. The last to pass drew his finger across his neck, sending the unmistakable message, *We're going to cut your throats.*

Farley swiveled his body and watched them go.

"Yup," he said in his unflappable tone of voice. "Time to get off this trail."

15

Every few miles we passed turnoffs, but so far none of them had looked right. They were all hardscrabble roads cutting into the forested woodlands at the base of the irregular mountain chain. If Dad's map was as close to accurate as I hoped, and if Farley was correct, we would have to leave the highway very soon. But where?

Then the route curved, and suddenly a massive gray rock came into view on the right, butting against the pavement. It was the size of a two-story house, with three tall birch trees rising from the turf on its crest. As we passed it, I noticed a smear of white on the rock face. It rang no bells for me, but obeying an intuition, I slowed to a stop, reversed as far as the rock, and idled in park. The other vehicles drew up behind me. Looking closely, I could see that the white smear was weather-faded paint, depicting a cross about three feet high with a two-foot crossbar. The big rock seemed vaguely familiar, but I couldn't recall seeing the cross before. The memory of my one short visit to the cabin when I was ten years old was a haze of impressions, mostly of forest and rugged landscape in limitless permutations.

After Calvary, Dad had written. How far after Calvary? I pressed the gas pedal and rolled forward. A hundred yards past the rock a turnoff appeared on the right.

I beeped the two-way radio and said, "This could be it."

With my truck at the head of the convoy, we turned onto a narrow dirt road that looked somewhat treacherous, as it wound away into the forested foothills with a number of blind curves in the offing. As the route didn't look wide enough for two cars to pass easily, this might prove to be dangerous. I decided to take it slow, keeping the speed at around twenty-five miles per hour and down to ten on the curves.

I strained to recall if I had ever seen this before, but nothing specific came to mind. It was all generic bush, one of ten thousand places just like it.

Within a mile, a gash in the terrain took me by surprise, cutting across the road without warning. I was forced to brake suddenly and came to a halt with my front tires on the rutted planks of a wooden bridge that looked none too stable. Most of its log guardrails were missing, either rotted or broken off by old accidents. Twenty feet below, a narrow creek roared through a gorge.

I radioed back to the others, "Rickety bridge. I'll go first. Proceed with caution."

When all four vehicles had safely crossed to the other side, we continued on at low speed.

Three miles farther along, I hit a deep pothole and bounced hard, my head hitting the cab's roof, an awful crack and clang coming from underneath the floorboard. The truck started lurching sideways. I braked to a full stop in the middle of the road and turned off the engine, thanking God that Annie was riding in Morrow's comfortable van. I debated with myself over turning the engine on long enough to ease the truck to the edge of the road, but saw that both its sides were flanked by deep ditches. There wasn't much of a shoulder, just a few inches of sloping gravel. It seemed unlikely that the poorly maintained route was frequently traveled, as there were more potholes in the wheel tracks ahead and tufts of dusty grass crowning the central ridge between them.

I got out to survey the damage, as the other vehicles

slowed and came to a stop behind me. The drivers—Rafe, Farley, and Richard—gathered around as I knelt and peered underneath the chassis, hoping that the problem was no more than a broken muffler, which would be noisy but not crippling. Rafe knelt down in the dust beside me and peered underneath.

"It doesn't look good, Cleve," he said in a tone that I recognized from our years of working together, those occasions when he wanted to assess a major breakdown objectively without letting himself get perturbed. "The muffler's ripped off and dangling, but that's no big worry. It looks like your drive train could have serious problems. It's possible the transmission's okay, but the driveshaft looks off-kilter and your differential's probably taken a beating too. There may be other problems. This truck's going nowhere for now, I'm afraid."

Trying to match his tone, I said, "Hmmm, and no service station or tow truck anywhere in sight."

"Pincher Creek had a gas station, but it's a long way back, and there's no guarantee it has towing or even if it's still open."

"And don't forget those two-wheel bandits from hell on the highway," said Farley.

Overcome with a flash of intense frustration, I clenched my fists and gritted my teeth. Just what we needed, I thought. Wasn't it always this way, your reliable servants betraying you at the worst possible moment!

I silently uttered a quick prayer, seeking the grace that would stop me viciously kicking the side of the Toyota or shouting something regrettable. Then out of nowhere I remembered Dad's dream and what he had said about me having to learn a big lesson, about going deeper into trust and higher into hope.

With a sharp pang I wondered about his welfare in the current crisis. How was he coping with it? Was he shaken by the lack of communications with his family? Was he frightened? Why wasn't I there with him? Why wasn't he here with us?

But in this, too, I knew I had to trust.

I took a few deep breaths and calmly said to the others, "Well, we can't let this stop us. How about we unload the truck and try to find space for my gear in your cars?"

All three men nodded. "Yeah, you could ride with me and Kateri, since we got one free seat left," said Farley. "Or we do some musical chairs so you can sit with Annie. We can also pack in some of your things. All of us are getting crammed full, but we'll do our best."

"We could strap a lot onto my roof rack," contributed Richard. "The leaf-springs on the trailer are starting to bend the wrong way, but if you have anything bulky that doesn't weigh too much, we can bungee it on top of the load. I have extra cords."

"Cleve, how certain are you that we're on the right road?" asked Rafe.

"About fifty percent," I said with a shake of my head. I reached into the cab and pulled out the map Dad had sent me, wondering if I had made a miscalculation somewhere. The four of us bent our heads over it.

"The rickety bridge matches one of his notes, but there could be a lot of rickety bridges in the area."

"And we passed a lot more side roads than your father marked," said Rafe tapping with an index finger the winding pencil line representing the road we should be on. "But the distances look right, in my estimation."

"Okay, I'll up my guess to seventy-five percent."

I told them about the three trees and Calvary.

"Sounds like a ninety to me," said Farley.

We had just begun unpacking my truck when we heard, before we saw, something coming around a bend ahead, thankfully engineless, the sound of trotting hoof beats. Within a minute a man on a chestnut horse appeared and approached steadily in our direction. Pushing back the brim of his white cowboy hat, revealing a shock of dusky blond hair, he reined in the horse a few paces away from us, swung a leg over the saddle, and dropped to the ground.

In a glance, I realized that this was not your usual cattleman. A lean, angular young man, he wore a white shirt with pearl snap buttons and corded pockets over his broad chest. His tan jeans were girded by a wide leather belt, buckled with a turquoise stone in a silver clasp. His leather cowboy boots were scuffed and cracked around the square toes; they looked well used, unlike the fancy snakeskin pointy-toes one often saw on male shoppers in Alberta malls, urban guys affecting a stylish western look. The way he handled the living horse confirmed his occupation, I thought.

A handsome fellow, he could have been anywhere from eighteen to twenty-five years old. It was his face that made it difficult to place his age, as his expression was so open it was almost childlike, like an eager boy off to his first rodeo. Not a hint of the tight-lipped antisocial demeanor of cowboys who seldom left their wilderness retreats and, when they did, were habituated to riding high above the frantic activities of conformist men. There was none of this in the young man's expression. If anything, he looked inordinately pleased by the chance encounter.

He stepped forward with an outstretched hand.

"Hi, I'm Luke Jacobson," he said in a voice surprisingly deeper than his years would imply. One by one he shook our hands with a firm grasp, and we gave him our names.

"Truck break down?" he asked, eyeing my old wreck.

"The drive train's messed up," I said. "Probably the end of the line for this old girl."

He dropped to his knees and then onto his belly and slid his head and shoulders underneath. With a click of his tongue he was back on his feet, dusting off his jeans and shirt with his hat.

He said sympathetically, "Looks bad. But we could tow it to my grandpa's place and he could take a look. He has a wrecker's yard out back of the station, and there might be a replacement part."

"A station?" said Rafe. "You mean a service station with a tow truck, way out here?"

Luke nodded. "Yup, way out here in nowhere. Course, in the nineteen thirties and forties, it wasn't as deserted as it is now. Grandpa's father built it for gassing up ranchers' trucks and cars. That's pretty much tapered off now, because most places hereabouts have gone back to bush, and the people still hanging on in the region drive to Pincher Creek for gas and repairs. Grandpa keeps the station going because he's always lived this way. It's his hobby." He cracked a grin. "It's his big love."

"Do you live around here too?" asked Farley, asking an obvious question, expecting an obvious answer.

"I'm here for the summer. My family's in Montreal, where I was born and raised. This past spring I graduated from university and came out here to help my grandpa."

"So you've got summer employment here in the hills," said Richard, "which is a very fine change of scene I would expect."

"Oh, it's not exactly employment," said Luke, turning to Richard with interest, perhaps intrigued by the British accent. "Not with the bit of income my Grandpa earns from time to time. Basically he survives on the Old Age pension."

"It's good of you to help him out," said Rafe.

"It's a privilege." The young man's smile grew tentative. "He's the most independent man I've ever known in my life. I'm learning a lot from him. I don't think I'll be heading back to university anytime soon."

"I've just left one," said Richard. "I don't think I'll be heading back anytime soon, either."

Luke slapped his hat against the side of his pant leg.

"Well, here I am telling you my life story. Sorry, folks, you have real worries, so let's see if we can do something about it."

"Where is your grandfather's station?" asked Rafe.

Luke pointed in the direction from which he had come. "Our place is about six miles that way. How about I ride on ahead, get the tow truck, and be right back? We'll get you off the road and see if anything can be done."

"This is a tremendous help," I said. "We're grateful for you taking the trouble. But wouldn't it be quicker if you leave your horse here and one of us drives you?"

"That could work, yeah."

Without further deliberation, he led the horse off the road by its halter, then down into the ditch and up the other side. There, he took loops of rope from the saddle horn, tied one end to a ring under the halter and uncoiled the rest until he had a twenty- or thirty-foot length extended, the end of which he tied securely to a poplar. That done, he spent a few moments talking to his horse, which nickered and dropped its head to feed on grass.

In the interim, we drivers returned to the other vehicles, where we found that all the passengers had disembarked for short bathroom breaks in the trees, or to stretch and walk about for circulation. Rafe explained the situation to those who were standing nearby. I went to Annie, and we took each other's hands.

"Time to get a new car," I said. "This is probably the bitter end for the truck. There's a glimmer of hope it can be fixed, but pretty slim, is my guess."

"We could get a horse," she answered.

"And a buggy." I squeezed her hand. "Are we having fun yet?"

"It's an adventure." Suddenly her eyes teared up. "Those poor children, Cleve. It's so awful, so evil. I feel so helpless."

"It's bad, I know," I said. "As soon as the situation settles down and systems get up and running, we'll try to find their relatives. And we need to contact the police somehow, at some point. But for now, all we can do is keep them safe."

"Cora's amazing with them. They instinctively trust her. Kateri's staying close, too, very motherish. The older boy and girl are warming up to them, little by little, though I think they're still in a kind of shock. Thankfully, they didn't see any of the horror. Fr. Peter is helping too."

"Good. As young as he is, there's a reassuring presence about him."

"Yes, a man of few words, but as his auntie says, he's deep waters. I can tell he's praying. All the time he's quietly praying. He anointed the children's foreheads with holy water, very gently, and prayed over them. They didn't shy away from it, just looked up at him with wide eyes. It seemed to help. He wants to offer a Mass of thanksgiving when we get to our destination, Kateri says. So the Lord will be giving us Himself soon, and then we'll be stronger when we face whatever's going to happen."

"How are the runaways?"

"Mute. But the change in their faces is surprising. Instead of brooding, they're looking . . . how should I put it? . . . they're looking *interested*. Something real is happening to them, and maybe that's sparked their interest."

"For a change, they're no longer problem-central; their lives aren't swamped by adults talking over their heads and shuffling documents that determine their fate."

"Yes, they're beginning to look outward, instead of obsessing on the inner darkness . . . Who is that boy on the horse?"

"He's more young man than boy. Name of Luke. His grandfather has some kind of backwoods gas station farther down the road. We're going to drive there now and get their tow truck." I leaned over and kissed her. "I have to go, honey."

"Okay. Don't rush."

When I returned to the other men, who were still in discussion with Luke Jacobson, I learned that Farley had arranged for us to take his SUV, which had four-wheel drive, more stable on this road. He and I and Luke would pick up the tow truck and drive right back. Six miles or so each way, no more than half an hour. In the interim, Rafe would stand guard at the rear of the convoy, armed with Farley's shotgun, though the likelihood of the motorcycle brigands making an appearance was slim—they were highwaymen, in more senses than one.

Farley at the wheel eased his vehicle carefully around my truck, with Luke beside him in the front passenger seat. I sat in back, studying Dad's map and trying to match it with twists and turns in the road.

"We'll have to take it real slow," Luke cautioned Farley. "The surface is like a bombed out battlefield. And this is the *good* part of the road."

"Ten m.p.h. all right?"

"You've got high suspension, but five might be safer."

"Okay, down to five," said Farley, creeping along and concentrating on weaving around the worst of the potholes.

"So, are you all on a camping trip?" asked Luke.

"Something like that," answered Farley without taking his eyes from the road.

"What's happening in the world? Anything interesting going on?"

"Don't you have internet or cell phone?"

"Used to. But my grandfather took the battery outta my laptop and smashed my cell phone soon as I arrived here last spring."

"Woah, you mean deliberately?"

"Deliberately."

"Without your permission?"

"Uh, well, you have to understand about Grandpa. He's kind of eccentric. Not crazy by any means, just . . ."

"Different."

"That's right. He says that cell phones make it possible for the government to track you. He's not a conspiracy theorist or anything like that. But he does take a stand on certain freedom issues. Thinks the surveillance society is mentally and socially morbid, not to mention downright dangerous. He speaks his mind a lot, so I hope you won't take anything he says the wrong way. He can be cranky."

"Oh, I can be cranky, too, even downright crabby, my wife says."

Luke laughed. "That's good. You should get along fine."

"You look happy enough, despite the loss of communications," I commented from behind their heads.

The boy nodded emphatically. "I am. It really took me aback when he went all Luddite on me. But now I can honestly say I'm grateful to him. It was like swift surgery. And life out here is so real, so healthy. I feel like I'm getting my self back, or maybe a better way to put it is I'm finding out who I should have been from the beginning. The real me."

"From the beginning . . ." I echoed, remembering the

phrase Rafe had used in one of our early discussions. I had presumed at the time that he meant God's intention for his life, the unique identity that he could and should have. I had seen no signs that Luke was a religious believer, however. There was an unusual purity or innocence about him, but that could be more a case of natural qualities than of faith.

The service station wasn't what I had thought it would be. It stood back from the road a stone's throw, fenced with sagging wooden rails and overgrown with high weeds. Posted beside a wide open cattle gate was a sign that read:

CLOSED IN PERPETUITY

Exceptions made for the lost, the desperate,
and the utterly disoriented.

Also for close friends and relatives.

But then I repeat myself.

"He doesn't really mean it," said Luke pointing to the sign. "He'll open up for anyone who happens by. Sad to say, no one has during the time I've been here. You're the first."

Luke directed us through the gateway into a broad yard before the station building. It looked like an old-fashioned country store, with a sitting-and-spitting porch across its whole width. Two antique gas pumps in faded red paint stood close to its front steps. Cardboard signs were tied to both with baling twine; on them were scrawled in marker ink, *Dry wells*.

Beyond the building, a larger two-story structure looked like a garage where trucks and farm vehicles were serviced. There were additions left and right, and sheds out back, including a Quonset hut of corrugated metal with a badly rusted dome. To the left was a kind of wrecker's yard, an open field where dozens of vehicles were parked, all of them old and skewed at odd angles.

"Grandpa's not here," said Luke, jumping out. "Pard's gone too, that's his dog, so it looks like they headed up the road to see to the sheep. He should be back by lunch time."

"You have sheep?" I asked, surprised.

"We keep about forty in a paddock on some acreage nobody owns any more, a quarter mile from here. Three horses, too, plus a bunch of goats, including a really bad billy."

"So you have a farm as well as the service station."

"As I said, it's not ours. It's not anyone's. It was a foreclosure ages ago, so maybe a bank somewhere still owns it. As far as I know, no one's ever come out to look it over, and I doubt you could find an interested buyer. Fields are shrinking with new-growth trees. The house has fallen down, the barn's caving in, but the old shed's still solid."

"You're taking a risk trespassing like that," Farley pointed out.

"I know. I raised the question with Grandpa, but he believes the status of the property is debatable, probably reverting to open range. Nobody's posted a *No Trespassing* sign, and there's no *For Sale* sign, either. He says at worst we're maybe guilty of a misdemeanor, but he insists it's an outright crime to waste good land."

This grandfather is an independent sort, I thought. *A rebel by the sounds of it. And despite what his grandson thinks, he probably is a conspiracy theorist.*

I silently wondered if he would turn out to be the type who shoots strangers on sight, thinking it only a misdemeanor to make a preemptive strike against anyone who might plunder his stash of ammunition and dried beans. For now, I would reserve judgment. I reminded myself that the accumulating signs of social breakdown during the past few days, the proliferation of gunfire and other manifestations of violence, including murder, all too easily inflamed the climate of suspicion.

Luke and I headed to the tow truck, a weathered 1950s era brontosaurus with a huge front hood. On its welded back bumper a sticker read:

Where are we going? And why am I in this hand basket?

I climbed into the cab beside Luke. The keys were in the ignition, and when he fired it up, the old engine rumbled steadily. He did a slow reverse into the yard, turned, and circled back to the gates and out onto the road. Farley followed at a safe distance. The ride was bumpy, to say the least, and the seats were treacherous with coiled springs about to break through the worn leather padding. The ride back to our cavalcade was mercifully short.

There, Luke performed a truly amazing feat getting the tow truck reversed without letting it slide into the ditches on either side. Within minutes, he had my pickup chained and the front end lifted. Farley also did a precarious reversal with his SUV. I realized now that he could have waited at the station and avoided all the bother, but he probably had been worried that the tow truck might break down. In any event, he drove off again, heading back the way we had come.

In the interim, everyone piled into the other vehicles.

"Mission impossible accomplished," said Luke with a satisfied smile. He pressed the gas pedal and eased the truck forward, taking it slow. The other vehicles followed at a sensible distance.

"What about your horse?" I asked.

"Oh, she'll be happy there all day. I'll get her later."

When we reached the station, Luke parked at the entrance to the wrecker's field beside the main building and got out to release the Toyota. Farley and I went to the rear of the tow truck to watch him manipulate the hydraulic lift. My truck settled onto the ground with a clank just as the other vehicles in our caravan turned into the yard and parked in a line behind us—all of them had made it without mishap. I noted a dusty all-terrain vehicle parked by the front porch, a single seater with no engine hood and no roof.

There were now twenty-four people standing around (baby Longworth made it twenty-five) with no idea about what to do next. Luke bounded up the porch steps and went inside. As we waited for his grandfather to appear and magically fix my wreck, I said a prayer that he was a skilled auto mechanic.

Before long, Luke reappeared, and alongside him came a black and white border collie with a whisking tail. Behind them, an enormous old man now stepped onto the porch. He was well over six feet in height, six-foot-eight in my estimation, three hundred pounds, dressed in farmer's overalls and stained tee-shirt, carpet slippers on his feet and a straw sun hat on his head. His huge belly was half covered by an untrimmed white beard. Pinned to his overalls beneath it, dead center, was a large white button with red lettering, reading, *Thought Criminal.*

Exhibiting no surprise at seeing a crowd in his yard, he squinted through wire-rim spectacles and said in a rumbling voice:

"What's the trouble, folks?"

I stepped forward and explained. He listened without interrupting, glancing from time to time at my truck with a look of stern disapproval.

"I haven't had my lunch yet," he said grumpily when I had finished. "And I never work on an empty stomach." He swept the crowd with his eyes. "It's hot out here. Come on in and put your feet up. I'll take a look at your truck after I have a bite."

He turned abruptly and went back inside. We all followed him into the shadows.

16

THE INSIDE OF THE STATION wasn't what I had expected, that is, a small cramped place with a mini-counter and digital cash register, possibly a few auto parts hanging from hooks and a glass-topped case with an array of chocolate bars and cigarettes. It was nothing like that. There was, indeed, a cash register, but it sat at the near end of a long counter stretching away into a voluminous room. It was a hulking antique, nickel plated, and manually operated with large typewriter keys, hand crank, and bells. Beyond it was a hybrid of hardware and general store of the now-vanished country variety, an emporium extending back into the far reaches of the interior of what had seemed from the outside to be a conglomeration of smaller mismatched structures patched together. Through a wide double doorway at the end of the room, I spotted a wood-burning cooking range and a refectory table. Closer at hand was a potbelly stove with a rusty chimney rising straight up into the shadows above. Fly tapes were dangling everywhere, buzzing with their captives. Unlit coil oil pressure lanterns of ancient make hung from the rafters. Mounted on the room's wood plank walls were several antlers, mainly deer, a single caribou, and what was probably a mountain goat.

There were advertising signs too: a metal Coca-Cola ad, vintage 1930s; an aproned dairy maid displaying a lot of dazzling white teeth as she held up a can of Carnation condensed milk; a spiffy middle-age man in a fedora encouraging customers to buy Canada Savings Bonds to help support the war effort (which I guessed was the Second World War); a heroic-looking young man in a sailor's uniform with a bandage across his forehead, and the caption, *Loose Lips Sink Ships*. Plus a whole lot more, including some smaller signs hand-painted on wood, all of them quotations, such as:

> *If you don't read the newspaper you are uninformed; if you do read the newspaper, you are misinformed.*
>
> *(Mark Twain)*

and

> *Hoarding's not my game, freedom's my aim.*
>
> *(J. Jacobson)*

and

> *In a time of deceit, telling the truth is a revolutionary act.*
>
> *(George Orwell)*

I now began to get the picture. The old man's button *Thought Criminal* was straight out of Orwell's dystopian novel *1984*.

Ordinarily I was suspicious of self-actuated dramatic personas, but I now found myself warming to Luke's grandfather. I could live with the country curmudgeon act, as long as he truly was an independent type, and maybe an intelligent one. Hopefully he had no nasty right-wing baggage.

An inbuilt bookshelf caught my eye. A quick glance revealed a selection of titles atypical of a gas station's usual fare: Instead of *Mechanix Illustrated, Car Buyer's Guide*, and *Autotrader*, here were Plato, Aristotle, St. Thomas More, a few standard Orwells, Golding's *Lord of the Flies*, something titled *Summa of the Summa*, and one by Chesterton that I'd never read, *The Everlasting Man*. I pulled it out and opened to the flyleaf, where I found a few lines penned on the page: "To J-J, *Ex umbris et imaginibus in Veritatem*, from your friend and neighbor, D.L."

Rafe had been browsing too. I caught his eye and pointed to the book.

"Your favorite light reading."

"Interesting," he said.

"Very."

While we had been wandering around the room looking at all of the above, Luke and his grandfather had been busy welcoming the visitors and inviting them to find a seat. Clearly the establishment's version of a parliament or town hall meeting was around the potbelly stove. No one chose to sit in the large cane rocking chair beside the stove, because it was invisibly surrounded by an aura that proclaimed *For Proprietor's Use Only*. There were half a dozen captain's chairs in a semi-circle around it, and more wooden chairs along the closest wall, beneath shelves full of kerosene lamp chimneys, boxes of sulfur matches, striped bib overalls, workmen's gloves, and all manner of sundry other items. In addition, four wooden benches were now drawn forward by Luke, expanding the circle. He smilingly encouraged people to sit wherever they liked (feeling no need to mention that the rocking chair was off limits). The grandfather brought a thick cushion and put it on the seat of a captain's chair and indicated that Annie should sit down on it.

"Thank you," she said. She sat and drew the little girl from the Burnt Café onto her lap.

That done, the old man seated himself on his rocker with a sigh. Pard the dog, having finished his survey of sniffing the visitors, flopped onto the floor beside him. The old man absentmindedly scratched his ears with a hand bigger than the dog's head. He beetled his brows and peered around the assembly. It looked like we were about to become an audience.

"My name's Joseph Jacobson, and I own this place," he rumbled. "If you're forced to linger a while, don't get too cozy and don't start calling me Joe. I'm curious to know who you all are."

I think everyone was so surprised by the man's appearance and manner, no one immediately spoke up.

"Who's the leader here?" Jacobson asked, setting his chair to slow rocking.

No one replied. Then, one after another we all cast glances in Rafe's direction.

"Ah," said the man. "I should have guessed. Tall, strong, handsome, self-composed. An observant and highly intelligent look in the eyes, though capable of fearful sternness, given the occasion. You're accustomed to giving orders, but my guess is you do it nicely, am I correct?"

Rafe smiled, said nothing.

I answered for him. "You're uncannily right, sir." I leaned forward and offered my hand for a shake. He met mine with a catcher's mitt of a hand, cracked and weathered, with a vice-like grip. "I'm Cleve Longworth from Calgary, and the impressive fellow standing over there is my boss. He owns the construction company I work for."

"I work for him too," contributed Farley, standing with arms crossed at the edge of the circle.

I continued, "Nobody's appointed him our leader, at least not on this trip. He's more a friend than a boss, but it can't be denied he has certain qualities, which—"

"I can see it well enough," said Jacobson, still rocking, eyeing Rafe.

Rafe stepped forward and extended his hand for a shake.

"Raphael Morrow, sir. And we thank you for opening your station for us. We'd be grateful if you could take a look at Cleve's pickup and see if anything can be done."

"I surely can do that, after lunch, as I said. The world's too much in a hurry, don't you think? Having and getting before it cloy."

"We don't want to take too much of your time."

"Time's something I got plenty of. And maybe you people should take a few deep breaths, relax a little, have lunch with me. You'll be my guests. I have a truly impressive larder and am renowned in these parts for my culinary skills."

Luke stepped in hastily, "Uh, Grandpa, why don't I make lunch for everybody?"

The old man chuckled silently, his belly fully involved.

"My grandson here, he doesn't think too highly of my recipes and experimentations. He disapproves of skunk soup. He's trying to save you from my excesses."

Smiles flickered around the room.

"There's no skunk soup," said Luke, trying to reassure everyone. "It's all going to come out of cans—beef stew, right, Grandpa?"

"Right," Jacobson replied with a wave of largesse. "Go ahead, do what you will."

Cora spoke up, "I could help make a meal, if you wish."

"So can I," said Colleen Lyon.

Richard, too, rose to his feet and offered his assistance.

"My husband's an excellent cook," said Colleen.

"We'll bring in all our food so we don't use up your own supplies," Cora said, "if we could just borrow your stove, please."

"No need, no need," said Jacobson with another wave. "Of course, bring in whatever you like, but I have tons of rations to spare. Luke, we've got ten industrial-size cans of that beef stew in the cupboard. Crank it all open and get a fire going."

Luke led those who had offered to help away toward the kitchen. Some of the children followed. The remaining young ones, clearly fascinated by the old man, stayed on their benches or cross-legged on the floor, looking at him with upturned faces. The older Lyon boys perused the bookshelves. The two runaways kept to their bench, mute, watching. The little girl from the Burnt Café rested against Annie's huge lap, the child's face streaked with tears, Annie's arms around her, stroking her hair. The little boy still looked stunned, no tears, but he allowed himself to be held by Kateri, enfolded in her arms. Alice jounced Babby up and down on her knee, making him chortle.

"Now, down to business," Jacobson said, looking suddenly grave. "There's the indelible watermark of serious strain upon all your countenances, though you're doing your best to mask it. I may be wrong, but it strikes me that you're not out here in the boonies for a happy camping trip."

"No, we're not," said Rafe.

"We're actually heading to a cabin owned by an uncle of mine," I explained. "I'm not sure if we're on the right road, but maybe you've heard of him. His name's David Longworth."

Jacobson gave an affirmative jerk of his head. "Oh, you're on the right road, boy. I knew Dave pretty well. Died a few years back. Your uncle, you say. Sorry for your loss."

"Thank you. The map we have isn't all that precise. Could you direct us to his place?"

"No problem there." With an outstretched arm, Jacobson pointed vaguely west. "Nine miles farther along the road you come to a river. Used to be a bridge over that river, but it collapsed in the bad winter of . . . oh, I forget when. Anyway, the spring flood was so high that year it swept away anything that was left. Never got rebuilt. And the road on the other side has since gone back to bush. No harm done, though, because the ranches back there were already deserted. Good land, but the economy since the sixties, seventies has got more and more diabolical, pardon my mouth, but that's another topic altogether." He paused to wipe irritation off his face with an open palm. "Anyway, where was I?"

"We've come to the river," prompted Farley.

"Right. Well, there's no way any vehicle smaller than a Sherman tank can get across it now, and even the tank might not make it. But that doesn't matter for your purposes, because Dave's road is *this* side of the bridge—or where it used to be. I fished off that bridge when I was a boy, caught plenty of trout there, courted my wife, Dora, there—God rest her soul, she's buried in St. Michael's graveyard up at Pincher Creek; a hard battle with the cancer; she was a rancher's daughter; their place was down at the end of the road another ten miles or so. The family's all gone now, died off or moved away." He sighed deeply, eyes drifting toward the front window. "Everyone's gone, except for me. I'm the last holdout."

"You mentioned Dave's road," I said.

"Yup. So, about a hundred yards before the river—by the way, are you metric or imperial?"

"I try to think in both, sir."

"I'm purely old school. Imperial. Anyways, a hundred yards before the river, that's around three hundred feet, Dave's lane cuts in on the right and climbs up into the hills. It's just a rough trail now, starting to get overgrown. I take the ATV up there once every few weeks, to make sure no hikers have broken in. I made him a promise I'd keep an eye on it, because he told me he was going to leave it to his brother in his will. He was already fighting the cancer when he told me that."

"Yes, he left it to my father. My father's very ill too, and he's leaving the cabin to me."

Jacobson nodded solemnly.

"It's a nice place, the cabin's a dandy, terrific view of the Rockies close up on one side, and if you squint your eyes on a clear day you can see the prairies on the other. In addition to the cabin, there are twelve acres of woods and rock, and some sweet springs in the little valley below it."

"The property borders on crown land, I understand."

"Federal parkland, no neighbors, leastways not the two-legged kind. Okay, I get it, you're wanting to see your inheritance."

"That's right."

"An awful big gang of you for such an outing. You look like a boatload of refugees."

To which none of us offered a reply.

"What's happening out there? What's the world done to itself this time?"

"It's a long story, sir."

"I got time."

17

I BEGAN BY SAYING my father had recently mailed me a map and told me the cabin would soon be mine. I went on to relate how my boss, Rafe, and I had planned a brief excursion just to see the place.

"Very brief," said Rafe. "A week, no more, because this is our prime building season, and we had to get back to work. But soon after we hit the road, the situation quickly changed. So much has happened in the past two days, all of it unexpected, it's hard to describe. You asked what's happening out there in the world, Mr. Jacobson. Well, in short, civil order seems to be breaking down."

I cut in, "More rapidly than we could have imagined. It's only a five or six hours' drive from here to Calgary. But along the way, we've encountered more and more disturbing incidents. We don't know why it's happening. We can't get any news because digital communications and phones are totally down."

"Good," muttered Jacobson.

"Only cash works now."

"And I wonder how long that will last," said Jacobson.

"Of course, it may not be anything sinister."

"Or it may be maximum sinister, but there's no way of knowing. And if it *is* sinister, this mass ignorance is of great benefit to the Big Brothers who launched it."

"It could be caused by something natural, like an intense solar flare," I countered.

"Or it could be a cyberattack by China or Russia, North

Korea or Islamic terrorists—or by our own governments here in the Last Best West. Paralyze the nation, scare it to death, then reshape the docile masses."

Clearly, Jacobson was bringing us into the territory of conspiracy theory, which none of us visitors wanted to pursue at the moment. It was a mental fly tape, a Möbius strip of convoluted conjectures.

"How many of you are carrying those devilish little parasites?" he asked abruptly. Seeing our incomprehension, he growled, "The cell phones!"

Rafe and Farley removed their phones from their jacket pockets.

"Show me!" the old man barked.

They stepped forward and held the instruments out to him. He took Rafe's and inspected it closely. The screen glowed, but remained blank. Jacobson handed it back. He glanced at Farley's. "Turn them off!" he commanded.

I felt a flash of irritation. The man's rudeness was not only offensive, his mood swings were setting off an alarm bell in me, eroding any shred of confidence I might have had in his goodwill. Rafe, however, kept his equilibrium. Matter-of-factly he opened his phone and turned it off. Farley did the same. Grudgingly, I did too.

Alice and Theresa looked at each other, extracted their cell phones, and turned them off.

"Grandpa, that'll help, but it's not enough," said Luke with an apologetic look at the rest of us. "In crime novels they show how police can still locate a phone by pinging it."

"What the heck's *pinging*?"

"It's complicated. The only way to go totally invisible is to take out the battery and the SIM card. But with these late-model cells, you need a special tool to open it up and remove the power source."

"Didn't know that," grumbled Jacobson.

Colleen, who had been standing by the kitchen door, half listening to the foregoing, came into the room and showed Jacobson her phone.

"I've always hated these things," she said. "So useful, so efficient, and so always demanding attention. I felt it was starting to own me. I thought I was being irrational about it, but now I'm not so sure. My husband has one too."

"Turn 'em off."

"They're off."

"Okay, but we still got this pinging business. Mind if I smash them with a hammer?"

"Um, well, perhaps later," she said uncertainly.

Meanwhile, the runaway American girl, Lucy, had pulled a phone from her jean jacket pocket, and was trying surreptitiously to tap on it. The runaway boy named Garfield or Son was leaning close to her, whispering in her ear.

"You two!" Jacobson roared. "What are you doing?"

They froze and stared at him.

"You, boy, what did you just say to that girl?"

Son cleared his throat and nervously stammered, "I . . . I . . . I . . . t-told her to t-turn it off. The c-c-cops can track you with it."

"Damn right they can track you with it. Give it here."

Surprisingly, for all her stubborn sullenness, Lucy complied. She walked over and hesitantly handed it to Jacobson. In short order, he took it from her, got up, and rummaged in a drawer behind the cash register, where he found some kind of mini screwdriver. With this, he proceeded to open the instrument's back without asking her permission. He pried out the battery and pocketed it, then handed the cell back to her. Looking cowed, she returned to the bench and sat down beside Son

Becoming angrier by the minute, I thought to myself, *What have we got ourselves into*?

Jacobson threw the screwdriver onto the countertop and pointed at it.

"Do it yourselves. I ain't gonna make you. But if you don't take those batteries out, you could be killing us all."

He plunked himself back down in his chair and scowled.

Oh, really, killing us all? I thought sarcastically with a curl of my upper lip.

Again, Luke stepped in. "Uh, Grandpa, it's not just the batteries. Some late model SIM cards have their own power source. And they can be located within feet now, maybe inches. How about I make a Faraday?"

"A what?"

"Something to block any wireless signals or pings reaching our devices. We've got aluminum foil, and if I could use one of your metal tool boxes—"

"Okay, do whatever! I just want those bloodsuckin' leeches dead."

As Luke went off to get the materials he needed, I realized that I knew very little about electronics and microwaves and such, and that it might not be a bad idea to humor our idiosyncratic host. Luke returned to the room carrying an old metal tool box and a roll of aluminum foil. We all extracted our devices and handed them over to the young man. He wrapped each one carefully in foil, and placed them in the toolbox, closed it, and then wrapped the whole in more foil.

As he made the Faraday blocker, I continued to fume. It was not the deactivation of the cell phones that bothered me so much; it was Jacobson's churlish attitude. Ready to tear a strip off the old man's hide, I was preparing to jump in at that point, but fortunately Rafe acted first, bringing us back to our narrative:

After shooting me a look, he said, "The farther we went, the more incidents of violence we came across, erupting on the roads and even in the towns."

Following his lead, Cora added, "It felt like we were on the crest of a tidal wave, things getting worse every step of the way. As we went along, we kept meeting people in need of help, and they've joined up with us."

Farley said, "Rafe and Cleve here, they started out yesterday morning from the city with seven people, eight counting the baby. My wife and I and our nephew joined them at Fort Macleod . . . Now we're twenty-four, the last I counted."

"Uncanny," said Jacobson with a furrowed brow. "What do you mean by violence?"

Taking turns, we gave him verbal sketches of the troubles we had encountered, including the drive-by shooting at the young women on the highway, the bikers tossing Molotov cocktails at our vehicles, the mini-riot at the mall, and the fires and gunfights in Pincher Creek. After checking to make sure the Hearne children were not in earshot—Babby was now asleep in Alice's arms, Susan asleep in Annie's arms, Sam had been led away to the kitchen by Kateri—Rafe described the scene at the Burnt Café. As he listened, Jacobson slowed his rocker to a halt and leaned forward, peering intensely at us.

"I know that couple," he said. "Me and Luke ate there a couple of times. That place was their dream. They're murdered, you say? Where the hell are the cops?"

"Busy shutting down cities," Farley answered dryly.

"You're a cop," said Jacobson suspiciously, pointing at Farley's shoulder badge. His hostile expression left an unspoken question hanging in the air: What did *you* do to stop the crime?

Farley made a valiant effort to ease the tension. "Ee-yup, I'm a cop. You know those television series, good cop, bad cop working as a team to soften up suspects?"

Jacobson glared at him. "Don't know what you mean. I never had tee-vee when I was a kid and not when I raised my own. Just a movie now and then, whenever my wife dragged me against my will to the picture house at Lethbridge." He paused to draw breath. "So what's your point?" he snapped.

Pard sat up on his haunches and whimpered.

This was a new face of the man's rudeness. I wondered if his attitude had its roots in backwoods anti-native bias, but then considered that he didn't seem like your garden variety redneck. It was possible the frustrated outburst was due to his upset about the murder.

Farley seemed to take it in stride. I couldn't claim to know him well, but in all my interactions with him in the past, and on this journey, he had struck me as a classic stoic type, even-tempered, non-emotive. His face now became expressionless, looking like an unassailable fortress.

"My point is, I'm a good cop," he said with half-hooded eyes, slowly drawing out his words. Then, nodding his head in our direction: "And this is my team. Not a bad one among them."

Jacobson mulled it over, rocking and frowning until finally he grumbled, "My apologies. Bad habit of mine, shoot first, ask questions later. The mouth being my weapon of choice."

He extended a hand toward Farley, implying that a shake would be in order.

Farley took a step forward, extended his own hand, and they shook on it.

"Farley Crowshoe's my name. I'm a constable up at Siksiká. I don't have legal jurisdiction to investigate murders in these parts."

"Of course you don't," Jacobson murmured with a contrite look. "Sorry, constable."

"That's okay. We're all a bit on edge."

I broke in at that point and recounted the incident of the Hell's Angels making threatening gestures, and how they might have done worse if Farley and his shotgun hadn't been there to warn them off. I finished by mentioning that this had happened a couple of miles before Calvary rock.

"That's pretty close to home," said Jacobson. "We'll have to do something about that."

But what he meant exactly was left dangling, as Luke walked into the main room, holding up a square cowbell and banging it with a fork.

"Lunch is ready!" he called. "Come and get it!"

"You all go eat," Jacobson said to us. "I'll take a look at your truck."

Everyone went into the kitchen, myself included. By the time we all had returned to the main room and were well into our meals, a steaming savory stew served in metal bowls, along with what was left of the food we had brought with us on the journey, Jacobson returned and lowered himself onto his rocker.

He looked red in the face and winded, his hands blackened with grease. Shaking his head, he said to me, "Bad news. The exhaust system's ripped out. No big problem there, but the worse damage is your drive train. Transmission's okay but the rest is shot, needs total replacement. With ordering foreign parts, you have a long wait these days, and you pay a king's ransom. Worse, you've got a cracked axle. You drive it that way, and you're driving a coffin."

"Oh-boy," I said, trying to maintain my serenity, at least the outer appearance of it.

"That truck's going nowhere except the way of all flesh, which is to say, into the graveyard out back, if you need a place for a decent burial."

"Well, it brought us this close to our destination, so I guess it's earned a rest. The truck's yours if you want it, Mr. Jacobson. Maybe you can strip it down for parts."

Richard now entered the discussion. "Cleve, we've already distributed your gear among the rest of us. We can find a seat for you. In any event, we probably should get going as soon as we can. The day's more than half gone, and we need to reach the cabin while there's still light to set up tents, make meals, and try to figure out where everyone's going to sleep."

"You're right. We can't stay here."

Jacobson stood up and arched his back, making cracking noises along his spine.

"You sure *can* stay here, if it's to your liking. Of course, go or stay, it's your choice."

Colleen stood and introduced herself. "You don't have space for twenty-four people," she said. "Moreover, it's completely uncertain how long we'll be stuck here. The social unrest could settle down within a few days, or it might take longer."

The old man grimaced. "And if the settling down out there means loss of all freedoms, would you want to go back? Would you want to take your kids back into it?"

"But we'd eat you out of house and home."

Strangely, Jacobson chucked at this. "You wouldn't. I guarantee it."

"Huh?" said a few among us. And all faces looked curiously at our host.

Cora said, "Mr. Jacobson, we can't thank you enough for your hospitality. It's uncommonly generous and kind, and we realize you hardly know us. We're strangers and we don't want to be a burden on you, use up all your resources. We're very grateful for lunch, but, good heavens, it's like feeding an army, so as soon as we can get mobile, we'll be on our way. Could you give us directions to Cleve's uncle's place?"

"I already gave directions to your menfolk here, ma'am. However, it's not as cut and dried as it seems. We'll think about your options after everyone's finished getting food in their bellies. As for my resources, I can show you that too. Luke, why don't you take Mrs. Morrow and Mrs. Lyon and anyone else who's interested and show them the larder."

Luke led the way back to the kitchen, the ladies following. Annie remained in the seat beside me, holding my hand. The little girl was still asleep on her lap, whimpering in a dream, the doll clutched tightly in her arms. None of us men said anything for a few minutes. We watched some of the younger children ferreting about in a free-standing shelf full of toys, opening up boxes, inspecting see-through plastic packages. A couple of parents rose to put a stop to it.

"Let 'em play," said Jacobson. "That stuff's been sitting there gathering dust for more'n ten years. It's time to put it to good use."

The parents backed off, and the children excitedly began opening the packages—dolls, trucks, cars, teddy bears, picture puzzles, multicolored Lego and Duplo blocks . . .

Theresa took Sam Hearne by the hand and ambled over to join the fun. Unconcerned about her dress, she sat down on the unswept floor among the children and caught Sam's interest by examining a boxed collection of miniature racing cars.

"*Vroom-vroom*," she said with shining eyes, offering him one. The boy took it in hand and dropped to his knees.

"*Vroom-vroom*," he whispered, making the car speed around him in circles. Crawling on all fours, he drove it out of the group of children and into another aisle, where more faint *vrooms* could be heard as he made his circuits.

Ten minutes later, Luke and the women returned. The wives looked subdued, even a little stunned.

"Any questions?" asked Jacobson.

They shook their heads in unison.

Rafe caught his wife's eye with an inquiring look.

Cora said, "The larder's actually a warehouse built onto the back of the garage. It's stacked full of cases and cases of canned food, a mountain of it; also bins of dried grains, rice, beans, sacks of flour."

"It's yours for the asking, people," said Jacobson. "No cost to you. My treat."

Standing beside him at the potbelly stove, Luke nodded up and down to confirm the old man's offer.

"This place here used to be a general store as well as a gas station, so I guess you could call the larder my stock. Started building it up a couple of years before the turn of the century, and just kept adding to it year after year." He rocked and chortled. "A heck of a lot of it's past the eat-by date, but that never bothered me none. I ain't been killed by it yet."

"We dip into the older stock first," said Luke. "And hey, I'm still alive, too."

"You people probably think I'm crazy, eh?" said Jacobson, with a suspicious look around the room.

Clearly he was expecting an answer. The shaking of several heads seemed to satisfy him.

"Just think about it. In this country, you don't go strolling around under palm trees expecting coconuts to fall into your lap."

Suddenly Jacobson covered his face with his hands, rubbing it fiercely as if to rid it of useless distractions. Looking up, he said:

"Three weeks ago I wrote letters to all my kids, also to anyone who'll still listen to me. I told them a storm's rising, and it's going to be a bad one. Told them to get yourselves out this way by hook or by crook and do it fast. We'll make room for everybody, I said. Don't you worry, I said, I've got lots of camping gear and food. I been preparing for this since Y2K, and that was a big scare to be sure, but it fizzled out in the end."

"Maybe it was a trial run," Luke suggested.

"Uh-huh, that's probably it. Before you were born, boy, before you were born. For me it's just yesterday. I was old then, and I'm old now, but time keeps whipping on by. Anyway, like I say, we should always be ready, keep oil in our lamps, never forget the seven lean years and seven fat years and the bowing wheat like the dream in the Bible and pharaoh and the bad brothers when famine came upon the land, and God prepared aforehand that his servants might—"

"Mr. Jacobson," Rafe interrupted, "do you know how many of your loved ones will be coming?"

"Not a word back yet, and nobody's showed up, except you folks. Maybe they're packing their bags or they're already on the road. On the other hand, maybe they've all written me nice notes saying they can't come at this time but hope to visit me soon. Et cetera. And so forth. Everybody has excuses. It's my fault, really. A case of me crying wolf too many times is my guess."

"Everybody loves you, Grandpa," said Luke.

"Well . . . thanks, lad. You have a good heart. But anyone can feel a fondness for eccentrics—from a distance."

"You're not an eccentric, Grandpa."

Jacobson turned to me and squinted. "Your uncle once called me a 'colorful character'. Nice, eh, *a colorful character*. So I said to him, 'Dave, I may have suspenders and a belly and I talk funny, but, fact is, you're a way more colorful character than I am, sitting all by yourself on that hilltop, content to see nary a soul for months on end. Thinking your thoughts, writing whatever it is you write all day long. You're dignified, you're tidy, you're introspective, you don't say much, and when you do, it's with good vocabulary and cogitative tones, none of which applies to my good self.'

"So, he shoots back, 'Well, Joe, character ain't in the eye of the beholder.' He used *ain't* instead of *isn't*, you see, just to rile me. Oh, he wasn't trying t'get my goat, he was just upping the ante because I'd used some items from *his* dictionary, like *cogitative* and *introspective*. We liked to spar like that now and then, along with the sipping whiskey he brought along for the occasion. And I usually had to chew on what he said. There was always something solid in it, even the jokes."

"I never knew him well," I said. "He lived on the other side of the country when I was growing up. But he sounds a lot like my Dad."

"I met your Dad, too, a couple times. Yup, they were a lot alike."

"Why do you think a successful man like that chose to

spend four months alone in a cabin every year, all year round after he retired?"

"Because he was as sick as I was of the way civilization was slowly mutating into anti-civilization. He once told me, 'Joe, when you're *inside* the belly of the beast, you can't see where you are. You have to be spit *outside* the beast in order to recognize it,' he said. He was a lot less flamboyant about resistance than I was. He aimed his bullets carefully, nah, more like a scalpel; gave me copies of his articles and a couple of books he wrote. They were good. They were dang good, but by then no one was reading any more—leastwise not real reading."

"Real thinking," Richard interjected.

"Uh-huh," Jacobson nodded. "Then if you add to the psychotropic drug the whole world seems to have ingested—mainly politicians and the people who elected them, not to mention the mainstream media—add into the mix the fact that everybody, simply everybody, was writing books and publishing them."

Luke raised his hand with a playful grimace. "Guilty as charged," he said.

Jacobson pointed to a stack of paperbacks beside the cash register. "See that display, front and center? That's Luke's detective novel. Philosophical private eye. Deep. Wrote it when he was nineteen years old."

Everyone turned and looked at Luke with new interest.

"Self-published," said the author with an embarrassed flush on his cheeks. "Grandpa paid for it."

"Now, now, it wasn't an act of pity, lad. I really enjoyed the story and characterization. It deserves to be a best-seller. And, hey, it's on its way to being one."

"Forty-eight copies sold in five years," said Luke lifting

his shoulders theatrically and slumping in resignation. "All of them bought by family members and my college pals."

"Anyway, you see my point," Jacobson continued as if Luke's remark was of no consequence. "If this nation hadn't sold its birthright for a mess of pottage, your uncle would have been one of the country's brightest lights. I told him that once, made him blush redder than this grandson of mine. All he said was, 'Joe, the truth must be spoken, even if no one listens, no one hears.' He never counted the cost, you see. That's the kind of man he was."

Yes, that was the kind of man he was, if he was anything like my father. I had read my uncle's books back when I was an unbeliever. I had been impressed—or half-impressed, thinking I could have written a better critique of the state of the world. At the time I was a bubbling pudding of arrogance. He was a Toronto university professor, with a big reputation as a scholar, low reputation as a social critic, the favorite whipping boy of big journals and newspapers, the opinion-piece writers and editorialists who slyly demonized him as a fascist, which he wasn't. My uncle was what you might call a classical liberal in the true meaning of the word. But he had the habit of weaving short biblical phrases into his essays, which to modern readers tended to be opaque. When he wrote about "prodigal sons gorging on rationalist porcine slops", they didn't know what he meant. The powerful older "liberals", who were the real nouveau fascists, got the references plain enough and went for blood.

"Uncle Dave was a strong believer, a regular churchgoer," I now said to Jacobson. "But you say he never saw a soul for months on end, which doesn't sound like him."

"Oh, that's just me exaggerating to underline a point. Your uncle drove in to Pincher Creek every Sunday for

Mass. We had a lot of discussions about religion, and after a time I started going with him. Realized I was long overdue to get back to the faith of my fathers. I made the longest confession ever heard at St. Michael's. Set a record, is my bet."

"I'm sorry to tell you the church in Pincher Creek was burned down last night," said Fr. Peter.

"No," Luke groaned.

"What! Who would do a damn foolish thing like that?" Jacobson growled with pain in his eyes.

We shook our heads.

"It's been brewing a long time," said Rafe.

"Well, it had to boil over sometime," said Jacobson.

Then, as if going deeper into himself, he said in a low voice, "I don't have dreams or visions or visits by angels, but I know you're here for a purpose."

Cora tilted her head curiously. "What purpose do you think that is?"

He took a few moments to ponder. His answer, when it came, did not seem to fit her question.

"I've seen this coming for years. Dave saw it coming too. Dora? Well, nobody beat her in that department. We didn't know when it would happen, didn't know how, but we knew it would come. So I been preparing. Oh, and just to reassure you good people, I'm not a prepper with a cave out back full of guns. I have a .22 for squirrels and racoons, and an old beat-up .303 to scare off bears, but that's not my basic attitude. Seven fat years and seven lean years is my attitude. Hoarding's not my game, freedom's my aim. A secret stockpile of food just for myself and my pals, and damned be everyone else, is an idea straight from hell. It'll poison you unless you're willing at every moment to give it up to help others—to help strangers. As I said, I don't have dreams, and I don't have visions, and I don't pay attention to visionaries and whatever their imaginations come up with."

"It may not all be imagination," said Fr. Peter.

"Oh, it's a mixed bag, I'm sure. I used to read a lot of it twenty, thirty years ago, so did Dora. Maybe some of it was pure gold, but too much of it was guesswork mixed up with mental musings mistaken for the voice of God, Bible prophecies interpreted any which way, getting people galloping this way and that. It worried me then, and it worries me now."

"Why?" asked Richard.

"Because the sound of thundering hoofs always makes me nervous. Buffalo stampedes are all about hysteria. All about the hunters spooking the quarry, getting the poor critters in a state of confused panic so they can move in for the kill."

Rafe pointed out, "We may look like a stampede to you, Mr. Jacobson, but each of us—each in his own way—has responded to a quieter kind of grace. For us, it's not about self-preservation; it's about faith and obedience. We don't know where it's all leading, but we want to follow."

"Hmmm, now *that* I can trust. Yup, give me faith every time." Jacobson straightened his spine and slapped his knees with his oversize mechanic's hands, preparing to get to his feet. When he was upright, he absentmindedly combed his long beard with his fingers.

"The past three weeks," he said, "every morning I wake up with this knowing inside me." He thumped his chest with his big fist. "No dreams, no visions, just a kind of certainty, without me hearing any words as such, just a meaning. And the meaning was pretty simple and straightforward. *They're coming soon*, it told me. *They'll need help. Get ready.*

Luke looked surprised. "I've been hearing it too, in my heart. Every morning the past couple of weeks, and again when we have night prayers together."

The old man looked censoriously at his grandson. "And you didn't bother to tell me, boy?"

"Didn't want to spook you, Grandpa," Luke replied with a wry smile.

18

OKAY," SAID JACOBSON. "We gotta think about options. First and foremost, we need to deal with the Hell's Angels."

And how will we do that? I wondered silently. *One shotgun and a couple of rusty rifles won't ward off an invasion.*

"Luke, I want you to drive back to the junction where our road joins the highway. Cut down a whole lot of small brush, evergreens only. Stand it up across the end of the road, make it look natural, so nobody driving by will notice there's access here. And for added insurance, buzz down some bigger trees across the road."

"Grandpa, what if Mum and Dad come?" asked Luke with a worried frown. "What about all the others you invited?"

"The whole family knows Calvary rock, so they'll figure it out and find their way here without too much trouble."

Luke didn't look convinced. "On foot? If I block the road with big trees, they won't be able to drive far."

"Oh, and you'll need to break up the bridge," said Jacobson, without answering the objection.

"The bridge on Deep Creek? You can't take that down! If any of the clan gets as far as the junction and clears away the brush, they'd only be able to drive one mile before the bridge. That's nine or ten miles from here."

I mentally retraced our journey from the highway: one mile to the bridge across the ravine; three miles farther on to the pothole and truck breakdown; the gas station was six miles beyond that. Total, approximately ten miles. And ahead of us lay nine more miles to a river at the road's end, plus a couple more miles climbing a lane to the cabin.

Bringing my mind back to the argument, I saw that Luke was still disputing with his grandfather. "What if they bring Grandmère in her wheelchair and Uncle Amédée with his bad hip? You can't ask them to walk all that way. It's crazy, Grandpa."

"That bridge is a death trap," the old man answered with a scowl. "A disaster just waiting to happen. It's more likely to kill innocent bystanders than marauders. I've been procrastinating for years about taking it down. So, looks like it's time to do it. We'll think about making a new one when this emergency's over."

"I'll take a tent and camp at the junction till they arrive. After that, I'll fall the big trees and take down the bridge as soon as they're across."

"No, you're not taking a tent with you. I don't want you standing guard alone out there, overwhelmed by Mongol hordes."

"I'll bring the .22."

"Nope, you let that gun alone, and you get back here pronto, soon as you finish the work."

"I could leave a message on a stump or something. I'll tell them to send their fittest person to come get us, and then I'll drive down to pick everyone else up."

"It's a long shot *anyone's* going to show up. For now, we need that road camouflaged at the junction and some bigger timber brought down across the road as backup, to stop hell-raisers getting in on wheels. Soon as you fall the trees, you do the bridge."

"Grandpa!" exclaimed Luke with a note of exasperation.

"You're not hearing me! How is the family going to get across the ravine?"

"Leave a couple of planks on the far side so they can make a footbridge."

Luke rolled his eyes and shook his head.

"Take the chainsaw with you," said Jacobson, "and there's plenty of crowbars and a couple of long pry-poles out in the garage."

"You mean right now?"

"Yeah, right now. And scrape up some volunteers to give you a hand."

Instantly, the Lyons' three oldest boys jumped to their feet. "We'll come."

"Boys, I don't know . . . ," said their mother, looking worried.

"Let them go, Colleen," said Richard. "Knights in training, remember."

There followed a wordless communication between husband and wife.

"I'll go with them," Richard added.

"How are you planning to get your crew there?" Farley asked Luke. "You're talking three men and three boys. That ATV looks like it can seat two at best. And you can only squeeze three into the cab of the tow truck."

"Oh, right."

"Let's take my four-wheel-drive. It seats six, and seven in a pinch."

I noticed Jacobson looking at Farley with new respect. "Good thinking," he said.

Son stepped forward. "Uh, can I help too?" he asked uncertainly.

"Great," said Luke. "We'll need all the muscle we can

get, if we're going to get this done quickly. You sure you're strong enough?"

Son lifted his chin and broadened his shoulders.

Luke smiled and clapped him on the shoulder. "Yeah, you're strong enough."

For the first time since we had met him, Son's stony countenance broke. He returned the smile—tentative but genuine.

Rafe and I also offered to go with them, but Luke declined. Interestingly, he suggested that Richard also remain behind. "To guard the fort," he said to the three of us.

"I've got my A-team. And Mr. Crowshoe'll be with us standing guard."

The Lyons looked uncertain, but acquiesced.

"Don't worry, we'll be fine," Luke reassured them. Turning to his crew, he said, "All right, you guys, let's go."

And off they went to gather tools. Not long after, I heard Farley's vehicle rumbling out of the lot.

Without voicing my concern, I wondered how wise it was to let them go back so close to the highway. But I knew, as well, that Farley was a level-headed, fearless man and would keep his loaded shotgun at the ready. Perhaps as important was the injection of energy into the youths, the experience of camaraderie in the face of danger, the rewarding sensation of accomplishing an urgent task with courage.

"Now, let's consider your options," said Jacobson.

Rafe, Richard, Fr. Peter, and I sat down on the captain's chairs facing him.

"First of all, you're a lot of people for one small cabin," he began. "There's a single bedroom and another room Dave used for an office, his writing space, which could be cleared out and used as a second bedroom. I have a few camp cots you can use. But even if you lay a mattress or two on the living room floor and use the couch, I don't see many people crowding into the place."

"Is there plumbing and electricity?" I asked.

"There's an outhouse behind the woodshed. No running water, just a hand pump that draws on the springs, and barrels for collecting rainwater. He's got a solar panel and batteries, but it produces just enough juice to power a few lamps and his computer. I don't know if it's still working."

"A few of us have brought camping tents," said Rafe, "but they're small."

"Don't forget our dome tent. It sleeps six," said Richard.

"Even so, I doubt we're going to be able to shelter everyone, cabin and tents combined."

"There's another thing to think about," said Jacobson. "Up there on the hilltop, it's mostly rock and slopes, not a lot of flat ground to pitch tents. Some of you can stay here with me and Luke, if you want. There's my bedroom but, sorry, that's sacred ground. My two girls had one of the other bedrooms, but that's Luke's room now. Dora and I also had four sons, and they built themselves a bunkhouse beside the Quonset hut; I can show you it later. The mattresses have gone moldy, and we'd have to sweep out the squirrel nests, but it could do for makeshift. Otherwise we can rearrange this big room here, spread some mattresses around. Did you bring mattresses?"

"I believe some of us brought thin foamies."

"Thin mattress, thin sleep, I always say."

"You're very generous, sir, and we may need to take you up on your offer. For now, I'm thinking that our people will want to stay close to one another. It's been a stressful few days."

"That's your call. Anyway, all I'm saying is no one needs

to sleep out in the bush. And here's another possibility. I have three old HBC tents—Hudson Bay Company issue—nine by twelve foot each, heavy duck. They look like little huts, cute as a button. Hope the mice haven't got into them. Plus, a few years ago I bought a high-walled military tent from the Army Surplus store up in Calgary; it shut down some time ago, but I got this great deal at the closing sale. Forty foot long, heavy canvas, olive drab, screened windows. Bug proof and, hey, maybe even bomb proof."

We smiled at the joke. However, no one said anything, as these various details were a lot to take in at once.

"If you want to take it all up the lane to Dave's place, you're welcome to try," said Jacobson. "But, as I said, there's no real level ground to pitch them on his hill. You might think about making camp down by the river. That's flat meadow and close to a water supply. We can pack all the things you need and drive it there, no problem. I don't know if we can get any vehicles up to the cabin, other than the ATV and the constable's SUV."

"Mr. Jacobson," said Rafe. "I'm curious about your own transportation. Your tow truck doesn't have license plates, I noticed."

"You're a sharp observer."

"How do you get in and out when you need supplies from town or go to church? It's a long way to Pincher Creek on an ATV, a pretty miserable ride in winter I would guess. Do you catch a ride with neighbors?"

"There ain't no more neighbors," said Jacobson with a grimace. "My main transport's a '57 GMC pickup parked in the garage out back. V8, half-ton, gas guzzler, but it never let me down till now. Blew a piston head last month, plus the bearings are shot, and I'm still waiting for parts. Couriers refuse to drive out this far, not on our road they won't, so the parts are being mailed to my post box in Pincher. I just have to figure out how to get in there to pick them up." He paused and wiped sweat from his forehead. "Well, maybe it's too late for that."

He rocked forward and backward, silently musing on some additional idea. The sound of the playing children filled the gap, their chatter sweet to the ear. Given the instability of our current situation, their innocent trust in the adults was especially poignant.

I glanced across the room at Annie and the little girl still asleep in her arms. She smiled at me. I smiled back. She patted her tummy. I replied with a thumbs up.

Since our wedding, we seemed able to read each other's thoughts without the aid of words. Her eyes now sent me a message: *We've made it this far.*

I nodded, returning the same message. With facial gestures I added a postscript:

Keep laughing, no wailing.

She sent me another smile. She was being brave; she was making an effort. But I knew that in the depths of her maternal heart she was aching for the three orphaned children.

Suddenly, Jacobson brought his rocker to a halt and slapped his forehead. "What's wrong with my brain? I shoulda thought of this before. We can get the Bluebird up and running."

"The bluebird?" I asked, feeling a quiver of déjà vu.

Jacobson catapulted to his feet. "Come on, let me show you."

We four men got up and followed him out the door onto the porch. Fr. Peter and Richard went on ahead, side by side with Jacobson as they walked through high grass toward the side yard full of dozens of wrecked and otherwise defunct vehicles. With great animation, Jacobson was describing something about engine sizes and fuel capacity, diesel versus gasoline, et cetera.

I held Rafe back for a moment.

"How stable is this man?" I asked him in a low voice. "His accent slides all over the place, his vocabulary expands and contracts without rhyme or reason. He's quirky, moody, too."

"And abrasive at times," said Rafe. "But I think he's reliable."

"You sure about that?" I said uncertainly. "These eruptions of rotten temper are disturbing. He's nice as homemade pie one minute then barking at people the next."

"Oh, he might bark at us, but it's unlikely he'll bite."

"He does a whole lot more talking than listening."

"That can happen with people who've spent too many years alone without other people to share their thoughts. He's been terribly lonely, I think. Thank heavens the grandson came to stay with him a while."

"There was my uncle Dave."

"An introvert, if I heard correctly."

"Oh, they had their occasional whiskey all right, and the world's going to hell in a handbasket discussions, but maybe it wasn't enough for a grieving widower."

"Probably not. I think our host is a man who grieves about many things. He's sorrowing over the loss of a way of life, the decline of children and family life, and the steadily corrupting state of society. Most of all, he's worried about his own children, and with this present crisis it's become a major anxiety. He's afraid—though he's doing his best to hide it."

"Okay," I admitted. "I guess the bottom line is that he's welcomed a troop of complete strangers with open arms, offering all his resources to help us. What kind of person does that?"

"A good person."

"A good person in need of politeness training."

"Good people come in all shapes and sizes, Cleve, all kinds of personalities. Joe Jacobson's a big personality, rough around the edges . . . but a kind of giant in his own way."

I looked at Rafe curiously, but we said no more, as we had now caught up with Jacobson, Fr. Peter, and Richard, who were standing in waist-high weeds before a small, superannuated school bus, its original bright yellow faded and spotted with rust. It listed a little, and I noticed that the left front tire was flat. Positioned centrally on the front grill was the logo of a flying blue bird.

"Built by the Bluebird Company in 1975," said Jacobson, slapping the hood with his open palm. "This model's a Microbird-T, twenty-five passenger, built to last. It has the best suspension on the lot, and it rides high, so it won't be scraping dirt with its underbelly. We'll use it to take everything you need down to the river."

Not a bad plan, I thought, but the challenge of getting the old school bus operational would be no small one.

"I'll pump up the tire. The battery'll be dead, but we can try to jump-start it." He glanced at me. "And if it won't keep a charge, we can try switching the battery out of this man's lame duck."

"I'm fine with that," I said. "The duck is yours now anyway."

"Dora drove this for fifteen years," said Jacobson looking at the bus with great fondness. "There was a schoolhouse at Twin Butte in the early days, and after it closed down, she had a longer haul picking up the kids from the ranches on this road and along the highway, taking them to Pincher.

To make a long story short, the last of the kids on this road grew up and moved away, our own moved away one by one, and the ranches were shutting down, no one could make a living at it any more. Then the school board mandated a better bus and a driver from Pincher for the handful of kids still living on the highway south of town. So we packed it in. I bought this old Bluebird for a song, and then we parked it here in the graveyard. I never could figure out why we did that. Nostalgia, maybe. Or we hoped there'd be a better time coming, families having kids again. But that didn't happen."

For a few moments he was preoccupied with staring into the distance or into the past.

"Well, let's get busy," he said, shaking off memories, opening the hood.

The remobilization of the Bluebird entailed a series of tasks. First, Jacobson inspected the oil stick and pronounced, "Good enough."

Then came the battery. As he climbed into the bus, it groaned and swayed off center. Turning the key in the ignition did nothing but produce a click sound.

"Dead as a doornail," he said.

"I have jump-start cables," I said. "I'll go back and get them."

"Bring one of them vehicles with you. We need a live battery to spark this one."

Richard said, "You can use mine."

I retrieved the cables from behind the seat of my Toyota. Richard unhitched his trailer then carefully drove his low-slung Eurovan through the high grass and parked it nose to nose with the bus.

Connecting the cables produced sparks but did nothing

for the bus's battery. The ignition gave a few more clicks, but no *rrrr-rrrr* and no rumble of an engaged motor.

"I could trickle-charge it overnight," said Jacobson with a grimace.

"Without electric power, how would you charge it?" asked Rafe.

"I can get the generator running out in the shop."

This was new information. "You have a generator?" I asked.

"Course I got a generator. Hardly ever use it, mind you. It burns gas like you wouldn't believe. And I have to get all my gas at Pincher Creek. Got a 45 gallon drum on the back of the GMC, welded a spigot onto it, fill it up every time I go to town. It's empty now. Maybe I got a jerry can or two left with some juice in 'em."

It sounded like a laborious method to me. "Why don't we use the battery from my pickup. It's plenty live."

"Okay," said Jacobson, wiping sweat from his forehead and adjusting his straw hat.

I walked out of the lot and opened up the hood of the Toyota. I had brought my tool kit along on the journey, and I now used one of my wrenches to loosen the cables from the battery posts. Fortunately, the battery had a carry handle, which made my life easier, and I soon had it back at the bus.

After removing the dead battery, I installed mine and connected it. Once again, Jacobson heaved himself up into the bus and took the driver's seat. He turned the ignition. When the *rrrr-rrrr* was followed by a belch and a rumble from the engine, a cloud of dirty exhaust blew out of the tailpipe. The rumble skipped a couple of beats, then caught hold and steadied without further interruption.

We cheered:

"Hey-hey," said Rafe.

"Bravo! Well done!" said Richard.

"Thank God," said Fr. Peter.

"Space shuttle ready to launch!" said I.

"Better late than never," said Jacobson climbing back down to ground level, sporting a big toothy grin, missing a few teeth. "Okay, the ol' bird ain't dead yet. Gas gauge is on empty, though, and creeping into the warning zone."

"Where are your jerry cans?" asked Rafe. "I can go get them."

"You'll find them in the shop—the garage out back."

I accompanied Rafe to the garage, and when we entered its open doorway, I was moved to see the old 1957 GMC pickup sitting there in mint condition. Red body with black fenders, not a scratch or a dent. Redwall tires with shining chrome caps. It was beautiful, obviously a labor of love. The only flaw was a rusty blue drum in the cargo bed.

The metal jerry cans were on the dirt floor in front of a workbench as long as the deck of an aircraft carrier, its thick boards dark with age and stained by untold toil. It was overcrowded with tools for motor mechanics and woodworking and small engine repairs, most of them non-electric hand tools, some new, some vintage.

Rafe took one of the cans, and I took the other. They were full. I grabbed a gooseneck funnel, and we headed back to the bus.

Jacobson, Fr. Peter, and Richard were in amiable conversation when we arrived. Jacobson was holding forth, but Richard was standing his ground with lightning-swift ripostes, and I could see that Jacobson was enjoying the pushback. Rafe and I filled the gas tank.

"Ten gallons should get you to the river," said Jacobson when we were done. "There and back a few times, I'd wager. Now, our only remaining problem is this hobbled horse."

"Pardon me?" said Richard.

Jacobson pointed to the flat tire. "Mind if I borrow your cigarette lighter?"

"Ah," said the doctor of history with a smile of illumination, "an air compressor. I happen to have the very one you need."

"Good man."

Richard went to the rear of his car, found a small black kit in the trunk, and brought it with him to the bus's tire. There he snapped the hose valve onto the tire's air nozzle, and after that he unraveled a length of wire as far as his front seat. He got in behind the wheel, turned on the engine, and slid the wire plug into the socket of his dashboard cigarette lighter. A flick of a switch on the black box initiated a loud chattering as the compressor began its work. We stood around watching in hopeful expectation. Slowly, slowly the big old tire inflated.

Jacobson mentioned what the maximum pressure should be, and Richard took the cue, squatting down to check the pressure dial on the box. Within five minutes, he flicked the machine into silence and kept watching the dial.

"The needle's not moving," he announced with a smile. "No big leaks."

This was greeted by more cheers.

19

We were still listening to the Bluebird's satisfying rumble when the sound of another vehicle broke our concentration.

An older station wagon had come to a halt in a cloud of dust in front of the antique gas pumps. Its car horn beeped three times.

"What now?" Jacobson grumbled.

Richard backed his car out of the lot, while the rest of us walked to the station to investigate this latest development.

The driver of the station wagon got out as we approached—a tall man in his fifties, wearing sunglasses and a paunch. He whipped off the sunglasses and waved.

Jacobson increased his gait and threw his arms wide.

"Hardy-boy!" he called with a laugh. "You made it!"

"Hey there, Pa! Wouldn't have missed it for the world."

The two men embraced each other with thunderous back thumps. A woman got out of the front passenger side. Petite, dark-haired, smiling, she came up to Jacobson and timidly embraced him.

"Céline," said Jacobson with a tender look and held her tighter as the rest of us stood around gawking.

"Pa, we are so happy to see you," she said with a French accent. "It was a very long journey. Your letter—"

"Bring anyone else with you?"

"Grandmère and *mon oncle* Amédée. Pierre has come with us too."

"Not everybody, then?"

Hardy and Céline shook their heads with a look of regret. In the meantime, an eighteen-year-old youth who closely resembled Luke Jacobson had stepped out of the car.

"Grandpa," he said with a grin.

"Pierre-lad, what a surprise!"

No embraces and back thumps ensued, as Pierre was busy helping a dignified elderly gentleman to disembark. After standing himself upright with some effort, the old man said, "Joe!"

"Amady," Jacobson answered, mispronouncing the man's name, then going over to shake hands.

"And *Maman* also," said Amédée.

"Well, let's get the poor dear out of that sardine can, eh!"

This was already happening, as Hardy and Céline were now assisting a very ancient, very tiny lady to disembark from the rear of the vehicle. Quickly, Pierre untied a wheelchair strapped to the roof, brought it down to the ground and opened it wide. The old woman sat down on it with a flicker of pain crossing her face and a sigh of relief.

"Grand-mare," said Jacobson with a fond look. "Welcome. Ben-venoo."

"Big Joe, it's good to see you," she chirped in reply.

"I can't believe you drove all that way. How many days did it take you?"

"Five, but it pass swiftly. We have the good company with each other, and the card game. Pierre, he try to teach me the English grammar, which is impossible, but we have a nice time anyway. Like the old days. I bring a box of my special recipe to eat on the journey, the *éclair au chocolat* and a nice *gâteau opéra*."

"You save some for me?"

"Ah, Joe, it is a great pity—they are consumed. I regret that I make your son more fatter."

Everyone laughed as Hardy patted his belly. "It was worth it," he said.

Jacobson looked at their car.

"You drove all the way in from the highway," he said, stating the obvious.

"Grandpa," said Pierre, "Luke says to tell you he's going to cut down big trees now, to block the road. After that, he'll break up that bridge over the ravine."

"Well, well, incredible timing, you showing up not a minute too soon."

"It *is* incredible timing, Pa," said Hardy. "We made it to the turnoff just as Luke and his crew were setting up little evergreens across the junction, for camouflage. He got us through and across the bridge, and told us to head on up to the house. He'll be along soon." He paused and then said with a frown, "You've had your own share of troubles, I hear."

"Oh, yeah, plenty of those. These people—" Jacobson turned and made a sweeping gesture that encompassed the rest of us. "These people been through hell, some of 'em. They're good folks."

"I can see this is true," said Grandmère. "It is in the eyes. Always it is in the eyes."

"Did you run into any flak driving from Montreal?" Jacobson asked his son.

"Not until yesterday. Things started to look weird after the Ontario-Manitoba border. Traffic patterns going screwy. Insane speeding. Road rage. More and more cars parked on the side of the highway. Couldn't get explanations on the radio. Gas stations taking cash only, restaurants out of food. Some biker gangs, some army trucks on the road."

"See many people with guns?"

"Oh, yes, lots of people with guns. Standing in front of

supermarkets and gas stations, ordinary houses too. It was like someone flicked a switch, and suddenly the world went psycho. It's, like, one minute everything's ordinary, and the next minute it goes crazy. Things got worse as the day went on and we were into Saskatchewan. I took the bypass around Regina, but even the trans-Canada pit stops were cash-only and guarded. Around Moose Jaw we passed a police car on fire. We saw quite a few houses burning in Medicine Hat, Lethbridge, Fort Macleod."

"By then, we knew something very bad was happening," Céline contributed.

"Pa, you remember the big trucker's stop just north of Macleod, on the highway to Calgary," Hardy said. "It was totally in flames, clouds of black smoke like a volcano, like a huge oil tanker had exploded. I was getting real worried by then, because we were low on gas. Thankfully, I found a little station on a back street in Brocket, run by a native guy, one of those discount places, because there's no tax on the reserves. He and a buddy stood guard while I filled up, didn't overcharge me, and they took my cash, God bless 'em."

"Then we arrived at Pincher Creek," said Pierre. "Hard to imagine it was only a couple of hours ago. Things were crazy in town. Several buildings on fire. We took side streets to get onto a back road heading south, but even then we heard a lot of gun shots."

"Did anyone shoot at you?" Jacobson asked.

The newcomers all shook their heads.

"We were protected," said Grandmère, making a sign of the cross on her chest. "The whole journey we pray much. The angels travel with us."

Jacobson stared at the ground by his feet. Looking up, he asked, "Are any more family coming, d'you know?"

Hardy said, "I called all the family across the country to see if anyone else was heading west in response to your letters. I'm afraid, Pa, they all said they wouldn't be coming. Maybe later this summer, they said. Maybe in the fall when the leaves change color and the bugs are bearable."

"And maybe never," said Jacobson, with a sad shake of his head. "Maybe it was one too many times."

"Times?" asked Uncle Amédée.

"The boy who cried wolf. Chicken Little and the sky is falling. Is that why they're not coming, Hardy?"

"Well . . ." the son replied and averted his eyes.

"But *you* came."

"Uh-huh, we came."

Grandmère wheeled herself closer to Jacobson and put a little hand on his arm. "Big Joe, everyone loves you, those who come on this journey, those who stay at home. Do not be hurt in your heart."

"Oh, don't fuss about me. I got a hide like a rhinoceros."

"We, too, decide to stay home," she went on. "We discuss your letter greatly, many details, many sides to a picture. Pierre, of course, wishes to depart immediately. Amédée, who was once young, is also eager. Hardy and Céline are worrying very much; they say the journey will be too difficult for me, my wheelchair, my heart condition, the medications, you see. And I agree it is best I stay at home. I do not wish to burden them. I tell them, go, go see Big Joe, go see Luke. But they will not listen to me. They insist they remain in Montréal to look after me. They are *immeuble*, they are *pouvez pas les pousser*, you cannot push them to change their mind."

"I told them," Hardy said. "I told them, 'We are *not* going—*none* of us!'"

Jacobson peered at his son from under his lowered brow.

"You seem to be a long way from Montreal at the moment," he said.

"Ah, yes, it is so," said Grandmère. "Céline, *ma petite*, tell what happen next."

Céline said, "It is as my mother has told you. Hardy and I were immovable. The continent is very wide, and for an aging person, such a road trip would be an ordeal. We thought it too dangerous for her health."

"Then comes *le moment décisif*," said Uncle Amédée.

Céline continued. "*Maman* insisted we must not listen to our fears, but pray instead for a light to guide us. We desire only God's holy will, whatever it is, to stay or to go. She said we must climb the mountain of the Lord, which in our city is L'Oratoire Saint-Joseph, a place of many miracles, a fountain of graces that never runs dry. But of course we do not climb. *Maman* and I drive up the mountain in the car. Pierre comes with us. We go inside the Oratory to pray. We pray and pray, on our knees we are begging the Lord for light. Then Pierre has a little gasp of his breath. He tells us he is having . . . *une vision*. He whispers, *I see it, I see it, I see it with the eyes of my soul—mon âme, mon esprit—but also I see it with my own eyes*. Pierre is looking at the Blessed Sacrament, and his eyes are wide, tears are coming down his cheeks. I tell you truly, never have I seen my son like this. I ask him, 'What vision do you see?'

"He answers, 'The world is on fire . . . love is not loved . . . hatred spreads . . . souls are falling, falling, falling *aux feux éternels de l'enfer*.'"

With wet eyes, Hardy broke into the narrative: "Falling into hell."

"Then Pierre's tears cease flowing, he closes his eyes. He is very still, his face becomes beautiful, his whole body is quiet. There is an enormous peace in him, and it fills us also, *Maman* and me. Then comes the Mass and Holy Communion. More peace. And then we depart, because I must make supper for Hardy.

"We drive down the mountain to *chez nous*, our home. Not a word have we said since the vision. Nothing. Just peace. We come to our home, I open the door, and there stands Hardy in the hall. Before I say a word, he looks at me and he says, 'We are going. All of us'."

"I didn't have a vision," Hardy explained. "Nothing like that. I was just praying my rosary while they were up on the mountain. By the end of the prayers, I had peace inside me like I never felt before, and I knew. I knew without a shadow of a doubt that we were going."

"And here you are," said Jacobson.

"And here we are!" the visitors declared with smiles.

"We tried to convince Grandmère and Amédée to fly," said Hardy. "Told them we'd pick them up at Calgary airport. But, *nooo*, she dug her heels in, said she wanted to see the country from ground level, one last time."

"I can be stubborn," said the old woman with a playful smile.

Jacobson cleared his throat and shook himself like a wet bear.

"Okay, let's get you all inside. It's a hot day, and you must be hungry. I got plenty of beef stew. It's canned; hope you don't mind."

"*Magnifique*," said Céline.

"Memories," said Hardy in singsong.

"But who are all these dear people?" asked Grandmère, looking at the rest of us with keen interest.

Rafe, Richard, and I stepped forward to introduce ourselves. Our wives emerged from the station and joined us, hand in hand with a few of the children. Fr. Peter, humble as ever, held back until it was his turn. Introductions were still in process when Farley's SUV drove into the yard.

The four boys jumped out, red faced and elated, glowing with the satisfaction of mature men who have just completed a daring task. Farley stepped down from his cab with his usual slow intentionality.

"Any problems?" Jacobson asked him.

"It was good," replied Farley with a summary nod.

"No bandits?"

"Nope."

"Luke on the way?"

"Yup. He's bringing the horse."

"Well, it's gettin' on suppertime. Let's find some grub."

We were all inside the station's main room, eating more beef stew and getting acquainted when from the direction of the open front door came the sound of hoofbeats approaching at a trot.

I got up and went out onto the porch, in time to see Luke slide off the saddle with a happy, winded look. He tethered the horse to a newel-post and bounded up the steps.

"Great job, Luke," I said. "There's a family reunion inside, and supper's on the table."

"*Out . . . standing*! On two counts, yeah!" He grinned and went inside.

I lingered on the porch, examining the sky. A glance at my wristwatch confirmed the time—around 5 P.M. That meant approximately five more hours before sunset, and we needed to do a lot before the light faded. In addition, the mountains would block a portion of the sky, and we might find ourselves groping around in the dusk.

I found Annie talking with Rafe, who was keeping little Babby occupied by bouncing him on his knees. A detectable odor still hung about them both.

Addressing my wife and friend, I raised my concern about

the dwindling time, how we needed to set up a camp before nightfall. They agreed that we should get started as soon as possible. Rafe handed Babby off to Annie and left in order to get the Bluebird from the wrecker's yard. I went around the room, gathering our people. In the meantime, Jacobson, his son and two grandsons went off to various storage sheds to find the HBC tents and the army tent, plus additional blankets and sleeping bags. Fr. Peter, Richard, and the oldest teens went with them to give what assistance they could, Son among them. I was pleased to see his continuing progress.

They were still hunting when Rafe parked the Bluebird by the front steps. He retrieved a power drill and wrenches from the rear of his own van, then opened the back doors of the school bus. I jumped up to help him. We unbolted the passenger seats one by one and tossed them out. Finally Jacobson and company arrived bearing heavy loads, including three white canvas carry bags and a longer, olive-green bag containing the army tent. In addition to these were half a dozen folded camp cots. After we packed everything into the bus, I checked my watch again. A quarter past six. Time to get going.

When everyone had been gathered outside, Jacobson asked Rafe, "You need me to show you the place?"

"No, we'll be fine," said Rafe.

"Good, because I ain't going with you. I got my hands full settling my own family here at the station. You've all got your heads screwed on straight, so just figure it out when you get there. Luke, you go with them just in case."

"You bet, Grandpa."

Jacobson handed me a tarnished Yale key. "This'll get you into the cabin."

"Thanks, Joe," I said. He didn't acknowledge my sudden

switch to familiarity other than to hold my eye a few seconds longer before turning away and addressing the others gathered by the cars.

"That cabin's got enough space for the newlyweds here, and maybe for two or three more. But there's not much room on the hill for tents, and none for these big camp tents we packed into the bus. If you're going to put up a tent city for the rest of you, do it on the flat land down by the river, but not on the open meadow. Set 'em up under thick tree cover. Evergreen, not leafy. There's no way of telling how long you're going to be there. Maybe a couple of weeks, maybe a lifetime. I'd bet my last worthless dollar it's going to be a lifetime."

No one responded to that. The conspiracy theorist was back again—albeit a generous one. Like me, the others were probably considering the possibility that he might be right.

Jacobson continued, "Poplar, birch, cottonwood go naked soon as fall arrives, and then if any locusts from hell start flying over the hills looking for folks who escaped their jaws, they'll spot you. Those HBC tents are white, easy to see from the air. So, you'll need to go deep cover, cut lotsa spruce to lay over the tent roofs. Park your cars out of sight; you can drive into the trees on a couple of bush trails back there."

"Good advice," said Rafe with a nod. "Luke can show us how to find them."

"Take the road real slow, all of you. Walking pace only, or I'll be forced to pick up more of your cars with the tow truck."

After a brief discussion, it was decided that Farley would go first, with Luke as his navigator. Then would come Richard driving the Lyons' vehicle, followed by Cora driving the Morrows'. Bringing up the rear, the school bus would be driven by Rafe, with me as copilot.

"Okay, you better get going," said Jacobson. "You've got a few more hours of daylight, but night comes faster than you'd think."

We all began climbing into our vehicles.

"Come back any time," he said. "Get rations from the larder whenever you need." After a pause and a wave, his parting words were, "Good luck. God bless you."

Off went the leading cars. With Rafe at the wheel of the bus, we chugged on after them. I glanced at the speedometer. The vehicles in front were maintaining a steady pace of five miles per hour.

"If I recall correctly, it's nine miles to the river," I said.

"Sounds right," said Rafe, keeping his eyes fixed on the road ahead, swerving now and then to avoid the larger potholes.

The land through which we traveled was flat, the route occasionally winding around ponds and swamps and bordered by forest crowding close on both sides, mainly jack pine and spruce interspersed with light green stands of deciduous trees. Shortly after leaving the station, there appeared on the left a collapsing barn and a fenced field with grazing sheep—the Jacobsons' farm of dubious legality. There were few other signs of human habitation along the way, some broken rail fencing, a couple of abandoned ranch buildings with roofs caved in, their rangeland reverting to scrub brush and encroached by new-growth woods. It was a dismal sight.

Though I could see that Rafe was concentrating on keeping the bus from mishap, I broke the silence, hoping to make our slow progress pass more quickly.

"You've been preternaturally calm through all of this," I said. "I'm really impressed."

I *was* impressed, but too late I realized that my tone had sounded patronizing.

Without taking his eyes from the road, Rafe tilted his head pensively, smiled his almost-smile, and replied in perfect imitation of my tone:

"I'm really impressed by your own preternatural calm . . . despite a couple of near misses. I was glad to see how you valiantly overcame yourself before anyone noticed."

"Obviously you noticed." I shook my head, amazed once again by Rafe's sharp eyes and insight into people.

"We're all praying," he said. "Graces are flowing."

"True. I can feel it, Rafe. But some people have a greater reserve of natural confidence than others, and I think you won the lottery in that department."

"Do you?"

"We're a motley crew. Everyone's being brave. Farley with his stoic approach, Kateri serene and spiritual, the Lyons nervous but soldiering on, the college girls scared but doing their best to trust. Fr. Peter worried but relying on God. And Cora—well, Cora has you to rely on."

"And what about Annie?"

"I'll never plumb the depths of my dear lady. She's a phenomenon."

"Phenomenological," he said.

"Ontological."

"Metaphysical."

"Don't rule out the physical."

This made him smile.

"You're the philosopher," I said. "Tell me: If civilization is on the brink of self-destruction, do you think these terms will disappear altogether?"

"Hard to say. Let's keep exercising them and hope for the best."

A mile or two passed in silence. More bush, more swamps,

higher elevations rising to our right, towering cordilleras looming ahead.

"What about you, Rafe? Doesn't anything ever upset you?"

He met my eyes for a second, then turned his gaze back to the road.

"I feel shaken to the core of my being, Cleve," he said in a low voice, with a tone so calm it was entirely at odds with his words.

I said nothing, trying to comprehend what he was saying.

"We're twenty-five souls here," he continued in his thoughtful manner. "We all feel the need for reassurance, and for hope. But what is your and my part? How should *we*—you and I—react to the collapse of all securities?"

"You're saying we shouldn't show any signs of panic."

"Panic's infectious. So is confidence. The others need us to remain peaceful and steadfast. I can't afford to give in to my fears, my confusion."

It was hard for me to imagine Rafe ever being fearful and confused. He certainly didn't look it at the moment.

"So . . . what do we do?" I asked.

"We do the task that's put in front of us. One step at a time. Take responsibility without fanfare or other kinds of emotional noise. Meet each challenge as it comes. Do the duty of the moment. That is God's will for us."

"The duty of the moment," I murmured, beginning to understand.

He flashed a quick smile at me. "And next we have a city to build!"

20

AS DESCRIBED, THE ROAD ENDED AT A RIVER.

Luke and Farley made a circle left and drove the SUV along the riverbank through a grassy meadow speckled with white and purple clover. They parked a hundred feet from the road's end, and the rest of our vehicles came to a halt in the lead vehicle's tracks. Rafe parked the bus at the tail end of the chain, beside the rotted posts of the bridge that had once been the crossing to farms on the other side. There were no signs of these now, only copses of young trees, cottonwood and poplar, pale green with their June foliage, migrating toward the water's edge.

After disembarking, everyone made their way to the bank of the river. There was a ten-foot drop from the meadow to a shoreline of gravel and rounded stones, which rustled under the force of the racing current. The water was clear, tinted a blue hue that I thought must have come from a glacial source higher in the peaks to the west. Its span was no more than sixty feet from bank to bank, and its depth was not very great. It looked icy cold.

Insects hummed. Stellar jays raucously protested our presence. Smaller birds carved tangents in the air around us, twittering and warbling. Swallows darted low over the grass. A sharper cry caught my attention, and I looked up to see two eagles soaring high above us.

To our left, the east, a forest of evergreens bordered the meadow and stretched away into the south.

Luke cast a glance at the westering sun, which was now hovering above the highest peak.

"We should start setting up camp," he said. "Come on, I'll show you the way to the bush road."

The wall of dark forest looked impassable at first, but within minutes our pilot found a narrow opening into the trees at the end of the meadow. Driving at less than walking speed, Farley followed his directions, and within a hundred yards the brooding jack pines gave way to fat, jade-colored spruce. After these, the trail widened into a clearing full of waist-high grasses, wild rose, and low-bush cranberry. Beyond it, a patchwork of trembling aspen closed in.

Farley braked in the middle of the clearing and walked back to talk with Rafe and me.

"What do you think?" he asked.

"It's a good place," said Rafe, looking all around and up at the disk of sky above us.

"How far is the river?" I asked, wondering about water supply.

Luke pointed. Glints of reflected sunlight were visible at eye level. "Real close. The river loops around, so it's maybe a couple of minutes' stroll through the trees."

"Let's talk with the others," said Rafe, "and see what everyone thinks."

A consultation seemed unnecessary to me, because this site offered the best conditions we had found so far. Of course, the meadow by the old bridge would have been a preferable place to make camp, but it was too exposed to the threat of air surveillance.

Reflecting a little, I understood that Rafe was wise to respect the decisions of the others. A lesser man would have instinctively seized control, presuming upon his own leadership, driven by his ego or his secret insecurity. This, in turn, could have bred resentments and divisions among us. As I observed him talking with the adults who had gathered around, I realized that he was deferring to the right order in human affairs: The natural and spiritual authority over each family belonged with the head of the family, not with a dominant personality higher in a pecking order. A boss would impose order; a true leader would evoke it.

And Rafe was a true leader. Within minutes, all the husbands and wives were nodding their agreement.

The sun was perceptibly lower now. In short order, the four vehicles were driven into gaps between the trees and parked close to the clearing. Our bus lost paint on both its sides, but we wanted to make sure it would be as invisible as possible.

Unloading began.

The HBC tents came first, and then the heavy army tent. A platoon of young helpers assisted the men in erecting the white canvas huts under the trees. Lucy and Son threw themselves into the task, their faces revealing their earnest desire to be of use. Alice, Theresa, and Annie helped keep the littlest ones from running away and getting lost in the bush. Annie kept her eye on Babby especially, waddling after him as he careened about the clearing, piping his high-pitched squeals and burning off energy too long contained during the car ride. As I pounded tent pegs, I blew her a kiss.

Kateri commissioned the younger Lyons and Morrows to help her find stones to make a fire pit. Back and forth they went to the river's edge. The children displayed energetic enthusiasm for the work, and even Susan and Samuel Hearne wanted to do their part, still solemn but diligently carrying smaller stones. Indeed, everyone seemed to thrive on doing something constructive. Kateri supervised the fire pit's assembly, situating the ring in the center of the clearing. When that was done to her satisfaction, she led her little followers into the woods to gather twigs and dry moss, and any other kind of kindling they might come across.

Next, those who were able to assisted in erecting the army tent. Forty feet long, sixteen feet wide, it proved to be too large to fit between any bordering trees. We might have chopped down a few spruce to make space for it, but, after consultation, it was agreed by all that the massive shelter should stand in the clearing itself. If viewed from the air, its camouflage material would provide sufficient cover. With an abundance of willing hands, putting it up took an hour to accomplish, and by the time we were done, the sun was behind the peaks and dusk was settling over the compound.

From our combined resources, three hatchets and a single axe were gathered. However, it was now too dark to go hacking branches safely out of the surrounding trees for covering tents and car roofs. Thankfully, throughout the day there had been no sounds of aircraft, near or far. It was decided that the first task in the morning would be to make ourselves as invisible as possible.

Flashlights had appeared here and there; people were emptying their cars of luggage and discussing where they should put it, who would sleep where.

The Lyons claimed their dome tent and a smaller annex tent where Edmund and Gregory would sleep. The boys encouraged Son to bunk in with them, and he accepted gladly, their bond already developing through their shared adventure blocking the road earlier that afternoon. One of the Jacobson sleeping bags was located and stuffed inside their burrow.

The Morrows had one of the white huts, with their stretch van for family overflow. Alice and Theresa took another, with the three Hearnes under their care. Kateri and Farley had the third hut, and Lucy was invited to share it with them. She made no fuss and helped find sleeping bags for all of them.

This left Fr. Peter, who chose to stay with his one-man pup tent, which he put up beside the entrance to the army tent.

Kateri and her disciples got a fire going in the circle of stones, feeding it broken pieces of deadwood, making it grow. Soon its cheery flames were crackling and spreading incense.

I wondered about the wisdom of lighting a fire, which might be spotted by aircraft, but then I reconsidered. Our people had no physical need for the fire, but there was a more profound need in the mind and heart. There was symbolism in it, though analysis escaped me for the moment.

Young and old gathered around the growing bonfire.

"I'm hungry!" complained Susan Hearne.

"Me too!" said Penny Morrow and Elias Lyon.

Several of us went back to the vehicles to scrounge for the remains of our travel food. We were still rummaging in the dark when the sound of a motor came roaring from the direction of the bush trail, followed by the rise and dip of approaching headlights. The moment of alarm passed when we saw Jacobson's ATV enter the clearing. It stopped with a screech of brakes, the engine died, and Jacobson himself materialized, slowly maneuvering his body onto the ground with grunts and groans.

"Grandpa, what are you doing here?" yelled Luke. "How did you find us?"

"Find you, boy?" He pointed at the compressed grass. "You left tracks like a herd of bison."

"Great you could join us," said Rafe.

"Helluva long ride, but I broke the speed limit, such as it is. Near broke my back, but I wanted to get you some grub, seein' as how supper was a long time ago."

"That is so thoughtful of you," said Colleen.

"Ah, don't blame me. Old Grandmère and Céline, they made me do it. Threatened a revolt if I didn't obey. The old lady was holding out on me, too. She sent a box of her chocolate clares she forgot to tell me about."

"We had a very generous supper at your place, Mr. Jacobson," said Cora, "but the little ones are hungry again, so we really appreciate it."

"No problem. Look, I got a pot of the stew strapped on here. Some of it spilled along the way, but there's plenty left. It's still warm. A couple loaves of bread. A can of goat milk."

A chorus of thank-yous greeted this.

We unloaded the black, cast-iron soup pot he had strapped to the seat beside him as well as an old-fashioned, three-gallon milk can and a cardboard box full of bread loaves. A single pound of butter sat on top.

Jacobson extracted an oversize pocket watch from the bib of his overalls and peered at it. "It's gettin' late, after ten. I'm goin' home."

He got his body back onto the ATV and fired it up as Luke climbed in beside him. Without further ado, they made a three-point turn and roared away, chased by our waves and shouted good-byes.

After eating, everyone gathered by the campfire again. The warm light drew us and comforted us. Women sat on the grass with the younger children in their arms, a few of the little ones fast asleep. Theresa and Alice held Babby and Susan, who were lost to the world. Sam lay curled in fetal position beside them, sleeping lightly, from time to time whimpering in his troubled dreams.

Fr. Peter stepped forward and stood in our midst.

"We should pray," he said.

As heads were bowed, Fr. Peter lifted his voice, thanking God for guiding us all to this place, for protection along the way, for food and shelter, and, not least, for each other's company.

"We have entered the desert," he said in conclusion. "None of us knows how short or long our stay here will be, nor what additional trials we may face. But we are not alone. He is with us. We must not let our uncertainty about what lies ahead drag us into fear and despondency. When we begin to fear, we must look up and renew our trust in Him. *Sursum corda*, let us lift up our hearts."

Murmurs of *Amen, amen* arose from the gathering, and signs of the cross were made. Using a bottle of holy water, Fr. Peter sprinkled everyone in the names of the Holy Trinity, and then he walked around the clearing, blessing it all, including the brave little residences that had been erected in the trees.

Finally, he opened the entrance flaps of the army tent and went inside, still sprinkling holy water. When he came out again, he said:

"It's a great gift. A canvas wall divides the tent into two parts. We can use the front section for a kitchen or dining hall. There's plenty of room for storage as well. In the morning I'll make a chapel in the other section. We'll offer our first Mass there."

Faces brightened all around.

"The tent of meeting," said Rafe.

Fr. Peter flashed him an appreciative look. "A name with layers of meaning," he said.

Kateri, who had been tending the fire, rose to her feet and whispered into her nephew's ear. He listened with solemn attention and then nodded. Kateri went away to the Crow-shoes' car and returned shortly, bearing what looked like a large disk, three feet in diameter, with a wooden handle and covered with stretched animal hide. Painted on its surface was the image of a heart entwined with thorns and capped by a cross. In her other hand she held a wooden drumstick in the shape of an elongated cone.

She held the drum high and struck it once, listening to its resonating boom.

She struck it again. Then a third time.

In a pause, Kateri said in a low voice, "*Nitsínixki.*" After another drumbeat she said something that sounded like "Ah, sis-tee, ah!"

Farley, who was standing beside Annie and me, turned to us and explained:

"She says, 'I will sing.' It's a song she makes just now. She calls it *Aa, sisttsi, Aa!*, which means, 'Yes, little bird, yes!'"

Now increasing the pace of the drumbeats like the sound of a beating heart, Kateri began to sing. Her voice was high-pitched, with nasal pulsations on longer tones, a considerable rasp, and some melodious ornamentation.

Between each line of the lyrics, Farley translated for us as best he could.

Kateri sang:

Yes, little bird, yes!
Water pours from fractured mountains,
it flows into brooks and rivers,
it sleeps in pools and roars on seas.
but this good quenching is not what I come here to see.

I see the giant in his powerfulness
striding over the horizon's arc.
With a little bird in his hand enchained with thread,
he is the one enchained,
till hurling it up to set it free,
he is freed by its lifting wings.
Yes, little bird, yes!

The bird is blue as sky light,
its song's weaving is a sweet braid,
it turns to gold with each sun's rising,
and lays a balm upon my soul.
I raise my arms and rise to follow,
the chain that binds us sets us free.
Yes, little bird, yes!

On this old rock that my feet travel,
with this small bird in my hand,
it leaps from my fingers into sky-blue
and pulls me high above the land.
With earthbound waters far below me
I plunge into the waters above.
So together we may swim among the stars.
Yes, little bird, yes!

Water flows in brooks and rivers,
it sleeps in pools and roars on seas.
The Living Water pours not from fractured mountains,
but from the breast of the Beloved,
his hidden face I soon will see,
Aa, Aa, rising, rising, I soon will see!
Yes, little bird, yes!

Silence followed. All of us were moved, though the lyrics had been incomprehensible to most. I was moved, as well, by Lucy Medicine Stone, who at one point early in the song had come unobtrusively to Kateri's side. Clearly she had no difficulty understanding the words in the original language. She stamped her feet in rhythm with the drumbeat, and at every repetition of the refrain, she raised her voice and sang along with Kateri—*Aa, sisttsi, Aa!*

Now they both fell silent. Kateri's face remained lifted to the sky, her eyes still closed, still drumming, though the heartbeat was softer now. Lucy dipped her head and made a sign of the cross on her chest. Farley glanced at Annie and me, clearly stirred by his wife's song, though I could see by his uncertain expression and the tilt of his head that he wanted to offer a qualification.

"In *Siksikáí'powahsin*, our Blackfoot tongue, the words she sings are like music. Like flowing water. I tried to make the English rhyme, but it doesn't work right; it's too jumpy and doesn't much fit like poetry. I hope you got the meaning."

"I think we have the meaning, Farley," said Annie. "Thank you for it. It's beautiful."

"And true," I added.

Annie turned to me with tears in hers. "Your dream, Cleve."

"I know. It seemed so totally irrational at the time."

"We've just learned that it was *supra*-rational."

"Maybe the bluebird in my dream represented the Bluebird brand of school bus," I mused.

"I don't think so. It's a nice touch of the feather, but I believe your bluebird represented the Holy Spirit guiding us, bringing together people from different backgrounds, not united by origins or blood, but by . . ."

"United by the Precious Blood," said Farley, completing the thought. Annie and I nodded in agreement. Having finished her silent prayers, Kateri now opened her eyes and turned to us all.

"We are here," she said. "The Spirit has brought us to a place of safety. The Hidden Face looks upon us. He sees us. Always He sees us."

Fr. Peter Ahanu spoke up. He said:

"God prepares. He looked upon us in our weakness and began gently to touch us, each in his way. We did not understand. We wanted certainty. But instead of giving us certainty, he asked faith from us. Each of us followed a thread—blindly, in hope that it would lead us somewhere."

"And it surely has," I said. "Thanks be to God."

Others now stood and went to Kateri, thanking her, embracing her. Even Lucy received hugs from a few. Embarrassed, she looked away, though there was a shy smile on her face.

Annie gripped my arm. "Cleve, I need to sit down."

"Ayah, ayah!" exclaimed Farley. "Sorry, Annie, sorry! I'll drive you up to the cabin."

When she was settled into the back seat of the SUV, I climbed into the front with Farley.

"Is she bleeding?" he whispered to me.

"No, just tired. It's been quite a day, and she and the baby need rest."

"Okay, let's go then!"

We were about to depart when Richard and Colleen Lyon appeared at my window. When I powered it down, Colleen anxiously asked if Annie was all right. I reassured her and said that we were heading up the trail to my uncle's cabin, where we would spend the night.

"I think we should go with you," said Richard.

"All right. Hop in."

"No, I mean, we'll walk on ahead of you. If that lane is as bad as Jacobson implied, you could get into trouble—ditches and obstructions and all manner of disagreeable surprises. We'll be your spotters."

"Farley's SUV is pretty good for rugged terrain, Richard. We should be fine. I wouldn't want you to walk it; it's supposed to be a couple of miles, and how steep it'll be is hard to say. Also, it's getting late."

"Don't worry about late, Cleve," said Colleen. "We're night owls, and besides, we try to have a power walk before sleep every night, and we've missed it the past few days. We're getting sluggish."

"They might save us some grief, Cleve," Farley said.

"If you're sure," I said.

"We're sure," they replied with large optimistic smiles. I now noticed Edmund and Gregory standing behind them. Both of them carried hatchets. All of them carried flashlights.

"We've brought our torches, Mr. Longworth," the older boy declared.

"And we haven't walked in the Rockies yet, like Mum and Dad promised us," said the younger.

I laughed and said, "Okay. The more the merrier."

The Lyons walked on ahead of us through the bush trail, illuminated by our headlights. The boys swept the surrounding trees with their "torches", probably eager to see elk or deer. Ten minutes later, we were back on the road, idling with the nose of the vehicle pointing upward along the lane's wheel ruts.

"Ready?" I asked our scouts.

"Ready, ready, ready, ready" came the four replies.

Richard turned and faced the lane.

"*Per ardua surgo*," he declared. Colleen took his hand, and side by side they began the ascent. The boys followed behind at first, then the hero-veterans of the bridge forged ahead of their parents with energetic strides.

"The knights," said Colleen, and Richard smiled in acknowledgment.

With studied concentration, Farley drove on behind them. As the gradient steepened, there were a few bumps and a couple of hairpin turns, but nothing very hazardous. Along the way, Edmund cut down a few slender saplings growing on the center ridge between the ruts. His brother Gregory argued for equal rights and chopped down a few of his own. From time to time, Richard turned to look back at the car, giving the thumbs-up sign. Colleen gave a V for victory.

We were now definitely in foothill country. The lane dipped and rose, all the while climbing higher and higher. Finally, almost before we knew it, we arrived at our destination. The headlights picked out the shape of a log cabin with steep-pitched roof and gables, a covered porch, a row of stacked firewood beside the door, and two front windows. Its foundation was a slab of rock. The yard was very small, with only enough space for a car to turn around, and no real room for erecting tents—just as Jacobson had described it. The boys swept their flashlights this way and that, revealing that the cabin stood on a rise immediately surrounded on all sides by steep slopes and old bent evergreens that seemed to hover protectively.

The three of us got out of the car and joined the Lyons, who were expectantly waiting by the front steps. The air was growing chilly, though it was still perfumed with the scent of foliage baked in the day's heat. The ground underfoot was carpeted with red pine needles.

"Shall I carry you across the threshold?" I asked Annie.

"Better not, buddy."

The key opened the front door without a hitch, and we all went inside.

A switch by the door produced no electric light, but Richard spotted an oil lamp on a table next to it. Producing matches, he lit it. The boys went through the ground-floor rooms with their flashlights, searching for more. They returned with another lamp and a candle in a brass holder, which were promptly lit. As the interior glowed with the increased light, we saw that we were standing in a small living room, furnished with a sofa and two easy chairs, one facing a plate glass window. A sheepskin rug partially covered the bare plank floor. Shelves of books lined the walls.

Beyond this room was a kitchen with a wood-burning stove, a small table with two chairs, and a refrigerator with a propane tank hooked up to it. The fridge was empty, its door propped open. A third room was Uncle Dave's writing place, containing a cot, an office chair, and a dust-coated desk on which sat a computer and printer. On a shelf lay an unopened ream of letter paper, 500 sheets.

The last and largest room was a grungy-looking bedroom with a four-post bed, its mattress protected by a plastic sheet. I pulled it off, raising a cloud of dust and revealing a multicolored quilt and pillows. There was a crucifix on the wall above it; wooden rosary beads dangled from a bedpost. The only other furnishings were a dresser, another oil lamp, and a braided rug on the floor.

The decoration was austere: framed pictures of Dave's heroes—Chesterton, Tolkien, Cardinal Newman—and a photo of himself and my father as young men, arms around each other's shoulders, grinning as if all their lives ahead would surely be full of wonder and daring feats. Mountain peaks crowned the background, a strip of wild water in the foreground. They both lifted strings of the fish they had caught from the alpine river.

Two old men, one dead, one dying. From this late perspective, had it seemed to them that their lives had passed too swiftly? Too swift for full comprehension, too noisy for contemplation? Was this why my uncle had chosen such an isolated place for his final years, and my father his solitary bachelor's apartment?

My heart constricted with a sudden ache. Where are you, Dad?

This was followed by an inrush of additional anguish. Where were my brothers and sisters and their families? Where were Annie's? Why had my hardness of heart put up so many barriers during my years of unbelief? Why had I missed so many opportunities to love? Why had Dad left the cabin to me, the least worthy of his children?

Farley broke into the flood of confused emotions. "Well, Cleve, you made it. We'll leave you to your own devices now."

Annie and I walked the others out to the SUV. I thanked them all for being our pathfinders and told them I hoped to see them in the morning.

"I'll pick you up in plenty of time for Mass," said Farley.

"Or we'll send runners up to get you," said Richard with claps on his sons' backs.

"Dad, we'd have to carry Mrs. Longworth on a stretcher."

"I'll come get you by taxi," said Farley at his driest and drollest.

We wished each other good-night and God bless and then watched as the SUV made its difficult about-face for the return journey to the river. When the red tail lights disappeared, Annie and I went back inside.

I felt a desire to repeat the words we had spoken when we entered our little bungalow after our honeymoon.

We're home, Annie had said, a joyful light shining through her.

Something now kept me from saying it aloud. How long would this be our home? How long our temporary open-ended? Days, weeks, months?

This is not home, I thought. *This is shelter.*

The yearning for shelter had been with me since I was very young. It was not fear that impelled me then but rather the glee of a child playing at hide-and-seek. Now, the gratitude I felt for this place of refuge was not unmixed with worry for the safety of my wife and child. There was no glee in it, and I knew that the hide-and-seek could very well prove to be real.

While Annie unpacked our travel bag in the bedroom, I got a fire going in the kitchen stove, and another in a compact wood-burning heater in the living room. Its glass front allowed the flames to send dancing amber light around the pine-paneled walls.

After that, I went into Uncle Dave's office. The computer sat there waiting to spring to life, as computers always do, our loyal servants, our minders and conditioners. There was no awakening at the press of the *on* button, no response to my touch of the keyboard. Nor did any of the electric lights turn on. The desk drawer contained a collection of pens and pencils, USB thumb drives, and a single cell phone. The phone was dead, but I removed its battery nonetheless.

Desiring to investigate the solar panel and batteries, I used the tiny LED flashlight on my keychain to light my way outside. Around back of the cabin, I came upon the pole that supported the panel. Despite its cement foundation, it leaned askew, and the panel itself had been shattered by fallen tree branches.

"So long, twenty-first century," I said, shaking my head.

After opening the door of a shed attached to the pole, I scouted around inside, finding a few tools, including an axe, spade, and snow shovel. Also, two sacks of cement, one of them unopened. The solar batteries were tucked away in a corner with an insulated cable running into the ground. But the batteries were disconnected and probably dead.

The loss of the solar panel was a concern. More serious was the issue of water. And I wondered how long the community's gas supply would last, enabling our taxi rides up and down the hill? And what about oil for our lamps?

I returned to the cabin.

"Cleve to me," Annie called from the bedroom.

So I came to a bedside near her, and we smiled at each other. I noticed that she had unpacked the silver crucifix her parents had given us on our wedding day. Along with it she had brought the bronze heart with our names engraved on it, a gift from my father. She laid both of them on the bedside table. To this she added the book of Psalms that Rafe had given me shortly after my conversion.

I blew down the lamp chimney, and the flame went out. Stars began to crowd through the bedroom window.

We undressed, slid under the homely quilts, and pressed close together. I put the palm of my hand on her belly. A little knee or elbow pushed back.

"Hello," I said.

21

THOUGH I HAVE COME TO THE END of this narrative, I cannot fail to make a little addition about the events surrounding the arrival of our firstborn.

On a day some weeks after our first night at the cabin, I had spent the morning at the encampment by the river, as I did most days, helping the others to settle in. At that point, it was uncertain how long we would have to remain here, but we thought it prudent to prepare for an extended stay. Among other tasks, there was a great deal of firewood to be cut for the coming winter, and with a few other men I had been engaged in this during the past weeks.

By noontime I was bone weary, all my muscles aching. Our work team broke for lunch and headed to the campfire in the clearing. There, the ladies fed us warm stew they had cooked in a billy can on a tripod over the fire and unleavened bread baked in the coals. We ate our meal standing and in haste. It had become a habit to limit the time spent on cooking, as there was worry about the smoke being spotted. Our eyes constantly swept the sky, on the alert for helicopters. In the first weeks, we had seen three formations of them flying low over the forest to the south of us, but they did not veer in our direction. There was also concern about satellite surveillance in geostationary orbit over our region. There might also be orbiting satellites regularly passing overhead, but without instruments or a telescope to spot them, we couldn't know their tracks and schedules. Though Luke had removed all SIM cards from our vehicles, this was no guarantee of absolute invisibility. Our only hope was to keep out of sight as much as possible.

After lunch, I took a solitary walk through the trees bordering the river and sat down on the embankment.

It was soothing to listen to the rustling current, the faint chatter of water lapping the pebbled shore. Birds were rioting in the nearby woods, mingled with the voices of happy children at play. A soccer ball was being punted about the clearing. The sun beat down on my face.

I closed my eyes and prayed, thanking God for bringing us through the chaos, for providing a place of refuge. I begged him to keep all hostile eyes turned away from our little group of refugees. I prayed for Annie, whose due date was only two weeks away. Kateri and Lucy were now staying temporarily with us at the cabin, Kateri as midwife, Lucy as a runner in case labor commenced prematurely while I was away from home. I wanted to assist at the birth, and she would fetch me.

"Preserve us, Lord, preserve us in your kindness," I said aloud. "Do not let the lambs fall into the mouth of the beast!"

As I was praying thus, I felt all sounds slowly fading. I was not asleep, not even slipping into a light doze. I was fully conscious. Time seemed to dissolve as if I were suspended in an eternal present. I had never before felt anything like it, and yet its strangeness did not feel in any way strange. I was aware only of a surrounding stillness. Tears slid unbidden from my eyes. Soundless, consoling, it was the weeping neither of sadness nor of exultance.

Then a voice spoke to me. I heard it within my soul, but it came from outside of me, from beyond the realm of the senses.

Rise up now and enter the water, it said.

I rose to my feet, uncertain, but still at peace.

Enter the water and cross to the other side, the voice came again, a command or an invitation, it was not clear, though it spoke very gently.

I stepped into the water fully clothed, with my shoes on, wondering a little over my behavior, wondering if an angel or God himself was asking something of me, an obedience, an action that was beyond my comprehension but had meaning greater than it seemed. The water curled around my ankles, swift and cool. I waded in deeper, up to my knees, then my waist, and still farther into the current until my chest and neck were immersed. Then I began to swim, aiming for the farther bank.

In mid-river, I was pulled under by the current, my feet touched the stony bed, and I sprang upward, breaking the surface, propelling myself forward again. I reached the other shore, stumbled out, and sat down on the pebbles, catching my breath.

When I had rested a few moments, the voice came again.

Enter the water, it said.

I stood up and waded in, going step by step until the water reached my chin, and then I plunged, swimming underwater now.

Though puzzled, I remained without thoughts, sensing only the rightness of this irrational act of obedience. The peace continued. My head broke the surface, I reached the other shore and sat down on the beach.

When I had rested a little and my breathing eased, the voice came again.

Enter the water, it said.

Three times I crossed the river and back. On the third and final return, I was swimming underwater midway when I was suddenly enveloped in darkness. I could feel the surging current around me, knew my eyes were blinking rapidly, straining to see anything that would explain what was happening and would orient me to the distant shore. I was afraid, but not in panic.

And then something new was given.

It was not a spectacle for my eyes or ears, nor was it a dream like the bluebird that began the whole drama of our rescue. Swept along in the current, I was both submerged beneath the water and suspended above it. And in my soul's eye, I was praying with my arms lifted to the silent heavens and the watching lights of Paradise, the stars that I could not see with the eyes of the flesh. And I saw gates before me, but they were closed. I cried out to the presence behind those gates, *Open to me, please open to me!* But my pleading was met by silence.

As I floated, I felt absolutely alone, separated eternally from my loved ones and abandoned by God.

Do not leave me, do not leave me! I cried.

Then came a mighty roaring in my ears, and I was lifted up through many waters into the heavens above all heavens. I heard the chiming of countless small bells, I saw emerald lights flashing, and I heard a voice once more.

The Father is here, said the voice.

And I knew that the silence was not one of absence but one of Presence, and it was listening. Then this presence spoke, and words of a prayer entered into me like a living stream and out of me again as I offered it up with a cry:

You have called us out of darkness, O Lord, into your wonderful light. Nourish us unto eternal life!

The sound faded, I lowered my arms. Time resumed its flow. Was I awake, or was I asleep, or was I adrift in the realm between the two? Had I drowned, or was my body still alive? I opened my eyes and saw fish swimming past me. I saw the light of the sky above me.

I kicked, and my head broke the surface, my lungs gasping for air, my arms flailing as I swam against the current, striving for shore. I stumbled up onto the embankment, my heart pounding and tears running down my face.

I groped through the trees to the clearing, where I came upon Rafe and Richard sitting, talking by the campfire. When they saw me, they rose to their feet with worried looks. I collapsed onto my knees beside them.

"Cleve, you're soaking wet!" said Richard. "Did you fall into the river?"

I nodded but could not speak.

"What happened?" asked Rafe with a hand on my shoulder.

Minutes passed. I could not explain anything that happened, for I did not understand it myself.

"I think . . . I think . . . I was given a prayer that we all have to pray."

"What do you mean? Where did it happen?"

"Under the water. No, *above* the water. No, it was both—yes, it was both."

"You're shivering," said Richard and went off to find something warm to cover me. Rafe continued to stare at me with a reflective look. He said nothing. Richard returned and draped a blanket over my shoulders.

"I'm not sure if it was real," I whispered at last. "But I think it was."

"Real in a way that's not our usual understanding?" asked Rafe.

I nodded, still seeping soundless tears.

"Was it a vision?"

"I don't know what it was. I can't describe it, can't explain it. The only thing I know is that it was good. I didn't make it happen—I just obeyed and then—"

But I could not finish, because Lucy Medicine Stone ran into the clearing and shouted:

"Cleve, Cleve! Annie's in labor!"

I leaped up and ran. I ran faster than I had ever run in my life. I did not feel the distance and the steepness of the hill, nor the chill of my soaked clothing, nor the ache in my lungs, nor my drumming heart.

I was just in time for the delivery. I held my newborn son in my hands while Kateri knotted a thread around the umbilical cord and severed it with her pocket knife, and Annie gazed at me with her hand on my cheek, exhausted and flushed, her eyes shining.

"Hello," I said to our child, and I knew that he heard me, and I loved him.

"Your name is John," I breathed.

PART III
Legend

"All of these died in faith, not having received what was promised but seeing it and greeting it from afar, acknowledging that they were strangers and sojourners on the earth."

Hebrews 11:13

22

TIME, TIME, O SWIFT-FLOWING TIME!

Decades upon decades ago I completed the account of our "flight into solitudes", which I had provisionally titled *Letter to the Future*, a bulging great manuscript stacked nearly three inches high, now safely cached in the cave below the cabin. There was too much to tell, and I had never been one to stint on words—a lingering encumbrance from my erstwhile years, no doubt. In it, I had laboriously recounted a mere two days of our lives. They were significant days, to be sure, but the narrative had abruptly ended with Annie and me arriving at the cabin, with a short postscript describing the birth of our first child.

In writing it, I had been compelled by the hope that, despite everything that had happened, future generations of our community would one day read it. I wanted to explain, I wanted them to understand. Was there also a subconscious desire to self-exonerate or to acquit the guilt of my generation? This, of course, was impossible, as few were the souls who had been free from blame, fewer still who had been entirely innocent. Our civilization had turned its back on millennia of prophets and divine revelation sent to us and ended by rejecting our Savior himself. Instead, we had believed the lies and flattery of unseen powers and principalities operating through their human agents.

I had thought of our story as a torch hurled across an abyss in the hope that it would be caught, against all odds, by an open hand and an informed heart. It was my attempt to warn the children of the future about the consequences of self-deification. I wanted them to know how we were rescued—and, by implication, *why*. But my manuscript had not described the events that followed.

Annie and I brought seven children into the world, all of them endlessly surprising us with their unique characters and temperaments, their gifts and weaknesses. They made us laugh, and they made us cry, but always there was joy. My heart was at times broken by them in the places that needed to be broken, and healed by love for them, and by the love they gave in return.

As if they occurred only moments ago, I see again the births of each of our children. I see their eyes opening for the first time. I hear their first cries. I feel their tiny hands wrapping around my index finger. Then my mind swims, and I see the house crowded with small, rambunctious people overflowing with energy, full of tricks and delights. I remember how they strengthened me even as they eased my afflicted heart and pointed me toward the future. They taught me to die to myself each day, that I might be reborn each day.

They taught me, as well, to be a storyteller. No more dreaming of writing novels, no more angst-ridden editorials, no more regurgitative self-absorption. The bedtime stories I composed for them were about life's happy surprises and daring adventures, about drama and characterization and fun and frolic, about courage and kindness—about the wonder of being alive in a vast and marvelous universe.

First there was John, and then came Miriam, and after her came Talitha (one of our granddaughters is named after her), then Gordon (my father's given name), followed by

Colin (named for Annie's father), then David (named for my childless uncle), and finally Raphael.

Annie and I never had favorites, we loved them equally. She would say to them, "The heart is a palace with many rooms, and each room is larger on the inside than it is on the outside"—a riddle they loved but could not understand until they were older. And whenever a new baby was born, she would sing, patting her breasts, "Oh, oh, oh, I can feel it! My heart and daddy's heart just got bigger!" And I would thump my own chest enthusiastically, *boom, boom, boom.*

In their teen years, the children loved to tease me affectionately, with wit and whimsy. And I loved that kind of teasing. It was not uncommon for one them, Colin or Gordon or John, let's say, to pass by me carrying a log or an armload of firewood, whistling a tuneless melody and looking innocent. Without warning, they would shoot me a mischievous glance, muttering under their breath, *Boom, boom, boom.*

Their mother they adored, and rightly so. I did too.

I learned to be gentle in my instinctive firmness, as Annie learned to be firm in her gentleness. Each of our children inspired awe in me, and not one of them failed to engender the unspoken questions: *Who are you? Where have you come from? Who will you become?* I was often stunned by the awareness that there was a time when they had not existed. Now they were present, with active minds, vigorous bodies, and unique personalities written on their faces. They looked so different from each other. Each of them *was* different, a phenomenon, an incarnation of the limitless creativity of God.

Yes, now they were here.

I was a man alone, and who has given me all these?

From the vantage point of years blurring into years, decades melting into decades, it seemed to me that we had always lived this way, immersed in noisy love, and the past no more than a fading nightmare. Beyond counting were the times we had knelt together and prayed as a family, the times we had sat together and told stories, consumed our humble feasts, wept together and laughed together, joked and teased and comforted each other, and all the while Annie and I tried our best to pass down the truths of our Faith.

I am writing this on our cabin porch. John and I, with the help of Gordon and Colin, built it when John was eighteen years old and I was fifty. At my back, the Rocky Mountains rise from north to south, timeless and majestic, always stirring me with their singular beauty. The view in the other direction is moving in its own way: in the foreground the slope falls from the rock on which the cabin was built, through juniper bushes and pine saplings, then the foothills undulating lower and lower until they are banded by the Little Jordan River, and beyond it the beginning of the plains, and still farther, over the horizon, the burned lands. I have contemplated this view for most of my adult life, always alert to the possibility that some new calamity might arise out of the regions of darkness. Nothing has ever come since the holocaust, or the rebirth, as the young ones call it, they who were born into the world as we now know it. For them, the horrors of the past are the stuff of legend. For we old ones who lived through it, the past is still present. When the bottom has fallen out of your universe, it is hard not to fear that it could betray you again—and do so by surprise. The mind knows this will not happen, but the heart has its wounds.

As I mentioned at the beginning of this second, much shorter manuscript, I have decided to remedy the omissions of the first. Whereas the *Letter* mainly covered a period of a few days, this later writing must attempt to record piecemeal a multitude of events that spanned the half century that followed. Hopefully, the remaining sheets of this old letter paper, which, like me, have grown brittle and sallow with age, will be sufficient.

I will begin with the Great Mercy that fell upon mankind.

It happened in late summer, some weeks after John's birth, about three o'clock in the afternoon. We were scattered here and there, some at Jacobson's station, some at the encampment, Crowshoes fishing, Lyons unpacking books from the trailer, their boys and Son knocking the soccer ball around the clearing, Morrows preparing to cook the evening meal, Fr. Peter praying his Divine Office in the army tent, me cutting down trees, Annie nursing the baby in the cabin—all of us transfixed in the midst of our activities.

Without warning, an impenetrable darkness covered the sky. One moment we were in broad daylight, the next we were blind. Suddenly an immense cross of light appeared, a crucifix in fact, with even brighter rays of white light pulsating from the wounds of the body. The rays from the heart were red as well as white.

With this apparition came a grace that penetrated everyone who was alive at the time, an illumination that revealed to each of us the condition of our souls, the faults we habitually indulged, and the sins we had committed but had minimized and not repented of. Our flawed dispositions, our failures in love, the inner zones where we had been indifferent to one or more aspects of truth. Thus, in shock, and compelled by shame and grief, we fell to our knees, covering our faces. Then, the unimaginable Presence of the living God offered to each one of us the gift of his mercy. We accepted it, wept over it, and were changed forever.

It lasted an hour. Then the cross disappeared, the darkness drew back like a curtain, and the sun shone brightly in an empty sky. Every one of us, except the babies and very little children, made their way to the tent of meeting to find Fr. Peter. He heard confessions throughout the remainder of the day and long into the night. All those in the Jacobson party arrived the next morning, and they, too, made their confessions. Each person's spiritual state was different, but without exception we seemed to have been touched at the core. People were subdued, disinclined to discussion, trying to absorb what had happened, even as we continued to care for each other's practical needs.

None of us could now doubt that God existed. We were still free to accept or reject the Savior whom the Father had sent to redeem us, but there was a finality about our experience, for we knew we had been given a definitive grace. Over the following years and decades, we learned through the fragments of news filtering through to us that it had indeed been given everywhere—across the face of the entire earth, we believed.

Forty days after the illumination, the holocaust began. Once again it was three o'clock in the afternoon. The sky was open and deep blue. Without warning, a deafening roar filled the air all around us and shook us to the marrow. The earth trembled, the mountains seemed to quake, the forest swayed violently, and stars like fragments of burning planets appeared in the sky, and to our terror-struck minds they seemed to be raining down upon the earth. Roiling clouds, thicker than any ever before seen, black and purple and sickly bronze, engorged into monstrous thunderheads that rose higher and higher and then spread, convulsing in tortured mayhem above us, as lightning flashed unceasingly, thunder blasted like cannon fire, and a sound like mighty trumpets blared. Minute by minute the darkness deepened.

I ran up the hill to be with Annie and met her halfway as she stumbled down the lane with the baby in her arms. Together we ran to the encampment, where all our people were gathering in the hope of finding shelter. No one sought to hide in their own tents; they headed straight to the tent of meeting, and when all of us had been gathered inside, Fr. Peter zipped closed the front door and secured it. Quickly he tied down the window flaps, and then he lit candles and brought forth the Blessed Sacrament and asked us to kneel and pray. All of us did as he had bidden, save for the children, who fell asleep. Their sleep was mysterious, for the noise outside continued to be volcanic, wave after wave that vibrated the tent continually and shook it violently at times. Tidal waves of lurid red and orange light passed over us, so bright and horrid that even the thick canvas walls glowed like translucent parchment as each wave passed. There were waves of intense heat as well; they did not ignite the tent, but they increased our terror.

We were too stricken to voice our questions. Was it the end of the world? Had a nuclear war begun? And if it was the long-dreaded, long-delayed nuclear holocaust, would the missiles reach us, and if they did not hit us directly, would they send their solar heat and destruction sweeping across the planet? Would there be deadly fallout afterward?

Then the darkness fell. It became absolute. Inside our frail shelter, there was no light other than that of the beeswax candles. The flashlights would not work. For three days and nights we prayed unceasingly, and our priest led us in every prayer that was known to us, and he offered others, reciting aloud from his breviary and Bible. Over and over he recited the prayer of the three young men in the fiery furnace of Babylon, and the Psalms, and the rosary. He anointed all the walls and the doorway with holy water and blessed salt.

When voices began crying outside, sounding human, calling our names, pleading for us to open the door and permit them entrance, some among us believed that the people at Jacobson's place had come to find shelter, but Fr. Peter stood immovable before the doorway and would not allow it to be opened. When weaker ones pleaded with him to let those outside come in, he cried out with great force:

"Do not open the door! Do not open the windows! There are demons outside!"

With his crucifix upraised, he recited prayers of exorcism. The screeching became howling mixed with blasphemies. Little by little the hideous voices ceased, though the roaring thunder and raging wind continued.

On the morning after the third night, a calm descended. The tent ceased shaking, the rumbles receded into silence, and a natural light gently glowed through the seams in the tent walls.

Fr. Peter opened the doorway and peered out, his crucifix still upheld in his left hand and his right hand holding a bottle of holy water. After a pause to inspect what lay beyond, he stepped outside. Farley and Kateri followed close behind, carrying their rosaries. One by one, the rest of us followed.

The clearing was a shambles of torn branches, but on the whole it appeared to be unharmed. There were no signs of burning. The mountains were all in their places, monumental in their stillness, but their formerly white peaks were half melted, the remnant of snow and ice partly blackened. The sky was a sheet of leaden overcast. The nearby river was swollen with meltwater. Then birds began singing, uncertain and frail.

"The *Ksissta'pssi*, the Malevolent Spirit, is gone," Farley solemnly pronounced.

"We begin again, by the hand of *Á'pistotooki na*, our Creator," said Kateri.

"By the mercy of Jesus Christ," said Fr. Peter.

Then a light snow began to fall, sickly and gray.

For three years afterward, the pattern of the seasons seemed not only distressed but strangely unbalanced. The first winter came early and lasted seven months. The sky remained dark with an overcast so thick that we felt we were living in perpetual gloom. On the rare days when a hint of sun broke through the blanket, it was pale and distant, giving no heat. Whenever sunrises and sunsets were visible, they were colored with red and violet gashes, as if creation itself were bleeding. Falling snow had an oily texture, as did the rain when spring finally arrived in late April of the following year. As the snow melted away, it left a black film that smelled of burned chemicals, plastic, and rotting flesh. The wind, too, was tainted with a noxious smell for the longest time, as if the burning of forests had been combined with an inexhaustible supply of unnatural fuels. It was the stench of a burning civilization.

Joe Jacobson and the group of people at his place survived the holocaust. They had confined themselves to a windowless room, and, like us, they had blocked the door, had forced themselves to pay no heed to the screeching voices outside, and had prayed as they never had before.

The ladies sprinkled holy water they had brought from Montreal, anointed everyone with blessed oil from the Oratory, and frequently invoked the protection of the Mother of God and "St. Joseph the terror of demons." They drank a little water and ate nothing. Only blessed candles gave light.

In the years that followed, people tried to understand what had happened. Early discussions conjectured that we had survived a nuclear war, with ourselves on the fringe of multiple blast ranges. We had felt the effects of unthinkably powerful pulse waves of heat and light and pressure, though we had not been burned. While it was true that no initial sign of radiation sickness had appeared among us, surely we could not discount the threat of fallout. After all, had we not seen glimpses of plummeting missiles? Some among us thought that the "missiles" had been more like a rain of burning stars, perhaps fragments of a comet or asteroid breaking up in our atmosphere. It was also suggested that nature itself had revolted against us because of our sins. Others thought that God had directly sent a cleansing fire to rid the earth of evil. In the illumination, he had given a final grace, and the bulk of mankind had rejected it. He would not permit the culture of death to devour lives and corrupt innocence indefinitely, for to do so would not be mercy. But what about the demonic assault? Had Satan unleashed a diabolic holocaust as his ultimate stroke of hatred? Or had he tried to take advantage of the cleansing, raging because his time was short, lusting to take down as many souls as possible?

No matter how we considered it, the question remained: Was the holocaust of supernatural origins, purely natural, or simply man-made—or was it a combination of all three? No one knew.

Fr. Peter encouraged us to pray for light about the essential *meaning* of the events.

"It is understandable that we would instinctively seek to identify the source and the causality of the catastrophe," he said in his first homily after the events. "There is no harm in pondering these questions. However, they should not be our main concern. Regardless of the means God used, he has permitted it for the purification of mankind and the end of the reign of evil. The critical question before us is: How must we now live? How may we best reform our lives?"

The temperature that first winter was colder than any Joe Jacobson remembered. The river froze three feet deep, and we were forced to chip at the ice every day in order to keep a hole open for drinking water. The more vulnerable families with small children moved back to the service station for the duration, at Jacobson's invitation. He had two wood stoves and long rows of stacked firewood, hundreds of cords—not to mention the astounding larder. Alice and Theresa took the three little Hearnes to stay there for the winter, as did Cora with her girls, and Colleen with Elias, her youngest. Rather than overloading the already populous household, the majority of us chose to remain at the camp, to tough it out as best we could.

Luke loaned us the chainsaw, and this proved to be a lifesaver as it enabled the men to cut down a large number of trees for the firewood needed to keep us from freezing to death. By this time, the Jacobsons had no gasoline left at the station, but we had our vehicles with their gas tanks at least half full. The Morrows and Crowshoes had filled up at Fort Macleod, the Lyons at Lethbridge the day before, not knowing that within a few hours the world of certainties would end. My Toyota had been drained dry by Hardy and Luke in order to prolong the running of the station generator for a few days, but this last gasp of civilized comfort soon fell silent. The Bluebird produced a gallon and a half. From it and our other vehicles, we siphoned off every drop in order to keep the chainsaw going.

On his occasional visits, Luke sharpened the saw-teeth with his rat-tail files, cleaned the spark plug and oiled the machine, and helped with the endless porting of eight-foot lengths of tree trunks we cut down in the surrounding forest. He also constructed a sawhorse frame on which it was easier to buck up the poles into stove-lengths.

At first, the people at the encampment found solace in huddling around bonfires, but this was a grossly inefficient way of staying warm, especially when the deep winter fell upon us in October. Then Luke again came to the rescue. One day he and Pierre arrived by surprise, riding two of the family horses, breaking a trail through snow that was up to the animals' knees. Both horses were pulling travois poles on which were loaded a good deal of dried food, three pairs of snowshoes, and six sets of cross-country skis that had belonged to the Jacobson children before they left home years ago.

During that same week, Luke and Pierre made three more trips, thus improving the trail through the snow and, more importantly, bringing materials that would ensure the survival of the people who remained at the encampment: pots and pans for cooking, a wide-blade logger's axe, six bow saws still in their cellophane wrappers, and, most crucially, four lightweight wood-burning stoves, which were portable tin drums of the sort once used by trappers. They still had their fluorescent orange price tags gummed to their tops. Equally important, Joe had tossed in a few rusty stovepipes.

Our gratitude was boundless. Good ol' conspiracy Joe was turning out to be the patriarch Joseph in Egypt!

Prudently, just before the autumn's first blizzard, Farley, Rafe, Richard, Fr. Peter, and I had discussed the perils of the coming winter, to which our people would be exposed with only a little canvas to shield themselves. The decision was made to reposition the HBC tents as three sides of a square, with its fourth side the front wall and doorway of the army tent. This compound would provide additional protection from wind chill. Thankfully, the old HBC tents had been designed with a hole and thimble for stovepipes, and thus we installed the stoves within each of the "apartments", providing them with a heat source that would not be wasted. In addition, drawing on their own experiences, Farley and Fr. Peter insisted that we should cover all the outer walls and roofs of the compound with more layers of spruce and pine boughs. Though camouflage was now no longer necessary, the additional insulation could make the difference between life and death. More than that, they argued for embanking the whole with snow, as thick as we could pile it, because snow was a great insulator. Luke delivered shovels, and we went to work.

During that winter, Fr. Peter faithfully offered Mass in the chapel every day. On Sundays, he trekked the nine miles to Jacobson's, where he heard confessions and offered his second Mass. At first he walked there and back again, then he snowshoed for a time but came to prefer cross-country skis. Later, the Jacobsons convinced him to accept one of their horses, and from then on his Sundays were less arduous and time-consuming. True to his name, Goodrider, he became an excellent horseman.

The internal warmth, the strengthening and consolation we received from the Holy Eucharist was unlike any we had ever felt before. The shattering experiences of the holocaust would never fade from our minds, but little by little they found their place in a fundamentally altered architecture of memory, the true perspective of hope. The life now facing us, we presumed—we hoped—would be devoid of both spiritual and man-made terrors. The daunting challenges ahead were of the natural order. They would be hard, but they would be clean.

While the gasoline lasted, we employed the chainsaw in felling a large number of trees for the purpose of making log cabins the following year. For this project, Rafe's construction skills would stand us in good stead. My lesser skills would provide assistance. And though he lamented the absence of asphalt shingles, Farley thought that he could improvise roofing from tree bark and moss. Richard wanted to help too, and the esteemed professor seemed to thrive on becoming a manual laborer. He was never capable of heavy lifting, but his frame had its own sinewy toughness, which, combined with his analytical mind, made for a valuable addition to our work team. All of us grew stronger, though noticeably leaner, and even Farley was no longer overweight.

Thus we were making strides in providing shelter, heat, and sufficient food for survival. Our simple diet was augmented by Farley's hunting skills. With his shotgun, he took down geese in the early autumn and quail and partridge during the winter. He shot three deer during that first winter, using the .303 rifle he borrowed from Jacobson. He also snared rabbits and ground squirrels and made stews of them, seasoned with salt and sage. The back of the Bluebird bus became the community meat locker. When spring returned at last, Farley explored farther south along the river and a half mile from the encampment came upon a shallow ford.

He built a stone fish weir there and throughout the summer captured a good many brook trout and whitefish, and once an Arctic grayling. He hosted fish fries, and though doubtless all of us would have liked to devour every morsel of his catch, he patiently explained the necessity of preserving as much as possible in preparation for the coming of our second winter. He and Kateri constructed drying racks of sapling poles, on which the split fish bodies hung suspended like clothespins over a constantly smoldering willow fire. Later, we were grateful for their wise restraint.

By the second year, all gasoline and ammunition had run out. Hunting larger game demanded bows and arrows and spears. Firewood would be obtained with a bow saw, and future cabins would be crafted by axe.

One does not replace a vanished civilization. At best, we could attempt a reconstruction of small components or adaptations provided by the materials that came to hand.

Richard commented at one point: "Well, it looks like we've just been teleported back to the tenth century."

Rafe replied: "And unless we get busy, we're going to find ourselves in the Stone Age before long."

And so we got busy. Beyond price were the tools and amenities we had once taken for granted, had barely given a thought to in former times. Axes, shovels, saw blades, chisels, lighters, needles, thread—and, not least, artificial light. The batteries died in flashlights and cars. Jacobson had a few boxes of paraffin candles, which he liberally shared, but they were gone within a year and could not be replaced. At the station, the last can of kerosene kept a single pressure lamp radiating its harsh light throughout the worst of the winter months, and his oil lamps survived until the first spring. I estimated that my pack of butane lighters would stand us in good stead for four years, but after that, it would be essential to maintain a fire at all times, lest we be forced to rub sticks together in desperate hope of a spark.

Continuation of the sacraments was as crucial as any life-support materials—actually more so. Fr. Peter had brought on the journey a small amount of Communion hosts and a liter bottle of wine, but these did not last long. Grandmère and Céline industriously applied their baking skills to producing hosts from the rather large amount of flour Jacobson had stored. Wine, however, was beyond anyone's ability to produce.

I recall the Sunday in December when I skied with Fr. Peter the nine-mile hike to the station, where he intended to offer his second Mass of the day. Farley had sighted a gray wolf prowling along the road the day before, and I thought it best to accompany our priest as his armed guard. I brought Farley's shotgun with me, loaded with the last remaining shell. Fr. Peter carried a hatchet. We saw wolf tracks in the snow, but nothing of the animal that had made them.

Fr. Peter prepared for Mass in the main room of the emporium, setting his chalice, paten, Bible, standing crucifix, and candles on the table that was his makeshift altar. The potbelly stove roared beside him, its superheated top plates glowing orange. Before the opening prayer, he apologetically held up the wine bottle, showing everyone that less than an inch of wine remained. From the beginning of our exile until now, he had taken the precaution of using only a few drops of wine in his chalice, hoping to prolong the time in which it would be possible to offer the Sacrifice validly.

"I've got something might help you with that," said Joe diffidently. He spoke in such a subdued voice we didn't at first understand what he said. He had changed since the illumination; he was a quieter, humbler man, and, to his own embarrassment, given to tears at inopportune moments. He shuffled off to his living quarters, and when he returned he was pushing a cardboard box with his carpet slippers, sliding it across the floor toward Fr. Peter.

"Just remembered these," he murmured. "Stored 'em in my bedroom closet years ago, after Dora died. Had to hop on the wagon, or it was belly-up the way I was going. Anyway, here's ten bottles of homemade mare-lot."

"*Merlot*," Luke corrected.

Surprised by the appearance of exactly what we needed, feeling a bit literary, too, I said, "Whew, *Deus ex machina* or what!"

Fr. Peter looked at me and said, "*Deus ex pane et vino*."

After Mass, we gathered around the stove, drinking black tea tempered with goat milk (Jacobson had a stash of ten pounds of Ceylon tea). Colleen announced that she had just thought of something that might be of help. Without explaining, she ran off to the bedroom in which she and Elias were staying and returned with a look of triumph.

"I'd forgotten all about these," she said, holding in her hand a lump of something desiccated, possibly organic. "Last summer when we were driving from Winnipeg, I bought a bunch of grapes for the trip. I'd packed so much snack food we didn't eat it all. Well, these have been sitting in the bottom of my tote bag ever since, drying out."

"Raisins!" said Elias, peering at the pebble-like things in her hand.

"Seeds, actually," said his mother. She laughed. "I can remember how irritated I was when I discovered they weren't the seedless variety."

"Can I have some, Mum?"

"Hands off, dear. These could be the origins of a giant vineyard."

"Hmm, a long shot," said Joe with a frown. "This ain't Italy."

"No, of course not, but with some tender loving care, they just might sprout. They're vines after all, and vines are tough survivors. Let me give it a try."

To make a long story a little shorter:

"Can I help you?" asked Luke. "I have a degree in botany—plant physiology, genetics . . ."

Twelve terra cotta pots were filled with thawed soil and set on a table before the station's front window, where there was the most light. Under Colleen and Luke's watchful ministrations, the raisins were thoroughly soaked and then planted. They were kept warm, they were watered, they were coddled and anguished over, and within a few months they sprouted. In the spring, Hardy and Luke decided to build a greenhouse attached to the front of the building. Joe directed them to a stack of old sash windows he had stored in the Quonset hut, and with these and other glass scavenged from around the property (including windshields from the wrecker's yard), they crafted an effective nursery for the precious seedlings.

There was little direct sunshine during the first three years after the darkness, but it gradually increased, and the fourth summer was blessed with wide-open skies and a glorious sun that gave unusual warmth. The seedlings struggled to survive at first, but as the sun waxed ever bolder, they took hold and began to thrive. With careful pruning, the vines grew and grew and were eventually transplanted to prepared ground with southern exposure, on the hillside above the wrecker's yard. Because of the climate, they remained vulnerable to frost, and deep freezes could kill them, so as winter approached each year, the vines were heaped with hay and covered with plastic sheets.

The first harvest occurred in August of our fourth year, producing a few quarts of purple-black grapes of an unknown variety. They were not large, but they had a certain sweetness combined with a woody flavor. These in turn were planted and babied until the following year. The harvest increased after that, and by the sixth year produced twelve baskets full. The vineyard spread, and Luke and Pierre perfected the art of wine-making.

I cannot forget the reinvention of artificial light, if I may put it that way. Most of Joe's sheep flock had survived the first winter, and in spring a few lambs were born—not as many as usual, but a hopeful sign. That autumn he slaughtered a number of the older animals, distributed meat and hides to all the families, and encouraged them to eat as much animal fat as they could. Fat, he said, would become increasingly important, as our bodies now had greater need of it, due to our physical labors and the degree of exposure we suffered in this cold climate. Indeed, people were ever hungry for fat.

Nevertheless, it was by singular inspiration that young James Lyon had an idea. As he explained to a gathering of adults one day, while they were cutting up a carcass, the sheep fat could be used as fuel for lamps—a special kind of lamp. He had seen a documentary once about the life and culture of the Inuit people in the far north. For thousands of years they had burned seal oil in a shallow stone basin shaped like a half-moon, with a ridge for carrying a wick. The wick looked like a twist of white yarn. Maybe it was wild tundra cotton. He and his brother Gregory had explored the region around the encampment and had noticed a kind of bog cotton in the wetlands. Maybe it could be used.

Throughout that first summer after the darkness, the boys spent all their free time chipping away at half-moon slabs of stone, chiseling them into the shape of shallow basins. With trial and error, and plenty of finger cuts, they persevered until they were satisfied with their basic creation. Then they rendered down sheep fat that mothers gave them, creating a kind of lard and, from this, a liquified oil. Experimenting with wicks, they eventually succeeded in producing a crude lamp that functioned adequately. Pushing onward, they perfected a method of further refining the sheep oil, and the results were used as fuel for the old chimney lamps. Its flames were smoky and of low luminosity, but they gladdened the heart. If medals could have been awarded, James and Gregory would have scooped them all that year. It would be another decade before the community reached the stage of domesticating wild bees, the harvesting of honey, and the processing of wax for candle making. Until then the boys were our local heroes. They beamed with the pleasure of their achievement and the community's praises, and it spurred them on to further inventions.

Not all their inventiveness was purely practical. Even now I cannot help but smile whenever I recall the Lyon boys kicking their soccer ball around the meadow that first summer, their shouts of triumph when a goal was scored, their laughter, the way they recruited Son to join the game, their father coaching, running along the sidelines and blowing a whistle that Farley whittled for him out of an aspen shaft.

The soccer ball lost its air over the following winter and was no longer inflatable. Edmund and Gregory spent hours making a replacement from sheep hide, cutting the pieces and stitching them together by the light of their stone lamp, filling the cavity with loose wool. When it was completed, they waded thigh-deep into the snow in the clearing and launched a game. Exercising tremendous energy, they forced their way back and forth across the open space, using foreheads and knees and elbows to propel the ball, not without attempts to use their feet for kicking, though this almost always resulted in backwards sprawls and uproarious laughter. The rules of the game were fluid. They called it "snow-footy."

Yes, in this and a thousand other ways, we moved forward, slowly crawling out of the physical and psychological traumas that could so easily have crippled us, driven us into dismay and despair, to apathy and eventual extinction.

How did we resist the suction of hopelessness? It was grace, of course, that strengthened us and inspired ingenuity. It directed us into the future, enabling mutual dependence to grow among us all—and, in time, a profound mutual gratitude for each other. Though the darkness had passed, we did not at first understand the full reality of our liberation. The shadow of former times lingered, in the sense that we did not yet know for certain that it was gone forever, or at least for the duration of our lives. In low moments of extreme fatigue, the old fears tended to resurface: Would vestiges of the evil era return? Would its agents find us in the end? Though these worries nagged at times, for the most part we did not dwell on them overmuch because we were faced with the immediate tasks of caring for those who were more vulnerable than ourselves. They needed us to remain confident and strong. The duty of the moment, as Rafe had called it. God's will.

23

I AM VERY OLD AS I WRITE THESE FINAL NOTES. I am now in my mid-eighties. Looking back across more than fifty years since the catastrophe, I face a nearly impossible task, considering the short time left to me and the rapidly dwindling sheets of paper I once desperately hoarded. I am seeing images, fragments, scenes that stretch and contract, faces appearing in a glow of light and then receding from the foreground as they are succeeded by others, all of them beloved. Children becoming adults, adults maturing, and through them new souls coming into the world, destined for eternity. We knew then, and we know now, that each of us must do his part to carry the children into the future without fear. It is our duty and our joy to carry them.

The demons have vanished from the earth. Satan is enchained in the pit, and we pray earnestly that he will never again escape from it. Mankind has been given a day of rest, and it is our hope that this day will be as a thousand years.

It would be misleading to give the impression that this present era of grace is without ongoing hardships; nor does it lack the abiding challenge to resist the disordered impulses of our fallen natures. For us older ones, resistance is easier now in the absence of the constant barrage of temptations we once dealt with. It is easier still for those who were born after the tribulations, for grace and a radically purified environment have enabled them to choose the good more freely. Squabbles and disagreements arise at times, quickly resolved; occasionally resentments of short duration will fester, but these leave no lasting marks. Now and then, one sees evidence of venial sin, but it is always followed by genuine repentance, never brought about through shaming or shunning by others, and unfailingly accompanied by mercy. Of mortal sin I have seen no sign whatsoever. Nevertheless, our humanity remains with us all. God never pushes our nature aside, but seeks instead to ennoble and perfect it.

For the sake of avoiding confusion—and my tendency to leap back and forth across time—I will roughly divide the post-holocaust period into three stages: the early years, the middle years, and the recent years. These correspond approximately to the generations that came to us like phenomena, like the miracles they are.

From the day we arrived, Annie and I lived in our cabin up the hill. For the rest of our lives, we walked to and from the cluster of cabins by the river—which little by little expanded into a village—and we hardly noticed that the distance seemed to shrink the more we traveled it. We grew stronger with all that walking and with the constant breathing of purest air. I should qualify this by saying that the air gradually improved throughout the first three years, and only by the fourth year had the seasons corrected themselves and the skies become clear. In wintertime, I snowshoed down to the village and back, keeping the trail open. During her pregnancies, Annie seldom ventured forth from the cabin, except to attend Sunday Mass. I crafted a sledge on which I pulled her and the babies, learning to go downhill without letting it plummet out of control and hauling it back home with slow, arduous effort.

From time to time, people fell critically ill or suffered broken bones and needed constant nursing. Whenever this happened, we used one of our bedrooms as a temporary hospital ward, our children sleeping for the duration in the living room like a pile of puppies. Even before I met her, Annie's medical skills had been more developed than that of an ordinary nurse, and now her knowledge continued to increase. She became a kind of paramedic to the community and, on occasion, a surgeon—a task that filled her with trepidation but challenged her to pray more than ever. Kateri Crowshoe was often her assistant, and, as the years went on, Lucy helped too. These ladies never lost a patient. They were midwives at the births of dozens of children.

Luke Jacobson and Theresa were married the year after the darkness fell. For a time they lived in the bunkhouse behind Jacobson's service station, a residence more comfortable than the dwellings of our people who lived by the river. However, after they adopted the Hearne children, the survivors of the Burnt Café, they decided to make a home in our settlement where the children would have playmates and a larger community to help raise them. Luke and Rafe and I constructed their first log home.

Coping with the ongoing effects of the orphans' trauma demanded much patience and wisdom. Babby was always a jolly little fellow, and he became a jolly man, who later married our daughter Miriam. They parented nine of our grandchildren, who now number thirty-eight.

Susan Hearne was ever a thoughtful girl and a loving mother, for she married Elias Lyon, with whom she had seven children. She became an accomplished weaver and also instructed many a young girl in the knitting of intricate, decorative patterns for mittens, scarves, and sweaters. Despite the tragedy of her origins, she was a very happy person and throughout her life she spread that happiness to everyone who knew her.

Samuel Hearne, however, had a more difficult time growing up. He was prone to nightmares and screaming fits during his childhood; and then to rebellion during his adolescence. I understood him better than most people did, remembering my own rampant will when I was young. When he and his siblings were conditionally baptized, Luke and Theresa asked me to be his godfather.

Sam and I often went hunting together during his teen years. With painstaking effort, with trial and error, he and I constructed two crossbows, which were our pride and joy. We never spoke together about what happened to his family. By nature or by temperament, he eschewed conversation, though it was plain to see that he found solace in the companionship of our sorties into the wilderness and great pleasure in taking down game to bring back to families in the village.

He and his brother and sister were victims of a darkness so deep it defies explanation—the mystery of iniquity, Fr. Peter called it. How could we describe to their innocent minds the horror that had ended their parents' lives, for to do so with any accuracy would have increased the damage. Yet we had to explain their absence. Annie was very good at this. At the appropriate time for each of the children, she and Luke and Theresa worked as a team to explain to them that their parents had died of a "sickness of those days." This was true. Yes, the sickness that had destroyed millions of lives, the lightless vortex of delusion that attempted to solve the human condition by murder in various manifestations.

At a profound level, trust had been broken in Sam's young heart, for into his early twenties he suffered intermittent feelings of terror and abandonment whenever he recalled that fatal day at the Burnt Café. He had seen very little of the events, and nothing of the murder itself, but he had absorbed enough to realize eventually that "sickness" was an inadequate explanation. Fr. Peter would sometimes pray over him and anoint his head with oil, and over the years the boy received a good measure of healing from this.

Little by little, maturity took hold. He loved to be the provider, the rescuer. Always willing to take on the hardest community tasks, it was he who initiated the plan to make a dam across the river at the place where the old bridge once stood. The river was narrowest there, the water racing through with great force. Above this channel, the embankments drew apart, offering the potential for a broad catchment basin which, when filled, would be a deep reservoir.

Three years of Sam's life were spent hauling stones to make the dam. And when that was done to his satisfaction, he ingeniously designed a sluiceway that would one day turn the waterwheel, the hand-carved gears, and the grinding stones of a grist mill. Later, after he and Lucy were married, he became designer and builder of the mill and miller for life. This was in the middle years, and by then our people had long been hacking back the saplings that had invaded the rich soil on the far side of the river. Acre by acre, the land was being restored to grain fields, pastures, and the cultivation of other crops. In our northern climate, root vegetables prospered, and potatoes especially became one of the major sources of food. Above all, grains were the staple most needed, for the making of our bread and as supplementary feed for our livestock.

I should add that, shortly after completion of the dam, Sam and Son plotted the building of a bridge across the narrows and galvanized a work crew that completed it within a month. I think it was also these two lads who first called the river the Little Jordan, a name which quickly caught on and became permanent.

Though Son was seven years older than Sam, they grew to be as brothers, forging a working relationship, and later a close friendship, that bore fruit in numerous benefits to the community. When the first cabins were built in the early years, the fireplaces and chimneys were inexpertly raised and clumsily mortared, but as Sam and Son's expertise with stone developed, they offered to take over the task. The majority of our chimneys were built by them and, to this day, are the most durable and the best for drawing smoke.

In the early years, Son had his own internal turmoil to deal with, but after his baptism at age fifteen, his inherently resilient character steadily emerged. Self-sacrificing and generous, he was content to leave his troubled past behind as he looked toward the future with quiet dedication to the needs of others. He chose *Martin* as his baptismal name, in memory of St. Martin de Porres, a great saint who had been born out of wedlock. He also eventually revealed his surname, Levinson, which was his mother's, for she had been a single parent. Thereafter he was usually called Martin by most people in our community, though many continued to call him Son, especially those who had strong maternal or paternal feelings for him, like Annie and me. The boy was at ease with both names.

His healing came more swiftly than Sam's, but they understood each other very well. He was stricken with infatuation for a number of young women, Lucy at first (before Sam claimed her heart), then the Lyons' daughter Clare, though these affections came to nothing. In the same year that Sam married Lucy, Son and Rose Morrow fell headlong into a great love that has lasted to this day. They remain the doting, inseparable parents of eight and the grandparents of thirty-five. I believe I recently heard that the Levinsons are soon to become great-grandparents. Their farm and their family grow and grow.

Farley and Kateri? Oh, what can I possibly say about those extraordinary people! I came to love them so dearly that I grieved over their passing more than I had over that of my own parents. Farley lived for fifteen years after the catastrophe, before dying of heart ailments. Kateri died seven years later. Early on, Farley built a sturdy log cabin close to the river, in a patch he had hewn out of the spruce trees south of the original clearing. The days of explosive ammunition were long gone, but he made himself a mighty bow and long-shafted arrows, and during the years remaining to him he brought down many deer, five black bears (thankfully no grizzlies prowled our environs), and a single moose. Every autumn Kateri made pemmican and venison sausage, which she cured over willow embers in the smokehouse that Farley built for her. Much of it she gave away as Christmas gifts to everyone in the village, which people were now calling *Sursum Corda*.

As he had been in former times, Rafe remained "crazy" about their venison sausage. And we all were crazy about Farley and Kateri, whom we not only loved but revered. Both of them were givers who never hung on to price tags, not even emotional ones. Neither of them had a hysterical bone in their bodies. They were ever ready to comfort others and never sought human comfort for themselves. It was surely a suffering for them to be parted from their family, though they never spoke of the absent ones. This was a grief we all went through, for not a soul among us could forget that out there in the darkness where the holocaust had fallen hard, many people we loved were missing, their fates unknown to us.

Of course, the Crowshoes had their nephew Fr. Peter, whom in light-hearted celebrations they called *Ahanu*, Laughing One. Indeed, our self-effacing pastor did slowly reveal his sense of humor, which was as unobtrusive, as droll as his uncle's. A few times a year, Kateri would bring out her drum on festive occasions, around bonfires in summer or in the community longhouse during winter. The longhouse had replaced the army tent that wore out and blew away on the wind, bit by bit over time. She composed a new song for every such event, always in her first language, always translated by Farley and accompanied by Lucy, and later by Lucy's little daughter. When Farley died, the gift of song seemed to die within his wife. She converted it into new dimensions of prayer, I believe, essentially contemplative.

She was a grandmother to all the young, consoling hurt hearts, listening to children's small-scale stories about their adventures, and telling her own to them. She taught bush skills, imparting knowledge of the seasons, and oversaw communal berry-picking as various species ripened—wild strawberry, raspberry, bearberry, thimbleberry, black currant, blueberry, cranberry, and a host of other varieties, each with its particular genius, each with its need for special handling. Air-drying was the main method of preservation, but throughout late summer and into autumn, the making of jam was an additional highlight. We had few jars and lids for canning, so perforce the jam was entirely consumed. Kateri used honey after our sugar supplies ended. She also taught us how to make bannock, a pan-bread fried in purified sheep lard, spread with jam or, that rarest of treats, maple syrup. The sugar maple was uncommon in our neck of the woods, so to speak. Birch sap, however, was readily available, and though its natural sweetness was far more diluted and demanded great volumes for rendering down, it did produce a palatable syrup.

During the final years of Kateri's life, Lucy and her husband, Sam, helped with the annual fish harvest. Each year I tried to give her a day or two of labor, and my sons liked to spend even more time down at the river and drying racks.

They loved Kateri, and they loved the work—and they really loved the bannock.

I remember the last time I saw her. I had spent a good part of the day up to my knees in water, impaling fish with a two-prong spear Farley had made ages ago. Coming up onto the river bank, I noticed Kateri standing there watching me. I waved, but she didn't return the gesture. Instead, she walked toward me, put her arms around me, and gave me a gentle hug. She was a little lady, so she had to reach way up to accomplish this.

I was startled by the unexpected, unprecedented intimacy. She had never been a demonstrative person; her love was always in her eyes and her sacrificial labors.

"I'll miss you, Boy," she said. *Boy* was her name for me, never *Cleve*. I was fifty-seven years old, and she was still calling me Boy.

"Are you planning a holiday in Hawaii, Kateri?" I asked her.

She dropped her arms and stepped back, with a smile to reward me for the joke.

Then, growing serious, she said, "The veil is thin, Boy, the veil is thin. There's no *this place* and *that place*. We're always walking in eternity. We just don't have the eyes to see it."

I wasn't sure of her meaning.

"You're not fixing to die on us are you, Kateri? You'll see Farley again someday."

"Oh, he's waitin' for me, I know. Got a little debt to pay off, that man, but it won't be long."

Abruptly she turned away and returned to the tent in which she slept during fishing season. A moment later, she returned with a slab of bannock in her hand, the pan biscuit glistening with lard and smeared over with blueberry mash.

"Eat!" she commanded.

She observed me as I ate the bannock.

"I'm proud of you," she said. "You grew up."

These few words meant more to me than a million other words I had heard in my life. I met her eyes and nodded, but I couldn't speak. And seven days later, I was one of the pallbearers at her funeral.

It would be inaccurate to say that the village's liturgical life was an important cultural factor. It was far more than that. It was vital. It was the central axis around which the year revolved. It was our strength and consolation. The community had built a log chapel in the fourth year of our "exile", the fourth year of our coming home. The "longhouse", most of us called it, the "Godhouse", according to the children. This replacement for the original "tent of meeting" could hold sixty to seventy people, but our numbers kept increasing. By the time I was in my late middle age, the chapel ceded place to a stone church that could seat a hundred and fifty. It even had a wooden steeple with a bell donated by Hardy Jacobson.

In the first year after the darkness, Hardy and Pierre Jacobson fashioned a tabernacle out of the hardwood of an ancient upright piano that had fallen on hard times, keys missing, strings sprung and irredeemable, and what remained of its former glory so hopelessly out of tune that it was an acute suffering to listen to it being played. They cut down the cherrywood soundboard and from it fashioned a beautiful box with ornamental motifs engraved in the wood, a door in front, all edges trimmed with brass strips (there was no gold to be had). Decade after decade, this little "ark of the covenant", this seat of mercy, first reposed in the army tent and then the longhouse and then finally was borne in procession to its permanent home in the stone church, bearing the radiant Presence, as it had from the beginning.

I remember the day, decades earlier, when we were still

worshipping in the tent of meeting, and a little child (Penny Morrow, if I recall correctly) stood up in our midst after the final blessing. With a beaming face she raised her arms high and cried out:

"Our church needs a name!"

Our "church" was by then beginning to break down under the cycle of the seasons, with thinning canvas, rips appearing at the seams, and holes in the roof poked by branches. Its once waterproof floor now leaked badly in spring melts and rainy periods.

The child's declaration was met by murmurs of agreement and some silent brain-storming, but no one put forward a name.

Kateri had brought the Sacred Heart drum with her that day, and she took it up and began to beat a gentle rhythm. The spirit of prayer fell upon us, we all knelt, and a hush of silence ensued. Moved by implication or inference, many of us, myself included, considered suggesting the name Sacred Heart.

Then Fr. Peter stood and said in his quiet way: "It is in my heart to name our parish after the Apostle John. He rested on the Lord's breast at the Last Supper, and he surely must have heard the Sacred Heart beating in his ear. He was inspired to write the most sublime of the Gospels, and it was he who gave us the great vision of the Apocalypse. What say you all?"

The rightness of the suggestion was obvious to everyone. One by one we answered, "Yes! Amen!"

And that is how our tent, and then the longhouse, and eventually the stone church came to be called St. John's.

In the early years, Joe, Grandmère, and Uncle Amédée died and were buried in the family cemetery beside the wrecker's yard. Hardy and Céline grew older and older, but no less affable, ever generous with the dwindling supplies in the "larder." As the mountain of goods in the shed melted away, a cache of precious seed was found inside mouse-proof metal bins—spelt wheat, corn, rye, barley—which they exchanged for our firewood, deer hides, smoked venison, honey, and beeswax (we were cultivating dozens of hives by then, the wild bees in the region being numerous). The economy, if one could call it that, was loosely based on barter, but it should be noted that the exchange of goods and services was never sly or grasping, never miserly; indeed, all parties tried to outdo each other in generosity. In this way, the flow increased and general abundance spread, and no one lacked for essentials.

Pierre remains a singular presence among us, first as a luminous young man, and then a wise older man, and eventually a sagacious elder. He is a person of constant prayer, and full of love. He maintains that in his entire life he was blessed with only a single vision, the one he was given on Mont Royale. He and his wife Alice have six children. Their oldest they named Joseph and the next André, in memory of the vision. Another two sons were Jean de Brébeuf and Isaac Jogues, named for the Jesuit martyrs, the first saints of the new world. Their youngest, both girls, are Marie and Marguerite, again named after early saints of New France. Alice and Pierre are now the grandparents of seventeen.

Pierre continues to work in his grandfather's shop and wrecker's yard, creating arrow- and spear-heads out of what he calls "kar-métal", which he cuts from the obsolete automobiles with hacksaw and files. He has built a mini foundry and blacksmith shop. He has retooled two ancient band saws, the kind once used for cutting ice, eight feet tall, with new wooden handles and teeth refiled for the sawing of wood into planks. Whenever he forges a new axe head, it is an event acclaimed throughout the community. Likewise, the successful completion of a bow saw is a cause of widespread rejoicing. Without these, the cutting of firewood would be a crushing burden. There is a brisk trade in his wares up and down the valley.

The Lyons are very dear to Annie and me. They are our peers, and, along with Rafe and Cora, they are our closest friends. Richard and Colleen taught all of our children in their schoolhouse. We are now approaching the third generation who learned language skills and mathematics under them, with elements of rudimentary science, including the readily accessible nature studies and geology and, to a lesser extent, chemistry. Above all, history. With the dashing vitality of his teaching style, added to his humorous wit and his abiding capacity to engender deep understandings of man and history, Richard is not only a popular teacher but a beloved one. Colleen is equally loved by her students, but for different reasons: her approach combines her brilliance with her fundamental empathy, a sensitive intuition regarding the inner conditions of souls and their stages of development. Their own children are among the most secure and happy in the entire region, which bears testimony to the excellence of their parents.

Penny Morrow grew up to become a graceful woman, as bright and shining as she had been as a child. She has never married and has dedicated her life to teaching the lower grades in the schoolhouse. Cora, who had been a teacher in the before-times, assists her daughter whenever she can. In the early years of the school, Alice Jacobson, who had studied childhood education at university, also taught, but after she married Pierre, she moved to the old service station, which was too long a way to commute. Nevertheless, she never misses a graduation ceremony.

Edmund Lyon is married to the Morrows' daughter Josie; they have four married children and numerous grandchildren (forgive me, I have lost count). He is a farmer, and has had some success in breeding ponies, which he caught running wild in the southern rangeland and brought home to domesticate.

Some years ago, the Lyons' middle boys, Gregory and James (re-inventors of the stone lamp, if you recall), discovered veins of iron ore higher and farther west in the mountains and have established a very small mining operation there. Their natures are intrepid and impelled by devouring curiosity. They return home on weekends for Mass—and for proper feeding, as their mother says.

Efforts to reconstruct a little of our lost civilization were manifold (a village choir, story-telling at community gatherings, poetry memorization, Scripture studies), but I cannot fail to mention the books in Joe Jacobson's service station. For years the people of *Sursum Corda* borrowed them, with much wear and tear and a loss or two. Not long after Joe's death, Hardy donated the collection to the schoolhouse library, where it remains to this day, some of it used for classes, some for the enjoyment of the reading club, some for personal enlightenment. I also sent Uncle Dave's collection down to the school. Books are so great a treasure that their handling is carefully overseen by the Lyons. If one is lost or damaged beyond repair, there will be no replacement.

The same holds true for a far greater treasure, the five copies of the Bible in the community's possession. Three are in the English language, one in French, and one in High German (if there are enough sheets of paper left over from this writing, I will explain how two of these came to us).

For now, I can't help remembering the way I undervalued the Sacred Scriptures in the before-times. I had been indifferent to them during my years of unbelief, and though my Bible became of utmost importance to me after my conversion, I had neglected to bring it along on our journey. Moreover, I had failed to notice the gradual disappearance of Bibles from the mainstream of our society—marginalized under the pressure of malicious reformers, and then banished. First they were removed from the schools, then from courts and government forums, then libraries and bookstores and bedside drawers in countless hotel rooms, and above all in homes where the internet had become the savior from boredom, the reigning oracle, the Luciferian source of light. This famine of the Word of God took hold of an entire culture with hardly anyone noticing. We had not been paying attention.

Of Rafe and Cora, I have so much to say that I scarcely know where to begin. My boss, my friend, my mentor. Our undeclared, unelected leader. And the very wise woman who sustained him all the way. They are old, bent with arthritis, and walk with canes. Both of them have white wooly hair above intricately wrinkled, dark brown faces made darker by their years of toiling under the sun. Their eyes are as old and wise as the ages.

This is the point in my account where I may best mention the sheep, for they became a cornerstone of the life that took root and grew strong all around us. In the early years, Hardy gave ten ewes and a young ram to Rafe and Cora, asking that the Morrows be the custodians of this subsidiary flock and that in the future they would prudently apportion lambs for the establishment of yet more flocks, as well as distribution of mutton, wool, and hides to the other families. Thus, Rafe's first years were consumed with setting up sheds and paddocks, haying and shearing, and extending pastures—in summer, he brought his flock up into the cooler hills by our cabin; in winter, he kept the sheep down by the river, where he had his home, which was, of course, a well-built, expansive log residence filled with life.

I had to smile whenever I recalled the dream that Theresa told us about when we first met her on the highway where she and Alice were attacked.

St. Thérèse of Lisieux had appeared to her and encouraged her to drive into the west without reason or known destination. "Have no fear," the saint had said. "A shepherd will help you."

I remembered Rafe's remark at the time: "I'm not a shepherd, but I think we're the ones sent to help you."

Which brings me to the topic of clothing. Needless to say, the commercially produced garments we had worn on our arrival, along with those in our meager baggage, did not last more than a few short years. There were overalls, work gloves, and other oddities from Jacobson's emporium that lasted longer, but item by item these, too, disappeared from our midst, replaced by hand-sewn trousers and tunics made of deer and sheep hide. As the sheep flocks increased in number, the annual harvesting of wool made woven fabrics possible. Looms were constructed, carding and spinning skills developed. The resulting cloth was warmer and more resistant to rain and snow than synthetics had been. Woolen blankets, cloaks, and socks were greatly valued. Herbal dyes were used to introduce colors into the yarns. Deerskin moccasins became the standard footgear, one that never went out of fashion. Kateri and Lucy taught many young women how to make them. Thread was obtained from the sinews of both wild and domestic animals killed for food.

Oh, did I mention Pard the border collie? Yes, I think I did. Joe Jacobson's dog. Well, Pard was a canine gentleman, needless to say, and lacking a mate he seemed fated to be the last of his line. It was an immense blessing, therefore, when a female collie wandered into the station yard two or three weeks after the darkness. She was emaciated, frightened, whimpering and limping. Her paws were bleeding from a long and arduous journey. She had probably wandered away from a home or farm where she had been involved with people—people whose end we could not imagine. She sidled up to the Jacobsons' front porch, quivering and crying and explaining in dog language the sad story of her travails. When Pierre and Luke fell to their knees in the dust of the yard, embracing her, patting her, murmuring sympathy in her ears, she adopted them on the spot. Pard edged closer and sniffed.

In the ensuing months, what began as carnal desperation became a kind of romance between Pard and his mate. Luke named her Sally (as in sallied forth, he explained). She had one blue eye, one brown, which indicated a certain amount of interbreeding in her ancestry. Before any of us came into his life, Joe had invested effort in training Pard as a sheep dog. The natural herding instinct of border collies had become so refined under Joe's tutelage that he could leave the dog alone with the flock all day on his farm of dubious legal status—now legal, we presumed, though what legality meant was no longer certain.

The mingling of Sally and Pard's genes produced puppies of high sensitivity, intelligence, and ability to learn. These in turn gave birth to a long line of excellent herders, a number of which Rafe acquired. On rare occasions, one of the offspring was lured into the wilderness by a wolf and came home pregnant, a cause of concern because the hybrid offspring might prove to be a threat to our flocks. We need not have worried, however, as these pups grew to be fine hunting dogs.

In the early years of the settlement, whenever he could spare some time from his sheep, Rafe assisted Luke and me in the building of several log homes. Indeed, this was to become my life's work, Luke's as well. In the middle years, when he was gradually handing off the flock management to his children, Rafe was even more involved in helping us. Yes, he had become the employee, and I the employer. He enjoyed calling me "Boss". Now, in our later years, he has become one of those knowledgeable old chaps who in times past would sit beside construction sites, leaning on their canes, scrutinizing the comings and goings of laborers and offering unsolicited advice. His advice is always good, and younger men listen to him. In my latter years, I, too, have become one of those figureheads, as my strength is failing. Hopefully, my mental faculties will last a little longer. I still feel exhilaration whenever I observe the hearty young fellows lifting notched logs into place, and sometimes as I watch them I doze on my tree stump, half asleep, remembering, remembering . . .

I see again the hand-painted quotations on the walls of Jacobson's emporium. What has become of them? I see the rocking chair. Is it still there by the potbelly stove? I see the vintage pickup truck in the garage, shining and red, as mint-new as it was a hundred years ago. Has it been cut down into arrowheads and axes, scythes and ploughshares? I see the dissolving of my antipathies, and the garden of wooden crosses in the cemetery, where some of our early founders now sleep, awaiting the final day.

The terms "gas station" and "service station" faded into

obscurity very early on. Thereafter, people called it "Jacobson's place" or "the Jacobson homestead". Hardy, Luke, and Pierre called it "Joe's Freehold" long after Joe had died. It was also the name my father had used on his map, and I concluded from this that he had picked it up from Joe and Uncle Dave.

Since their marriage, Pierre and Alice have always lived there. They taught their children at home, determining that an eighteen-mile round trip to the Lyons' school was too great a distance. All internal combustion engines had died long before their first child arrived, and though they had the horses, they felt that the journey would consume far too much of each day. Even so, when their children reached their mid-to-late teenage years, invariably they begged permission from their parents to study under Richard Lyon. Always an admirer of raw intelligence, Richard recognized that these growing minds were awake and hungry for mental stimulation. It became a tradition that the Freehold youngsters would be weekly boarders at the school.

At some point in the middle years—I'm guessing twenty years after the holocaust—a concerted effort was made to fill nine miles of potholes and to slash back the encroaching trees, restoring what had become a bush trail to its proper condition and status as a road—our single road. A work "bee" of thirty men completed the task in three weeks. After that, horse and foot traffic increased, and then came a sprightly horse-drawn buggy. I believe there are now, in these latter years, seven or more such buggies in regular use.

This brings me to one of the more remarkable happenings that took place in the early years. It occurred a month after the holocaust. On a day in early September, the runaway boy named Son was wandering despondently along the river bank, weighed down by his internal anguish, his aloneness, and perhaps also by the lowering sky so laden with the debris cast up by the universal catastrophe. There was no longer any place for him to run.

As flakes of grimy snow began to fall, he heard human voices talking on the far side of the river. He froze, very afraid that bad men would find the encampment. He tried to make himself immobile, invisible, but then a man and a woman came out of the willows on the opposite bank and stopped in their tracks when they spotted him. They too froze, gazing at him in silence.

The woman held a baby in her arms. The man had a pack upon his back, and behind him came a horse he had been leading by a tether. The young couple looked startled—and frightened.

At last the man spoke. He raised his right arm in greeting and hailed the boy from across the water.

"May peace be with you!" he called.

Son did not reply, though his curiosity was aroused.

"Are there Christian people living near here?" asked the man.

"Yes," said Son.

"Would you show us where we may meet them?"

Without replying in words, the boy gestured downriver, turned and began to walk along the embankment toward the shallow ford. The man and wife and horse followed on the other bank.

At that time of year, the water was low, and at the ford it was about two feet deep. With amazing strength, the man lifted his wife and child onto the back of the horse, then led it into the water and waded slowly and carefully across to the other side, wet to his knees.

When they came to Son, he swallowed his fear, as he now

could apprehend that their faces were good. They wore black clothing, the man in trousers with suspenders, a white shirt and a straw hat on his head, and mud-caked boots. The woman wore an ankle-length dress and a large black bonnet on her head, secured with a ribbon tied beneath her chin. They seemed to him very strange in appearance, though he noted their eyes were clear and kindly.

"Do you live on a farm?" asked the man.

"No."

"Where, then, do you live?"

"With the others," said Son, and abruptly turned and walked away in the direction of the encampment. "Come."

They followed.

There was much astonishment when Son led them to the group sitting by the campfire, myself and Rafe included. We stood and greeted the newcomers, saying, "God bless you."

At this, their faces thawed and they recounted their story. They had been members of a community of "brethren" called Mennonites who farmed in a region of southern Alberta not far from Lethbridge. When, without warning, the behavior of "the English" became strange, they had quietly continued with their lives, for they had no need for electricity or telephones or automobiles. When the shooting of firearms and burning of farms began, the community had dropped all their labors and retreated to their house of prayer, where they commenced to read Scripture and prayed for protection.

Then the police had come and arrested their pastor and elders, who had refused to sign the affidavits that would limit their preaching and teaching. They had also rejected the government programs aimed at re-educating their children. After that, rioters plundered the brethren's houses of the little they possessed and then torched the buildings. No one was killed, but the people were suddenly homeless. They set off by horse and buggy in convoy, hoping to reach another Mennonite community farther west, where they might find refuge. They traveled by back roads for three days, pausing at Amish and Hutterite communities which were also in dire need, as they had been similarly pillaged. Along the way they saw numerous houses in flames and violent men racing in trucks, shooting guns in the air. No one bothered the brethren at first, which they attributed to God's protection, as he had helped the three young men pass through the fire of the evil king's furnace.

On the fourth day, a gang of motorcycle riders surrounded the convoy on the road and spoke defilement and blasphemy, insulted their women, and shot with guns some of the husbands and fathers, killing them. Then those who survived lashed their horses and scattered in all directions across fields and into woods.

"The ones on motorcycles chased some of us, but my wife and I were hidden from their eyes," said the young man. "They did not follow us."

Rafe was the first to introduce himself. "I am Raphael Morrow, and you are welcome here."

"Thank you, sir. I am Menno Gerbrandt, and this is my wife, Sarah, and our daughter."

"You are safe with us. We are happy to offer you shelter and food for as long as you wish."

The couple dipped their heads in acknowledgment, reticent yet grateful.

"Surely you must know about the events that have occurred in recent weeks?" Rafe inquired.

"The heavenly events, you mean? Yes, we know, for we passed through the purgation. Before this, because the roads were unsafe, we sought a place to rest for the night and went on a lane that led us to a farm. It had been burned, the people within the house were dead. The stone barn stood unharmed, and we hid in it for days, and no living being did we see.

"Then in a dream I was commanded to rise up and take my wife and child and go into the desert places. A voice in the dream warned me that the evil one seeks the life of our child, for the devil intends to destroy all innocence from the face of the earth. Now does Satan make war against those who obey God's commandments and follow Jesus."

"This is true," said Rafe. "We are at war."

"The voice told me that I would come upon the children of the Lord, and though they are not of the brethren, they are of God, and I must trust in this."

"And you obeyed."

"Yes, I obeyed, for in obedience is found the narrow gate to freedom. It is the will of the Most High."

"Mr. Gerbrandt, all those you see gathered here believe the same. Our Savior is our life and our hope."

The man smiled for the first time. "I am very glad of it, sir."

"Still, I wonder how you have found us in all this vast wilderness."

"He led us, though we were blind. We hid in diverse shelters in the wilderlands while the devils raged, and we remained hidden from the eyes of evil men. Then one afternoon at the third hour, the great darkness came, and fire fell from the heavens as we were caught betimes in an empty silo. Throughout those three days, we prayed until the angel of death had passed by. When the light returned and calm settled upon the earth, we ventured south through a region of ashes and came to other roads. And when we passed a forest lane not many miles from here, a lane that led into woodlands and swamps, I knew it was the way we should go. At first I was in fear, for it seemed strange to me that it would be a place where men tilled the soil. But the voice had not departed from me; it was gentle within me, and it assured me that I must follow this path. When it ended in the trees, I left the buggy behind, and we continued onward by foot. This morning we came to the river, and there stood your boy, waiting for us."

"Yes, he is our boy," said Rafe warmly, "our Son."

Son blushed and looked at his feet.

The memory now yields to a later scene. It takes place in the newly built stone church several years later. It is a moment of great rejoicing, the baptism of one of Menno and Clare's children.

Clare Lyon had married Menno after he was widowed. He and his first wife, Sarah, had converted to the Faith in the year following the holocaust, and Sarah lived three more years after that. When she died of pneumonia (we had no antibiotics, and no herbal remedies were able to halt the disease), Clare had taken the Gerbrandt's newborn baby and the older orphan into her heart as if they were her own. With her parents' permission, the nineteen-year-old girl had daily walked to the homestead, rising before dawn and returning home late at night, caring for the children while their father worked in his fields, whenever he was able, or wandered aimlessly in a heartbroken daze. By then, the Lyons owned one of Pard and Sally's pups, which had grown to be a smart, bold, and reliable young dog, with one brown eye and one blue. Daily it loped along beside her on the two mile walk to the Gerbrandt farm. Clare was never bothered by dangerous animals, though she often saw fox and deer. Only once did she see a wolf, which stopped in mid-stride to peer at her, sizing her up as prey, until the dog caught the scent and launched a frenzy of barking and chased it off.

Menno hardly acknowledged Clare's presence in his cabin, rarely meeting her eyes, giving only monosyllabic responses to her greetings. That was all right, because she was there for the children. A year and a half went by before Menno recovered from his devastating grief, opened his eyes and understood what was being given for his family's sake. He and Clare married and had four more children together.

Menno had spoken a great deal at our first meeting, but this was not his habit. Godly in every aspect, devoted to Sacred Scripture (his German language Bible was his paramount possession), he afterward resumed his natural disposition, that is, a man of minimalist speech. A robust and tireless worker and as patient as a mountain, he had cut his small farm out of raw bush and thrown himself into sheep raising on the rough pastures that he managed to grub from the reluctant soil. Long years passed as the reclaimed land spread, succumbing foot by foot to the relentless onslaught of his mattock and plow, and all the while he endlessly picked stones from the turned earth, constructing field walls as he went. In addition, he laid miles of traditional rail fencing that zigzagged across his expanding acreage. He raised a barn and sheds and eventually a large extension onto their cabin, in which he and Clare hoped the elder Lyons, Richard and Colleen, would live out their last years. And all in good time, this came to pass.

With the coming of Menno into the life of the community, the profession of cartwright was resurrected. He made a four-wheel cart for the community and another for himself, a sturdy burden-bearer that bounced and bumped along the rough track from his farm to the bridge over the Little Jordan. In this way he was able to bring his family to

Sunday Mass, and later, when the road to Joe's Freehold was repaired, he took Clare there to visit her friends and for his discussions with Hardy and Pierre about horses. In due course, he crafted a fine two-wheel buggy that was the forerunner of the ones now in use.

Far back in the earliest years, the Jacobsons had three horses, two mares and a stallion. Need it be said that these creatures were fruitful and multiplied, until with time Hardy had a sizeable herd that he wanted to find homes for. Not everyone needed a horse in our village, but outlying farms were eager to obtain one.

After the passage of many years, Hardy and Pierre began their series of ventures beyond the confines of our safe haven, leading four horses at a time. To the west rose the mountains, to the south and north were more mountains, but it was possible that people still lived in the regions extending northeast to southwest. Their first sortie was to retrace the steps that the refugees had taken in obedience to their dreams and visions. They found that the ten miles leading to the junction with the old highway had grown over with deep grass, willow and poplar, and was frequently obstructed by fallen trees. The ravine posed a major obstacle, but they had brought along planks strapped to the backs of the horses, and with these they made a narrow bridge sufficiently strong to bear the animals' weight. In the final mile before reaching the junction, the big trees that Luke had cut down were still blocking the way, but they were partially decayed and could be jumped by the horses.

At the junction, they came to the old highway that once led to the U.S. and were surprised by how much it had deteriorated. The tarmac was fractured and crumbling and reduced to less than half its former breadth. Though it was still navigable, walking or riding it demanded a winding course, due to the numerous saplings that now grew out of wider cracks. Eventually they passed, unknowingly, the site of the Burnt Café, which was by then no more than a hump covered with undergrowth. When they came to Twin Butte, they found nothing remaining of the buildings and saw that all the surrounding fields had been reclaimed by young woods. There was evidence on the hills of a great fire that had scoured through the region, either natural in origins or supernatural or both. They went no farther north. After turning back, they happened upon the head of a footpath that had earlier escaped their notice. It led into the east, and it showed signs that it had been recently used.

The path ended at a cluster of farmhouses and humble fields and gardens beside a small lake. Living there was a community of thirty-five souls, young and old, some of them scarred with burns, some unscathed. Hardy and Pierre were welcomed with jubilation, with copious tears and prayers of thanksgiving. These people had had neither priest nor sacraments for more than twenty years, but their faith was strong. They had named their little hamlet *Pacem in Terris*.

They offered to trade furs and cornmeal for a horse, but Hardy, moved by their poverty, was loathe to accept anything from them by way of exchange or payment. The meeting itself was the great blessing, he felt—they all felt. He and Pierre enjoyed a meal with them, and prayed with them, and they traded their news. The families did not know anything about the fate of Pincher Creek, nor about any points north or south. They simply marveled that there were other people still living in the world and seemed awed by the descriptions of *Sursum Corda* and its enterprises. Hardy promised to return the following year and also gave directions to our village in case any of them wished to venture westward. He left two of the horses with them as a gift. The people of Pacem gave in return a pair of live turkeys, male and female, and four egg-laying hens and a rooster. The transplanting of these priceless fowl to Freehold and Sursum inaugurated another turning point for our people.

A sturdy little bridge was soon built over Deep Creek, and headway was made in clearing the trail to the highway. It was never again a road, but the route became fairly passable. From then on, a trickle of traffic began between the two communities, though it was sporadic because of the distance. The journey was probably little more than thirty miles, which in the old days would have taken half an hour by car.

I hesitate to write more about Fr. Peter, lest even the highest praises fall too short and succumb to the lure of platitudes. Let me say, at least, that throughout these many long years he has remained faithfully busy about his Father's business. His Masses are worshipful, in no way infected by personality, and they are always an immersion in timelessness and peace. His homilies give consistently clear instruction and inspired insight. His counsel is the same. He takes little rest for himself; he is early to rise and late to bed, and many hours each day are spent praying in the church. He is one of those hidden saints whom everyone appreciates, but no one knows the full measure of.

He will accept no payment for his unceasing service, other than the food that people give him, and sometimes new clothes when his old ones have been worn to tatters. As always, he takes nothing for himself, not even those little luxuries that have returned to daily life (honey on risen bread, duffel moccasin liners, non-sacramental wine), and he is certainly indifferent to strokes to his self esteem. His one-room rectory is a place of utmost simplicity, his bed is bare planks and a blanket or two. His meals are austere.

During the middle years, he rode his horse the long, demanding route to Pacem, bringing the sacraments there, baptizing and marrying and confessing its people, feeding them with the Bread of Life, and on occasion standing vigil at their deathbeds. He has never failed to offer Sunday Mass at Jacobson's, which is now a hamlet of seven homes. In later years, as he aged and his walking pace declined, even as the demands on his ministry increased, he took to riding everywhere, even the short distances to outlying farms. Over the years, he owned three horses, the last two broken to the halter by our resident wrangler Luke Jacobson. Luke also built him a corral and a small barn beside the rectory, and every summer the entire community harvests hay to fill its loft.

Fr. Peter's interior life must be very rich. There is always a smile on his face. Even so, there have been occasions when I caught glimpses of a struggle. Once in the middle of the night when sleep eluded me, I got up and walked to the village in the dark and went into St. John's seeking strength and consolation from the Lord's Presence. Entering silently, I saw by the light of the vigil lamp the figure of Fr. Peter face down on the floor before the tabernacle, his arms spread wide as in a cruciform. I heard groaning and pleading in the Blackfoot tongue, or Cree perhaps, mixed with a little Latin.

I prayed for him and then silently left.

Among the few wanderers who came to *Sursum Corda* out of the wilderness, Menno and Sarah Gerbrandt were not the first, but they were the only ones who stayed. I have always wondered why the others chose to go on. Could they not believe that civilization, as we had known it, was now ended? Did they fail to understand that a society built from top to bottom on sin could not last? Perhaps they were repelled by our community's poverty and hardships and were unable to see the wholesome beauty that was growing here. Perhaps they yearned to be reunited with loved ones surviving elsewhere or to find more comfortable places to live. With thanks for the food we gave them, they headed off into the forest, following uncertain paths into the east and north. None of them returned.

First among the later arrivals were two physicians who stumbled by accident into our midst, a few days after we had set up the camp—this was before the illumination of conscience and the holocaust. That evening our entire company was gathered around the bonfire, praying the rosary.

The doctors, a man and a woman in their mid to late thirties, had seen the glow of our fire in the twilight and followed it. They were bearing recreational camping gear on high-backed aluminum frames, a new red tent, and rolled sleeping bags; they wore fashionable hiking clothes and expensive footwear. The man held a one-year-old child in his arms, its chirpy face peering out from a carry sling. The parents' faces looked very anxious. When they noticed that we were praying, the man and the woman fell to their knees, removed rosaries from their pockets and joined in our prayers—in another language.

Afterward, they explained in their halting English that they were from France and had been hiking in the Waterton Lakes on holiday. They had been camping on the heights above the town of Waterton when their cell phones ceased working. Within hours they began to hear gunfire and saw several fires break out in the residential area below them, and then they were shocked when the great luxury chalet on the lake, the Prince of Wales Hotel, erupted in flames and became a roaring inferno. They had stayed in it the night before and had taken an "English tea" there the next morning. Hesitant to go back down into the town after the troubles erupted, they were now trying to find a way to the highway.

We told them about our own experiences and what we thought about the emerging situation in the country, which might also be taking place throughout the world. Rafe encouraged them to stay with us until signs of improved conditions were apparent. They stayed three days, but they were distressed throughout. They pitched their tent by the fire and prayed with us again, but in the end they decided to leave. They had their responsibilities in their homeland, they explained; they had patients at the hospital and clinic where they worked; they had families waiting, surely concerned about their welfare now that communications seemed to have failed. Perhaps the airlines were functioning.

We gave them directions back to the highway, with plenty of warnings about physical hazards and the prevalence of marauders on the roads.

I do not know if they ever found their way home or if they were among the countless casualties out there in the regions of chaos. I could not help but think they would have done better to remain with us. I was also thinking of the approaching birth of our child. But they did not stay, and I had to leave them to God's hands.

A solitary man arrived in the summer of our second year, stumbling across the ford and collapsing onto the ground near the Crowshoes' fish weir. Farley and Kateri left aside their drying racks and rushed to him. I was helping with the fish that day and witnessed it all. They gave him water and food, which he devoured desperately, and when he had sufficiently revived, he sat up and tried to speak. His face was disfigured by poorly healed burn scars. His matted hair was long and gray, tied at the back into a ponytail, his bedraggled beard reached to his waist. He wore the remnants of a tattered black robe. His feet were bare, cracked, and bleeding in places. A torn blanket covered his shoulders. A bronze cross with the three bars of eastern Christianity was visible beneath the rim of his beard.

At first, the man could not get his words out.

We three tried to reassure him that he had reached a place of safety. That he was no longer alone. That all those who lived here were followers of Christ.

When he heard this last, he buried his face in his scarred hands and began to weep.

His story came out in bits and pieces that day. He had been arrested at the church where he had been a pastor, in a community in southern Alberta. He had been taken to a "civilian internment camp." There he was interrogated and tortured, mined for information about the hiding places of Christians, and when he could tell them nothing, he was held in an isolation cell for weeks. Finally released into the larger camp, he was put to work filling pits in the prairie soil.

"Many bodies, hundreds of bodies I threw into the pits," he explained in a choking voice. "In my thoughts I prayed for each one's soul, for I hoped that there was still a thread of sacred authority in me. And I prayed also for my own corrupt soul. I begged God to let me die, but he would not let me. It was in punishment for my sins that I was not permitted release from the hands of those human devils. It was payment for my divided heart in the time when I thought only of my pleasures." He could say no more for a minute as he again choked and wept. Finally, he said, "For my pride and my passions. For preying upon the flock of the Lord. For my unrepented evil."

"Would you like to speak with a priest?" Farley gently asked.

"I *am* a priest!" the man cried out in anguish.

Later that day, Fr. Peter came and spoke with him. The wandering priest explained that in the mid-afternoon of one day during his captivity, he had seen his soul exposed; it had terrified him, his heart had nearly given out when he saw the condition of his soul in the eyes of God. He begged for mercy and received it, and from then on he tried to help the other prisoners and the guards deal with the shocking illumination that had come to them all. In both parties there was a divergence between those who accepted mercy and those who rejected it.

Then came the fire and darkness, and the gates of that place of torment were blasted open, and he ran. He struggled onward day after day, through fields and forests; he waded swamps and swam across rivers and came at last to the highway leading into the south, where he hoped to find refuge. But refuge eluded him, and he knew then that God in his mercy and his justice was calling him to a pilgrim path, to wander through the desolation until his death, making reparation for his own past life and for the sins committed in these lands. Obeying an inner command, he had left the highway and entered the regions of bush and swamp, and arriving at the river, he had spotted the two old native people tending a fire by their fish racks.

Fr. Peter heard the man's confession and absolved him. Then he, too, knelt down on the ground and asked the visiting priest to hear his confession. I do not know if the man was an Eastern Catholic or Orthodox, but it seemed that ancient divisions evaporated that day. The visiting priest absolved our Fr. Peter, and when the final prayers of the sacrament were completed, they stood and embraced each other.

"I must go," said the man. "There may be souls out there who need me."

"Go in peace," said Fr. Peter, blessing him with the sign of the cross.

The man left by the way he had come, and we never saw him again.

The third late arrival stands out in my memory. He simply walked into our compound a few days after the illumination of conscience, about a month before the holocaust. He was a well-groomed man in his fifties, trim and silver haired, proud of bearing, dressed in a suit and tie and overcoat, as if his travels through the forest had not left a scratch on him, save for his expensive looking shoes, which were scuffed and muddied. He wore a large backpack strapped to his shoulders, and in one hand he gripped a heavy nylon bag of the kind used for carrying sports equipment.

Taken by surprise, not knowing where he had come from or what his loyalties were, we men rose quickly to our feet.

"Greetings," he said, his face poised, with a cautious academic mien. "I intend no harm. I merely wish to ask directions to the nearest highway."

"Where have you come from?" asked Rafe.

"From the United States of America," the man answered, pointing vaguely toward the south.

"Is the border open now?" I asked.

"I imagine so. When I passed through it a week ago, the only guards I saw were unfortunately dead. The same on the

Canadian side. A rank indifference to burial of bodies seems to prevail at the present time. Thus, I entered your country without the usual irritating delays and customs duties." He patted the carry bag with a sarcastic expression.

"Please sit down," said Rafe. "Are you hungry? We would be happy to give you something to eat."

"A little refreshment would be most welcome, thank you."

With a show of some reluctance, the man sat down on the ground beside the fire, after sweeping the sod clear of ashes and twigs. A bowl of stew and a mug of tea were brought to him. After a few moments of deliberation, the man consumed them without haste.

Finished with the meal, he took the pack off his back and opened its flaps. Then he opened his carry bag.

"Let us have no illusions," he said, showing their contents, which were books. "I am not bearing gold in any material form, if it is survivalist gold you are hoping to plunder."

"We do not want gold from you," I said. "You're in no danger of plunder from anyone here. We merely wish to help you."

"But why?" he asked, fastening his impassive eyes upon me.

"You are human."

"Am I human? Yes, perhaps a scrap of humanity remains within me. It would be necessary."

Intrigued, Richard spoke up: "Why would it be necessary?"

Turning to him, the man said, as if from a great height, bordering on the supercilious: "An automaton would be ill equipped to complete the task I have set for myself, which is the preservation of *intellectual* gold, the birthright of our civilization. Can you direct me to any towns or cities that have libraries and universities?"

"Some of us are refugees from universities. Some of us taught in them."

"Ah, the political mills, the money mills," said the man in a tone of loathing.

"Indeed. But to answer your question, sir, we suspect that there are no places remaining where you could donate your treasure securely."

"This is disappointing news. America is in chaos. I had thought that this placid land of yours might be a place of refuge."

"Our country is in chaos like yours. Lawlessness prevails. We are safe here for a time, perhaps a long time. You are welcome to stay with us for as long as you need."

The visitor looked all about the encampment, surveying it with a critical eye.

"I think not," he said at last.

"As you wish," said Rafe, his face a mask. I knew the expression in his eyes. Neutral, courteous, but holding back a deep aversion. I could see some pity in it too. He stood up and the man stood with him.

"Do you not understand the grace God has given us—which he has given to all mankind?" Rafe asked.

"Grace? I see no grace. I see everywhere the empirical evidence of his indifference."

"Surely your conscience was illuminated a few days ago, as ours were."

"My conscience is a maze of byzantine complexity."

"Then here is your opportunity to become as a little child."

"I think not," he said again.

Reaching into his carry bag, he removed a volume bound in red leather. He looked at it with disapproval and tossed it onto the ground.

"I am an archivist of futile tales," he said with a bitter twist of his mouth. "And I must now be about my business."

"I'll show you the road to the highway," I said.

"No need. I'll find my own way."

Nevertheless, I accompanied him as he walked with his burden through the encampment. At the head of the road where it ended by the river, I told him that the route was rough, but after twenty miles in that direction he should come to the highway. There would be fallen trees and a ravine to cross, I said, and there might still be dangerous people roaming about. He acknowledged the information with a nod.

I wished him farewell and God's blessings, but he turned away without replying and walked off down the road.

Returning to the campfire, I found Rafe and Richard showing the leather-bound book to Fr. Peter. It was a Bible.

Two physicians and their child, a wandering pilgrim, and an archivist of futile tales. Five souls who might have made a good life with us, but went searching elsewhere for a succor that they didn't realize they had already found.

When I think of the Gerbrandts and all the life that came from them, the children and grandchildren and souls yet unborn, as well as the other benefits they brought to the community, I ponder the ones who left, and I wonder what unforeseen blessings they would have brought, and found, among us. Our village should have numbered more than its present two hundred souls. It should have become thousands. An entire people should have been saved, but it was not saved because men called evil good and good evil and they chose the path of disobedience and clung blindly to their illusory lordship.

Sometimes when I am alone, I weep for those whom we could have helped, and I weep from the pain of not knowing their fates.

24

ON A PERFECT SUMMER'S DAY, a Saturday morning in the Year of Our Lord, twenty- . . . I forget the year! No matter.

As I was saying, it was a perfect summer's day in a Year of Our Lord. I was seated on a chair that I had crafted a long time ago, from willow saplings held together by wicker cords. The table in front of me had been constructed from rough pine planks, which Annie, now deceased, had helped me fashion at a time when we aspired to rebuild token remnants of civilized life. The table was worn in places by countless meals and radiant with memories. Our children had all eaten there. I saw their shining faces before me still.

The sun was climbing in the sky, the warmth of the day increasing, the air freshly scented with wild flowers in the valley of springs below, mingled with the tang of the swaying pines.

"There's a breeze," I remarked, as if to Annie, for the illusion of communication with my beloved was a consolation I indulged in whenever I found myself alone, or thought I was alone. I could hardly bear to think of her death. She had died peacefully in her sleep in her early eighties. Even now I can't write about it.

I was startled from my reverie by the thumping of feet approaching at a gallop from lower down on the path to the village.

"Grandpa!" called a deep voice.

"On the porch," I called back. "Come on up and sit a while."

"We just wanted to give you a heads-up," answered a second voice, another grandson.

My son Raphael's oldest boys.

"You've got visitors," he added.

"I can see I've got visitors, lads, and welcome ones at that."

They laughed and scrambled up the rock and onto the porch, where they stood huffing and puffing before me. Stalwart lads. *My steadfast men*, I called them in my thoughts and sometimes to their faces. Because the old are permitted such indulgences, they never raised an objection whenever I did so, though I knew that the praise both embarrassed and pleased them.

"Dad sent us to let you know, and to bring this so you can serve them something nice," said the elder of the two.

Onto the table he placed a loaf of bread and a crock of the sort we use to decant wine.

"Bread and wine," said the younger. "Mum wants to know if there's anything else you need?"

"Nothing that I can think of, except information. Who are these guests I'll be entertaining?"

"We're not supposed to tell you. It's a surprise."

"A surprise," I said with an attempt at a smile. Actually I was leery of surprises.

"They're slow on their feet and kind of creaky, Grandpa, but they'll be here in a few minutes. Tally's showing them the way, in case they've forgotten."

The two young men bade me farewell, and I listened to their quiet talk as they went down the rock and onto the lane, these sons of catastrophe, born in exile, content and happy in their vitality, facing the future with confidence.

Presently, the shapes of slow-moving, bent forms appeared on the lane. A little girl was leading them, my granddaughter Talitha.

"Halloo, hallooo!" they called simultaneously when they spotted me.

My eyesight is no longer the best, but I recognized one of the voices. I called back, "Is that you, Boss?"

"Indeed it is I, the fearless leader of your band of merry men!"

Long ago I was one of Rafe's employees, in a time that has become a collage of imagery, the time before the world fell apart. He now lived with his daughter Penny on the far side of the river, a mile to the southwest of *Sursum Corda*, close enough to the village but no small walk for a very old man. Hopefully someone had guided him safely across the bridge.

Wondering who the other man was, I shouted directions for an easier way to climb the rock to the cabin's back entrance, then through it onto the porch. Within minutes we three were face-to-face for the first time in ages. Tally stood to the side, observing the reunion with her eager smile.

The second visitor was my old friend Richard. His presence meant that he had walked from his home on the frontier of the cultivated lands bordering the southeast wilderness. Since their retirement, he and Colleen had lived there with their daughter Clare and her husband, Menno.

"Yo, Lion-hearted!" I exclaimed, very glad to see him. Of course we saw one another at Mass, but visits to each other's homes demanded energy that we no longer had.

"Yo, yourself, pal," Richard said, his voice thinner and higher than Rafe's, his hand grasping mine and shaking it. I felt its frailty, though the spirit that impelled it was still strong. He had once been a university professor, teaching history until the tsunami of history itself swept him and his family out of civilization and into the desolate places. I recalled how he had looked when we first met on the road of escape. A man prepared to defend his family to the death, armed with a hockey stick. A fighter with a large mind inside a large skull, and learned Oxford eyes atop a compact body with quicksilver reflexes, a dynamic soccer player (I would later learn), a brilliant scholar, an author, and father of a large family.

"Well, sit down, boys, sit down," I said, very pleased to see them.

They found seats on two chairs across the table from me.

"Well, here we are, three old survivors murmuring in our twilight years," I said, which made them smile, as we fell without effort into our decades-old habit of banter.

"Twilight years? Speak for yourself, old man," said Rafe, his neck bobbing rhythmically with Parkinson's disease, his hands shaking with involuntary tremors.

"What brings you this way?" I asked with a laugh.

"I'm taking notes for posterity," said Richard. "I have my paper and pen."

"Paper?" I exclaimed. "Where did you get paper?"

"A private stash. Sometimes being a secret hoarder has its benefits. I really do want to take notes of our conversation."

"Well, I'm a hoarder too, down to my last few sheets, but don't waste yours on me, buddy."

"I'll be the judge of that, Cleve. There are a few questions I need to ask you."

"Always more questions. Haven't you written enough books?"

My two friends chuckled. The last book published by Richard had appeared in print only months before civilization had chosen to self-destruct. Though he had fled the city carrying his six various titles along with him, each of them had been burned during that terrible first winter to keep our families from freezing to death. Our survival skills weren't developed in those early years, and paper of any sort helped ignite damp kindling. It was interesting in retrospect to see that he had chosen to burn his own treasured books instead of his secret hoard of blank pages.

"Of the writing of books there is no end," Richard said, quoting Ecclesiastes, his mind as swift as ever, the traces of his British accent lurking within the intonations.

"Mmmm, looks like that's no longer the case," said Rafe.

"Don't be so sure. Deerskin manuscripts will serve the purpose, with the added benefit of hearkening us back to the age of vellum in the medieval period. And if that fails, there's always birch bark at our disposal."

"Ah, irrepressible progress," I said. "Give us another century, and we'll invent the printing press."

"Someone, somewhere, is surely working on it."

"Another thousand, and they'll be inventing cell phones," said Rafe with his most ironic tone.

"They'll come in two attractive models," Richard quipped, "*incubi* and *succubi*."

Though I remembered how both men had once been critics of the directions Western culture was going, each in his particular way, it was rare in these later years to hear them slip into that old resentment.

"What is a cell phone, Grandpa?" Tally piped up.

"Ah, sweetie, it was a thing that was used by people of the past to talk to each other. It was a kind of machine, with pictures and words in it."

"A machine with pictures and words?" she repeated,

puzzled. "But the water wheel is a machine, isn't it? And the windmill and metal forge. There're no pictures and words in them."

As Rafe tried to explain the technology to the girl, with no great success, Richard and I turned to each other.

"O time, time, time," I whispered, feeling tears come unbidden to my eyes.

"Are you all right, Cleve?" he asked.

I waved away the question, intent on demonstrating that I was hale, if not exactly hearty, and, though prone to lapses into unwelcome emotion, I was still *compos mentis*.

Rafe leaned forward and placed a rolled parchment on the table. "You must have heard the wonderful news about the little monastery that's been founded at Jarrow. Eleven men now. Each of them made his way there from isolated places—following threads of inspiration, as we once did. Two of them are Dominicans, one a Franciscan, another a Jesuit, and even a Carthusian who arrived after a year's journey on foot from the wastelands of Colorado. The others are diocesan priests from the burned cities here in the northlands. They follow the Benedictine rule now."

Walkers and horsemen had begun to pass through *Sursum Corda* in recent years, interrupting their journeys long enough to take a short rest and receive our hospitality. From such itinerants, we had garnered fragments of news. We had learned that the town of Pincher Creek was utterly destroyed, but that a village had arisen a little farther north and east of the ruins, on the banks of the Oldman River. The village had been named Jarrow. As industrious as our own people, its residents had dammed the river and renamed it New Man River. Behind the dam, a lake was slowly filling and expanding; it had been baptized with the name Galilee. It was full of fish. The buffalo were returning to the region in surprising numbers. The once fertile grain fields were being reseeded.

We had learned, as well, that the national highway was little by little being swallowed by woodlands, its pavement fractured and gradually covered by windblown soil. Years might pass without seeing a single wanderer making his way along the route, coming out of nowhere, searching for an undefined refuge, any place that might offer an end to dreadful isolation. Yet, at intervals, such people continued to arrive. Many of these solitaries had been burned or maimed, but without exception they carried a flame of holy faith within them.

All of this passed through my mind while Richard continued.

"Fr. Peter has just returned from a visit to their foundation," he said. "Living among them is a bishop who arrived last summer, after journeying five months on foot from the east. He is instructed to establish a diocese for the entire western lands."

"This is tremendous news!" I exclaimed.

Richard and Rafe glowed with their own feelings of elation.

"You can imagine how Fr. Peter feels after so many years of ministering alone," said Richard. "The bishop has offered to send one of his priests here, if Fr. Peter should choose to retire."

Rafe said, "Our pastor says that he doesn't know the meaning of the word *retire*. He wants to serve until his final breath."

"Long may that breath be delayed," I said.

"There's more good news," said Rafe with a smile at our friend.

Richard said, "One of my great-grandsons, Anthony

Gerbrandt, has been discerning his vocation with Fr. Peter. Since childhood, he has yearned to become a priest, but, until now, it seemed impossible to explore the question. After the autumn harvest, Fr. Peter and Anthony will go by horse to Jarrow and meet with the bishop."

"After all these years, green shoots spring up from the ashes! Blessing upon blessing. We'll pray for him, Richard."

"Thank you, Cleve." He paused and lowered his eyes, shaking his head in wonder.

"Who could have foreseen all this?" I said, thinking back to the desperate, barren years, when we had struggled daily to retain hope.

"Who could have foreseen?" Richard echoed. Inhaling deeply, he looked up and glanced at the rolled parchment. "In any event, I've brought you a letter from the prior of the new foundation. He's a young man, born after the holocaust. He wants survivors to jot down their memories of the before-times."

"Seeing as how we'll soon be gone."

"Yes. Gather the oral histories before they're lost forever."

"I have no argument with that, but I'll read it later," I said, shifting the scroll to the side of the table. "How often do we get together, you guys? Let's have some bread and wine."

"I'll butter the bread," Tally piped up, removing a muslin packet from the pocket of her dress. "Mama sent it for you."

I went back into the house and collected four clay cups and a knife to cut the bread. When we were settled around the table again, we offered a prayer of thanks and then got underway with the repast. The rare treat of wild berry wine was most welcome, and for the girl I had a flagon of spring water flavored with the last of my raspberries. She buttered our slices of bread with the short wooden knife I had carved for her last Christmas. She carried it everywhere and used it for all manner of purposes.

Occasionally, one or another of us engaged in recalling stories of our shared adventures, a "re-past", as Richard the ever-articulate pointed out. We touched on highlights of our flight from unleashed terror into the fearful unknown. Mainly we talked about our "pied piper children", as we called them, all of them now well-grown, some living nearby, others farther afield. As we shared what news we had of each one, we found the unspoken bond between us as strong as ever. We were the pipers, and those rescued children were as beloved to us as our own flesh and blood.

Finally Richard recalled the little blue bird of my dream, which both he and Rafe had frequently heard about over the years.

Yes, little bird, yes!

"On such small things the fate of the world so often hinges," Richard said, his face growing meditative.

"Without that bird," said Rafe, "none of us would be here."

"Perhaps," I said, musing. "Or perhaps not. The Lord's Providence ensures that when one way is blocked, he will open another."

I mentioned the truth that Providence flows in countless streams beneath and behind and through the ordinary events of life—and the extraordinary, too. Richard suggested that while *streams* was descriptive, it would be more accurate to say that we are always immersed in the *oceanic*. Rafe mused a moment and then in his deep bass he said, "It's both."

We three laughed, for this had been the pattern between us

from the beginning—each of us playing our role to produce a triangulation of thought and, hence, depth perception.

Then Rafe put forward the idea that while the veil hiding the hand of God's movements in human affairs is parted at crucial moments, as it had been for us, it prevails just as powerfully when it is hidden from our eyes and understanding.

Richard and I agreed with him.

Glancing at Tally, I noticed her glazed eyes. We were putting her to sleep. I reached over and gently shook her shoulder.

"Sweetie, thanks for bringing Mr. Lyon and Mr. Morrow to see me. It's time you headed back home."

She stood up. "Okay, Grandpa. Mama says the black ewe will go into labor today, and we think it will be twins. I want to be there to help. I hope it will be two black lambs. You can make patterns when you're knitting black wool with white wool."

"That's wonderful, Tally. Let's hope for two black lambs."

"I'll knit you a new scarf."

I already owned three scarves she had made for me as Christmas and birthday gifts.

"I can't wait to see it," I enthused.

She kissed me on the cheek and patted my shoulder, as if I were the child and she the grown-up, evoking a faint memory that I could not quite recall. Then she was off at a trot. I stood by the railing and watched her scramble down onto the path, where she turned to give one final wave before heading off in the direction of the village. I waved back and gave a hugging gesture, and she was gone.

We three old men remained in comfortable silence for a time, sipping the last of the wine, adrift within our resurfaced memories.

The bird, I thought, seeing that ancient dream so clearly, as if it had flown into my mind only last night. I followed its flight through everything that followed. For a few minutes, maybe longer, I lost all awareness that my friends were with me.

You have called us out of darkness, O Lord, into your wonderful light. Nourish these generations unto eternal life!

"Are you asleep?" asked Rafe.

"I'm awake," I said, opening my eyes.

"Something just happened to you," said Richard.

"I was remembering," I slowly replied.

"Anything in particular?"

"I was thinking about that time I went into the river, not long after we got here."

"Ah, yes, you fell into the water the day John was born."

"I didn't fall," I said. "I was *called* into it. Three times I went under."

"A kind of baptism," mused Rafe.

"Yes, like that. Beneath the water I had the . . . you know . . . the. . . ."

Richard quietly supplied the missing word. "The *vision*."

"I wouldn't dare call it a vision."

"A light, then, or an inspiration. It was about memory, if I recall correctly."

"You recall well."

"Half a century ago, and I remember it too," said Rafe.

"Whatever it was that happened to me, I think it was about more than memory. It was about the vigilance needed if we hope to remember rightly."

"I think you mean to say that, just because some of us survived, we shouldn't presume that mankind is now immune."

"God was telling us to pray," I said. "He told us we have to keep praying without ceasing."

"The illumination came, the holocaust fell, and now we always pray," said Richard.

I listened to the soft flow of the breeze, the music of the insects and birds swelling their chorus. In the strange ways of the imagination, I could almost hear the sound of my people as they went about their work in the houses in the village down by the river—their breathing, the drumming of their many hearts. I heard faint bells. I heard the distant river roaring in my ears, and I was beneath the water again, drowning and rising three times—as fresh as if it happened only a moment ago.

"I have nothing more to give," I said to my two friends, glancing at the scroll on which I was supposed to record my memories of the before-times.

"Cleve, you always have something more to give," said Rafe. "That's your nature, man. You said we should pray, but it has to be more than that."

"We think we're safe now. The devils are all cast out, the earth is cleansed. It would be so easy to sit back and say to ourselves, There, that nasty business is over with. Now let's enjoy life."

"Nothing wrong with enjoying life," said Richard.

"Nothing at all, if there's real joy in it—and truth. What I'm trying to say is, I think we're supposed to pray for heaven's help more than ever."

"More than ever?"

"So we won't forget the lesson mankind just learned."

I could see Rafe digesting this.

"Quite a lesson," he sighed.

"It was an education all right," Richard murmured.

"More than ever—so our descendants will not repeat our mistakes," I said.

Silence stretched long as we contemplated the horrors we had witnessed.

"We've known each other many years, Cleve," said Rafe at last, "and we've endlessly rehashed what happened, and still we understand so little about it."

"Do we need to know everything? You told us once, Rafe, that we would know what we need to know *when* we need to know it."

He nodded. "I remember."

"The years flow onward as a river," I said. "We swim in it for a while, and in the end we're taken into the great sea. There, we'll be given understanding in full."

"The sea is near for all of us," said Rafe.

"Why were we chosen?" Richard asked.

"If we were chosen, it was because we were ordinary," I said, "nothing special."

"And because we listened," said Rafe.

My mind drifted.

I saw myself waking up one fine morning, Annie expecting our first child, me with a good job, the spreading madness in the world kept at bay but creeping closer and closer, like deadly gas. I saw myself packing up the truck, and Annie and me abandoning our home and heading off into the unknown, drawn by a dream, an intuition, and a whiff of what proved to be well-founded paranoia. A temporary permanent we had called the excursion. Or was it permanent temporary?

I saw my terror at the time. For years afterward, I was plagued by the questions: Why did the catastrophe fall so severely upon humanity? Why were we spared? Would some of the spared out there in the world revert to their former ways? What if the persecution erupted again? What if marauders from the burned lands appeared without warning? What if we the survivors and our children and their offspring forgot the hard lessons that were learned?

"I wrote the story of what happened to us all," I said to my two friends. "Don't worry, I hid it in a secret place. They'll never find it."

"The *theys* are all gone, Cleve," Richard said.

"It's a kind of letter—a letter to the children of the future."

25

MY FRIENDS LEFT THE EMPTY SCROLL WITH ME, encouraging me to consider making a contribution of insight and memory. They would ensure that travelers would return it to the new abbey. For days I looked at the scroll with uneasiness, not touching it, wondering how I could possibly compress a lifetime into a few lines. What could I tell those who might read it some day? What legacy, what inheritance, what testimony of a life seasoned and, hopefully, purified; of a world chastened and, hopefully, resolved to strive for a better path.

We hobble along half-blind, ever-repenting, trying to love in all circumstances. Invoking the supernatural grace of Hope, converting fear into trust. Practicing thankfulness for all things, the sweet and the bitter, the soft and the hard. Offering to others our little bits of bread, baked in the kitchen of our weakness.

The bulky "letter" I wrote several decades ago was a little bit of bread—my attempt to tell a story that would leave a trace of historical perspective, to pass on to the coming generations an account that would help them understand what had happened to us, before it faded from memory. It is stored in the chamber beneath my feet. I will soon add these final pages to it.

With the passage of time, I have come to believe that there are different ways of imparting truth. At this late stage of my life, with swiftly dwindling sands in the hourglass, I understand that the forms of speaking are manifold. By which I mean that, from the crucible of countless years and momentous events, one may distill essences, simplified, clarified, expressed through the language of ultimate thoughts.

I do not mean the writing of literature (I long ago abandoned that persona); nor do I mean philosophical arguments to change people's thinking (at which Rafe was a master); nor do I mean historical data and analysis for the informing of minds (at which Richard was a prodigy). I mean instead our own deepest heart-soul words—living *logos*.

As Rafe once told me, the children of the future need us to remain peaceful and steadfast—not in denial of the dark realities from which we have come, but rather by keeping our feet planted firmly on the Rock and our eyes on the true horizon, which is Him.

We do the task that's put in front of us, he said. Taking responsibility without fanfare or other kinds of emotional noise. Meeting each challenge as it comes, one step at a time. Dying to ourselves a little each day, and each day being reborn. Doing the duty of the moment. That is God's will for us.

And so, my distillates:

> *Give life, as life was given to you.*
> *Love always.*
> *Forgive everything.*
> *Fear nothing.*
> *But when you begin to fear, turn to Him.*
> *Trust! The greater the darkness, the more complete our trust should be.*
> *He is coming, He is near.*

I remain always, my children of the future, your friend and your father.